PRAISE FOR JOHN SHARER'S
THE COCKNEY LAD AND JIM CROW

"...John Sharer is an especially gifted novelist who can engage the reader's full and informed attention through a deftly crafted story that is an accurate portrayal of the antebellum south's brutal segregation and murderous oppression of African-Americans. A compelling read from beginning to end and one that will linger in the mind long after the novel is finished and set back upon the shelf. Very highly recommended...."

> — James A. Cox, Editor-in-Chief,
> *Midwest Book Review*

"...Smashing....Don't miss this one - it is a super read - I devoured it in three days. I haven't read his first book but look forward to picking it up."

> — Patty Smith, *Union Jack*

"Gripping historical fiction about a London teenager who relocates to a Jackson Mississippi that's rife with the horrors of racism and which inevitably alters his life forever. A lawyer as well as an author, Sharer's passion for justice shines through the book."

> — *Indulge Magazine Online*

"Sharer is, once again, a master story teller. This time about an English youngster's shocking experiences with racism and all of its injustices and violence and how he handled it. He handled it well. He made a positive mark for understanding and some acceptance between the races long before the Civil Right's movement was even a thought. It's a good read." — Amazon reviewer

"This easy read presents a picture of racial prejudice in the south through the eyes of a young man from England.... He stands up against what he innately knows to be wrong. A thoroughly enjoyable and thought provoking story." — Amazon reviewer

"I bought and read this book and it ruined my Sunday: I could not put the damn thing down until I finished it." — Amazon reviewer

"Being an expatriate, arriving on these shores in the early 60's, I enjoyed the authors insightful & interesting retelling of his experiences both here & in England. Whether it was all true or not I found it a very enjoyable read." — Amazon reviewer

"Really enjoyed *The Cockney Lad and Jim Crow*. The story moved well and fast paced. A great twist at the end." — Amazon reviewer

PRAISE FOR JOHN SHARER'S
HONOR KNOWS NO BORDERS

"A compelling and historically fascinating fictional account of a pivotal point in World War II. Intense, thrilling and riveting. I can't wait to see the movie, which is sure to be a blockbuster."

> — Ted Olson, one of Time Magazine's 100 most influential people in the world.

"... The thing about this book and its values is that it is as current today as it was in 1941."

> — Richard Reisberg, former president of MGM/ UA Television and of Viacom Productions

"... grabs hold of our attention and will not let go. Sharer treats us to action, suspense and psychological insights that challenge conventional assumptions. The reader is in for a stimulating treat that lingers."

> — Arthur Gilbert, Author of *Under Submission*

ALSO BY JOHN SHARER

Honor Knows No Borders (2010)

THE COCKNEY LAD AND JIM CROW

JOHN SHARER

Wompetias Press

THE COCKNEY LAD AND JIM CROW by John Sharer

Published by Wompetias Press

First Edition, May 2015

Author Services by Pedernales Publishing, LLC.
www.pedernalespublishing.com

Cover by Andrew Campbell

Library of Congress Control Number: 2015934995

ISBN: 978-0-9961142-6-4 Paperback Edition
         978-0-9961142-8-8 Hardcover Edition
         978-0-9961142-9-5 Digital Edition

Printed in the United States of America

CONTENTS

While some of the following is based on the author's own experiences, this is a fictionalized story concerning life in the Deep South and elsewhere over a half century ago. It involves race relations as they were at that time. While race relations today throughout the United States are not perfect, they are vastly improved over what they were all those many years ago and nothing in this book is intended to demonstrate otherwise.

PROLOGUE

WHAT FOLLOWS is the story of Peter Mason, a young cockney boy from the east end of London who left war-ravaged England in 1950 and somehow ended up in totally white-dominated and completely segregated Mississippi. This is not a story of freedom rides. There weren't any. This is not a story of sit-ins, lie-ins or any other kind of "ins." There weren't any of those either. Nor is this a story of voter registration drives for Blacks, or African Americans, if you prefer. Polite Southern society in the early 1950s referred to them as "Negroes." Somewhat less polite societies referred to them as "Nigras" and those who did not qualify for either society referred to them as—well you know what they referred to them as.

In any event, there were no voter registration drives; no protest parades; no refusals to move to the back of the bus; no attempted use of the other guy's drinking fountain or of the other guy's toilet facilities. James Meredith's attempt to integrate the University of Mississippi came ten years later, as did the advent of the freedom riders.

Brown v. Board of Education was a few years away, as was Lyndon Johnson's signing of the Civil Rights Act. It took even longer for those momentous events to have any significant impact in the Deep South, and indeed in other parts of the country. In 1950, relationships between the races in Mississippi and in the rest of the Deep South were ostensibly calm and peaceful. The calmness and peacefulness did not result from mutual respect or a belief in the equality of all men. It was born out of Black acceptance, although with some reluctance, of enforced subservience.

Peter Mason did nothing deliberately to change any of this, but he did do some things that could have gotten him killed had it not been for the fact that, among other things, he was young, new to the South and, perhaps most important, English. Many white southerners of that era (and perhaps even today) were proud of their distant English ancestry and many of them, but certainly not all, grudgingly forgave the boy for his violations of the apartheid protocol, sometimes referring to him as "that crazy English kid." He found that the time-worn adage that England and the United States were two countries with much in common, one of which was not the language, to be woefully inadequate. He found, at least initially, that he had virtually nothing in common with his new-found neighbors and workmates. This was not just a culture shock to the boy caused by moving from one country to another. A culture shock was traveling more than a hundred miles from his home. A culture shock was going from London to New York. Going from London, England to Jackson, Mississippi was more like moving from one planet to another.

The boy had no humanitarian, altruistic or save-the-world reasons for ending up in Mississippi. He was touring the country on a shoestring, ran out of money in Mississippi and simply needed a job.

WHERE IT ALL STARTED

THE BOY WATCHED in horror as one of the robed and hooded men pushed the Negro off a stool. A second man kicked the stool away. The Negro's body jerked. It swung back and forth and then it was still. The only sounds heard at that moment were the rustling of leaves in nearby magnolia trees and the boy's muted sobs. He knew that what had happened was his fault and he would live with the scars in his mind and on his back until he died.

It had been three and a half years since he had last traveled from London to the port of Southampton. He stood on the pier waiting for the passengers to disembark from the New Amsterdam. It was the same pier from which he had sailed for America when he was seventeen. He looked around at passengers leaning on the ship's rail and seamen carrying trunks and suitcases down the gangplank, and he remembered. This is where it all started.

THE SUIT

PETER HAD NEVER SEEN anything that big before, at least nothing that moved. The French Line, *Liberté*, would take him to America, thousands of miles across the Atlantic. The ship stretched the length of what seemed to be several football fields and towered above him. Sailors in horizontally striped jerseys and typical French berets and stewards in white coats bustled about loading supplies, luggage and people. It was organized pandemonium. He had just made the longest journey of his life, London to Southampton, a distance of less than a hundred miles.

It was November the fifth, 1950, Guy Fawkes Day. In 1605 Guy Fawkes and others had plotted to blow up the Houses of Parliament. The plot had failed, but ever since, English children celebrated the event by making life-size images of Fawkes out of straw, old clothes and anything else they could find. All day on the fifth, the children pushed their concoctions through the streets in wheelbarrows imploring passersby to "spare a penny for the guy." At the end of the day, they would burn their creations on bonfires. On the boat train from London, as the sun went down, Peter saw bonfires everywhere. The war had been over for five years, but the fires brought back memories of other fires that did not have their origins in a delightful centuries-old childhood tradition.

His family had survived the war without anyone being killed, but not without one painful casualty—his mother.

Her nerves, shattered by the incessant bombing, she had literally shriveled up. At war's end she was forty-four, but looked decades older. His father, returning from army service abroad, could not reconcile himself to the fact that the vital, attractive and healthy woman he had left, no longer existed. If he paid any attention to her at all, it was to shout at her for some perceived, but non-existent, grievance. Mostly he ignored her. He had no job to return to and seemingly made little or no effort to find one. During the war he had become an officer in the British army, a surprising development since his exposure to formal education was fleeting. Having commanded large numbers of soldiers and having achieved a level of importance that he was destined never again to attain, his return to the same mediocrity that he had left was unbearable for him. For months after his army discharge, he continued to wear his uniform with its ribbons and the emblems of his former rank. He left the house for days and sometimes weeks at a time for places and for reasons he never revealed. Finally he left and didn't return. The boy never saw him again and never wanted to. Months later his mother died. Doctors were not able to explain to him the medical reason for her death. They said it was some sort of mental disorder whose name he could not pronounce, much less spell, secondary to wartime trauma. To the boy and his sister the doctors' explanations were gibberish—the medical equivalent of doctors shrugging their shoulders and saying it's "something that's going around."

Peter watched as the first-class passengers boarded the liner. The women were elegantly and expensively dressed in the latest London and Paris fashions. The men, for the most part, wore suits made by Savile Row tailors, each costing more than the average British workman earned in a year. Peter was also wearing a Savile Row suit that had been individually tailored and had cost a small fortune. However, it had not been made for the boy, but for his only rich relative, an uncle who owned several shops from which he sold expensive dresses to the wealthy.

He had rarely seen his uncle and had been to his house on only two occasions. However, upon hearing that Peter was going to America, the uncle, in a uniquely charitable moment, gave him five twenty-pound notes and one of his own suits. The uncle was over six feet tall and weighed close to three hundred pounds. Peter was five feet eight and weighed one hundred and thirty-five pounds. Two boys of similar size could have simultaneously fit into the suit with room to spare. Peter took the suit to a tailor he knew in the neighborhood who held it up, looked at him, then at the suit and shook his head. "I'm a very good tailor," he said, "but I'm not a very good magician." He did his best and the results were not bad. He successfully reduced the waist from forty eight inches to twenty-nine inches and narrowed the back of the coat so that it fit more snugly. There was little he could do to reduce the shoulder spread or the circumference of the trouser legs. Peter could literally take a stride in the trousers without them moving an inch.

He stood in his Savile Row suit watching the first-class passengers board the *Liberté* with the remains of the hundred pounds now converted to dollars in the suit pocket, and waited for the third class passengers' turn to board. He felt small and scared. It wasn't just the size of the ship or the mass of people, none of whom he knew, that frightened him, it was the loneliness and the trepidation at the unknown that lay ahead. His sister had wanted to come with him to Southampton, to see him off. He convinced her not to. The return fare was expensive, and she would have to take a day off from work without pay. In truth, he was afraid that her presence would make him change his mind about going. Even without her being there, the thought of getting the next train back to London gnawed at him. With difficulty he resisted it.

BETH MASON

FOR A LONG TIME Beth stood in her brother's room with tears streaming down her face. She was now all alone in the only home she had ever known. The slow emptying of the pitifully small apartment was now almost complete. It called to mind the Haydn *Farewell Symphony*, only on a much smaller scale. She was a devotee of classical music and in particular, of Haydn. She had taken violin lessons for many years and occasionally took out the scarred old violin that her mother had bought for her, second-hand from a peddler in Petticoat Lane. She had watched the *Farewell Symphony* at the Royal Albert Hall several months earlier and had focused intently on the first violinist as he played some of the solo pieces. She practiced so hard on her old scarred second-hand violin but even if she could have afforded high caliber professional tutoring, she could never have hoped to approach the exhibition of exquisite artistic skill she was hearing. It wasn't envy. It was unreserved admiration. Candles provided the only lighting in the hall, with one in front of each musician.

As the Symphony continued, one by one the musicians blew out their candles and left the stage. Finally just one musician, the first violinist, remained with the only illumination in the massive auditorium, the last candle. As the Symphony concluded, that musician blew out his candle and left a totally dark theater. There was momentary silence, then massive applause. Her father was the first to leave, then her mother and now her brother. No candles were extinguished and there was certainly no applause but the sense of finality was very real.

Beth was a petite girl, two years older than Peter and quite pretty. While she had even less education than Peter, having left school early to work for a West End dress designer, she had inherited her mother's wisdom. Despite her diminutive size and quiet voice Beth was strong-willed and exercised almost maternal control over Peter's sometimes unruly antics. Peter ran with a pretty wild bunch of chums who smoked and drank and frequently partied until the early hours. Although Peter argued with her, he nonetheless obeyed her edict that he not smoke and that he drink only an occasional beer and that he be home at a reasonable hour.

When Peter had first voiced a desire to see America, she had encouraged it, although she resisted his imploring her to go with him. She wanted to pursue her dress designing career. Her employer had often told her that she had the talent to be a big success. As important, she had started seeing a young man she met at the local athletic club. They were both decent runners and they frequently trained together. She liked him more than a little but felt that it was too early to tell whether that relationship would go anywhere. They spent a lot of time together. He was fun to be with and made her laugh.

Peter had only been gone for a few hours but already the flat had taken on an aura of loneliness. Beth half smiled as she looked around the room. There was nothing out of place. She had often chastised Peter for his messiness—clothes dropped wherever he removed them, and books and papers thrown carelessly around. She missed the chaos already. She wondered whether she was right to have encouraged him to leave. He wouldn't have gone if she hadn't pushed him. By now he was probably getting ready to board the ship. She was sure he was thrilled and anticipating his impending great adventure.

She was only partially correct. He was, in fact, having second thoughts. Was this a sensible thing to do? While he wouldn't admit it to anyone, he was afraid. He had been through far more frightening times during the war. Nonetheless, he was scared. His heart raced and, despite the chill in the air, he felt clammy and a little shaky. During the war he was with people he knew—family, friends, neighbors and teachers. He had even experienced closeness to strangers. They were linked by a common peril and they shared a kind of camaraderie. Now here he was, going on a ship with people, none of whom shared the same concerns he had or shared any link with him. He was going to a country that had over a hundred million people, not one of whom knew him or cared whether he lived or died. He had left his home barely a few hours ago and was already encountering a new terror—gnawing, abject loneliness.

THE "ROADS" SCHOLAR

PETER HAD NEVER had a real conversation with an American before he met the man with whom he would be sharing a cabin for the five day voyage to New York. In third class, individuals traveling alone were required to share cabins, even if they didn't know the other person. The only Americans he had ever seen, outside of motion pictures, were GIs stationed in and around London during the war. GIs were constantly pestered for sweets (candy) and chewing gum by young English boys, and sometimes girls. Candy was severely rationed and the long-suffering and good-natured Americans would share what they had with the children, whose introductory line was almost always, "Got any gum, chum?"

"What's your name, kid?" said his new cabin mate in an unmistakable American accent.

"Peter, Peter Mason. My mother didn't like people to call me Pete. What's yours?"

"Charles Bradley, but I'm known as Chuck by everyone, even by my mother."

Chuck looked at the skinny kid in the badly fitting suit. He watched as the boy heaved his battered suitcase onto the lower bunk. The bag was held together and tied with several strands of thick string.

"Peter, are you traveling alone?" he asked.

"Yes, I am," the boy replied.

"Who's meeting you in New York?"

"Nobody, I don't know anyone in America. I've a visa and I want to travel around. I've never been anywhere before."

Chuck drew a deep breath. "Peter, America's a big country. How old are you?"

"I'll be eighteen next month."

"You look like you're twelve, for God's sake."

"Well you're not that much older," Peter said, somewhat defiantly.

"I'm twenty-three, and the difference between eighteen and twenty-three is a lifetime. Take it from me, I've been both. Do your parents know what you're doing?"

"I don't have any parents. They're both dead," he said. His father, though technically alive, was, as far as he was concerned, dead.

Chuck fished around in his wallet and pulled out a card. "Here Peter, take this. It has my address and telephone number in Boston. You get into trouble, you give me a call. Okay?"

Peter put the card in his pocket and nodded. "You're American. I've never known any Americans. Why were you in England? Were you on holiday?"

"No. I was at Oxford. I was there on a Rhodes Scholarship."

"Why would you come to England to learn about roads? I've seen pictures and newsreels about the highways in America. They stretch forever. You could drive sixty to seventy miles an hour, easy. Our roads are nothing. Most are worn out and still have bomb damage."

Chuck laughed. "Not r-o-a-d-s. It's R-h-o-d-e-s. Cecil Rhodes was an empire-builder and philanthropist. Rhodesia is named after him. He funded a scholarship in his name to allow worthy young Americans to study at Oxford. I'm not sure how worthy I am, but I got one of the scholarships and I've been studying international relations at Oxford for the last year."

Peter was embarrassed by his mistake. "I knew that," he said defiantly, although he didn't. "I just forgot. Sorry. "

"There's nothing to be sorry about. Say, let's go get something to eat. I'm starved. I haven't had a bite since this morning. I think the dining room closes in fifteen minutes."

Chuck got up from the bunk. He was over six feet, about the same height as Peter's uncle. Had he been a hundred pounds heavier he could have gotten into the suit without the need of any tailoring.

THE DINING ROOM

After several meals in the third-class dining room Peter learned that it was always filled with a diverse crowd. He saw groups of young Americans going home either from studying at English universities or returning from their holidays. According to many of the English travelers, the Americans drank too much, smoked too much and talked too much. During the war, some resentful English people referred to the GIs as being over-sexed, over-paid and over here. Peter didn't agree. They may have been over-sexed and over-paid, but the vast majority of English people, including Peter, were grateful that they had been "over here." He knew that many of the thousands of GIs stationed in England were later killed on Omaha Beach, during the Battle of the Bulge, at Anzio and in a hundred other places. Peter liked the GIs, or the "Yanks" as the English called them, and he liked listening to the young Americans in the ship's dining room. Of course he didn't understand everything they were saying; they used a lot of words he'd never heard before, and talked about things he knew nothing about, like baseball. It didn't matter. They were always in good spirits and funny.

Peter saw that most of the other diners were English families immigrating to America to look for jobs and new lives. Except for their young children, they were quieter than the Americans, somewhat older, and not nearly as well-dressed. Many of the men were veterans of the war. They had come home to grim, unrelenting austerity and to severely bomb-damaged Britain. It was a cold and bleak homecoming, with continued shortages of food and housing—not the hero's welcome they expected. They looked tired and older than their years. They could not find jobs in their own country and while there was nothing for them at home, they were uneasy at picking up stakes and moving into the unknown.

The Americans were constantly complaining about the food. Although it was a French ship and the first-class passengers were feasting on the finest French cuisine and vintage French wines, the third-class passengers were provided a constant diet of bland, overcooked meats and cheap wines—the kind that had caps that unscrewed rather than corks that were removed with corkscrews. In their country, even the poorest of the young Americans were used to better, while in England, the English were used to less and worse. During the war, food had been in very short supply in England and virtually everything was rationed. Ironically, in the years following the end of the war, food was in even shorter supply. The country had suffered some of the worst weather in its history. Crops were decimated. The means of production, massively damaged by German bombing, were recovering at a snail-like pace. Returning military personnel found employment hard to get, and inflation was the order of the day.

The English travelers did not complain about the food. The quality of the food was better and the amount larger than the older people had seen in many years and better and larger than the younger ones had ever seen. The availability of abundant helpings and even seconds was a totally new experience for Peter. Chuck picked listlessly at what he considered to be unpalatable food, while looking at Peter with quiet amusement as the young English boy devoured his meal with obvious relish and went back for more.

The cabin that Chuck and Peter shared was tiny. It had two bunk beds, a small table and a single chair. There was no place to hang clothes and no drawers for underwear and socks. It had no porthole, no carpet and no toilet facilities. The bathroom and the separate lavatory were down the passage way and there was always a line to use either. There was no air conditioning and no fans. Despite the fact that this was November and they were sailing through frigid weather in the North Atlantic, the cabin was always hot. To compound their discomfort, there was some type of machinery that seemed to be directly above the cabin. Chuck said he thought it was a large turbine. It made a constant loud thumping noise and the cabin vibrated incessantly.

The weather in the North Atlantic in winter was never ideal, and it was particularly bad on this trip. The noise, heat, vibrations and rolling of the ship made Peter slightly nauseous, but he was proud that he did not feel like actually being sick. The excitement of where he was and the anticipation of where he was going and what he would see when he got there overcame all of the difficulties. His fear and loneliness had evaporated, at least temporarily.

THE VOYAGE

DESPITE THE CONFINES of the tiny cabin, the noise from the turbine, the vibration, the heat below, the freezing cold above and the queasiness from the pitch and roll of the ship, Peter found the voyage exciting and memorable—even magical. He especially enjoyed the time he spent with his cabin-mate. The two of them soon became close friends. Chuck had been everywhere; Africa, China, South America, all over Europe. Peter had gone nowhere, unless you counted the two hour trip from London to Southampton. The two of them spent hours together talking, having meals, and exchanging life stories. Chuck also taught Peter the fundamentals of playing chess, a game he had never played before. Peter didn't think he had much to tell, but Chuck insisted that Peter's life was fascinating—the bombing, the search for food, for shelter, for safety; the difficulties of getting an education under such circumstances, and the very attempt to stay alive day-to-day.

Chuck got his cabin-mate's permission to have some

of the other young Americans listen to Peter's wartime history. Their fathers and other older relatives had told them some of their experiences, but listening to an English boy, younger than themselves, was at least as interesting, maybe more so. He told them of the German bomber raids, the V-1 "Buzz Bomb" attacks and how these pilotless planes were sent over London to crash on random targets when they ran out of fuel. He told them of the V-2 rockets and how one hit a block of flats in East London killing 134 people, including one of his close school friends. That boy had played football with Peter on the school playground one day, and the next day was dead. Peter wiped away a tear, as did several of the listeners.

Throughout the war, Peter was in school. His sister had left school and gone to work before the war ended. His school had suffered damage, and several other students and two teachers were killed at various times. The memories were clearly painful. As Peter spoke, Chuck put a consoling arm on his shoulder. He continued on, telling of the difficult time his mother had in the war and how she died as a result of it, although well after the war ended. He told of his closeness with his sister and how she was a steadying influence on him despite the slight difference in their ages. It was not lost on Chuck that Peter barely mentioned his father. Chuck surmised that there was a story there, but didn't push it.

Chuck told Peter that his father was the president of a construction company, though he had come out of the post-Depression years with nothing. He worked as a common day laborer picking up any jobs he could and was always unsure where his next paycheck would come from. As the years went by, he developed skills in carpentry and bricklaying. He started his own construction company with just himself and a partner to do all the work. After years of only very marginal success, one day the business began to boom.

Chuck said that the company now employed two hundred people and they were involved constantly in a number of important building projects around the country. The family now lived in a large colonial house on several acres. They had horses, a swimming pool, a tennis court and separate servants' quarters. Despite all of those trimmings, Frank "Red" Bradley had never forgotten his roots. Although the headquarters of the Bradley Company were in a skyscraper and he was surrounded by secretaries and well-dressed executives, Red always appeared in work clothes. He wasn't just trying to look like one of the workers; he *was* one of the workers. He spent a good part of several days a week hammering nails or laying bricks on one of the projects. He knew the names of all the workers and they knew him simply as "Red."

"Why'd they call him 'Red?'" asked Peter. "Did he have ginger hair?"

"What's ginger hair?"

"We call red hair, ginger."

"You had better learn to speak English," Chuck said with a smile.

"I am speaking English. You're speaking it with a funny accent." Peter said, also smiling.

"Well you'd better learn to speak American English. Anyway no one knows why my dad is called Red. Even he doesn't know. He never had red hair and now he doesn't have any hair at all. He was good with his fists when he was young. Some people say he was always ready for a fight and the 'ready' became 'Red.'"

Chuck was going home to work in the company and one day he would own it. Just the same, his father required that he start at the very bottom; carrying tools, delivering plans, running errands and even getting coffee for the men. Someone else with Chuck Bradley's credentials and family connections might resent such menial assignments, but not Chuck. He fully understood why his father was doing what he was doing, and he was grateful.

Chuck and Peter showed each other family pictures. Chuck had a large number of them, including pictures of the family home. Peter's photo offerings were less impressive. He showed a picture of his sister and one of his mother taken before the war. He had a picture of the block of flats he lived in, but he shoved it into his pocket, not wanting to reveal the austere and dreary place.

RESENTMENT

PETER SPENT TIME with the young Americans in the dining room, on deck when the weather permitted, and in the recreation hall. He was embarrassed at first. They were older, well-educated, sophisticated and relatively wealthy. He had left school at fifteen and had worked as an errand boy for two years for a large real estate agent. He brought the bosses coffee and tea, delivered plans and keys to potential clients and even collected rents from prostitutes occupying apartments in Soho.

His new-found friends had studied in universities in America and England and a few had attended classes in France and Spain. Nonetheless they accepted him. They liked him. They involved him in their conversations, in their games and even in their meals. They explained American football, which the English referred to as "gridiron" because of the marking on the field. In return, he explained the highlights of "real" football and they argued good naturedly about the superiority of one over the other. He even spent the better part of an hour unsuccessfully trying to unveil the mysteries of cricket, a game that, of necessity, one had to be born to. They laughed at terms such as "silly mid-off" and "leg before wicket."

Try as he might, Peter could not make them understand the difference between a bowler delivering a "leg break" as opposed to a "googly." Conversely, he chided them about all the pads and masks that American football players wore and why they would have the audacity to call their game "football" when the foot only touched the ball sporadically. They taught him how to hold and throw the American football. It was skinnier and more pointed at the ends than a rugby ball. They threw it back and forth on the third-class passengers' deck until one of Peter's erratic passes went over the rail into the North Atlantic. He apologized over and over. The owner of the ball told him not to worry. It was an old scuffed up ball and he was planning to leave it behind anyway when they got to New York.

On the third day out of Southampton, Reg Brown, one of the older Englishmen, confronted Peter. At Alamein, shrapnel from a German Tiger tank shell had shattered his left knee. He now walked with a stiff leg and a perpetual frown. He had made his living in civilian life driving a lorry for a brewery. That was now out of the question and the brewery had no other job for him. He could not support his family. He was bitter and resentful that his country's lack of help was forcing him to leave after he was crippled in its service. What was infuriating to him was the loud joviality of the young Americans. It didn't help to see the young English boy joining in their laughter and loud talking. As Peter walked by his table in the dining room one evening, Brown grabbed him.

"Why are you hobnobbing with those bloody Yanks?" he asked. "Don't you know they look down at us poor English? They've got all the money and we've got nothing. They didn't suffer in the war like we did. Why don't you stay with your own people."

Peter was shocked. He wanted to tell Brown that he had it all wrong and, furthermore, who he associated with was none of Brown's business. He didn't. He had seen Brown limp in and out of the dining room on previous days. He had seen the pain in his face, and sensed that it was not just from his war wounds. His wife was thin and drawn and his children did not play and laugh like children of their age normally did.

That night, Peter sat for some time with the Browns listening to their story of difficult times; about his war wounds; his medals for bravery, which he had pawned to buy food for his family; and about his futile search for work of any kind in the country he had fought for and in whose service he had been crippled. Occasionally Peter came up with something he hoped would be reassuring, although he had no basis for the things he said.

Brown looked older than his years, at least seventy, but Peter knew that could not be true. He had young children and, even as desperate as the British military had been during the war, they wouldn't have taken a sixty-year-old-plus man. His face was lined and his eyes had that moist rheumy look frequently associated with the aged or the drunkard, although Peter had not seen Brown drinking anything stronger than a cup of tea.

Peter felt it necessary to explain his own feelings. "It's not their fault that they've more money than us, that they were too young to be in the military or that they didn't suffer like you and your family obviously have. You shouldn't hold that against them. I like them. They make me happy. I know you and your family will be all right. I'm sure when you get to America you'll do real well. I just know that. I've heard it's the land of opportunity and you'll make your fortune there."

After his probably unsuccessful attempt to comfort Brown, Peter got up, put his hand consolingly on the older man's shoulder, smiled at his wife, and then walked over and sat down with Chuck and some of the young Americans. As usual they were laughing, joking and talking loudly.

"What's the matter with that guy?" Chuck asked.

"Nothing really. He just had a very bad time in the war."

"What kind of bad time?" asked Brian, one of his newfound friends who had recently graduated from the Harvard Law School and had taken a couple of months off before starting his legal career with one of the prominent Philadelphia law firms.

Peter explained about the war injury that was preventing Brown from working in his old job or to find a new one; his anguish at the difficulty of providing for his family and his bitterness that his country seemed to have abandoned its returning veterans.

The laughter, jokes and loud talking stopped. The rest of the meal was eaten in relatively uncharacteristic silence at the American table.

GOODBYE TO NEW FRIENDS

DURING THE VOYAGE, Peter had changed first into a football goalie's jersey that he had kept from his school days and then into a striped open-neck shirt and a pullover that his mother had bought him a month before she died. Unlike the suit, the shirt and pullover were a bit too small for him. Chuck told him that in America, a "pullover" was called a "sweater." Peter thought that sounded a bit crude. They should at least call it a "perspirer," he thought. He soon found that perceived unintended crudeness was not a one-way street. He was explaining to the Americans that some now forgotten event was a complete "bollocks." The use of that word drew much laughter. One of the Americans explained that in America, bollocks was a word sometimes used to describe a particularly personal portion of the male anatomy.

"This is going to take some getting used to," Peter said, shaking his head.

Although he was eager to start his journey around the new world, he found himself sad at the thought that the ocean voyage was drawing to a close. His new-found American friends gave him their addresses and phone numbers. He gave them his sister's address in London. She had no phone. He would be in touch with her from time to time and provide her with his whereabouts.

He and the Americans pledged to stay in touch and they exacted promises from him that he would come to visit in their hometowns. He came to understand later that those types of offers and promises were frequently made, and made in good faith, but the truth was that no further contact was really anticipated and no further contact was ever made, except with Chuck. He never saw any of the others again.

Chuck roused him on the night before they landed so he could see the Statue of Liberty come into view. It was a sight Peter would never forget and he was grateful to Chuck for making sure that he saw it. The next morning they prepared to disembark. Peter was wearing his uncle's suit. He had not told Chuck, or anyone else, about the history of the suit and how he came to have it. He didn't have to.

Chuck watched as Peter stowed his few pitiful possessions in his beat up suitcase, and tied the long piece of string around it.

"How much money do you have?" Chuck asked.

"Oh, I have lots," Peter replied.

"How much?" Chuck repeated.

Peter pulled out some bills and a few coins.

"Never mind the coins, how much in paper?"

"Eighty-eight dollars."

"Eighty-eight dollars!" Chuck said, unable to keep the surprise and exasperation out of his voice. "How far do you think you'll get on that?" Without waiting for a reply, Chuck pulled out his wallet and extracted three one hundred dollar bills. "Here, take this."

"No, I can't," Peter protested.

Without a word, Chuck reached over and put the bills in Peter's top jacket pocket.

"I can't take this. I may never be able to pay it back."

"I don't want you to pay it back. It's a gift." Chuck hesitated and then said "But there's one condition. You have to promise me that when you become a great success, as I know you will, you have to help some other struggling young person. Do you promise?"

Peter started to protest again, but Chuck cut him off. "You don't take it, I'm going to throw you overboard and you can swim around and try to find that football you lost. I don't want to hear another word other than you saying you promise."

Peter was close to tears at this extraordinary act of kindness. In a low voice he whispered, "I promise."

As he said good bye to the Americans and especially to Chuck, he turned his face away. It was not seemly for a boy on the verge of his eighteenth birthday to be tearing up.

THE IMMIGRATION AUTHORITIES

Before landing in New York everyone was required to fill out a form. Those who held American passports were given a shorter form than those who didn't. One of the questions initially stumped Peter: what was his address in the United States? Chuck seemed a little concerned about that question when Peter showed it to him. Maybe the authorities would take a dim view of allowing entry to a seventeen-year-old English boy in a suit several sizes too large for him, carrying a battered suitcase held together by string, with little money, no accompanying adults and no address in the United States.

"Use my Boston address. The one I wrote down for you. If the immigration fellows ask you who you know there and how, give them my parents' names. Here, write them down. If they ask, tell them they're close friends with your parents. If they ask you how long you're staying with my parents, tell them it hasn't been decided yet, but it will be for some time."

Peter dutifully wrote down everything. Chuck had

also found a baggage tag with string attached—the kind that was usually tied to a piece of luggage to identify the owner of the baggage. He wrote his parents' names and address on the tag and then tied it to a button on Peter's jacket. "It might make it appear more certain where you are going than just the same information on the form," Chuck said. Peter objected "This makes me look like a piece of luggage."

Chuck grinned. "Don't knock it. A piece of properly labeled luggage has a slightly better chance of getting past immigration officers than a seventeen-year-old, pardon, almost eighteen-year-old, English kid with no visible means of support." To spare Peter from embarrassment, he didn't mention the additional possible obstacles posed by the ill-fitting clothes and the battered suitcase.

The immigration process was conducted in a huge hall with several booths at one end. The room was dimly lit with a series of naked light bulbs hanging by wires. Exposed pipes extended across the ceiling. The linoleum floor was a non-descript color and in parts was worn through to the wooden floorboards from the passage of thousands of travelers. The walls, originally light blue, were now closer to a dirty grey. A number of immigrants had recorded their names on the walls in pencil or ink. It appeared to Peter that the names had been painted over periodically, with little concern for matching the existing color. The windows were encrusted with dirt as though they had not been washed in years, if ever. Adding to the depressing aura was a peculiar smell, suggesting a combination of body odor and decayed food. The hall, though necessary for proper processing of travelers, was not the greatest introduction to the wealthiest country in the world.

Passengers were ushered into one or another of several lines. Each booth had instructions in various languages as to who should be in which line. Another ship had docked an hour earlier. It had sailed from Rotterdam shortly before the *Liberte* had sailed from Southampton. It had been packed with an eclectic collection of people from various European countries. The cacophony of various languages was deafening. Peter's geography teacher, a much traveled man, had told the class that when the English cross the channel from Dover, Folkestone, Harwich or other ports, they would tell people they were going to Europe, ignoring the fact that England was, itself, in Europe. Geographically, England and the rest of the British Isles were indeed part of Europe, but culturally and as a political and practical matter, most of the English people never thought of themselves as European. Whether it was arrogance, isolationism or something else was irrelevant. It was a fact.

There were lines for Americans and lines for foreigners. There were lines for first-class American passengers which were much shorter. By the time Peter finally got to the head of his line all the Americans had long since been processed and had disappeared. Without looking at him, the immigration officer, a bored looking, middle-aged, heavyset man in a dark blue uniform, held out his hand and said, "Passport." Peter figured this officer had already said that word several hundred times that day and many thousands of times over the course of his employment. Peter handed over his passport, which contained his visa, to the man who still didn't look at him. After thumbing through the pages, the officer looked at the man and woman in line behind him, and asked, "Are those your parents?"

"No."

He looked around impatiently. "Well, where are they?"

"They're dead."

"Give me the form." He almost snatched it out of Peter's hands. He glanced at it briefly and asked, "This Mr. and Mrs. Bradley, do they know you're coming to stay with them?"

"Of course they do," replied Peter somewhat testily, annoyed by the man's disdainful attitude.

"Don't get smart with me, kid. Just answer the questions," the officer said sharply. He reached over and snatched the tag off Peter's jacket, tearing off the button it was attached to. Without apologizing, he looked at the tag, crumpled it up and threw it on the floor. Then he reached for one of a number of metallic stamps, stamped a page of Peter's passport and gave it back to him. "You can go," he said without emotion, then looked over Peter's shoulder and shouted, "Next."

"How do I get to New York?" Peter asked.

"This is New York, kid. Where did you think you were?" the officer retorted.

"I mean the middle of New York, where all the shops and hotels are."

"What do you think I am, a travel agent? Get moving."

Peter "got moving." He had just met his first unpleasant American. It would not be his last.

THE STRAWBERRY CHEESECAKE

BUSES LEFT FREQUENTLY for Manhattan from the docks. Peter climbed aboard one with the sign "Midtown." The fare was 35 cents. One of the American students had told him about a cheap hotel called The Drummond. He said it was plain but clean and that it was within walking distance of a lot of interesting places to see in New York. The bus driver told him where to get off and how to get to the hotel. It was two turnings, or as he came to understand, two blocks, from the bus stop.

The lobby was small, with four or five rather well-used upholstered chairs and a vending machine for Coca Cola. The desk clerk, a bald-headed man wearing a shirt that looked like he had slept in it, sat in a corner behind the desk reading a newspaper. As Peter approached, he noticed a well chewed unlit stub of a cigar protruding from one side of the man's mouth. The clerk did not immediately look up.

"I'd like a room, please."

A couple of slightly seedy-looking men sitting in

the lobby and smoking cigarettes glanced up with mild interest when they heard Peter's cockney accent.

"Where you from boy, Boston?" asked one.

"A bit further east than that," replied Peter, with a smile.

"There ain't nothing further east than Boston, unless you live on a boat. Don't you know no geography?" the man asked.

"England, I'm from England and that's a lot further east than Boston."

The man grunted. "I thought you talked funny."

"You got money, boy?" The room clerk, who had finally finished reading and had put the newspaper down, asked.

"Yes sir," said Peter.

The clerk looked Peter up and down and said, "Cheapest room I got is $3 a night. You got that kinda money, son?"

"Yes sir," Peter repeated.

"How long you staying?"

"I'm not sure."

"Well, you pay $3 in advance every day, starting now."

Peter fished out $3 from his pocket. The clerk gave him a key and told him the room was on the third floor and the bathroom was at the end of the hall.

The room was even smaller than the cabin on the *Liberté*. There was a narrow bed, a chest of drawers and a rod with metal hangers dangling from it. There was a naked light bulb hanging on a wire from the ceiling and a small table beside the bed that had a lamp and an ashtray. The room reeked of stale cigarette smoke. The American student was right. It was cheap and it seemed clean, but there wasn't much else you could say about it.

Chuck and the other Americans had told him of the places to see in New York—the Empire State Building, Central Park, museums, the shops on Fifth Avenue, Grand Central Station, Madison Square Garden and other points of interest. They told him he could eat cheaply at the Automat where you could see different food behind little windows and put coins in the slots to pull out food. They told him to be sure to get the strawberry cheesecake at Lindy's but not to buy anything else there because it was expensive.

It was getting dark and he was hungry. He got directions to Lindy's from the room clerk. It wasn't far. The traffic was heavy—cars everywhere, lights flashing, horns blaring. There were miles and miles of skyscrapers; it was like being in a tunnel without a roof. Peter was fascinated by the multitude of neon signs; some big, some small and some enormous, some flashing, many in a variety of colors advertising all kinds of things—restaurants, cinemas, clothing, live theaters—anything and everything. In London during the war there had been no lights. Everything was dark. Even years after the war there was almost no neon advertising.

Everywhere in New York Peter saw people, crowds and crowds of people, and they all seemed to have to get somewhere in a hurry. They came at Peter in swarms and seemingly without any effort to go around him. He ducked and weaved and crossed several streets. He had been warned about cars driving on the "wrong" side of the road in America. He had become so used to cars driving on the "right" side of the road that it was second nature, when crossing the road, to look in the direction from which you anticipated cars approaching. He forgot and his trip to the United States nearly ended almost before it started. He stepped off the curb and a taxi swerved to miss him with the driver yelling out the window, something to do with his backside.

Even as a very young boy, Peter was adventurous, or, as his mother would say "full of mischief." When he was four, he was left with a babysitter while his mother and sister went to the wedding of a friend. Not to be left out, Peter sneaked out of the apartment and rode his tricycle to the church. Although it was only a half mile away, he had to cross a couple of busy streets. He sat in the back of the church, undetected, and, after the ceremony, rode his tricycle home. When he was ten he traveled by himself on two different buses to the grounds of the mighty Chelsea Football Club, went through an unmanned turnstile and, with twenty thousand fans, watched the entire game. He was fearless, which was both an asset and a danger.

As he made his way toward Lindy's, he felt neither adventurous, nor mischievous, nor fearless. What he felt was fear; fear of being thousands of miles from home with little money, no friends and no financial ability to get back to London. He wondered how he could ever be able to pay for a return ticket. *I'm being silly*, he thought. *This is a great adventure and I'm going to stick it out.*

He got to Lindy's and looked at the menu posted in the window. His friends weren't joking about the prices. They were frightening. The strawberry cheesecake was $2.00—almost as much as a night's lodging at the hotel. As an errand boy in London, he earned two pounds a week, which translated to around seven or eight dollars. He was about to buy a piece of cheesecake that would have cost him close to two day's pay in London. He went inside. The place was large, but it looked quite crowded. A man wearing a tuxedo approached Peter and looked him up and down. So many people did that to him. Maybe it was the suit. Maybe they admired Savile Row tailoring or maybe they didn't. Peter stared back at the man, assuming he was the headwaiter.

"What do you want?" the man asked in a not altogether pleasant manner.

"Well I want to get a piece of strawberry cheesecake."

"Oh you do, do you?" His tone was not becoming any friendlier.

"Yes, please." He felt a little like Oliver Twist even though he hadn't eaten anything yet, much less wanting more.

"All right, just this once but only this once. You wait outside."

Peter complied. Strange customs, he thought. Why would a restaurant serve food on the pavement? The place was crowded, but there were empty tables inside. There were no tables at all outside. In a few minutes the man in the tuxedo came out the door carrying a small cardboard carton, presumably with a piece of strawberry cheesecake inside.

"Here, take this," the man said brusquely. "And don't you come around here begging for food ever again. You got that?"

"But I wasn't—" Peter started.

"Beat it!" the man said. Peter hadn't heard the term before, but he conjectured it had something to do with leaving and he left. He began to wonder if maybe people weren't looking at the suit with admiration for the tailoring, but were seeing something only a beggar would wear. If that was the case, it had got him a free piece of cheesecake. Holding it carefully, he made his way back to the hotel.

"What you got there kid?" asked the hotel desk clerk.

"A piece of strawberry cheesecake from Lindy's."

"Wow! That must have cost you an arm and a leg."

"Want a piece?"

"Just a small bite," said the desk clerk, fetching some paper plates and knives and forks. The slice of cheesecake was big and Peter cut off a large portion for the clerk, who protested that he was being given too much, but took it anyway. They sat and talked and ate the cheesecake very slowly, savoring each bite. It was creamy and loaded with plump juicy strawberries. It was by far the best thing either one of them had ever tasted.

NEW YORK CITY

With the exception of five days on the Atlantic and now his second day in America, Peter had lived all his life in London. The room clerk had given him a map of New York City. Compared to London, the city was tiny. He was quite sure that he could walk from the Hudson to the East River in a couple of hours and from the Atlantic to the Harlem River in an afternoon. You couldn't walk from one end of London to the other in days, and he didn't know anybody who had ever tried it. You could stick the whole of Manhattan into a small corner of London and most Londoners would not even know it was there, except, of course, for the incessant noise. He had been awakened at three in the morning by music coming from different places, people talking and car horns—always car horns. He decided that he was the only person in New York City who had gone to bed that night.

Soon it was Monday morning. He had been walking around for two hours with no particular destination in mind. He was on Park Avenue going toward Grand

Central Station. He seemed to be the only person going in that direction. Legions of people continually streamed out of the station almost all heading in the direction opposite from his. It was like going up the down escalator on the London tube. When he was younger, he and his chums used to do that, to the great annoyance of those travelers who were proceeding in the right direction. He found himself being bumped, elbowed and generally pushed around. His only other option was to step off into the street and almost certainly get hit by a car. At times it appeared that there were even more cabs than people, and yet people trying to hail them seemed to have little success.

He had lived in London all his life and knew it was much bigger than New York not only in size but also in population. Why then did he feel like a yokel in from the country on his first visit to the big city? Maybe it was the skyscrapers—they were enormous and everywhere. Maybe it was the cars. London, in 1950, still had few privately owned vehicles and the price of petrol was prohibitive; New York probably had ten times more cars than all of England. Maybe it was the incessant noise. In truth it was the people, millions of them all packed into an area not much larger than the size of Hyde Park. They were crammed together like sardines and all in motion, all going who knows where. Wherever it was they were going, they did it with an almost frightening ferocity of purpose.

He had heard that the finest shops were on Fifth

Avenue. It was to New York what Bond Street was to London. The difference was that the shops on Fifth Avenue were overflowing with all manner of merchandise and numerous customers, whereas those on Bond Street still had very little to sell and few customers.

He went in and out of the shops all morning gawking at the jewelry, clothes, toys and dozens of other things. It was clear that he was not a real customer and yet the sales personnel were infallibly kind to him, did not look down their noses at him, and always asked him if he needed help. Given the rudeness he had encountered at Lindy's, he was pleasantly surprised at how nice the sales people were in the shops. Maybe the fact that he was not wearing the "suit" caused people to have a different reaction to him. He had put on a blue shirt and a sweater although he still found the name funny. Unlike the "suit," they fit him well. His infrequent visits to London stores had not always been quite so pleasant.

After a while he got a little tired of the shops. It was interesting at first but he got a bit frustrated looking at things he couldn't afford to buy. He decided to go look at things that wouldn't cost much. He remembered a movie his mother had taken him to where the people went to the top of the Empire State Building. He asked direction from a policeman. It wasn't a long walk. He went up an elevator to the top of the Empire State Building and spent a nickel to look through a telescope. The sights fascinated him and he spent a half hour before remembering what Joe, the desk clerk, had told him about other things to do and see. After coming down from the roof he took a city bus to the Brooklyn Bridge and then paid fifty cents to sit on the top deck of an open-air tour bus that conveniently had stopped right by the bridge.

Finally, he got off the tour bus at the entrance to Central Park and bought a hotdog and a bottle of Coca Cola from a street vendor. He sat in the park for a long time, eating and watching the people—women with children in tow, men and women walking dogs, people in track suits running and children playing. Before Peter left England, his uncle had told him not to be openly critical of the Americans. They are, he said, prideful, insular and resentful of anyone who doesn't think that America and everything American are the best in the world. They talk funny, he said, you might not like them; they are loud, brash and ill-mannered and their food is not very good. These emphatic opinions came from a man who had never been to America, had never eaten American food, and had never met or talked to an American.

Things seemed very different, on this bright sunny day, than they had the night before walking to and from Lindy's. Yes, the people did seem to be loud and maybe even pushy. Yes, they weren't all nice, but nor were the English. Yes, New York was a noisy, crowded place and, despite the fact that he was a big city boy, he was intimidated by it all. But he had come to a surprising conclusion, albeit based on very short acquaintance. He loved it; loved the people, loved the food, loved the noise, the congestion, the cars. In short, he loved New York and, while he was not prepared to say that America and all things American were the best in the world, he already loved America.

THE SCAM

TUESDAY MORNING was magical. Peter had taken the ferry to Staten Island and then a tour boat around Manhattan. He had now seen New York from the top of the Empire State Building; from long, exhausting walks; from an open-air bus; and now from the tour boat. That latter trip was suggested by the room clerk, who was obviously very knowledgeable about the ways to see the city. Later that day while walking through Times Square, he was stopped by a nicely dressed man who looked to be in his late twenties or early thirties. The man looked around furtively and said almost in a whisper, "You wanna buy a ticket for the hit musical at the Carlton?"

Peter smiled. He said, "No, thanks," and started to walk away.

The man grabbed his arm. "Look, you can't buy tickets to this show for love or money. It's sold out for months. My little girl is sick and my wife and I can't go. I sold one ticket and I have just this one left. It cost me $6 but I'll let you have it for $3."

Peter again said no, this time a little more firmly. Again, he started to walk away.

"All right," the man said resignedly. "It's a steal, but $2."

For reasons he could not quite explain to himself, Peter reached into his pocket, gave the man $2 and took the ticket. The man turned and hurried away.

Peter got back to the hotel later that afternoon and was greeted by the room clerk. He still looked like he had slept in his clothes and still had what appeared to be the same unlit cigar stub stuck in his mouth, but he was now much friendlier. Perhaps he was still enjoying the memory of the cheesecake.

"Well, Peter, what've you got planned for this evening?"

Peter explained the fortuitous meeting with the man who sold him the ticket for that evening's performance.

"Uh oh! That sounds a bit suspicious. That's the hottest show in town. People have been scalping tickets for three or four times the face price. Why would this guy sell you a ticket for a third of the price on the ticket? I hope you haven't been taken."

But he had. When he got to the theater and presented the ticket, the person in the kiosk looked carefully at both sides of it and then picked up the phone. The theater manager quickly appeared and was handed the ticket without a word being said. The manager also scrutinized both sides of the ticket, held it up to the light and said to Peter, "I'm sorry son, but this is a counterfeit ticket. There've been several people selling clever forgeries around Broadway and Times Square and I'm afraid you bought one of the fake tickets."

An older grey-haired gentleman and his wife, both elegantly dressed, overheard the conversation. The man said, "That's too bad young fellow." The couple then walked off a few steps and whispered to each other. The man walked back to Peter and said, "Look, we have an empty seat in our box and we would be delighted for you to join us."

Peter was overwhelmed and stammered out his thanks. They took an elevator and were greeted effusively by a theater employee, who was obviously familiar with the elderly couple, and ushered them to their seats. The view to the stage from the box was excellent. During the two intermissions, Peter explained to his benefactors where he had come from (although his accent was a dead giveaway) and about his plans to see America. The older couple introduced themselves as Mr. and Mrs. Hamilton. They were captivated by the young English boy and they marveled at the courage it must have taken for him to strike out on his own at such a young age. When the show was over, Peter thanked them both profusely and started to say his farewells.

"Won't you come and have a bite with us, Peter?" Mrs. Hamilton asked. "We're going to have a light supper in our apartment and we'd love to have you join us." Peter readily accepted. A chauffeur-driven Rolls Royce picked the three of them up outside the theater and drove them to the Hamiltons' apartment on Park Avenue.

"I hope riding in this British car won't make you homesick," Mrs. Hamilton gently teased. Peter smiled somewhat weakly. He had ridden in a private car only once in his life and that was when their next door neighbor had driven him and his mother to the hospital in his rickety old Austin. After they arrived at a tall residential building and went up many floors in an elevator, the door to the apartment was opened by a maid and they went into an enormous room with leather couches, deep plush armchairs and other elegant pieces of furniture. There was a Steinway grand piano in one corner and a dark-stained bookcase covering one whole wall filled with hundreds of books. Mrs. Hamilton saw Peter staring at the piano. "Do you play?" she asked. "No," Peter answered, a little wistfully. "I took a few lessons but it wasn't for me. My sister plays the violin." "I bet she's good at it," said Mrs. Hamilton. "Not too bad," replied Peter.

While Peter was no expert on art, he was sure the paintings on the walls were worth a fortune. He was also sure that the interior of Buckingham Palace could not have been more impressive. The apartment occupied the whole of the penthouse. It had views of all of New York. Mr. Hamilton took Peter out on the balcony and pointed out various landmarks. "There's the Empire State Building" Mr. Hamilton said. "I was up there this afternoon. Doesn't look as big from here," said Peter. "You two better come in out of the cold. It's nice and warm in here," Mrs. Hamilton called. The three of them sat and talked for a couple of hours while the maid brought them a procession of soups, salads, various meats and desserts. *If this is a light supper,* Peter thought, *I wonder what a big meal would look like.* Peter told the couple about his schooling, how he got to America, what things he would like to see and how much fun he had had so far. They told him of what else he could see in New York, what their grownup children were doing with their lives and how they spent much of their time in their second home in what they referred to as "The Hamptons."

Finally it was time for Peter to leave. He again thanked his hosts for their kindness and assured them he could find his own way back to his hotel. Mrs. Hamilton would have none of it. She buzzed for the maid and told her to have the chauffeur take Peter back to his hotel. Mr. Hamilton gave Peter his card and made him promise that he would keep in touch and let them know how he was getting along in America. Mrs. Hamilton insisted that Peter call her if he ran into any trouble or needed any help.

As they drove to the hotel the chauffeur said to him, "Do you know who you just went to the theater and had dinner with?"

"Well yes," said Peter, puzzled by the question, "Mr. and Mrs. Hamilton."

"But do you know who Mr. Hamilton is?" persisted the chauffeur.

"I suppose not," said Peter, still puzzled.

"He's the president of Dockhouse Industries and one of the ten wealthiest men in the entire country."

Peter had recognized that the Hamiltons were very

rich people. The theater box, the chauffeur-driven Rolls and the fabulous apartment told him that. He had no idea just how wealthy they were until the chauffeur told him. His three hundred pound uncle, the only relative of his with money, was like a homeless man compared to Mr. Hamilton. With all their money and important people they knew and important things they had to do, they still found the time to befriend a lonely English kid.

Later when he wrote and told his sister of the evening with the Hamiltons, she urged him to drop them a line, thanking them for their kindness. He sent them a postcard and, over time, they corresponded. Eventually the correspondence became less frequent and ultimately ended. Peter was sorry to lose touch with them. They had been kind and generous to him, as had Chuck Bradley, but they had their own families, friends and lives. They had touched his life and he would never forget them.

"Well, what happened?" The room clerk was eager to know.

"It's late Joe. It's a long, truly unbelievable story. I'll tell you all about it tomorrow."

THE BACK OF THE BUS

"Well Joe, I'm moving on."

Peter had packed his things, tied his suitcase shut and checked out at the front desk. He had been in New York for less than a week and had been everywhere and seen everything, at least everything one person with very little money to spend could see in this busy, crowded city in five days.

"Sorry to see you go, Peter," said the room clerk. "You are what the English call 'a lovely blake.' I heard it in a British movie."

"That's 'bloke,' not 'blake.' And you, Joe, are what the Americans call 'a swell guy.' I saw that in an American movie."

"I'm going to miss you. You take good care of yourself and come back and see us again," said Joe.

"Thanks for everything, Joe. I would've had a much harder time finding all the sights without your help." He scribbled his address in London on a piece of paper and gave it to Joe. "Come to London one of these days and I'll return the favor."

"It's a deal! I always wanted to go there and see all them 'blokes' and 'blokesses,' particularly the blokesses." Both laughed.

The Greyhound bus was half empty as it pulled out of the station and crossed the Hudson River heading south, initially through northern New Jersey toward Philadelphia. Peter found a window seat and stowed his suitcase in the overhead rack above it. New Jersey was passing by and he was surprised at how beautiful it was. There were many trees, and the route took the bus through small towns, some quite reminiscent of small towns in England.

There were signs everywhere: how far it was to wherever, names of towns, notification of exits and many others. Peter thought how different things were in England with the total absence of directional signs during the war. The government had ordered them all to be removed. This was intended to confuse the German troops, assuming an invasion. It was, of course, too much to hope that the Germans would simply leave and go back to Germany because they couldn't find their way to Piccadilly Circus and because no patriotic Englishman would give them directions.

The bus stopped fairly frequently and started to fill up. By the time it stopped in Philadelphia it was pretty near full. An elderly Negro man walked down the aisle, looked around then stopped and asked Peter, "Would you mind if I sat next to you, sir?"

Peter was more than a little taken aback by being called "sir." Nobody had ever addressed him that way before. "Not at all," he replied and the man sat down, positioning himself so close to the aisle that Peter feared he would fall out of his seat.

"My name's Peter, Peter Mason. I'm visiting from England. Going to try to see all of America, if I can."

The man smiled, but didn't say anything.

"What's your name?" asked Peter.

"Solomon Broward."

"Are you from Philadelphia?"

"Yes." The man did not seem to be unfriendly, nor did he seem to want to talk. Still Peter persisted.

"I'm going to stop for a day or two in Washington, DC," Peter said, "the nation's capital," he added unnecessarily. "Then maybe I'll go farther down south to Atlanta and New Orleans. I want to see everything in your country."

As Peter prattled away in what was essentially a one-sided conversation, Broward's obvious discomfort finally started to melt away.

"I'm going to Jackson to see my son, daughter-in-law and my grandchildren," he finally offered. "I don't go there very often and I'm really looking forward to it. My son's name is Joshua."

"I never heard of Jackson. Where is it?"

"It's in Mississippi. It's the state capital. I was born there, but moved up north after the war. Actually, I've been to your country. I was in the army over there in a transportation company; drove a truck in England and then in France and Italy."

"We had lots of Yanks in England during the war. Maybe I saw you."

"Maybe you did," Broward said smiling.

"Jackson, sounds like someone's name. What's it like?"

"It's small for a state capital. It's different to what you're used to. You might not like some of what goes on down there. You want to be careful and not get sideways with white folks down there. They wouldn't take kindly to that. Things hasn't changed much in over a hundred years and you've got to go along with it. They're set in their ways. Life is slower. You just came from New York where everything is rush, rush. Jackson is different. People walk and talk slow-like. They take their time eating and reading. Most don't travel much. A lot of them have never been out of the state of Mississippi. Their likes and dislikes in food are very different from up North."

"What about how whites treat Negroes? I've heard some things but I don't know much about it. We don't have many Negroes in England. Of course there were a lot there during the war."

Broward hesitated. "I think I'm going to let you find out about that yourself. It'll be part of your education. If you go down there, you'll see and hear things you probably never heard or saw before. You'll understand it better by seeing and hearing it than by me telling you about it."

Their conversation continued, each telling the other about their lives and their families. Solomon had been wounded in combat, received a Purple Heart and was hospitalized in England for some time. He now worked in Philadelphia as a clerk in one of the courts, although he would be retiring in a year or two. His wife had died several years earlier and he lived with his sister and her husband.

Peter told Solomon of his life in England during the war, where he had gone to school and that his parents were both dead, although that was only half true. He told him what he had done and seen in New York and whom he had met there. The passengers in the nearby seats didn't say anything to either Peter or Solomon, although the white man in the seat immediately in front of Solomon turned around several times with what appeared to be an angry look on his face.

When they got to Baltimore and pulled into the Greyhound station, the bus driver came down the aisle and stopped by Solomon's seat.

"OK, boy," he said in a loud voice, "get out of that seat and get to the back of the bus."

"But I like this seat," protested Peter. "Why should I change?"

"I ain't talking to you, sonny, so butt out. I'm talking to the guy sitting next to you," growled the driver.

"But why?"

The driver ignored Peter. "All right boy, let's move now," he said threateningly.

"Why does he have to move?" Peter asked politely, although it was now clear to him what was going on.

"Look kid, I ain't telling you again. Shut your face or I'll kick you off the bus and you can damn well walk to wherever the hell you're going." Turning back to Broward, he went on, "And I'm going to kick your ass off, boy, unless you move back there in the next ten seconds."

Solomon reached under the seat in front, pulled out his small, cloth-covered bag and slowly got up. He leaned over toward Peter and said in a quiet, gentle voice, "Peter, you'll learn a lot of lessons in this country. Some of them will be pleasant—some won't. You have to be prepared for those not so pleasant ones. You will learn about "sir" and "boy" and many other things. Don't get into trouble, and may God bless you."

With that, he walked toward the rear of the bus. Peter turned and saw that all of the last four rows were now occupied by Negroes. He was stunned by what had just happened to this pleasant, kindly old gentleman. He was also surprised that the bus driver's rudeness did not seem to bother the other passengers. Conversations had stopped briefly, but quickly resumed. Peter sensed no discomfort among the white passengers nor, indeed, among the Negroes.

Within a few moments, a heavy-set white woman in a flowered dress, wearing too much makeup and smelling of cheap perfume, sat down next to him. "Do you mind changing seats with me?" she asked.

"I'm sorry but I like the window. I've never been here before and I like looking out the window," he responded.

"But I don't want to sit in the seat that the man who

just left sat in."

"No, I won't move," said Peter.

"Well, I can't say as I blame you for not wanting to sit in this seat given who was here last," she snorted.

"That's not the reason," Peter replied. He didn't say another word to her until the bus arrived in Washington, DC. As he got off, he turned to wave to Solomon Broward, but he wasn't able to catch Solomon's eye.

THE HOSTEL

"YOU LOST?"

Peter looked up and saw a fellow, perhaps a couple of years older than him, leaning up against a battered old car. Peter had come out of the bus station in Washington, DC and was standing on the curb, wondering where he should go and how he should get there.

"Yeah I'm lost," Peter replied.

"Where do you want to go?"

"I haven't a clue. I'm going round the country looking at things. I've never been here before and I haven't got much money. I've gotta find a very cheap hotel."

"Are you Australian?"

"No, I'm English."

"Ever stay in a hostel?"

"No. What's that?"

"Well it's not very fancy. You'd have to stay in a room with a bunch of other guys, share a bathroom with a whole lot of other people, make your own bed and pay in advance. It's cheap though, half the price of even the worst flea pit in town."

"Cheap is what I'm looking for. So long as I've my own bed, I can put up with the rest."

"What's your name?"

"Peter Mason. What's yours?"

"Fred Stegel. I'm waiting for my buddy. He's coming in from Pittsburgh. He'll be in any minute. We're going to stay in that hostel and we'll give you a ride." Peter's mother had warned him to be wary of strangers and not to accept rides from anyone he didn't know. Since very few people in postwar England had cars, nobody in England had ever offered him a ride and his mother's caution was never tested.

They didn't have to wait long. Fred's friend was on the next arriving bus. "Doug, say hello to Peter. He sounds like an Aussie but he says he's a limey."

"I didn't say I was a limey. I said I was English," Peter retorted but good-naturedly.

"Same thing. Let's go."

Both of Peter's new acquaintances seemed like nice fellows and there didn't seem to be any way he was going to find the hostel without their help. They were lucky. The hostel was only half full. They were assigned to a room with six beds, but the three of them would have it to themselves. The room was large and Spartan, but clean. The room clerk was a jovial woman who people might describe as "pleasingly plump." She expressed the hope that Peter would not be offended by having to share the bathroom. Since Peter in his whole life had never had his own bathroom, the sharing requirement was no hardship.

Fred and his friend, Doug Atterbury, told Peter that they were between their junior and senior years at the University of Minnesota and had taken a semester off to travel around. Peter had never met anyone in England who had gone to university. Well that might not be completely accurate. He didn't know for sure whether the owners of the real estate agency he worked for in London had gone to university. They might have, but if they did, they never told him. One of the tenants in his block of flats was an accountant. He might have been to university, but probably not. He was the only person in the flats who had a car.

That evening the three of them went out to get something to eat. They stopped in a bar and had hamburgers and beers. The waitress didn't ask to see IDs, although Peter, and perhaps the other two, were under age. As they lingered over their drinks, Doug asked, "Where are you going from here, Peter?"

"I thought maybe I'd go to Jackson, Mississippi."

Fred exclaimed, "What?!"

Doug choked on his beer. "Mississippi!" Doug said still coughing and spluttering. "Why the hell would you go there?"

"Why not?"

"First of all, there's nothing to see and nothing to do there. Second, the food is awful, grits and collard greens and stuff like that. Third, even we can't understand what they're saying and we're Americans. Think what problems a limey like you would have," said Fred.

"If I don't like it I don't have to stay long."

"You'd better be careful down there—that's the Deep South," warned Doug.

"Why does everybody keep telling me that and what does the Deep South have to do with it?"

"Boy you are green," said Fred in exasperation. "They have their own ways. They don't like outsiders. They don't like us northerners. They don't like Negroes and they aren't going to like you. You be plenty careful or you'll be in a heap of trouble and I'm talking physical trouble. You run afoul of their ways and they'll beat the shit out of you, or worse. I wouldn't go near the place."

"Me neither," agreed Doug.

"You ever been there?" asked Peter. Both had to admit that they hadn't, but they nonetheless claimed a lot more knowledge than Peter had. That wasn't hard since Peter had no knowledge. Fred and Doug were right. He was green. He was also a little scared—well maybe a lot scared. To his recollection he had never even seen a Negro until he was eleven years old. The only Negroes he had seen from age eleven until he arrived in America were American soldiers sent to England to prepare for the invasion of Europe. They were seen in restaurants and pubs. Many of them went out with white English women. They had no restrictions as to where they could go and with whom they could associate. He had heard of segregation, but he knew little about it. In his school there was no class on American history. He had heard of the American Civil War, but to an English boy, the Civil War meant the War of the Roses. His education into the South really had its start with Solomon Broward and had just been supplemented by his two new friends. Strangely, the warnings only strengthened his resolve to go there, but it didn't dissolve his fear. Maybe it was merely curiosity, but he'd made up his mind. He was going.

The next day Peter toured the sights with his new American friends. They went to the Lincoln Memorial, the Washington Monument, and looked at the Capitol, the Supreme Court Building and the White House, although they didn't go inside any of them. They went to see the law school at Georgetown University where Doug was thinking of going when he graduated from Minnesota. They walked the length of the Mall from the Lincoln Memorial to the Capitol, and when they found an old tennis ball, they took time out and threw it back and forth for a while. Exhausted, they went back to the hostel and collapsed on their beds.

The next day the three of them left Washington.

"Peter, why don't you come with us?" said Fred. "We're going to drive back to Minnesota by way of South Bend, Indiana. Doug wants to consider Notre Dame Law School as a possibility. There's a lot of great things to see on the way. If you want to see the Mississippi River instead of the state of Mississippi, we can go that way, too. How about it? It'll be a lot safer than going down South."

"It's tempting and thanks a lot, but no. I think I'll go to Jackson. I may end up going to Minnesota, so give me your addresses and phone numbers. Who knows? One day I might show up on your doorstep."

They wrote down the information on a piece of paper, but Peter never went to Minnesota and never saw or spoke to them again. He never forgot them, even though he knew them for only a short time, but they were part of the experience he was seeking and part of the education he was receiving. It was as Solomon Broward had said, "There will be good experiences and bad experiences." This was one of the good ones.

He watched as their car disappeared, both of them waving out of the windows. He was alone again, and that empty feeling in the pit of his stomach returned. He could have gone with them. Instead, he was going by himself to a place that sounded strange, and might indeed be dangerous. He doubted that anyone else in his position would have made that choice and he could not come up with a very persuasive reason why he had. He'd received very similar warnings about going to the Deep South from two very dissimilar sources; somewhat more subtly from an elderly Negro who had lived there for a long time, and from two young northern college students who had never been there.

THE BOARDING HOUSE

THE FIRST THING he did when he got off the bus in Jackson was to look for a drugstore. He thought that drugstores probably carried local newspapers and that, if they were similar to English newspapers, they would have sections listing rooms to rent. In New York he got some puzzled looks when he'd asked for "the chemist shop." He now knew that Americans called it a "drugstore." He bought a local newspaper. The man at the cash register thanked him, smiled and hoped that he would have a nice day. Peter was quite taken aback at the friendliness of this total stranger, but had the presence of mind to wish him a nice day in return. He had gone to many chemist shops in England and one in New York. No employees had ever expressed the hope that he would have a nice day or given the slightest indication that they cared.

He found a bench, opened the newspaper and looked for the classified advertisements section on apartments and rooms for rent. He had decided to stay in Jackson for more than a few nights and a hotel room at $3 or even

$2 a night would be far too expensive. He found one ad that sounded attractive: a large room that opened onto a backyard, which he assumed was the English equivalent of a garden, and it had its own entrance. The price was $17 a month and the address was somewhere on North State Street. He stopped a passerby and asked for directions to the address. The passerby, as friendly as the cash register man had been, told him how to get there, and even offered to walk with him to the location. Peter thanked him, but said that accompanying him would not be necessary.

As he followed the route the man had described to him, he passed a number of people going the opposite way. Some of them smiled and several even said hello or good afternoon. *The warmth of these people is amazing,* thought Peter. Fred and Doug and even Solomon had it all wrong. There was nothing menacing or frightening here, quite the contrary. So far this place was the warmest and friendliest he had ever been to. Then he suddenly saw something which was not as warm and not as friendly, but was, in fact, chilling. He passed a petrol station—the first one he had seen in America. It hadn't seemed like New York or Washington had petrol stations, but they must have.

The station had lavatories with doors that were visible from the street. There was one that had painted on it 'White Women,' another 'Colored Women,' a third 'Colored Men,' and the last one 'White Men'

The fact of segregation in the Deep South came as no surprise to him. He knew of it before he left England, although only in general terms. He and Chuck had talked about it briefly. Fred and Doug had warned him about it and he had witnessed it on the bus. Nonetheless, seeing it in writing, professionally painted in a public place for the first time, came as a shock. He wondered what would happen if he walked into the men's lavatory that said "Colored" or if a Negro man walked into the one that said "White." The only attendant that he saw was an old Negro man. Would he call the police if the wrong lavatory was used? What was the penalty for using the wrong lavatory? He decided that if he was going to find out, he would do it another time when he wasn't carrying a heavy suitcase.

The door at the address on North State Street was opened by a woman of about sixty. She was thin, had grey hair pulled back tightly in a bun and wore thick horn-rimmed glasses.

"Yes?" she said.

"I've come about the room you advertised. Is it still available?"

"Yes it is," she replied. "Come in and I'll show it to you."

The room that she showed him was large; much bigger than his bedroom in England and twice as big as the cabin he shared with Chuck. There were French windows that opened into a large garden bordered by magnolia trees. There were carefully cultivated flower beds and a freshly mown lawn. The room had a double bed, a closet, a chest of drawers and a desk and chair.

"You'll share a bathroom with one other tenant. Each room has a door into the bathroom. When one of you is using it, the door to the other room can be locked. It's $17 a month. Do you want it or not?" she said rather sharply.

"Can I just rent it by the week?" Peter asked. "I don't know how long I'll be staying."

"No. It's by the month and payment is in advance," she retorted.

"All right, I'll take it," he said, as he pulled a $20 bill out of his pocket and handed it to her. She reached into a pocket in her apron and gave him three one-dollar bills.

"By the way," she said, "I can't place your accent. Are you from Boston?"

Peter was perplexed. This was the second person who thought he was from Boston. Chuck was the only person he had ever spoken to who came from Boston and, to Peter, he could not possibly be mistaken for an Englishman.

"No," said Peter. "I'm English. I'm from England."

Her face lit up and she smiled broadly. "My great-grandfather was English," she said. "And I had a distant cousin who came here from Scotland." She lowered her voice and almost whispered as though telling a family secret that she didn't want anyone else to hear. "You know, I think that one of my ancestors came over from England on the *Mayflower*. Here's the key. You seem like a real nice boy. If there is anything you want, you just let me know."

Somebody had once told him, he couldn't remember who, that many southerners, at least white ones, were very proud of their English ancestry. It looked as though his accent was going to turn out to be a real advantage, provided people did not confuse it with that of a Yankee from Boston.

71

THE ACCIDENT

FRED AND DOUG were right about one thing; there wasn't much to see or do in Jackson. Solomon Broward had told him that, unlike people in New York, those in Jackson seemed to do everything slowly. It hadn't taken him long to find out how true that was. People in New York always seemed to be in a frantic hurry to go somewhere and do something. Nobody in Jackson seemed to be in the slightest hurry to go anywhere or do anything. He enjoyed people-watching and he was slowly getting used to the language, although not completely. There were other things, not as enjoyable, he was not getting used to and never would.

One afternoon he stopped at a small café for lunch. He ordered a cheese sandwich and a coke. The waitress asked him if wanted "burr'n leds." He asked her to repeat what she said and she repeated "burr'n leds." Since he still didn't understand what she was saying, he concluded that economic prudence dictated that he decline "burr'n leds" for fear that it would be expensive and he might not like it anyway. Later he learned that "burr'n leds" was "butter and lettuce" and there was no extra charge for it. He finished his sandwich sans butter and lettuce and ventured out into the street. It was bitterly cold. He had incorrectly assumed that the south was always warm. He was bundled up in a lined jacket he had bought at a secondhand store the third day he was in Mississippi, a pair of gloves and a scarf he had brought from England, and a baseball cap he had bought from a sporting goods store. The cap said "Ole Miss" which the storekeeper had explained was the nickname of the University of Mississippi. If he didn't talk, he could pass for a native Mississippian.

He walked briskly down several streets and unwittingly crossed into what was the Negro section of downtown Jackson. He had come to understand that, not only were individuals separated by race, but the town was also split, with Negro housing, businesses, hospitals, restaurants, movie houses and other establishments in one part and white housing, businesses, hospitals, restaurants, movie houses and other establishments in another, completely separate part.

What happened next was inevitable. Lost in thought, he again momentarily forgot that traffic came at you from a different direction than was true in England. He looked the wrong way, stepped off the curb and the last thing he knew was hearing the screech of brakes.

People also heard the screeching and came pouring out of neighboring stores. The car that hit Peter stopped as did several others.

"It wasn't my fault," pleaded the driver. "He stepped right out in front of me. I couldn't help it. Did any of you see it?"

Peter had slammed face first into the pavement. A couple of people gently turned him over. What was visible of his face above his scarf was covered in blood.

"We've got to get him to the hospital right away," said one of the bystanders.

Several of them gently laid him down on the backseat of a Negro-operated taxi cab that had stopped. The driver took off toward Froman Hospital which was only four blocks away. Froman was a ramshackle building that was once a wholesale warehouse. It had been converted into a hospital shortly before the war and was staffed entirely by Negro doctors, nurses, administrators and other personnel. The cab driver ran in to get help and came out with two orderlies who placed Peter on a stretcher and carried him into the small and ill-equipped space that was used as an emergency room. The only doctor on duty told the two nurses present to undress the patient and clean the blood off his face. He went into an adjoining room to wash his hands and put on gloves. Suddenly there was a loud shriek from one of the nurses.

"Doctor, Doctor James!" she called. "You'd better get in here right now. We've got big trouble. This boy's white!"

Doctor James came running in, looked down at Peter and said, "Bring in the portable x-ray machine; I want a picture of his head and neck."

"But doctor, the boy is white."

"I heard you the first time. Do you think x-ray machines only work on Negroes? Get the machine, now!"

The hospital administrator, hearing the shriek, came in from his small cubbyhole of an office. He took one look and said, "Doctor, you've got to call Jackson General, tell them a young boy was brought to our hospital and that he was so covered up with clothes and blood that we didn't know he was white until we wiped the blood off his face. They'll send an ambulance for him right away and they'll know it wasn't our fault that he ended up here."

"Can't do that, Moses. This boy shouldn't be moved. He might have a serious head injury. We move him too much, we might kill him," said Dr. James.

"That's not our concern. We have to think of the hospital," argued the administrator.

"What do you mean, 'not our concern?'" Dr. James said angrily. "This boy is hurt, maybe seriously. You think of the hospital, Moses. I'll think of my patient. It might sound trite to you, but when they made me a doctor, I took an oath and I intend never to violate it. Now get the hell out of here. I need to examine him."

"But Greg . . . "

"Let me understand you, Moses. You want me to, perhaps, kill the kid by not treating this emergency and shipping him off to some white hospital just so I don't run the risk of pissing off some redneck big shot who wants to have my license because I laid my black hands on some white kid? Now move. You're in my way."

After a lengthy examination and review of the x-rays,

Dr. James concluded that there were no broken bones, no internal injuries and no skull fracture. Peter regained consciousness during the examination.

"Where am I? What happened?" he asked in a weak voice.

"You got hit by a car." Dr. James had learned how the injury occurred from an orderly who, in turn, had learned it from the cab driver. "You're all right. If it's okay with you, I'm going to keep you here overnight. You took a pretty hard knock on your forehead. I had to put in several stitches. I want to be sure you don't have intracranial bleeding; that is, bleeding inside your skull."

"Whatever you say, Doctor, and thanks a lot for helping me," said Peter.

Dr. James smiled and gripped Peter's hand. "You're English aren't you? You look *both* ways before you step off the curb from now on. Now you get some rest."

He took one last look at Peter's eyes before he left to see other patients. Both of the pupils were equal in size, reacted to light and were not dilated. The doctor told the on-duty nurse to wake Peter every hour, ask him some questions to see if he was coherent and wasn't slurring his words, examine his eye pupils, ask if he had a headache and call him if there was any difficulty. He then wrote orders and left the room.

Moses Brown, the administrator, cornered James as he came out of Peter's room. He was livid. "Don't play the great selfless hero with me, Greg. We've got a piss pot full of trouble now. It's one thing to give the white boy first aid when he comes in, unexpected. It's a totally different thing when you decide to make him your patient and keep him here in this hospital overnight. I've got a hospital to run and God knows it's tough enough without you pissing off the white medical community, if not the entire white population of this city."

"Just simmer down, Moses. This kid could still be in trouble. If I'm not going to do what is best for this boy and only think of what's best for you, me and this hospital, I might as well turn in my ticket to practice. You talk about 'selflessness' as though it was a goddam disease. That boy's staying here overnight because it's the right thing to do medically. If the white community gets pissed off racially, it's the wrong thing for them to do and I don't give a damn."

DOCTOR GREGORY JAMES

DR. JAMES FINISHED writing on the chart he had prepared for Peter. He leaned back in his chair, sighed and took another mouthful of coffee, which had gone tepid. He was born in Jackson, but had moved to California and had graduated at a top rated west coast medical school. After internship, he had done a four-year residency at a San Francisco hospital. He was board certified in orthopedic surgery and had a successful practice in San Francisco for several years. After Pearl Harbor, he had been drafted into the army. He was rejected for service as an army physician and was not even permitted to be an enlisted medic. Instead, he became an infantryman initially in an all Negro company. But with the many casualties incurred in the European Theater, he became a replacement in an all-white company. During the Battle of the Bulge, he was instrumental in singlehandedly eliminating a German machine gun nest. Although shot through the right shoulder, he carried a wounded soldier back to U.S. lines and saved the life of a second soldier by using his medical training to stem the bleeding from a torn femoral artery.

James's commanding officer had recommended him for the Medal of Honor, the United States' highest award for bravery. When the recommendation was rejected by his regiment, that officer told him that his actions deserved it and he would have received it if he had been white. That same commanding officer also recommended that PFC James be given a battlefield commission and transferred to the medical corps. That recommendation was also rejected. However, he was awarded the Silver Star, the third highest award for bravery. In view of his injuries, he was transported to the military hospital in San Francisco. When his wounds healed, he was given a thirty-day leave. He returned to Jackson to visit his elderly parents. To celebrate, he wanted to take his parents out for a fine dinner. He was now a sergeant, and despite wearing his army uniform, replete with ribbons depicting extreme bravery in the service of his country, he and his parents could not eat at any "white" restaurant in the town.

There was a German prisoner-of-war camp on the outskirts of Jackson. A few of those prisoners were given special dispensation to work on farms in the area and go into town, provided they returned to the camp at night. What made Sergeant (Doctor) James's rejection even more painful, while wearing the uniform of his country, was the sight of several German prisoners dining in restaurants where he was not welcome, while wearing the uniforms of *their* country.

After his honorable discharge from the army, he returned for a while to his medical practice in San Francisco. By this time, his parents were very elderly and his mother quite ill. He was their only son and he felt that he should be with them and help them in their old age. That is how he came to be in Jackson and how he happened to be at Froman Hospital the day that Peter Mason was brought in. He had left one of the most liberal-thinking areas of the country to return to his hometown in what must have been one of the *least* liberal-thinking areas in the country. He had suffered indignities as a child growing up in Jackson as a consequence of his race and suffered continued indignities for the same reason both when he returned as a decorated war hero and when he returned as a practicing physician.

It had gotten late. He had seen and treated a lot of patients that day both before and after the arrival of the young Englishman, and he was bone tired. His reverie was interrupted by the night charge nurse. She had been at Froman since it opened. Her gruff voice and stern exterior hid a kind and caring heart. Although she ran the night staff with a firm hand and would brook no nonsense, there was nothing she wouldn't do for them, the doctors and, most importantly, the patients.

She took one look at James and said, "Doctor, it's after ten and you look like you've been awake for days. Go home and get some sleep." She was a long-time experienced nurse and he took her sternly-delivered scolding for the kindness intended. She paused for a moment and then said, "I heard you and Mr. Brown going at it. If it helps at all, I think he's full of you know what. I know you did the right thing about that young Mason boy. I'm proud of you."

He smiled. "Thanks Becky; coming from you it means a great deal. I'm going. I'll take one last look around."

He stopped in on all of his patients. When he reached Peter's room, he asked the nurse if she had wakened him. She said that she had done so twice and on both occasions he showed no signs of intracranial bleeding. He pushed back Peter's eyelids and checked the pupils. He thought that Peter's color looked good and he smiled at that observation. Despite the doctor's examination, Peter continued to sleep peacefully. Then Doctor Gregory James did what he should have done much earlier. He went home and went to bed.

FROMAN HOSPITAL

It was just starting to get light when Peter woke up. Apart from a slight headache and some stiffness as he tried to move, he felt reasonably well. He was in a small room with two beds and a window with no curtains on it. There was a table beside his bed on which rested a glass with what appeared to be water. The other bed was occupied by an elderly Negro man who appeared to be asleep or unconscious. Peter noticed there was a tube coming out of his nose. He heard two female voices coming from the hallway, both speaking in what he had come to recognize as typical Negro patois. Initially, they were discussing a motion picture they had both seen. Then the talk turned to "that white boy."

"Dr. James should never have let him in here. There'll be the devil to pay when word gets around," said one.

"What was he to do? That white boy might have died if Dr. James didn't help him," said the other. The word "help" came out as "hep" but Peter knew what she meant.

"Do you suppose those white doctors would have cared for my Willie if he was taken to Jackson General after getting knocked down by a car?" the first voice said. She answered her own rhetorical question. "Not on your life. They wouldn't even have let him in the door of that place. Dr. James could be in real trouble and him a great doctor and a war hero. They treat him like dirt. They give him a medal, but he should've got the big one—the Medal of Honor."

"They're not gonna do nuthin' to him. He was only doing what any doctor would have done under the circumstances," said the second voice.

"Dream on, girl. Dream on. Just you wait. Get on with your work," said the first voice in a combative tone, obviously not liking to be contradicted.

Ten minutes later, a nurse came in and told Peter that Dr. James said he could have something light for breakfast, either a smallish portion of grits or a couple of soft-boiled eggs. Never having eaten grits or even knowing what they were, he opted for the eggs. Before she left to get his breakfast, she took his blood pressure and temperature and entered the results on a chart hanging on the end of his bed.

He had finished eating and was reading a magazine that the nurse had brought him, when Dr. James walked in, wearing a white coat with a stethoscope around his neck. He first went over to the old man's bed, looked at his chart, leaned over him and performed some sort of examination. He whispered instructions to a nurse who hurried out of the room. He then took the three steps to Peter's bed.

"How are you feeling this morning, young man?" he asked.

"Fine, Doctor, thanks. Just a little headache and some stiffness," Peter responded.

"Well let's have a look."

The doctor examined Peter's eyes; made him look in different directions; had him move his head around; listened to his heart and his neck with his stethoscope; had him move his arms and legs and felt various parts of his body, periodically asking whether anything he prodded hurt. Peter realized he was sore in a few places, but Dr. James said it would wear off in a few days. He had Peter swallow two yellow pills with a sip of water and then told him he was going to keep him in the hospital for two or three more hours to be sure everything was all right. He gave Peter the bottle of pills and told him to take two of them first thing in the morning and last thing at night for the next three days. "That will take care of the achiness," he said. Peter was instructed to engage in only light activities over the next three days and to rest for most of the time. Lastly he told Peter that the nurses would change the bandage on his head before he left and to keep it on for the next few days. He should then go to a doctor at Jackson General to take the stitches out.

"Can't I come back here and have you take the stitches out?"

"It will probably be better if you go to Jackson General."

"Doctor, are you in trouble for having treated me?"

"Of course not. Whatever gave you that idea?"

"I heard two women talking outside my room this morning. I think they were nurses. They said you would be in big trouble for having treated a white boy and that it was a shame because you're a great doctor and a war hero."

"They're just a couple of old chatterboxes," Dr. James said with a laugh. "Don't pay any attention to them."

"I could tell them at Jackson General that my grandmother was a Negro and therefore I have Negro blood."

Dr. James looked alarmed. "Don't do that, Peter." It was the first time he had used his first name. "I don't know how long you plan to stay in the South, but that could cause you a mess of ongoing trouble."

"Well what if I tell them that I wasn't a Negro, but I told you I was one so you would help me?"

"Don't do that either. It's not necessary and nothing bad is going to come out of this. I assure you."

"Maybe no one will ever find out I was here and that you treated me."

"There are no secrets in this town. Look I appreciate your concern, but really there's no need for it."

"Why do you stay in this town? Why don't you go somewhere else where you can practice medicine and white people won't treat you like dirt?"

"Who said I was treated like dirt by white people?"

"Those two women this morning."

"Oh them again. Pay no attention. Don't get involved in matters down here that you can't fully understand. It will only bring you trouble and grief. Things will change. Maybe not in my lifetime. Perhaps not even in yours. If it will make you feel better, I don't intend to spend my life in Jackson. One of these days I'm going back to San Francisco. Go there if you get the chance. You'd like it. It's a lot different from here."

Peter was discharged from Froman that afternoon. Dr. James had one of the orderlies drive him home. He took the pills as instructed and rested for most of the next three days, pleased that he had met and talked with Dr. James, although he wished their meeting had occurred for a different reason. He remembered some of the things that Solomon Broward had said. What he hadn't said was that Peter's experiences could be both pleasurable and some not so pleasurable at the same time. It was strange and mystifying, but these mixed experiences were the most painful.

JACKSON GENERAL HOSPITAL

On the morning of the fourth day following the accident, Peter presented himself at Jackson General Hospital. Unlike Froman, Jackson General was huge. It was surrounded by spacious lawns, obviously well-kept, and by numerous trees and flower beds. He had spent considerable time concocting various scenarios to explain how he came to have stitches in his head and who had treated him. He decided that the accident must have happened some place other than Jackson and that he was treated and stitched in that other place. Otherwise the logical question would be: why hadn't he gone back to the doctor who treated him for a follow up visit, and for removal of the stitches? No matter what happened or what he was asked, there was no way he was going to implicate Dr. James or Froman Hospital. They could put him in jail before he would do any such thing. Dr. James had assured him that nothing bad would happen if the white community found out that he had treated a white patient. Maybe he was telling the truth, but Peter didn't think so.

There was a series of windows in the lobby and behind each was an admitting clerk. In front of each window were lines of patients or prospective patients. He got in the line that appeared shortest. After ten or fifteen minutes he got to the window. A bored-looking admitting clerk asked him what he wanted.

"I was in accident a while ago and I was hospitalized and treated for my injuries. I now need someone to look at my head wound and take out the stitches," Peter explained.

"What's the name of your doctor?"

"I don't remember."

"Look, sonny, I have a lot to do," she said sharply. "Here's a list of the doctors on staff here. Look through them quickly and pick out the doctor who treated you." She handed him a document containing a long list of names.

"I wasn't treated here," Peter said.

"For heaven's sake." Her patience was wearing thin. "Why don't you just go back to the doctor who treated you, whoever he is and wherever he is, and have him finish up what he started."

"I can't."

"Why not?"

"I wasn't injured here. I was injured in Washington, DC."

"Well why didn't you say so at first? There are a lot of people waiting behind you." She fished out a form, handed it to Peter and told him to take a seat, fill out the form, return it to her and wait for his name to be called.

He sat and waited for two hours in a room filled with

people in wheelchairs, on crutches, with bandages on various parts of their bodies and others who just looked ill. Over the course of two hours, patients came and went; names were called and the owners of the names were ushered through a door at the end of the room and presumably went to one or other of the examining rooms. During the wait, perhaps forty or more patients were processed in that room. There were men and women, young people and old, children and adults. They all had one thing in common. They were all white. He noticed the lavatories were labeled "men" and "women," but were not labeled "white" and "colored." Peter conjectured that was because colored people were probably not allowed in the building. That turned out not to be completely accurate. He saw a Negro man sweeping the floor, and when he went to the lavatory there was a Negro man cleaning the wash basins. He assumed they had their own toilet facilities in a separate part of the hospital.

Eventually, a nurse opened the door through which all previous patients had entered.

"Peter Mason," she called out.

He went through the door and followed the nurse past several examining rooms until she beckoned him to go into one. There was a desk with a lot of files, a couple of hard wooden chairs, something that looked a little like a bed and a variety of mysterious-looking medical instruments. Peter sat in one of the chairs for a half hour until a man in a white coat came in.

"Well, young man, what seems to be the trouble?"

Peter explained what had happened.

"Well why didn't you go back to the doctor who treated you?"

That question again! Peter gave him the made-up story that the accident had happened in Washington four days ago, that he couldn't remember the name of the doctor that treated him and that he had then traveled to Jackson.

"I'm very surprised that the doctor didn't try to stop you from traveling with that nasty bump on the head. You could have had some serious complications."

"He did tell me not to go and to stay and rest, but I had to meet a friend here and I'm sorry I didn't do what he said."

The doctor removed the stitches, looked carefully at the wound, put on some sort of ointment, applied a patch and then said, "You're a very lucky young man. The doctor you saw must be a top man. This wound was treated superbly and the stitching is as fine a job as I have ever seen. As a result of his handiwork, you almost certainly won't have a scar and if you do it will be barely perceptible."

Peter couldn't resist one last comment. "Oh, and his nurse told me he was a war hero and got the third highest medal that the army gives."

"He must have been a medical officer in a front line area. I'd liked to have met him. If by any chance you ever remember his name, I would like to congratulate him both on his medical skills and on his heroism."

Well that's that, thought Peter. *Now they'll never find out that Dr. James treated me.*

THE LONELINESS

HE WOULD NO LONGER have to say he was "almost" eighteen or that he was seventeen years, eleven months, three weeks and so many days. It was his birthday. There was no cake, no party and no friends or relatives bringing presents. He would have called his sister in London, but she had no phone. He was sure that she had sent him a birthday card, but it hadn't yet arrived. He had sent her a letter, but she would only just have received it and he could not expect a reply for several days—perhaps a week or more, and that is assuming she wrote as soon as she got his letter.

Up until that day he'd had no time to brood. Now he had to admit that he was desperately lonely and bored. He knew nobody in Jackson, with the exception of Dr. James. Momentarily, he thought of dreaming up an excuse to go to see him. Maybe he could say that his head hurt or his back was still stiff, neither of which was true. He had finished the pills Doctor James had given him. Maybe he could say he needed more. He quickly gave up the idea of going to Froman. The chances were very good that nobody was going to find out that Dr. James had treated a white boy, and he wasn't going to risk being seen going into a Negro hospital.

With no friends, no job and little money he had lots of time to think. Why had he come to Jackson? He could have gone to Minnesota with the two fellows he met in Washington. They were a lot of fun and he had enjoyed himself with them. He could have gone to Hollywood and seen some film stars. He was told by people, who had never been to Hollywood, that you couldn't walk down the street without bumping into one. He still could go there, if he ever got any money, but why had he come here first? Maybe it was just because he had been told not to—that it was dangerous and he wouldn't like it. Perhaps he just liked to swim upstream. He had come to America against the advice of his uncle. He always had something of a defiant streak, doing things just because others said he shouldn't. With all that, he probably would be somewhere else if it hadn't been for Solomon Broward. The treatment Solomon had received on the bus had upset Peter, but it had also made him curious. He had come to America to see things that were entirely different from anything he had ever known. Certainly in New York and Washington he had seen and heard things he had never seen or heard before. But life in Jackson went beyond that.

The weather was dismal. It had been raining for days. He decided to go for a walk. It always rained in England, but it had never stopped him from going out in it, stomping through puddles, playing football with his friends or just walking around. Ordinarily he loved the rain. Living in London it was almost required that one like the rain, but here in Jackson it merely increased his sense of loneliness. He had no raincoat. A Londoner would not ordinarily be without a raincoat, but he had left his at home. He considered asking his landlady, Mrs. Grant, if he could borrow one, but decided against it.

She had told him on the day of his arrival that there were several other lodgers in the house, but he had not seen any of them. The only other time he had even seen Mrs. Grant again was when he returned from Froman with a bandage on his head. He told her of the accident and his hospitalization, but he omitted telling her where he was hospitalized, leaving her with the obvious unstated assumption that it had been at Jackson General.

He walked for over an hour. There was nobody else on the street, and only a few cars drove by. By the time he got back to the house, he was drenched. He decided that a hot shower would be a good idea. Getting out of his wet clothes, he carefully turned the doorknob to the bathroom. A couple of times he had done that and found it locked from the other side, signifying that the bathroom was occupied. This time it was not locked and he opened the door and saw a tall slim man standing there drying his hands on a towel.

"Oops, I'm sorry," stammered Peter, embarrassed both because he had barged into the occupied bathroom and because he was stark naked, while the other man was fully clothed. "I didn't know anyone was in here."

The man laughed. "My fault. I forgot to lock the door." The man put down the towel and held out his hand. "My name is Glenn Landers," he said.

"My name is—" as Peter reached to shake the man's hand, he knocked a glass off the side of the basin. It shattered with shards strewn about the floor. "I'm sorry," Peter said, for the second time. "That was clumsy. I'll get dressed and go ask Mrs. Grant if I can borrow something to sweep it into."

"Don't bother," Landers said. "I'll just push the bits of glass into the corner." And he did so with his shoe.

"But I need to get the glass off the floor."

"Not necessary, the Nigra will be here in the morning."

"What's a Nigra?"

Landers momentarily looked puzzled, then smiled. "You're not from around here, are you?"

"No, I'm from England. I've only been here a short time."

Landers explained, "The Nigra is the colored woman who cleans the house. She comes twice a week."

"Well, I'll leave her a note apologizing and maybe give her some money for causing her extra work. What's her name?"

"I have no idea what her name is. Don't be writing her notes, even assuming she can read. Most of them can't. You sure have a lot to learn," said Landers, somewhat sharply. "You were about to tell me your name."

THE SECOND ACCIDENT

IT WAS SEVERAL DAYS after Peter had met Landers and he was glancing idly through the daily newspaper when he saw in the entertainment section that the film *Double Indemnity* was playing at the Regent Theater on Porter Street. He had heard very good things about this film and decided to go. He had picked up a free city map at the bus station and was having no trouble finding his way around town. When he arrived at the theater, he realized it was in a Negro area and catered exclusively to Negro customers. The ticket seller looked at him strangely, but nonetheless sold him a ticket. Even with the use of the map, he had misjudged just how far away the theater was and by the time he was seated, the movie had already been playing for ten or fifteen minutes. When the movie ended, he sat through a cartoon, a newsreel and trailers for future movies. He watched the beginning of *Double Indemnity,* which he had missed, and then left the theater.

There was nobody on the street when he came out. The sun was just starting to go down. He waited a minute for his eyes to become accustomed to the light and then started walking back toward the house. As he approached an intersection controlled by traffic lights, he saw a man crossing with the light in his favor. There were no vehicles visible and no one else was on the street. Suddenly a car approached the intersection at a high rate of speed and, without slowing down, ran through the red light and struck the man, hurling him into the air. The car slowed for a second or two then sped away. Peter ran toward the fallen man. Before he could reach him, another man, whom he had not seen before, came out of the shadows created by a shop's awning, ran over and appeared to be going through the fallen man's pockets. As Peter paused, uncertain what to do, a police car approached from the opposite direction. Peter later learned this was a fairly high crime area and the police regularly patrolled it. The car which had struck the pedestrian had disappeared by the time the police car arrived. Peter stepped into the street and flagged it down. Two officers jumped out. The man bending over the victim got up and started to run, holding what appeared to be a wallet in his hand. One of the officers shouted at him to stop, drew his sidearm and fired a shot in the air. The man stopped and raised his hands. One of the officers handcuffed him and then searched him for weapons. "Hey Jack, lookee here what I found, an iron bar suitable for bopping people on the head. That's what you used you crud." He then shoved the suspect into the back of the police car.

The other officer knelt down beside the victim and

felt for a pulse. There was none. "This guy's dead. Better call for the meat wagon."

"Did you see what happened?" the first officer asked Peter.

"Yes, a car hit him and then the man you have in the police car came over and seemed to be going through his pockets. Maybe he was just trying to find out who he was," replied Peter.

"Oh sure," said the officer with a note of sarcasm in his voice, "and he tried to run away with his wallet looking for a phone booth so he could call the next of kin."

The second officer rubbed his chin. "I'm not saying you're wrong, kid, and it could have happened the way you say, but I've investigated lot of homicides in my time and it just doesn't look to me like he was hit by a car. It looks like someone hit him over the head with a blunt instrument with a lot of force and that Nigra had the weapon to do just that. There's blood from this poor guy's head all over the place."

He looked from the victim to Peter. "Young man, you had better come with us to the station and make a statement. One way or another, it looks like we've got a homicide on our hands."

When they got to the station, the suspect was locked up. The suspect was Negro. Peter heard a police officer say that the victim was white.

Detective Sergeant Rousseau was there to meet them. He told Peter, "I'm going to call in Miss Simmons. She's a certified shorthand reporter and she's going to take down the questions I ask you and your answers. Is that all right with you?"

"Yes sir."

After a series of preliminary questions, name, address etc., the questions and answers of a substantive nature began. "Where were you coming from?"

"I'd been to see the movie at the Regent."

"Let's start again. Where were you coming from? You weren't coming from the Regent. That's a Negro theater. Now once again, where were you coming from?"

"I told you. I'd been to see the pictures—I mean the movies at the Regent. They were showing a picture I wanted to see and it wasn't playing anywhere else. That's where I was coming from."

"Didn't you know that it was a Negro theater?"

"I didn't ask, but I figured it was because of the people who were going in. The woman who sold me the ticket looked at me kinda funny."

The stenographer and Rousseau looked at each other and Rousseau threw his arms in the air. The stenographer asked, "Sergeant you want me to type up what he just said?"

"Yeah, sure. Put everything down."

"Tell me something kid, are you nuts? Never mind! Don't answer. All right you were coming from the Regent," Rousseau said, sounding exasperated. "You say you saw a car hit the victim; what make of car was it?"

"I don't know. I'm just here from England and I don't know the makes of American cars."

"What color was it?"

"I'm not sure. It was a dark color, probably either black or dark blue."

"Did you get the number off the license plate?"

"No. It all happened very fast and the car sped away at once."

"Did you get any part of the number?"

"No."

"Were they Mississippi plates or another state?"

"I don't know."

"Can you tell us anything about the car, other than it was black or dark blue?"

"No."

"Did you see the driver; male or female; Negro or white?"

"I didn't see the driver."

"Was there more than one person in the car?"

"I don't know."

"Did you see where the man we arrested came from?"

"The first I saw of him was when he came across the road and bent down over the man and seemed to be going through his pockets. But I don't know where he was right before he crossed the street. It seemed to me that he must have come from the front of a shop that had an awning that made a shadow, I don't know for sure. It all happened so fast."

"Did you see him hit the victim?"

"He didn't hit him."

"At least you didn't see him hit the victim."

"I was watching him from the time he came across the road until he ran away and he never hit the victim."

"Okay. Peter, you wait right here and Miss Simmons will type this up and have you sign it. Is everything you have said true and correct?"

"Yes sir."

After about twenty minutes, Miss Simmons brought out the typewritten transcription of the interview and gave the original to Peter and a copy to Rousseau.

"Read it carefully Peter. If you see anything that you need to change let me know. If not, go ahead and sign it above your name on the last page and date it," said Rousseau.

There was nothing to change and Peter signed and dated the document and handed it to Rousseau.

"Don't leave town," Rousseau said. Peter smiled. It sounded like a line from gangster movies he had seen. "The district attorney is going to want to talk to you. Officer Rodgers will drive you home."

The events of the evening had not alleviated Peter's feeling of loneliness, but he was no longer bored.

THE DISTRICT ATTORNEY

THE ASSISTANT District Attorney, Roy Broderick, was short and stocky with a round face and a bald head. He wore a grey striped suit and a garish yellow and red tie on the day he first met Peter. Several days after Peter had given his statement to the police, Broderick had sent a car for Peter who then found himself in a conference room with two additional men who were not identified by name to Peter. He was told they were investigators with the department.

The county coroner had conducted an examination of the victim and had determined that death was caused by a blow to the head administered by a blunt instrument. He told Broderick that, since the cause of death was so clear, it had not been necessary to conduct a full autopsy. The report of the coroner would be an important exhibit in the trial of Jerome Washington, the man arrested at the scene of what Peter maintained was a car accident.

Broderick questioned Peter for the better part of an hour. At first, the questioning was more or less the same as that conducted two days earlier by Detective Sergeant Rousseau. It then went into more detail. Where had he come from? What was he doing in Jackson? What were his plans? Had he known either Jerome Washington or the victim, Jake Fleming, previously? He was shown pictures of both men. He had never seen either man before. He was shown pictures of numerous car models. He could not identify any of them as the car that hit Fleming. He was shown a map of the city and asked to trace his route to and from the movie house. He was even asked to describe what the movie was about, presumably to confirm that he was actually at the theater. Finally Broderick, the two investigators and a photographer took him back to the theater at approximately the same time of day that he had said he left the theater, attempting to duplicate the lighting conditions.

They walked with him along the route he had taken to return to the boarding house. They asked him to walk at the same pace as he had on the night of Fleming's death. They had him position himself where he had seen the car hit the man. They closed off the street and had one of the investigators lie in the street where Fleming had gone down. They had the other investigator follow Peter's directions as to where he first saw Jerome Washington; what path Washington took to Fleming's body; where Washington bent over; and how Washington put his hand into Fleming's pockets. All during the re-creation the photographer took pictures.

They then took Peter back to the office and had him

make and sign another declaration, this one much longer than the one he gave at the police station. He was told that his attendance at the trial of Jerome Washington would be required and, for the second time, he was told not to leave town. Peter's emotions were mixed. It was exciting, even thrilling, that he was to be a witness, probably the most important witness in a murder trial. On the other hand, the importance of his role in the case troubled and scared him.

After he left, Roy Broderick and the two investigators talked about Peter Mason and his story about a car accident. "Do you believe him, Roy?" asked the older of the two investigators.

"I don't know. He seems sincere, but Dr. Silvers is convinced it was death from a blow on the head from a blunt instrument and not the result of a car accident. He's prepared to so testify," said Broderick.

"Why would he lie, if he is lying?" said the other investigator.

"I don't know the answer to that either," said Broderick.

"Maybe he wants to help the Negro. He went to a Negro theater. What white guy would ever do that? Maybe he's just a nigger lover," said the first investigator.

"Joe, I don't want to hear that kind of language in here. Do you hear me?" Broderick reprimanded.

Broderick was born and raised in Jackson and had obtained his law school degree at the University of Mississippi. He had been with the Hinds County District

Attorney's office for all of the years since graduation. He was their top prosecutor. There was talk of him becoming the district attorney when Clarence Perkins, who was in his sixties, retired. Broderick's sharp reply to Joe's racial epithet was not necessarily born of some innate liberalism or belief in equality. It was more pragmatic than that. He did not want his office or himself to become known for racially motivated prosecutions, although it was strongly believed that at least some were. He had higher aspirations than just being the DA of Hinds County, maybe even on a national level. While racist epithets and racially motivated prosecutions might find favor with certain local elements in the South, they might not be as favorably received on a national level. He secretly loathed the state of racial relations in the South, but he kept those thoughts to himself. His views would not be well received by most of the local citizenry and, if known, his chances for advancement to district attorney would be over as, indeed, might his present position.

"Mason has only been in Jackson a short time. I want to find out more about him. He hasn't got a job and apparently hasn't made any friends yet. I'm going to see his landlady. Maybe she knows something about him. In any event, we are going to try Jerome Washington for capital murder and we are going to seek the death penalty," concluded Broderick.

THE DEFENSE COUNSEL

IT WAS TWO DAYS after Peter's lengthy session with the district attorney and his colleagues. The rain, which had stopped for a few hours the day before, had started again and was coming down quite heavily. Mrs. Grant answered a knock on her door. A Negro man wearing a raincoat and no hat was standing on the step.

"Good morning," he said pleasantly.

"What do you want?" she asked, not nearly so pleasantly.

"I'd like to speak to Mr. Mason, if he's at home," said the man.

"What do you want to speak to him about?" she asked, her tone not becoming any more pleasant.

"I'm the lawyer for Mr. Jerome Washington and Mr. Mason was an eye witness to an incident involving my client."

Mrs. Grant had read in the paper about the death of a man and Peter had told her he saw what happened. "MISTER Washington is it? Hah! Where do you get off calling murder 'an incident?'" Her tone had gone beyond unpleasant and had become belligerent.

"Would you please tell Mr. Mason that I would like to talk to him?"

"I'll see if he wants to talk to you."

There was no overhang above the door and the man was getting soaked.

"May I step inside while you fetch him? It's awful wet out here."

"No you may not," she retorted and closed the door in his face.

A few minutes later Peter appeared.

"Are you Mr. Mason?"

"Yes I'm Peter Mason." He frowned a little and said, "Eighteen-year-old boys are not usually called 'mister' where I come from."

The man laughed. "My name is Luther Adams. I'm a lawyer and I represent Jerome Washington. Could we talk for a little while?"

"Of course, why don't you come in? Mrs. Grant has a little sitting room. I'm sure she won't mind."

"I'm sure she will mind. She has already let me know that I wouldn't be welcome in her house. Perhaps we can talk in my car. It's right by the curb and we can get out of the rain."

Had he been told a few short weeks earlier that Mrs. Grant would not let this man in her house, Peter would have been surprised and perhaps shocked. While he didn't like her attitude, he was no longer surprised or shocked.

They sat in the car for over an hour going over the circumstances of Mr. Fleming's death in exquisite detail.

Luther Adams was one of a very few Negro lawyers in Jackson. He had graduated from a small unaccredited law school in Alabama and for several years the Bar Association refused to let him take the Mississippi bar exam as a result of the lack of accreditation of that law school. Finally they permitted him to take the exam, probably figuring that he wouldn't pass anyway, but he did. Adams told Peter that he was the only real chance that Washington had of avoiding the electric chair. He explained that Washington was not the ideal defendant, being a petty thief with a number of convictions for which he had spent a series of short sentences in the county jail.

"He never hit anyone or hurt anyone and he certainly never killed anyone," Adams said. "But with his record and his color, he starts out with two strikes against him." Adams had to explain to Peter the baseball analogy, which he had not heard before.

"Actually there is another bad fact that probably would be a third strike without you," said Adams. "The trial judge is Walter Carson. None of the judges here speak out for racial equality. They wouldn't be on the bench if they did. But Judge Carson is somewhat more extreme in his racial views than the others. He is an old line southern gentleman, tough as nails, with definite, unfortunate, frequently stated beliefs on racial matters. He has set the trial to commence a week from tomorrow. I hope you don't mind, but I have to serve a subpoena on you, which

I do now. No offense meant, but it is customary in order to insure attendance of witnesses."

Peter took the piece of paper. "No offense taken. As a matter of fact this whole thing is kind of exciting." Peter omitted to say that not only was it exciting, but it was also frightening.

They said good-bye. Peter got out of the car and extended his hand through the window. Adams, who could not remember ever shaking hands with a white man in Mississippi, took it.

When Peter got back into the house, Mrs. Grant was waiting. "Did that man want you to help him get a murderer off scot-free?" she asked.

"If they call me, I'm just going to testify to what I saw. It's not my place to help or hurt anyone. I'm just going to tell the truth."

"Well you be sure you do that and be careful who you associate with from here on."

Peter went back to his room thinking that Jerome Washington would have received the third strike that Mr. Adams was talking about if Mrs. Grant was on his jury. Of course it had not taken Peter long to realize that there were a lot of Mr. and Mrs. Grants in Jackson, Mississippi. It was unlikely Washington could avoid them all.

THE DISTRICT ATTORNEY - TWO

Assistant District Attorney Broderick arrived at the Grant house about two hours after Luther Adams had left. He decided to come alone so as not to overwhelm her. Mrs. Grant opened the door at his knock.

"Good afternoon," he said pleasantly.

"Good afternoon to you," she said equally pleasantly.

"My name is Roy Broderick. I am an assistant district attorney for Hinds County and I am investigating the death of Mr. Jake Fleming."

"Terrible thing, that murder. Won't you come in Mr. Broderick?" she said ushering him into the little sitting room. "You probably want to see the Mason boy. I'll go and see if he's in."

"Actually, I came to see you, Mrs. Grant."

"Oh really, how can I help you?" she said surprised. "Please sit down. May I get you something, some coffee or perhaps something a bit stronger?"

"You're very kind, but no thank you," he said, taking a chair. "We know that Peter Mason only recently arrived in Jackson. He is unfamiliar with our customs and he attended a movie at a Negro theater on the night that Mr. Fleming was killed."

"Well that is a bit shocking, but you know, he is an English boy; my own ancestry is English. One of my ancestors came over on the *Mayflower*, they say. I am sure Peter didn't know that he wasn't supposed to go to a Negro theater. I'm sure he won't do it again."

"Peter saw Jerome Washington leaning over Mr. Fleming and claims that Washington did not hit Fleming, but that Fleming was hit by a car," continued Broderick, ignoring the irrelevance of Grant's claimed ancestry. "We're just checking out the accuracy of Peter's account. Since he has been here such a short time, he is not really known to anyone. We thought you might know a little about him."

"Well since he went to a Negro theater one might think he was partial to the race. I don't know whether he is or not. Even if he was, I would never use the term 'nigger lover,' that's just horrible-sounding."

"No of course you wouldn't," said Broderick, thinking that she might not say it, but she probably would think it.

"There was something … I thought it was curious at the time," she said. "You probably saw that wound on his forehead. He was hit by a car. Isn't that a curious coincidence? He spent a night in the hospital. A few days ago, two bills came for him. Of course, I didn't open his mail, but the letters had those little windows and you could see the word 'bill' and a few other words."

"I did see that wound and Peter did tell us it resulted from his getting hit by car. Why did you think it curious that he got bills? Hospitals don't usually treat people for nothing."

"One of the bills was from Jackson General and the other was from Froman, which as you know is a Negro hospital. I thought that one might have been sent to him in error."

"You could very well be right. 'Mason' is a fairly common name and Froman's billing department probably got the wrong one."

Broderick spent another twenty minutes with Mrs. Grant, but learned nothing more of interest. He stood. "Thank you Mrs. Grant. I won't take up any more of your time. You have been most gracious and helpful."

"Come back anytime. I hope young Peter is not in any trouble."

"None at all," he said.

He hurried back to his office and called a team meeting.

"It turns out that young Mason was probably treated at two different hospitals, apparently for the same injury. If that isn't strange enough, one of the hospitals was Froman. His landlady saw bills addressed to Mason, one from Jackson General and one from Froman. She thinks the Froman bill may have been sent to Mason by mistake. I told her that I agreed with her, but I don't. Where would they get his full name and address?"

"It is strange, but what's it got to do with Washington?" said one of the investigators.

"I don't know. Probably nothing, but I intend to find out."

"You want me to go ask the Mason kid?"

"Not yet. Joe, you go to both hospitals and find out which doctor treated him. They'll give you that much information. Get subpoenas on the doctors and on the records from both places. Probably a wild goose chase, but sometimes the goose leads you somewhere significant."

THE TWO DOCTORS

JOE MOSS had been an investigator in the Hinds County DA office for eighteen years. For the last ten years he had been the lead detective on all homicide cases. He was a large, muscular man with a close-cropped greying crew cut. A scar ran down the left side of his face from the corner of his eye almost to his chin, a memento of a knifing inflicted by a triple murder suspect. He was known for his gruffness and for his persistence, which had earned him the nickname "the Hawk"—a name he didn't like and which was never mentioned in his presence.

On arriving at Froman, Moss was ushered into a small room with a plain wooden table and six stiff-back chairs. There were no curtains on the window, no pictures on the wall and no carpet on the floor. This austere area was used as a conference room by the doctors and staff. Moses Brown got up from one of the chairs as Moss entered.

"My name is Joe Moss. I'm an investigator with the Hinds County District Attorney's Office. I understand from your admitting clerk that you're the administrator of this hospital. Is that correct?"

"Yes that's correct. My name is Moses Brown. Is there something wrong?"

"I'll ask the questions, if you don't mind. We have reason to believe that recently a white boy was treated here for injuries suffered in a car accident. Is that correct?"

Brown hesitated for a few seconds and momentarily considered denying it. However, it was clear that Moss was just reaffirming what he already knew and, while Brown wanted desperately to say that Mason had never been there, he knew it would be worse than useless.

"Yes it is. I believe he was seen by our Dr. James. Do you wish to talk to him?"

"Yeah. Fetch him now."

In a few minutes, a white-coated Dr. James arrived.

"I'm told you have questions about a white boy who was treated here. What is it you want to know?"

"Why was he brought here and why wasn't he transferred to Jackson General?"

"The laws of this state prevent me from discussing treatment of patients unless I'm subpoenaed to testify in court. This state has strict confidentiality rules about those things. I'm pretty sure you already knew that."

"I believe you can, under the rules of this state, tell me if you did treat a white boy earlier this month."

"I can and I did."

"Thank you. I hereby serve you with a subpoena to appear at the time and place specified in the subpoena and to bring with you the complete records pertaining to the hospitalization and treatment of one Peter Mason."

Moss handed Dr. James the subpoena and, without another word, turned and left.

Somewhat the same scenario was re-enacted with the administrator and with Dr. Robinson at Jackson General, although the conversation was slightly less formal and there were "good mornings," "how y'alls" and "good-byes" which were noticeably absent in the meetings at Froman. Dr. Robinson also stood on state law in refusing to discuss the case of Peter Mason. He, too, was then served a subpoena, with an apology for having to do so, for his attendance at the first day of trial and for the production of records pertaining to the treatment of Mason. Moss met with Roy Broderick that afternoon to bring him up to date and to inform him that neither doctor would discuss their treatment until they testified at trial.

"Not surprising," said Broderick. "I would have been surprised if they had told you anything more than they did. We'll just have to wait, but we will get to see the records well before we examine Mason and the doctors at trial. There's something odd here and my gut tells me it's going to have a substantial effect on the trial. Now go and subpoena the Mason kid."

THE TRIAL OF JEROME WASHINGTON —
DAY ONE

THE LOCAL NEWSPAPERS had been full of stories about the trial. Two reporters had come to the Grant house on separate days representing different newspapers. They not only wanted to have Peter repeat his story of what he had seen that night, but also wanted to know a lot about him. Who he was, where he came from, how he came to be in Jackson, his plans for the future, how it came about that he was in the area where the killing took place, and so on. There had been no publicity about him having been at a Negro theater that night, or that earlier he had been treated at Froman for injuries suffered in a car accident, and he told them nothing about those matters.

Broderick had told him that he could talk to the media, but not to discuss what he had seen of the killing or what he had discussed with the DA personnel. Peter told the reporters general things about himself, but kept it short and somewhat vague. He told them that he didn't think it was right for him to talk about the case or what type of evidence might be presented. They seemed disappointed. They might have learned more about the involvement of the two hospitals in Peter's treatment from Mrs. Grant, but they were unaware that she had any such information.

Peter put on the suit to go to court on the day set forth in the subpoena. He had not worn it since his arrival in Jackson and it didn't fit him any better now than it did then. Oddly enough, he was not as nervous about testifying as he had been earlier. Perhaps it was because Broderick had told him he would not be on the stand on the first day and he was excited to see the start of the trial. When he walked into the courtroom, Mr. Broderick and three other men were sitting at counsel bench closest to the jury box. He recognized one of the men as the one who had served him with the subpoena. Luther Adams was seated by himself at counsel bench farthest from the jury box.

Both Roy Broderick and Luther Adams turned and looked at Peter when he walked in. Broderick nodded in his direction. Adams smiled and gave a slight wave. A woman holding a handkerchief to her eyes sat in the front row with a boy and a girl sitting on either side of her. Peter surmised that the woman was Jake Fleming's widow and that the boy and girl were her children. There was a man in a uniform inside the bar, a woman sitting with a kind of machine in front of her and another woman at a desk parallel to where the judge sat. Peter subsequently found out that the man in the uniform was the bailiff, the woman with the machine was the court reporter and the other woman was the court clerk.

A few minutes later, three doctors arrived— Doctor Gregory James from Froman Hospital, Doctor Lloyd Robinson from Jackson General and Doctor William Silvers, the coroner. The bailiff stood and said in a loud voice, "All rise. The circuit court in and for the County of Hinds is now in session, the Honorable Walter Carson, Judge presiding." Judge Carson took the bench saying, "Take your seats." He was a grey-haired man of about sixty, quite heavy, with a reddish face and a stern expression. At that point two uniformed police officers brought in Jerome Washington. He was shackled hand and foot and dressed in prison garb. He was seated beside Adams, his lawyer. The police officers sat in chairs behind him.

Judge Carson told the bailiff, "Bring in the jury panel." The bailiff left and in a few minutes he came back with about fifty people. Similar to the people Peter had seen in the waiting room at Jackson General, the group was composed of men and women of all ages, from early twenties to late sixties. There were, of course, no children. As was also similar to the waiting room at Jackson General, there were no Negroes.

The prospective jurors took seats in the front four rows of the audience section. The remainder of the seats were for newspaper reporters and onlookers.

Mr. Broderick rose to his feet. "Your Honor, there are four witnesses in the courtroom who are here pursuant to subpoena. It is apparent that they won't be called until tomorrow at the earliest. May they be released with instructions to return tomorrow morning?"

The court so ordered. The three doctors left, but Peter remained.

Judge Carson asked him if he was one of the witnesses and Peter said he was. The court told him he could leave, but Peter asked if he could stay.

"You're that young English boy who saw all this, aren't you?" asked the judge.

"Yes sir, I am," replied Peter.

"You can stay. When you go back to England, you can tell all your friends about how well American justice works and how we have carefully followed the Common Law precepts handed down by our English ancestors," Judge Carson intoned.

There were a few titters among the jurors, but mostly by DA Broderick and his entourage.

"One thing you must remember, young man, is that on no account can you speak to any member of the jury until the case is over. Do you understand that?"

"Yes sir."

The jury selection took a long time. At first Peter found it interesting and thought that both lawyers asked sensible, probing questions. But as the day went on, the jury selection process became repetitious and boring.

Roy Broderick asked if any prospective juror would have any difficulty imposing the death penalty if Washington was found guilty. None had any problem with that. Luther Adams asked if any prospective juror would have difficulty acquitting Washington because of the color of his skin. None voiced any problem with that. Broderick asked if any prospective juror knew anyone who had experienced the murder of a friend or relative where that friend or relative had left behind a grieving widow and young fatherless children. Peter concluded that the prosecutor was less interested in the answer than he was in reminding the jurors of the nature and circumstances of the man killed and stirring up animosity toward the defendant. Adams dwelt on the fact that the prosecutor had the burden of proving Washington's guilt beyond a reasonable doubt.

The prospective jurors, who at first seemed alert and interested, started to become restless and irritated as the same questions were repeated over and over again. The process then moved to challenging jurors. Each side had eight challenges, but the prosecutor only used three and the defense five. Peter did not understand how or why certain prospective jurors were excused and others were permitted to stay. It seemed to him to be totally unscientific and random. Finally eight men and four women were selected as jurors, and the rest of the panel was sent home.

After lunch, the lawyers made opening statements. Broderick used a lot of words like "heinous" and "inhuman" and waved his arms about, got red in the face and raised his voice in displays of real or feigned emotion. He stated that Washington, a repeat criminal, had come up behind Fleming with a metal bar that he carried in his pocket and had struck him a fatal blow on the back of his head and then had the cold-blooded gall to steal from this dead husband and father. He concluded by saying that there was an eye witness who saw the murder and that, in addition, the coroner, a famous doctor in his own right, would conclusively establish that death resulted from that aforesaid fatal blow. Broderick was eloquent, riveting and very persuasive. Peter was almost starting to believe him when he came back to reality and recalled vividly that it hadn't happened that way.

By contrast, Luther Adams was quiet and restrained but nonetheless quite persuasive. He readily admitted that Washington was a petty thief and had tried to lift the dead man's wallet. But he insisted that his client was no murderer and that there would be irrefutable proof that Fleming did not die from a blow on the head from a metal bar carried by Washington but, instead, had been killed by a speeding car that had left the scene by the time the police arrived. At the end of the opening statements, Judge Carson sent the jury home with instructions to return at nine the next morning. Peter left the courtroom convinced that his testimony would clearly exonerate Washington from having committed murder, but would also be instrumental in convicting him of the far less serious crime of attempted theft.

There were, however, a few twists and turns to come.

THE TRIAL OF JEROME WASHINGTON — DAY TWO

PETER DIDN'T SLEEP WELL. He knew he would testify the next day and the thought made him nervous. Logically, he didn't see how the jury could possibly convict Washington of murder after they heard from the only eye witness. On the other hand, he had seen how Mr. Broderick impressed the jury in his opening statement and he wondered whether charm and charisma could possibly trump hard facts. The jury had listened closely to Broderick. Several had nodded when Broderick detailed Washington's prior criminal record and they had smiled and laughed at Broderick's corny, down-home humor. They had listened closely to Adams also, but their body language and facial expressions did not convey the same warmth and affinity as they obviously felt for Broderick.

The audience benches in the courtroom were full. Indeed, a number of people were turned away. They were all there to hear the English kid. It was no secret that his testimony was expected to be pivotal.

The trial was well into the second day. The jurors had sat through, and at times endured, the selection process. They had sat through, and for the most part enjoyed, the opening statements. However, they had not yet heard from a witness. That was about to change.

The first witness for the prosecution was Washington's probation officer. He detailed Washington's criminal record; the six convictions for petty theft including two for breaking into cars; the fact that Washington had six jobs in the last two years and had been fired from three of them and had quit the other three. Adams had sought to keep all of this information from the jury, contending that it was in no way relevant to the only question, and that was whether or not Washington had killed Fleming. Judge Carson had perfunctorily denied that request. Adams cross examined the probation officer and achieved some limited success by establishing that none of Washington's convictions involved physical attacks on anyone, although the jury seemed unimpressed by that piece of information.

Having now blackened Washington's character in the eyes of the jury, Broderick then called both of the investigating police officers to the stand, one after another. They testified that when they arrived on the scene they saw a man lying in the crosswalk of Magnolia Street where it intersected with Branson Avenue. The first officer had brought with him a drawing of the intersection showing where the body was found. He then stated that he had seen no vehicle of any kind, but that he had seen a man running down Magnolia Street. He had called to the man, who did not stop until his partner fired a shot in the air. He had then taken the man into custody, handcuffed him, frisked him and found the metal bar, placed him in the back of the police car and found that the suspect had in his possession a wallet that they discovered, on inspection, belonged to the victim, Jake Fleming.

The second officer testified that he had determined that Mr. Fleming was dead. He related his conversation with Peter, but Broderick's questioning was limited to that part of the conversation concerning seeing the suspect lean over the man, take something out of the victim's pocket and then run away when the police arrived. Both officers testified that they had scoured the area for any sign that an automobile had struck Fleming. They found none—no glass from a broken headlight, no skid marks, no debris of any kind. Without a description of the car, they were not able to mount a search for what Broderick continually referred to as "the phantom car."

On cross-examination, Luther Adams asked the same question of both officers; "Did Peter Mason tell you that he had seen a car strike Mr. Fleming before Washington approached?"

"Objection, Your Honor. The question is beyond the scope."

"Sustained."

Adams protested, "But Your Honor, the officers have not described the complete statement that Peter Mason made to them."

"You should know better counsel," Judge Carson

snapped. "You can only ask questions relating to the direct examination. I heard nothing in the direct about the involvement of a car. All I heard was that there was no involvement of a car. If you want to ask about that you must wait for the presentation of the defendant's case."

The ruling was puzzling to Adams since Broderick had clearly asked the officers about a search for evidence of a car's involvement, albeit a non-productive search.

So restricted, Adams limited his cross-examination to establishing that, other than running, Washington did not resist arrest and did not fight with the officers. Again, the jurors seemed singularly unimpressed.

The next witness called by the prosecution was Doctor William Silvers, the county coroner. He was a very tall and very thin man with thick horned-rim glasses. When looking at documents, he had a habit of pushing his glasses to the end of his nose and peering over them. Mr. Broderick started his questioning by establishing Dr. Silvers's qualifications as an expert. "Not necessary to do that, Roy," Judge Carson interrupted. "We all know that Bill is highly qualified and one of the top medical examiners in the country. He's more than adequately qualified to give expert testimony in this case."

Peter was astonished with the informal friendliness with which the judge addressed Roy Broderick and Dr. Silvers. It did not go unnoticed that the friendly informality of Judge Carson did not extend to Luther Adams who was always referred to as "counsel."

Dr. Silvers testified that the dead man had suffered

a fractured skull as a result of a heavy blow from a blunt instrument. The iron bar that Washington was carrying was introduced and marked in evidence, after which Dr. Silvers said that, in his opinion, it was reasonably probable that the iron bar caused the injury. An x-ray ordered by Dr. Silvers was also marked in evidence and shown to the jury. Dr. Silvers got down off the witness stand, walked up and down in front of the jury demonstrating to them where in the x-ray they could see the fracture. Finally Dr. Silvers testified that the skull fracture was the immediate cause of death.

Peter, who had previously been nervous, was now also frustrated and angry. He knew categorically that Jerome Washington had not killed Jake Fleming and yet each succeeding witness made more certain that Washington was going to be convicted of a murder he did not commit. As he contemplated that likely outcome, Peter's nervousness reached panic proportions. If the jury didn't believe him, Washington would die.

Luther Adams tried to ask Dr. Silvers if the skull fracture could reasonably have resulted from the victim being struck by a car. Roy Broderick objected that the question assumed facts not in evidence and that there had been no evidence presented that the victim had been struck by a car. Predictably that objection was sustained.

Judge Carson had delayed the lunch hour to accommodate Dr. Silvers's busy schedule and to allow him to complete his testimony before the break. Broderick took Peter aside and told him that he wouldn't be asking him any questions about the car hitting Fleming and that he should not to jump in with an answer to a question that might be asked by Adams on the subject because the judge would not allow any such question. Adams had waited to talk to Peter and merely said that he would like to chat briefly with him in the lawyers' room first thing next morning before the trial re-commenced.

After lunch, Peter was the final witness for the prosecution. The afternoon session didn't start until after three o'clock because of the late completion of Dr. Silvers's testimony. Rather than get lunch, Peter had walked round and round the courthouse. He knew he should eat, but the very thought of food was repugnant. He bought a bottle of Coca Cola from a street vendor and sipped on it without interrupting his walking.

Surprisingly to Peter, his testimony was quite short. Broderick elicited from him that he saw Washington leaning over Fleming; that he saw Washington take something out of Fleming's pocket and that he saw Washington try to run away when the police arrived. Again, Broderick did not ask when and where he first saw Washington and, most significantly, did not ask about a car. Adams tried to bring up the car in cross-examination, but Broderick's objection, that the question was beyond the scope of the direct examination, was sustained.

That ended the second day of trial, and the jury was sent home with the directive that they should return the next day at 9:00 a.m. and not discuss the case with anyone. Peter was baffled. Wasn't Broderick merely delaying the inevitable? Surely when Adams called him the next day the story about the car would all come out. Peter, who had never been in a courtroom before this case and had no knowledge of English law, much less the law practiced in Mississippi, wasn't focusing on two things, which were later explained to him. First, juries frequently make up their minds early in a trial and subsequent testimony, even if strong, does not move them away from their embedded conclusions. Letting them go home without hearing about the car was a definite plus for the prosecution, even though the jury would hear about it later. It was well known among seasoned trial lawyers that it was usually, although not always, better to delay bad evidence as long as possible.

The second thing Peter had yet to learn would come as quite a surprise to him.

THE TRIAL OF JEROME WASHINGTON — DAY THREE

"THE STATE RESTS," announced Broderick when court convened the next morning.

"Very well," said Judge Carson. "Defense, call your first witness."

Adams jumped to his feet. "Your Honor, first I have a motion."

Judge Carson did not seem particularly pleased to hear that, but sent the jury back to the jury room. "You could have told me you wanted to address something out of the presence of the jury before I brought them in. Now I had to send them out and then I'll have to bring them back in again. You're just wasting time. All right counsel, what's your motion. Get it said and let's get it over with."

"On behalf of the defendant, Jerome Washington, I move for a judgment of acquittal on the basis that the State has failed to prove my client's guilt beyond a reasonable doubt."

Judge Carson did not wait for any argument. He said one word: "Denied."

"But Your Honor," pleaded Adams, "I haven't had a chance to argue my motion yet."

"You could argue your motion until you were blue in the face—well, for hours—and it would make no difference. Your motion would have absolutely no merit and you'd just be wasting my time and, more importantly, the time of the jury. Bailiff, bring in the jury."

Adams had told Peter that he had decided to put Washington on the stand. He also explained that, under American law, a criminal defendant couldn't be compelled to testify, but Adams had decided, on balance, that the jury hearing from Washington would help his case. It didn't. He further decided to put Washington on as his first witness. This was a serious error. It was a cardinal principle that you lead with your strongest and best witness. Peter was the strongest and best witness for the defense. Conversely, Washington was the weakest and worst. Had he led with Peter and had Peter been persuasive, as he turned out to be, he might not even have had to put Washington on.

Washington's performance was a disaster. He slouched in the witness chair; averted his eyes from the jury and, when cross-examined by the prosecutor, became belligerent and looked at Adams as if asking for help. It didn't take an expert to see that having Washington testify had the opposite effect than what was intended. Quite simply the jury was put off by Washington and resented his "uppity" attitude. He did, however, testify that he had not struck Fleming and that he saw Fleming hit by a car. Apart from Peter and, perhaps, Adams, it was clear that no one else in the courtroom believed him.

Adams hoped for better from Peter and he got it. In his English cockney accent, which seemed to find favor with the jury, he testified that he was on his way home when he saw a man crossing the street at the intersection of Magnolia and Branson; that the man had a green light; that a dark-colored car went through the red light and struck the man; that Washington then went up to the fallen man and seemed to put his hands in the man's pockets; that Washington then ran off when he saw the police car and stopped when one of the officers fired a shot in the air and was arrested, handcuffed and put in the back of the police car.

None of the jurors had taken notes during Washington's testimony, but most of them were writing furiously during Peter's.

"Did you see Mr. Fleming at all times from the moment he started to cross the street until he was struck by the dark-colored car?"

"Yes, I did."

"When you first saw Mr. Washington, was Mr. Fleming already lying in the street?"

"Yes he was."

"Did you have Mr. Washington in sight at all times as he approached Mr. Fleming's fallen body and up through the time Mr. Washington ran away?"

"I did."

"Did you at any time ever see Mr. Washington strike Mr. Fleming either with an iron rod or with anything else?"

"No I didn't."

"Are you absolutely sure of that?

"I am."

"Then I have no further questions of this witness," concluded Adams.

Peter's testimony had been, to put it mildly, extremely effective and the jury was clearly impressed. Therefore, to the surprise of everyone in the courtroom, particularly Peter, who had steeled himself for a withering cross-examination, Mr. Broderick announced, "No questions."

"Roy, are you sure you don't have any questions for this young gentleman?" asked an equally puzzled Judge Carson.

"Not at the moment, Your Honor, but I would ask that you instruct Mr. Mason to remain in the courtroom. I may have some questions in our rebuttal part of the case," responded Broderick.

"Then call your next witness, counsel."

Adams then announced that the defense rested.

Broderick's strategy on not cross-examining him puzzled Peter. Why hadn't he tried to undercut Peter's testimony? Peter didn't think there was any way that Broderick could do that, but why didn't he at least try? Later events were to establish that there were shrewd reasons for Broderick's strategy.

After the lunch break, Dr. James and Dr. Robinson arrived in the courtroom.

"From what you said before the lunch break, I assume the State has one or more rebuttal witnesses," said Judge Carson to Mr. Broderick.

"Yes, Your Honor. First the State calls Dr. Gregory James."

"Dr. James do you recognize the young man I am pointing to in the first row of the audience?"

"Yes sir, I do," responded James. "It's Peter Mason."

"How is it that you know Mr. Mason?"

"He was a patient of mine at Froman Hospital."

An audible gasp went up from the jury and a surprised look appeared on the usually stern face of Judge Carson. A white man being hospitalized at a Negro hospital in Jackson, Mississippi was completely unheard of. There were seven rows of spectator benches, all of them filled. Whispered conversations went on all over the courtroom and the bailiff had considerable difficulty quieting everyone. Judge Carson gaveled and the room fell silent.

"What were you treating him for?"

"He had been hit by a car and had suffered a severe head wound."

"How long did he stay at Froman?"

"Overnight. He was discharged on November 28."

"Your witness."

Adams then asked, "How did it come about that a white boy was treated in what is recognized to be an entirely Negro hospital?"

"It was a very cold day and Mr. Mason was heavily wrapped up. He had on gloves and a scarf around the lower half of his face. The top of his face was covered with blood. He was unconscious when he was brought in and remained so for some considerable period of time. It wasn't until his clothes were removed preliminarily to an examination that it was discovered that he was white."

"Why didn't you then have him transferred immediately to a hospital that treated white patients?"

"He had a potentially serious head wound. He might have had a skull fracture and/or intracranial or internal bleeding. It would not have been prudent to move him in his condition."

"No further questions."

"I have a question," said Judge Carson. "I heard what you said, Mr. Witness; why didn't you call over to Jackson General and have them send a white doctor. You said yourself you thought the boy's condition might be serious."

Dr. James bristled at being called 'Mr. Witness,' and at the judge's clear inference that James was professionally inferior to any white doctor. "My name is not 'Mr. Witness.' My name is James, Dr. Gregory James and I am a board certified physician perfectly capable of treating patients without the help of a white doctor."

Judge Carson was not used to having Negroes stand up to him. In fact this was the very first time that a Negro, in his presence, had failed to demonstrate the customary and expected subservience. "You keep a civil tongue in your head, Doctor, or whatever it is you want to be called. You can go," said a visibly angry Judge Carson.

Broderick next called Dr. Robinson. As Robinson walked toward the witness stand he stopped, took a step toward Dr. James and briefly stared at him. For a moment it seemed as though Robinson was going to say something. James returned Robinson's look and smiled slightly. Robinson's stern expression didn't change. The tension in the court was palpable as people leaned forward to try to hear what Robinson would say. Having looked at James, Robinson quickly turned away, without a word, and continued to the witness stand.

"Doctor, we have heard testimony that young Mason was discharged from Froman on November 28; do your records show if and when he came to see you at Jackson General?"

"It was on December 2nd."

"Why did he come to see you?"

"To have his head wound checked and, if appropriate, to remove the stitches."

"Did you ask him why he didn't go back to the doctor who put the stitches in to have them taken out?"

"Yes, he said the car accident had happened six days before in Washington, DC, and he was treated there by a doctor in a Washington hospital."

That piece of testimony brought further gasps and whispered conversations between the jurors and the note-taking, which had slacked off after Peter's testimony, picked up again.

Adams's cross-examination was brief. "Did you draw any conclusions as to the competence of the doctor who had previously treated Mr. Mason's head wound?"

"I don't remember doing so."

"With the court's permission I would like to read from part of Dr. Robinson's notes on his treatment of Mr. Mason. 'The patient seems to have received excellent treatment from the Washington, DC physician. The wound is healing well and the stitching was clearly performed by someone very skilled. As a result, the patient will probably have little or no permanent scarring.' Doctor Robinson you wrote that note before you knew that the prior treatment you were commenting on was performed by Dr. James, a Negro doctor?"

"That is correct."

"Would you have made such a laudatory comment had you known that fact?"

"Objection, irrelevant."

"I'll withdraw the question. Nothing further."

Broderick rose. "For our final rebuttal witness and perhaps the final witness in this trial, the State recalls Peter Mason."

THE TRIAL OF JEROME WASHINGTON — THE REBUTTAL WITNESS

MR. BRODERICK sat looking at Peter Mason on the witness stand for what seemed a very long time. He took a drink of water and then slowly got to his feet and stared at Peter. "Now Mr. Mason, you say you saw a so-called car hit Mr. Fleming. Is that right?"

"I don't know what you mean by a 'so-called' car, but yes, I saw a car hit Mr. Fleming."

"Well let's test that. You don't know what make of car it was, do you?"

"No I don't."

"You don't know what year or model it was, do you?"

"No."

"You don't know whether it was a four-door or a two-door or a no-door, do you?"

"I'm sure it must have had doors, but I don't know how many."

"You don't know whether the driver was a man or a woman, white or Negro, big or small, fat or thin, do you?"

"No."

"You don't know whether the car had Mississippi plates or the plates of another state, do you?"

"No, I don't."

"And you don't even know for sure what color it was, do you?"

"Well I know it was a dark color but I don't know whether it was blue or black."

"Might it not have been dark red or dark green?"

"I don't think so, but possibly."

"Maybe it wasn't a car at all. Maybe it was a horse and cart."

Laughter rang out in the courtroom. It appeared that Broderick was making Peter look less than believable. Peter felt that someone had turned up the heat in the courtroom. His head was clammy and he suddenly didn't know what to do with his hands. What had started out as an exciting, albeit nervous, experience had become an ordeal.

"Let's go to something else. You didn't go back to Dr. James at Froman for a follow up and removal of the stitches, did you?"

"Dr. James told me it might be better if I saw a white doctor. Somebody might be offended if I came back to a place that treated only Negro patients."

"I see. That's how you came to see Dr. Robinson at Jackson General, right?"

"Yes."

"When Dr. Robinson asked you why you didn't go back to the doctor who treated you for the head wound you said it was because that doctor treated you in Washington, DC, isn't that right?"

"Yes."

"And that was lie, right?"

"It was inaccurate."

"It was a lie?"

"Yes."

"The reason you lied and said that the treating doctor was in DC was because you thought that if it came out that you had been treated by Dr. James, a Negro doctor, it would get Dr. James in trouble, correct?"

"That's right."

"And the reason you lied about a car hitting Mr. Fleming was because you wanted to protect another of your Negro friends."

"Not true, I don't even know Mr. Washington and a car did hit Mr. Fleming."

Broderick was now shouting at Peter. "There was no car. You lied to Dr. Robinson when you told him where you were treated. You lied to the police about what you saw the night Jake Fleming was killed. You lied to the district attorney and now you have lied to this jury and this court."

Peter was now close to tears. He hadn't cried since the day his schoolmate and best friend was killed by a German bomb. Despite his anguish, he was able to say just above a whisper, "I'm not lying."

"Well, we'll let the jury decide that. No further questions."

Adams asked two questions. "Did a car strike Mr. Fleming?"

"Yes."

"Are you absolutely certain of that?"

"I am absolutely certain." But Peter was perhaps now the only person in the courtroom, other than Jerome Washington, who was.

THE TRIAL OF JEROME WASHINGTON — THE DECISION

PETER WALKED slowly out of the courtroom and headed toward the boarding house. Mr. Broderick had made a fool of him and, what's worse, had probably convinced the jury that he was a liar. He wished he had never gone to see that motion picture. Maybe he was being punished for having gone to a Negro theater. He hadn't eaten since that morning, but he wasn't hungry. A man was probably going to be executed for something he didn't do. He had read about things like that, but he was personally involved in this one.

Then it happened. He was walking aimlessly, not wanting to go eat and not wanting to go back to the boarding house. He was thinking of his own accident and how Dr. Robinson had said what a fine job the attending physician had done in treating him. He remembered that the treatment wasn't limited to his head. Dr. James went over his whole body, looking for broken bones, internal injuries, and anything and everything else. Dr. Silvers, the coroner, didn't do that. He was satisfied by looking at the head wound. Maybe there were other injuries, injuries that couldn't have been caused by Washington and his metal bar. *Why didn't I think of that before? Why didn't the lawyers or Dr. Silvers think of that?* he mused. *I have to tell Mr. Adams.*

In his rush to get to Luther Adams's office Peter bumped into an elderly woman coming out of the Piggly Wiggly grocery store, spilling her purchases all over the street. He apologized profusely while gathering up the fallen items.

"It's all right young man, nothing's broken, not even me. You shouldn't be in such a hurry. Wherever you're rushing to will wait."

But it wouldn't. Peter ran up the stairs to Adams office and breathlessly told him of his revelation. Adams put his hands over his eyes. "It's so simple. I can't believe I didn't think of it. I just can't believe that I could have been so stupid. Let's go see Dr. James and see if he can help us," said Adams.

Fortunately Dr. James was still at the hospital and listened intently to what Peter and Luther Adams had to say. Adams kept repeating how stupid he had been to overlook the obvious until Dr. James cut him off. "Luther, I know how you feel, but it doesn't do any good for us to agonize over things past. Everybody makes mistakes. We have to concentrate on what we can do from now on."

"How did Mr. Broderick and Dr. Silvers miss it as well?" asked Peter.

"Maybe neither of them did miss it," said Adams. "It would have seriously damaged the chances of convicting Washington if a full autopsy showed other injuries which couldn't have been caused by Jerome. They may have been devious, perhaps even unethical, but I am the only idiot."

James overlooked Adams's anguish and said, "The two accidents that involved Peter and Jake Fleming were undoubtedly very different. The car that hit Peter was certainly going much slower than the car that hit Fleming. Fortunately, Peter only suffered a head wound that turned out not to be serious. Silvers was probably right in that Fleming's head wound was fatal, but that doesn't mean it wasn't caused by a car or that he didn't have other injuries that were caused by the car and couldn't have been inflicted by Jerome Washington. There has to be a full autopsy."

The next day Adams put on Dr. James in surrebuttal. He testified, "I understand that Mr. Mason testified that the car was traveling very fast and when it struck Mr. Fleming it knocked him several feet in the air. It is my opinion that an impact of that ferocity would almost certainly cause additional injuries which could not possibly have resulted from an attack with an iron bar."

"This is all rank speculation," argued Broderick. "There is nothing but guesswork and no hard evidence."

Judge Carson sat for a long while, then said, "I can't agree with you, Mr. Broderick." (No more "Roy.") "I think Dr. James has a very cogent point." (No more "Mr. Witness.") "I am going to order that the body of Jake Fleming be exhumed and that a full autopsy be performed to determine whether there were other injuries to Mr. Fleming and, if so, whether or not they could reasonably have been caused by the defendant. I want you, Dr. James, to attend the autopsy."

The trial was adjourned for a day to permit the autopsy to be conducted.

When court re-convened, the three doctors were present: Dr. Silvers, who had conducted the autopsy, Dr. James, who had observed it and Dr. Robinson, who was now an interested spectator.

Mr. Adams conducted the examination of Dr. Silvers. "Before you testified several days ago that, in your opinion, Mr. Fleming had been killed by a blow to the back of the head administered by a blunt instrument and that instrument could well have been the iron bar carried by Jerome Washington, had you conducted a complete autopsy on Mr. Fleming's body?"

"No, I had not."

"Yesterday, after that testimony of yours, did you, at the request of Judge Carson, conduct a full autopsy?"

"I did."

"Other than the head wound that you testified about earlier in the trial, did you find any other injuries?"

Silvers shifted around uncomfortably in his chair, took his glasses off, cleaned them, drank some water, and finally said, "I did. I found a broken femur of the left leg, a fracture of the left hip, a comminuted fracture of the left ankle, three broken ribs and substantial internal bleeding."

"In your opinion, Dr. Silvers, could these injuries

have been caused by a human attacking the victim with an iron bar?"

Silvers cleared his throat several times and drank some more water. Judge Carson looked at him impatiently.

"Dr. Silvers (no more 'Bill'), I see you're drinking a lot of water and we all want you to be well hydrated, but is there any way you could get these questions answered a little more quickly? We'd all like to get home for dinner." Several people smiled, particularly Adams.

"A few of them maybe, but most of them . . . no, particularly not the broken femur, one of the strongest bones in the human body, and not the hip fracture."

"In your opinion are the injuries you found on autopsy, including the head wound, consistent with the victim being struck by a speeding car?"

"Yes."

"No further questions."

It was now Broderick's turn to try to salvage something.

"Doctor you testified earlier that the cause of death was the head injury and that it was, in your opinion, caused by a blunt instrument such as the iron bar that was found in the defendant's possession. That is still your opinion is it not?"

"Only partially. I am still of the opinion that the head wound was the cause of death, but I now believe that, while it is possible that the wound was caused by a blunt instrument such as the iron bar you describe, I think it is more probable that it, too, was caused by a speeding car."

The tables had turned. While Broderick made a brilliant closing argument, contending now that if a speeding car had hit Fleming it was while he was lying dead in the road after being struck a fatal blow by Washington. Even with the autopsy and Silvers's revised opinion, that argument might have prevailed but for the renewed faith of the jury in the accuracy of Peter's testimony about the car. The court instructed the jury and they retired to consider their verdict.

In less than an hour, they returned.

"All rise," intoned the bailiff.

"Has the jury reached a verdict?" asked Judge Carson.

The foreman, a large, florid-faced man in farmer's overalls, rose.

"It has, Your Honor."

"Please hand the verdict form to the clerk." She in turn handed it to the judge who scanned it and handed it back to the clerk.

"The defendant will now stand and face the jury while the clerk reads the verdict."

"We, the jury in the matter of the State of Mississippi versus Jerome Washington, find the defendant, on the charge of first degree murder, not guilty; on the charge of attempted robbery we find the defendant guilty as charged."

The judge immediately sentenced Washington to one year in the county jail, but, surprisingly, suspended the sentence, and then said, "Before I discharge the jury, I first want to thank them for performing their civic duty.

I thank counsel for their skillful presentation of their respective cases."

Walter Carson had lived his whole life in Jackson, Mississippi, except for the war years when he was a military judge serving initially at Fort Benning, Georgia, and later in the European theater. He sat in judgment on AWOLs, fights, petty thefts and the like. He was well-known for his harsher treatment of Negro soldiers than whites. When he returned to Jackson and resumed life as a county judge, he continued to favor accused white men over Negroes, as he had before, during and after his military service. The only Negroes that he had any association with, outside of his court, were his housekeeper Bertha, who had been with the Carson family for thirty years, and the service station attendant where he got gas for his Chrysler. In all the years he had been patronizing that gas station and been helped by the same attendant, he had only ever said the same three words to him: "Fill her up."

Next, Judge Carson directed his remarks at Doctor William Silvers. "Dr. Silvers, I would strongly recommend hereafter that the coroner's office perform a more extensive examination of decedents, particularly where a man is on trial for his life for allegedly having committed murder."

Silvers turned bright red, started to say something, but decided not to and gazed at the floor.

If the castigation of this prominent physician and longtime friend of Carson came as a surprise, what came next was a real shocker. "Dr. James, you have the court's appreciation for bringing the matter to my attention. Your actions were instrumental in preventing what could have been a tragic miscarriage of justice."

Dr. James got to his feet and thanked the judge for his kind words and then said, "Your Honor the thanks really belong to young Mason who came to me and asked whether the victim could have suffered additional injuries not attributable to a claimed attack by the defendant."

At that point Peter got to his feet and said, "If it hadn't been for how careful Dr. James was in treating me and how he checked me all over, I never would have thought of the possibility of other injuries. He should get all the praise."

Judge Carson smiled. "While the two of you are each trying to pass the praise to the other, let me thank both of you for bringing this matter to the court's attention and helping to see that justice is done. The jury is discharged and the court is in recess."

It would have been a mistake to believe that Judge Carson had experienced an epiphany and had shed his long-standing bigotry. He had not suddenly become a liberal-thinking advocate for racial equality and he never would. Nonetheless, a subtle, perhaps barely perceptible, change in his thinking had occurred.

Peter whispered to Dr. James as they left the courtroom together, "Maybe things are going to get better. Maybe there's going to be some real changes." James just smiled and whispered back, "Maybe." But there was no conviction in his voice.

However, when Judge Carson went to get gas that

evening on his way home from court he said five additional words to the old service station attendant. They were, "Good to see you, Jesse."

THE TRIAL OF JEROME WASHINGTON
— THE AFTERMATH

THE LOCAL morning papers were full of stories about the trial and the surprising outcome.

Their earlier stories had pilloried Washington as a career criminal and had virtually predicted that he would be convicted despite the anticipated testimony of Peter. After the verdict, the writers continued to focus on Washington's unsavory past and attributed the murder acquittal to the efforts of Peter Mason with only a brief reference to the involvement of Dr. James. The northern press, which had also covered the trial, referred to Peter and Dr. James as the unlikely duo and marveled at the oddity of a black doctor and a young English boy combining to save the life of an innocent man.

Several other equally unrelated persons added to the oddity of the drama: the Negro defendant who, given his long history of petty crimes, could hardly be referred to as "a credit to his race" and a judge who was called by white critics an "ultra-conservative" and, secretly by Negro critics, "a red-necked bigot." To add to the uniqueness of the situation, the "ultra conservative" or "red-necked bigot" had praised the unlikely duo for their role in preventing a miscarriage of justice. Finally, an all white jury had exonerated this less than upstanding Negro defendant. Altogether a remarkable news day.

Late that afternoon Peter was lying on his bed when there was a knock on the door. It was Glenn Landers and the four other young people who were boarders, two men and two women. Although he had lived at Mrs. Grant's for some time, this was his first meeting with any of the boarders, other than Landers. Like Landers, the other borders worked in Jackson during the week but spent most weekends in the small towns where they were born and where their parents still lived.

"Peter, you've been in this country for five minutes and already you're better known around here than the rest of us put together. We're going to take you out to dinner to celebrate," said Landers.

They all went to a local eatery within walking distance of the house. The restaurant, considered to be one of the finest eating places in Mississippi, was large and noisy. It was owned by a former football hero who had quarterbacked the University of Mississippi to great success and who had enjoyed a short career in the NFL. The walls were covered with pictures of football action and there were framed jerseys of some of the former stars of the university. In case the theme of the restaurant was lost on any of the patrons, the waiters and waitresses all wore replica football jerseys with the names and numbers of Ole Miss stars printed on the back.

The restaurant was crowded that evening, and the tables were quite close to each other. People at the two adjoining tables seemed to take a great interest in the conversation Peter and the others were having concerning the case. At one point a woman came over and asked Peter if he was the English boy who had testified in the murder case. When Peter said that he was that boy, the woman pulled out a scrap of paper and asked him to autograph it for her and say it was for "Ruthie." After Peter obliged, Landers again noted what a celebrity he had become.

One of the young women from the boarding house, Alice Renfrew, said, "I know the accident you were in must have been terrible, but it must have been completely awful to wake up in a Nigra hospital surrounded by Nigras." Peter responded, "The accident was scary. The people at the hospital were very good to me and very kind. The doctor was marvelous and helped me a lot."

"Well I wouldn't let any of them touch me. You never know what you could catch from those people." Alice's remarks finally dispelled any lingering thoughts that Peter might still have been harboring, that blatant racism was found only among the uneducated, low intelligent rednecks of both sexes. Alice Renfrew was an honors graduate from the University of South Carolina, and had received her Masters at that same university. She was taking a year off before pursuing a PhD in, of all things, psychology.

None of the other people at the table said anything,

although a couple of them nodded, seemingly in agreement, and one frowned. Landers broke the silence and said, "Alice, I'm surprised at you. Peter says he was treated well at Froman's, and from everything I've read, that seems to be right. Peter, now that the case is over and you are in the public eye, what do you intend to do next?"

"Actually I'm running out of money. What with the hospital bills I owe, the rent, and buying new clothes, I'm going to have to find a job, and soon."

One of the other boarders asked, "What kind of job would you like to have? Jackson's not like New York or London where there are thousands of businesses and lots of opportunities."

"I don't have much experience. I left school when I was fifteen and worked as an errand boy for a real estate agent in London. I've never been to university and I'm not really trained for anything."

Landers said, "Let me think about it overnight. I work for an accounting firm and we have several clients that might have an opening or two. We'll talk tomorrow."

The next morning, Landers came by and asked Peter if he would like to walk downtown with him to his office. When they got there, Landers had Peter wait in the outer office while he talked with some of his co-workers about possible job opportunities. Fifteen minutes later, he came out.

"I've got something. It's not much and it doesn't pay a lot, but it'll keep the wolf from the door until you can find something better. We have a client, the Robert E. Lee

Hotel here in Jackson. We do accounting work for them. They frequently have openings for lower level jobs such as bellhops, elevator operators and janitors. In a lot of places in the United States, jobs like those are often held by Negroes, even here in the South, but the Robert E. Lee has a policy of not hiring Negroes even for the lowliest jobs. I know it's not much, but it's the best I can come up with right now."

Peter thought for a moment and then said, "I don't think I want to work for a company that won't hire Negroes."

"Peter, Peter, you have to be realistic. This is the Deep South. This is the way it is and this is the way it'll always be. Take it or leave it. If you want it I'll get you a letter of introduction from my boss, although I'm pretty sure the people at the Robert E. Lee have already read about you."

"I'd like the letter of introduction if it won't be too much trouble. If I don't get a job soon, I'll be sleeping on the street. As much as Mrs. Grant loves her English ancestry, I don't think she is going to let me live in her house for nothing."

THE ELEVATOR OPERATOR

"Should we hire this English kid? We're short an elevator operator since Terry Graham quit." The manager of the Robert E. Lee Hotel was discussing Peter's application with his 7am to 3pm bell captain.

"He's the kid who came up with the idea that kept that miserable little thief out of the electric chair," said the captain.

"The guy had done a lot of things, but he didn't kill that man."

"You're the boss. If you want him, it's your call."

"He's got that English accent. That'll give the elevator a touch of class."

"All he'll be saying is 7th floor, 9th floor, ground floor, stuff like that. I don't know how much class that gives," grumbled the bell captain.

"Bring him in."

Peter came into the manager's office wearing the suit. He had gotten a haircut that morning; the first one since he left England.

"Peter, we've an opening for an elevator operator. Have you ever operated one before?" asked the manager. "They're a little tricky at first."

"No I haven't sir, but I'm sure I can learn," said Peter. From the explanation that Glenn Landers had given him of an elevator, Peter recognized it as what was called a "lift" in England.

"This is Ron Provost. He's the 7-3 bell captain and, if you get the job, he will be your immediate boss and will help you learn how to run the elevator. The job pays $20 a week payable each Friday and the workday is 7:00 a.m. to 3:00 p.m. with a half hour for lunch seven days a week. Do you want the job?" asked the manager.

"Yes I want the job. Do I ever get a day off?"

"I think I already said the work week is seven days. There are no days off, not even for Christmas, the Fourth of July or any other state or national holiday. You see, a hotel is not like most companies. It's open for business every single day of the year and twenty-four hours every day. You still want the job?"

"Yes, sir."

"You see the uniform Ron is wearing? Yours will be the same except that Ron's has gold epaulets on the shoulders and yours won't. When you start work on Monday morning, you'll be fitted for a uniform. You'll also wear a hat." He turned to Ron. "Do you have one handy to show Peter?"

The bell captain went out and came back with something that looked like the bottom of a very small hat box. It had a strap that went under the chin. The uniform jacket was grey with red piping and buttoned up to the neck. The trousers were the same grey color and had a red stripe on the outside of both legs. Peter thought that the East End boys that he chummed around with in London would really get a laugh if they could see him in that outfit.

"I have to wear that, do I?" Peter asked, hoping the manager would say, "Only if you would like to." But of course he didn't.

"Yes you do have to wear it, and by the way, it will fit you a helluva lot better than what you've got on."

There he was—one day a star witness in a murder trial, his name plastered all over the papers, with people (well, one person) asking for his autograph, and the next day he is to run an elevator wearing the most ridiculous getup, one that would have his friends rolling on the floor with laughter.

THE ROBERT E. LEE HOTEL

THE HOTEL WAS a fine example of fairly early southern architecture. No expense had been spared in constructing what the owners described, with some basis but also with a little exaggeration, as "The finest hotel ever built in the South." The service was impeccable. Uniformed employees were available on a moment's notice for any task requested by the well-heeled guests—carrying bags, running errands, walking the well-groomed and fussed-over poodles with their jewel-encrusted collars, and providing newspapers, magazines and toiletries. Room service was available twenty-four hours a day and only very rarely was a requested meal unavailable, even if it meant a late night search by employees for necessary ingredients throughout the town and the awakening of suppliers.

Being young and inexperienced, Peter had given no thought as to when, if ever, he was going to return to England. He was fairly certain that he would, but he had no timetable in mind and, what was more, he had no financial ability to pay for a return trip. It would be an impossibility to save any money from his $20 a week pay from the hotel. He had almost exhausted the money he had brought with him from England and the money given to him by Chuck, plus he still had the hospital bills to pay and he had no insurance. After paying his rent, food and other necessities, he had almost nothing left and frequently he was compelled to miss meals. Further traveling around the United States was, at least for the time being, completely out of the question.

One would think that riding up and down in an elevator eight hours a day, seven days a week would be incredibly repetitious and the height of boredom. There were compensations, however. It was repetitious, but it wasn't boring, at least not all of the time. A guest's request to be taken to a particular floor was not satisfied merely by pushing a button bearing the number of that floor. The operator had to operate a handle while watching the floors scroll by on a panel above the door. As the elevator approached the requested floor, the operator had to jiggle the handle so that the cab slowed and stopped precisely at the floor. While not analogous to painting a masterpiece, the ability to maneuver the handle so as to arrive precisely at the destination was an art form and one that Peter never fully mastered. Most of the time he would get close enough so that a jiggle or two would result in a satisfactory arrival. Once in a while the elevator would stop between floors and considerable manipulation of the handle would require an appropriate adjustment. Most passengers were amused by Peter's embarrassed apologies as he tried to remedy his misstep, and entertained by Peter's attractive accent. Some were neither amused nor entertained.

A few of the guests were permanent residents at the hotel. They were, of necessity, wealthy and mostly quite old. Since most of them were retired, delays in getting up and down to their floors were of no great moment to them. They were pleased to have the opportunity to chat for a minute or two with this "delightful young English boy." Occasionally, but not frequently enough to be meaningful, one or the other of the residents would slip him a quarter or a half dollar.

The hope of the elevator operators was that sooner or later they would be promoted to bellhop. That was where the money was. Guests checking in or out would have their bags carried up or down by a bellhop and would have the bellhop bring them ice, or soft drinks, or run errands for them. Each item of activity would warrant a tip that would have to be shared in part with the shift's bell captain. For persons with limited education and no particular skill, being a bellhop was a well-paying job and few of them ever left. While the elevator operators were all young, the bellhops were all quite a bit older. Peter was well down on the seniority list and his chances of being a bellhop in the foreseeable future were worse than dim.

At Jackson General Hospital, he had seen Negro janitors. At the courthouse he had seen Negro cleaning people and workmen. Even Mrs. Grant had a Negro maid who cleaned the rooms and she had an occasional

Negro handyman. The hotel was privately owned and as Glenn had told Peter before he went to work there, the owner often boasted about having absolutely no Negro employees. All the janitors, maids and shoe shine boys were white.

He didn't see much of the other residents at Mrs. Grant's house, but he did see quite a bit of Glenn Landers. He and Glenn would occasionally go out to eat in the evening and, since both of them started work at 7:00 a.m., they would frequently walk downtown together. Glenn sometimes talked about himself. He told Peter he was born on his father's farm in rural Mississippi where they grew vegetables and some cotton. He would go home to that farm almost every weekend and help his parents and the hired help with the farm chores. Peter, in turn, told Glenn of his experiences in England during the war and what it was like to be brought up in one of the poorest areas in London.

Days turned into weeks and then into months. Peter had saved no money and had not found a better paying job, but in Glenn Landers he had found a good friend. Glenn, like Chuck, was several years older than Peter. He had graduated from Ole Miss with a degree in business administration and, like Chuck, provided advice and guidance to the young foreigner that was both helpful and appreciated.

THE GROCERY JOB

"I MAY HAVE a better job for you," said Glenn. He had waited outside the hotel for Peter's shift to end. "Another one of our clients is the Mitchell Company. It's a wholesale grocery business. They have a massive warehouse down on Raglan Street. From there, the company supplies retail grocery stores and chains all over the place with every type of food stuff imaginable—canned goods, fresh produce, cereals—you name it, they've got it. They want someone on their unloading platform. They get a lot of freight cars in from all over the country with all kinds of products and they have to be unloaded and stored in the warehouse. You interested? It pays more."

"Wow! Yes, I'm interested. I haven't been getting much exercise, other than just walking around. Sounds like I could get back in shape lifting bags while making more money. Thanks, this is terrific."

"Hey, you're not hired yet. You may not be the only one looking for the same job. By the way, there probably won't be any lifting. They've got other people to do that.

I've got to get back to the office. I don't have an easy job where I can go home at three."

"Yeah, but you're not working seven days a week either," Peter retorted. They both laughed. They had developed a close relationship and both enjoyed each other's good-natured ribbing.

"I'll find out more details. Maybe we can catch a bite to eat this evening and talk about it."

As he walked home, Peter thought about the new job. Glenn hadn't said how much more money he would get, if he got the job, or whether he would still have to work seven days a week. One thing puzzled him: how could he be working on a platform unloading freight cars with sacks and boxes of products without having to do any lifting? Maybe they needed a forklift operator, but he didn't know how to drive. No sense guessing, he would find out soon enough. Maybe he wouldn't even get the job, particularly when they found out he hadn't learned to drive.

That evening, he and Glenn went to a cheap hamburger place where they had gone a few times before. Glenn said that Peter was to go for an interview with the warehouse manager, a Mr. Will Foster, the following day as soon as he could get there after his shift at the hotel.

Mr. Foster was a fat man with an enormous stomach that protruded over his belt. He had a wad of chewing tobacco in his mouth, which made his cheek bulge. Periodically, he would spit into a paper cup he had on his desk. It was obvious that his aim was not always perfect.

The desk had numerous stains, undoubtedly the result of misguided streams of tobacco juice. While Peter was slowly getting the hang of the Southern accent, and while he continued to run into a number of "burr'n leds"-type confusions, they were becoming less frequent. However, the huge wad of tobacco in Mr. Foster's cheek along with his pronounced Southern accent made understanding him a bit of a challenge.

Foster explained the job to him. He would be in charge of a team of "Nigras" on the platform. Every day, freight cars would be shunted in and the team was to unload them. The men had pushcarts onto which they would load whatever was in the cars, and take the bags, sacks, cases or whatever else into designated areas of the warehouse. His job was first to check that the freight car to be unloaded had been sealed. He was then to remove the seal and place it in a labeled box on a desk in a small wooden hut on the platform. The hut was his office. Each freight car would come with a manifest of what it contained. He was to check to see that the manifest agreed with the order sheet which a clerk would give him each day. As the team unloaded the cars with the pushcarts, Peter was to take the order sheet and check off the products going by him. After a car was fully unloaded, he was to sign the order sheet if everything on it had been contained in the car. If there were shortages or damaged goods, he was to note that on the sheet in red pencil. He was then to give the completed order sheet signed by him to the clerk in the front of the warehouse.

"Okay, you're hired. Pay is $32 a week, hours 7:00 a.m. to 4:00 p.m., Monday through Friday." Peter was delighted—an increase of $12 a week and no work on Saturdays and Sundays!

"Come on, I'll take you to meet your boys," said Foster, spitting one last time in the paper cup before throwing the wad and the cup into a waste paper basket. "Don't forget that you've gotta keep after them. Nigras are a lazy bunch."

Peter quickly found out three things: first the "boys" ranged in age from late twenties to late fifties; second, far from being a lazy bunch, they were the hardest working people he had ever seen. Being new and inexperienced, his checking of the goods coming by him was not as quick as it should be and the men had to slow down to allow him to count and enter. When it appeared that he needed help, they would call out to him what items they had on their pushcarts. The goods were frequently heavy—hundred-pound sacks of potatoes, for example. Soon after they started work each day, the men were covered in sweat, but they never slowed down except to allow Peter to count.

The third thing he found out was that he was making more money than every member of the team. Dave, one of the older members of the team, had been with the Mitchell Company for over twenty years. He knew everything there was to know about the warehouse, the loading and storing protocols and the various forms and how they were to be handled. When Peter was about to make a mistake in completing the forms or anything else, Dave would quietly suggest what should be done. While doing so, this forty-seven-year-old, long time and experienced employee would address this eighteen-year-old, know-nothing kid as "boss" or "boss man." Meanwhile, Foster and the other white employees would refer to Dave and the other Negro employees as "boys."

Glenn had told him that it would take time before he became accustomed to the way Negroes were treated and referred to. Peter didn't say so to Glenn, but he didn't think he would ever get used to it and wasn't going to try to.

DAVE

PETER HAD PREVAILED upon Mrs. Grant to pack him a lunch from time to time. She added a few dollars to his monthly rent for this service. The lunch she packed was fairly basic—a plain cheese sandwich, a small bag of potato chips (he had been weaned away from saying the English "crisps") and an apple. At first he ate his lunch in his "office" in the wooden hut. The team would sit on the platform with their legs dangling over the side. Occasionally he would join them. At first when he did so, their animated conversation would virtually dry up. Later, they would open up more readily and they would talk with him about their children, what they did in their spare time, how exciting it was that the major baseball leagues were beginning to use Negro players and many other things. They laughed at his total ignorance of baseball and they spent time explaining the game to him. Some of the explanations were visual, showing him how pitchers threw the ball and how batters swung at pitches. He probably learned as much or more about life in the

South in those luncheon conversations than at any other time.

The white employees of the company would ordinarily eat at a boarding house down the street from the warehouse. A number of times they asked Peter to join them and sometimes he would. He learned a great deal from those conversations, as well. While no one actually insisted, several times it was suggested that it would be prudent for him to eat lunch with "his own kind." Surprisingly, Mr. Foster, whom no one would mistake for a liberal thinker, told the white employees to lay off Peter.

"He's a good kid," he was fond of saying. "His team really likes him and they work faster and better for him than for anyone before. Sure he's got a lot to learn, but he's from over the ocean. He'll come around to act the way he's supposed to in time."

Dave was one of the most intriguing people that Peter had ever known. He was one of eight children who were brought up in a roughhewn shack on the edge of town. He had left school at the age of twelve and had taught himself to read and write. He had, and expressed, a type of gentle wisdom that would have been hard to duplicate, no matter the level of education. From Dave, Peter learned many things. One was that intelligence was not synonymous with education. They were two totally separate assets. The difference between those who were well- educated and those who weren't was more related to vocabulary. Dave didn't know a lot of long words, but conversations with him were frequently on a high level, provided that the language used was the language with which Dave was familiar. Peter came to realize that words like "subsequent" and "prior" were unnecessary and that "before" and "after" were at least as good and less pretentious. While Peter's education wasn't extensive, it was much more so than Dave's. But Peter didn't have to curb his use of long words because most of them weren't in his vocabulary, either.

It was a long walk from the warehouse to Mrs. Grant's house. Dave drove an old pickup truck and, if he saw Peter walking, he would stop and offer him a ride. Peter generally refused because he knew that his destination was a long way out of the way for Dave. Sometimes he was tired and accepted. On the ride they would talk of many things and Peter would quiz Dave on his reaction to the inequities Negroes were subjected to in the Deep South. Dave would tell him that all people, white or Negro, must accept with good grace things over which they have no control, and seek the goodness that he believed existed in all people. Dave was a deeply religious man and was firmly convinced that God put people to the test and looked for them to overcome adversity with grace and kindness. Peter had never met anyone with more grace and kindness than Dave.

Peter had never ridden in a pickup truck and would ask Dave questions about the operation of the vehicle. When Dave discovered that Peter couldn't drive, he taught him how. It took a while, since Peter was perhaps not the best of students. But ultimately he mastered it, went to the

Department of Motor Vehicles with Dave in his truck and passed the written and driving tests.

His Mississippi driver's license became a treasured possession, although he had no car. That license was just one of the benefits, and not the most valuable, that he got from knowing Dave. Peter was more comfortable with Dave than with anyone else he had ever known. They were so different in so many ways—color, age, nationality, background, almost anything one could think of. Yet Peter felt a sense of kinship with Dave that he could not explain even to himself.

THE BASEBALL GAME

DAVE WAS DRIVING Peter home one evening. They had worked late and Dave insisted that he had an errand to run and Mrs. Grant's house was not that far out of his way. They had driven in silence for some time, which was unusual. On other rides they had talked incessantly about a multitude of things, but not this trip. Several times Peter attempted to start a conversation, but Dave's responses were a grunt or one or two words.

"Is something bothering you, Dave? You're awful quiet. Did I say something wrong?"

Dave finally opened up. On his way home the night before, he had been stopped by a white police officer who told him that one of his tail lights was out. He had no quarrel with being stopped. The officer had every right to bring the problem to his attention, but it was the way he did it. He was approximately half Dave's age and used an insulting, patronizing and demeaning tone. He constantly referred to Dave as "boy" and used language suggesting that Dave was a moron with the IQ of a head of lettuce.

"But Dave, you've lived here all your life. You must have heard this type of talk lots of times. I know it's awful, but you must be used to it."

"I've heard it lots of times and I'll hear it lots more before I die. No matter how often you hear it, you never get used to it. I was tired last night and I guess it hurt me more than usual. I'm forty-seven years old. I've got a wife and three kids. We go to church every Sunday. I've worked at the same job for years. Never been late, never stole nothing. I've never had no trouble with the law. I pay my bills, I don't drink. Yet I get called 'boy' and get insulted daily by white folks and rousted by the police. You know what? It ain't never gonna change."

Peter wanted to ease the pain but was at a loss to know how to do it. He had come to realize that segregation and the demeaning treatment of Negroes in the South was age-old, deep-rooted, and not likely to change any time soon, but he had to say something, no matter how feeble. "I've been reading about Negro players coming into the major leagues in baseball after Jackie Robinson broke the color barrier in the National League and Larry Doby in the American League. Don't you think that's going to start something and things are going to get better soon?"

"Not down here and maybe not never. Even up north that's just a tiny exception for great ballplayers that can put money in the owners' pockets. Those players are booed everywhere they go, even by their own team's fans. They can't eat with their white teammates in most restaurants and can't stay in the same hotels when they're on the road.

You think that's some kind of breakthrough? I don't. And even that ain't never gonna happen here."

So much for trying to make Dave feel better! Peter wished there was something he could say, but he couldn't. It would have been easy to say that he knew how Dave felt, but it wouldn't be true and Dave would know that. He could see it happening and he could fume at the injustice, but he couldn't put himself into the minds of Dave or any of the others. The best he could do was to move to another subject.

"Tell me about baseball. We've got a game in England called 'rounders.' We play it in the street with a stick and a tennis ball. We make bases using lampposts and manhole covers. You hit the ball with the stick and run around the bases until you get back to where you started from or someone touches you with the ball before you get there."

Dave laughed. "Well it's close, but baseball is much more than that. Tell you what. A bunch of us get together most Saturday mornings at a field on the end of Lemon Street and we play baseball. Most of us are pretty bad and some of us are probably too old. Come and watch.

We start at ten. We'll teach you the game and maybe you can hit a few."

The next Saturday, Peter showed up wearing his goalie jersey, a pair of shorts and plimsoles, which he now knew to call "sneakers" although he puzzled at such a funny name. Many of the players he knew from the Mitchell Company; some worked with him on the platform. Those who didn't know him seemed a bit uneasy at the sight of a white guy on the field. They had been playing most Saturdays for years and no white man had ever watched or played there.

The baseball field was just that; a field. There were no base paths, no bases, no mound and no backstop. The players used their jackets to make the bases. They had worn-out mitts and a mask for the catcher. One of the players wheeled up his old truck to serve as a backstop, covering the side facing the field with a tarp to protect it from the impact of passed or foul balls or wild pitches (of which there were many). The appearance of the truck suggested that it had served that function a lot of times and the number of dents demonstrated that the tarp did not actually afford much protection.

Dave introduced him to the players he didn't know. The youngest was a tall athletic-looking man who Peter later learned attended college in a small school in Arizona. He was in town for a brief visit with his parents. His father was also playing in the game. "This is Maurice Lennox, but he's always been known as 'Mack' as long as I've known him," said Dave. "Mack, this is Mr. Peter Mason." Dave was not willing to drop the "mister" even on the baseball field, but Mack was. He held out his hand. "Nice to meet you, Peter."

Peter must have looked a bit surprised, but quickly shook hands and said, "Nice to meet you too, Mack."

Noticing the surprised look, Mack asked, "Are you offended that I called you by your first name?"

"No, I'm pleased you did."

"Why pleased?"

"I'm eighteen years old and, other than a doctor who treated me, you're the first Negro who has called me by my first name. I don't seem to be able to make others do that."

"It's the way it is. You'll get used to it."

"No, I won't and I don't want to."

"Now it's my turn to be pleased," replied Mack.

Dave and some of the others explained the game to Peter as it went along. While it became clearer, he still didn't completely understand all the nuances. After a while they persuaded Peter to get in the game. They laughed good-naturedly at his awkwardness at bat, and generously allowed him far more than the allotted three strikes. He finally made contact with the ball, although it only traveled a few feet. They applauded him wildly when he made a fine running catch in right field, albeit with his bare hand. He could not yet get used to the mitt.

There were just enough players for two sides and, although the game went on for hours, there was no real attempt to keep score or to play precisely within the letter of the rules. The field had very little grass and soon they were all covered in dust. While the pitchers threw hard at everyone else, they slowed their deliveries when Peter came to bat. He protested about the special treatment and they promised they would speed up the pitches the next time he played. Finally the game was over. Nobody had counted the number of innings. Nobody knew exactly how many runs had been scored and nobody cared, although they argued playfully about it. It had just been fun to be out there, teasing and arguing about whether a runner had been safe or out or whether a fielder had actually caught the ball. They were among friends and they had a good time.

After the game they put away the bats, balls and mitts and broke out cans of beer and sandwiches. All of the players contributed a few coins to pay for the food and drink. They refused to take money from Peter. They said he was a guest this time, but next time he could contribute. They sat around eating, drinking, joking and telling stories. Those who had never met Peter before wanted to know where he came from, how he liked Jackson and what he thought about baseball. A couple of them had briefly been in England with the U.S. Army before the Normandy invasion. They wanted Peter to know how much they liked England and how kind the English people had been to them. It had been a great day. Peter was sorry that it had to come to an end. He had learned a lot about baseball, but more about the people. He had played in the game, although poorly. He had joked, ate and drank with people, many of whom he had not known before. He went home dirty, tired and supremely happy. He was already looking forward to playing again.

FINDING THE BROWARDS

Having the weekends off was not quite the pleasurable development that Peter had anticipated. Since all of the tenants at Mrs. Grant's went home for the weekends, including Glenn, the house was as quiet as a tomb. The whole town seemed deserted. While only a relatively small percentage of the Jackson residents left on weekends, there was a sense of emptiness that pervaded the town. Peter couldn't find much to do that wouldn't cost more of his money than he could afford. He was trying to save a portion of his wages for the time when he would decide when and if to return to England. Even with the increased amount he was now earning, saving much was difficult given the other expenses he had, including the hospital bills which remained due and unpaid.

Peter's spirits were buoyed by a letter from his sister. He had felt guilty and sad about leaving her, even though she had urged him to go. He often thought of her coming home to the cold, empty and dreary flat. He had been concerned that his leaving had saddled her with the entire rent and, on her salary, meeting that obligation would not be easy. The letter told him that her good friend Janet Gilmore had moved in with her and was sharing the expenses. Janet worked for a travel agency in the same general area as Beth's workplace. They were now taking the bus and underground together, both coming and going. Peter knew Janet and liked her. She had a great sense of humor and made him laugh. Beth also told him that her relationship with the boyfriend was going well and was becoming a little more serious. Peter scribbled a quick reply to Beth, expressing relief that everything seemed to be going well and assuring her that he, too, was all right. He had not told her about his accident or the Washington case for fear it would unnecessarily concern her. She tended to worry a lot. In that way, she was much like her mother.

Peter often thought about Solomon Broward, their conversation that led to Peter's coming to Jackson and his first real confrontation with segregation. He had been anxious to visit the Browards and was hoping to do so before Solomon returned to Philadelphia. His accident, the Washington case and the seven-day-a-week job at the hotel had interfered with that plan. Peter had the piece of paper on which Solomon had written his son's address and he knew the location from looking it up on his map. It was not far from the Mitchell Company warehouse. He was sure that Solomon had long since ended his visit and had returned to Philadelphia. Still he could use his looking for Solomon as an excuse to call on his son. He had little to do on that Sunday afternoon and, if nothing more, it would be a nice walk.

He found the address easily. It was on a street of neat but very small houses. The Broward house had a small front garden, obviously carefully tended, with freshly mown grass and flowerbeds.

He knocked and the door was opened by the most beautiful girl he had ever seen. She was probably sixteen or seventeen. Her eyes were almond shaped and her smooth lustrous skin was the color of milk chocolate. She was tall and slim and Peter was so taken aback that he just stood and stared at her. The girl was also taken aback but for different reasons. Her neighborhood was a hundred percent Negro and the only white people she had ever seen in the area were police officers serving court papers or making arrests. Certainly no white man had ever come to the Browards' house.

"Yes?" she said questioningly, "you looking for someone?"

"Yes, I am" he said, regaining his composure. "I'm looking for Solomon Broward."

"That's my grandfather. He doesn't live here."

"Who is it, Christine?" came a male voice from further back in the house.

"It's a man looking for Grandpa."

The owner of the male voice then appeared. He, too, was tall and slim with a slight facial resemblance to the girl who must have been his daughter. He appeared to be in his early forties and he, too, looked at Peter suspiciously.

"Solomon Broward is my father. Why are you looking for him?"

Peter then explained how he had met Solomon; how they had talked on the bus all the way from Philadelphia until Solomon was sent to the back of the bus, and how they had exchanged addresses. "I was hoping he was still here, but I suppose he's gone back to Philadelphia."

The suspicious look had left Joshua Broward's face. He told Peter that his father had returned to Philadelphia some time ago. He invited Peter to come in and introduced him to the rest of the family, his wife Harriet and his twelve-year-old son Philip. The house was small and the furniture old and worn. It was, however, spotless. There were several framed family pictures on the wall, including one he recognized as Solomon Broward, and one of Phillip in his baseball uniform with his team. There was also one of Christine in a cheerleader outfit. Peter spent a little more time looking at that one.

Joshua told Peter that his father had recounted his meeting and conversation with what he described as a "very fine young English boy." The afternoon passed quickly. The Broward family showed great interest in Peter's roots and Joshua expressed some amazement about why in the world, with all the other attractive places to see in the United States, he would end up in Mississippi. Peter said that he wanted to see something as different as possible from what he had been used to. Harriet said that he had certainly found that place and they all laughed. Christine and Philip told Peter about where they went to school and what classes they were taking. The Browards got a laugh when Peter recounted his ineptness at running the hotel elevator.

Harriet insisted that Peter stay for dinner, which he did. She had made a lamb stew. It was served with hot steaming bread that she had just baked and home-churned sweet butter. It was definitely the best meal he had eaten since he arrived in Jackson and probably the best meal he had ever eaten. He learned that Joshua was an automobile mechanic; that Philip was in the sixth grade and Christine was a senior, both of them at all-Negro schools. In the early years of their marriage, Joshua and Harriet had spent some time in the North and were seemingly more at ease with a white man and did not demonstrate the subservience that Peter had found so disquieting in his contact with other Negroes.

It had become dark and it was time to leave. Joshua insisted that he drive Peter home. Peter said goodbye to Harriet, Phillip and Christine (especially to Christine) and at Harriet's insistence, promised to come back soon. However, on the drive back to Mrs. Grant's Joshua struck a more somber note. He warned Peter that it was not without some measure of danger for a white man, other than a police officer, to be seen visiting a Negro home. That danger, to the extent it existed, was not only for the white visitor, but also for the Negro family he was visiting. Peter assured Joshua that he didn't want to do anything to cause harm to the Browards, but Joshua said that all of his family wanted to see Peter again and he was cautiously optimistic that there would be no repercussions. He did, however, tell Peter to limit his visits, to come at night, and to be careful. Sunday was probably the best time since there were fewer people around.

FARMER LANDERS

"WHAT ARE YOU doing this weekend?" Glenn and Peter were walking to work together on a Friday morning.

"Nothing. I thought I'd read and maybe go to a movie." He had developed the habit of calling them "movies" rather than "pictures" because, as Glenn explained, if you say you're going to the pictures, people think you're going to an art gallery.

"Why don't you come home with me this weekend?" Glenn asked. I'll show you what rural life is like in Mississippi and I'll introduce you to my family. You can have your own bathroom for a couple of days and not have to share it with me."

"That'd be great. You sure it's okay?"

"Of course it is. Didn't I just invite you?"

"The farm" was not at all what Peter thought it would be. He imagined it would be a log cabin with a field of wheat, three or four cows and a chicken coop. Instead it was more like a scene from *Gone With the Wind*. At the end of a long driveway lined with magnolia trees was a magnificent house with huge white pillars, balconies and a Negro servant in some kind of uniform to open the front door. He fully expected Hattie McDaniel to come out to greet him or, better yet, Butterfly McQueen rubbing her hands together and crying "Oh Miz Scarlett! Miz Scarlett!"

Glenn was amused by Peter's open-mouthed amazement. "A little different than you thought?"

"A lot different. I'm a big city boy and I've never seen a farm before, but this doesn't look like the farms I've seen in the movies. Your parents must be very rich. Why do you live in the boarding house?"

"It's convenient. I am only in my room to shave, shower and sleep. As you know, I'm not there on the weekends and I don't want the trouble of taking care of an apartment. Besides, I like the people at Mrs. Grant's; particularly you. This isn't your typical farm, but we do have crops—wheat, corn, cabbage, a lot of cotton; and we do have animals—cows, sheep, chickens, horses. I'll show it to you tomorrow. Come and meet my folks."

They went into an enormous living room replete with chandeliers, couches, chairs, a grand piano and expensive-looking oil paintings on the wall. Mr. Landers looked very much like Glenn, only a bit heavier and grey-haired. Mrs. Landers was an attractive middle-aged woman who must have turned a lot of heads when she was younger and maybe still did. Glenn's sister, Laura, was about Peter's age. She was very pretty in a tomboy sort of way with blond hair and fair skin. She was wearing shorts and a blouse with two top buttons undone. She looked like she enjoyed the outdoors; horseback riding, fishing and the like.

"Glenn's been telling us a lot about you, Peter. I'm glad you were finally able to come and see us. How about something to drink?" Mr. Landers rang a bell and a maid came in. She also was wearing a uniform and had an apron and a cap. "What'll you have? We've got some of the finest sour mash bourbon in the whole U. S. of A. How about a snort? You're old enough. In the South, young men can have a drink or two so long as they don't go overboard."

"I've drunk beer, but my mother never wanted me to drink anything stronger than a shandy."

"What's a shandy?"

"Half beer and half lemonade."

"Sounds awful, but I'll have her mix you one if you want."

"It *is* pretty awful. I only had it once. I think I would rather just have plain lemonade."

Mr. Landers looked at the maid and she went off and came back with a glass half full of ice and filled up with lemonade.

"I forgot you limeys don't like ice. You probably haven't figured out how to make it yet." He laughed uproariously at his own joke. "Glenn told us you were English. Both the missus and I come from English background going way back to the *Mayflower*."

Peter was beginning to think there must have been a whole fleet of *Mayflower*s, or one *Mayflower* as big as all of Jackson to have carried all the ancestors claimed by only the white Mississippians. However, the Landers claim was possibly verifiable. The paintings on the wall included one that Mr. Landers said was Lord Gordon Landers and another one he said was Colonel Simon Landers astride a horse and wearing the colors and insignia of what Peter recognized as the Coldstream Guards. Over the course of the weekend, it became apparent that Mr. Landers was a bit of a blowhard and tended to exaggerate his own connections. Peter even entertained the thought that he had commissioned the paintings and had applied fabricated names to them.

The next day, as promised, Glenn and his sister took him on a tour of the estate. It was huge. There were a lot of Negro workers feeding the animals, currying the horses, cutting, hoeing, sawing and performing a multitude of other tasks. Interspersed among them were a few white men who were obviously overseeing the work. All they needed, thought Peter, for this to be a true re-enactment of *Gone With the Wind* was for the overseers to have whips. Perhaps Mr. Landers wished they could have them and could use them. Peter concluded that such a thought, perhaps not completely irrational, was probably unfair.

It was a great weekend. Glenn's sister Laura was outgoing, talkative, athletic and flirtatious. The three of them tramped over a lot of the 1,000 acres that made up "Landers Land," a title Mr. Landers invented and of which he was most proud. Peter dutifully expressed admiration for the creation of such a catchy, alliterative and descriptive name, while secretly finding the name and the discussion about its authorship particularly inane.

Glenn and Laura showed Peter the shed where the newborn lambs were kept, and they cuddled a few of them. Glenn showed Peter how to operate a large tractor and let him drive it for a few minutes. The fact that he almost drove it into a small lake, and came close to falling off, made Laura convulse with laughter. Laura had an old Negro farm employee saddle up three horses and they rode out to the northern border of the Landers property. Peter had never ridden a horse before and his "seat" and obvious discomfort again made Laura laugh and Glenn smile. After the ride, they walked back to the house. A more accurate description would be that Glenn and Laura walked, while Peter hobbled.

The rest of the weekend was spent walking, riding, fishing, eating and just talking. When he made his farewells, the elder Landers made Peter promise to come back and stay with them often. Laura threw her arms around him and kissed him on the cheek while whispering, "You'd better come back or I'll come and get you."

On the ride back to Jackson, Glenn told Peter that he had made a great impression on his parents, but particularly on his sister. "Don't mind Laura. She's a terrible flirt, but she's a real good kid." Peter thought about the difference between the palatial estate of the Landers and the tiny house of the Browards, but mostly he thought about Christine Broward and Laura Landers. They were both extremely pretty, but that's where the similarities ended. Laura was brash and talkative but Christine was shy and sweet.

LAURA

It had become close to a regular event. Almost every weekend, Peter would go with Glenn to the "farm." The Landers, and particularly Laura, were sad on the weekends when Glenn would arrive alone. They very much liked having Peter around and always encouraged Glenn to bring him. He would protest that he was intruding, but the Landers would insist.

While Glenn would spend time with Peter and Laura, riding, walking, talking and fishing, more and more he would excuse himself on the pretense that he had brought work with him from the office or that he was going to help his father or mother on some task or another. Laura would fix a picnic basket and she and Peter would sit by the lake, sometimes with a couple of baited hooks in the water and sometimes not. The lake was stocked with trout, but unless Mrs. Landers wanted fish for dinner, the hooks they used had no barbs and anything they caught was thrown back.

Peter and Laura talked for hours, sitting close to each

other. They talked of what they wanted to do with their lives, where they wanted to go, what it was like in England during the war and a hundred other things. They never seemed to run out of topics. Laura was in her last year of high school and she was planning to go to Ole Miss, but she hadn't yet decided what she wanted to study. She urged Peter to enroll there also, but he didn't know that he wanted to or could afford to. Laura insisted that her father would pay for his tuition and expenses, but he vehemently rejected the suggestion. She further insisted that she would talk to her father about it, whether he liked it or not.

There were discreet signs of affection between the two from time to time. They would often walk back to the house hand-in-hand. When he would leave at the end of the weekend, she would give him a peck on the cheek. One late Sunday afternoon, as Peter and Glenn were getting ready to leave, Laura grabbed Peter by the chin and turned his face toward her. The peck on the cheek that Peter anticipated became an open mouth long-lasting kiss that had left them both breathless and Peter a little stunned.

"Are all English boys as slow as you?" she hissed in his ear.

"What do you mean?"

"Do I have to start everything? Boys are supposed to be the aggressors, but not you," she said petulantly. It was true that Peter's experience with girls was limited. He had gone to an all-boys' school in London and his primary interests were in sports, particularly football, which the Americans called soccer. It wasn't that he was not attracted to girls. He was. But he had always felt shy and awkward around them. In the weeks to come Laura would remedy that shortcoming.

Another three weeks went by before Peter again visited the farm. One weekend the warehouse was uncharacteristically overwhelmed with freight cars and Mr. Foster had required Peter and his team to work both Saturday and Sunday. Neither Peter nor the team resented the overtime since they all got time and a half on Saturday and double time on Sunday. The following weekend Glenn had to go to New Orleans with his boss for some kind of meeting with a client. After several weeks of absence, they finally showed up at the farm and were greeted even more warmly than usual. Peter said he was quite tired and shortly after dinner he excused himself and went to bed. He was awakened by what seemed to be something pressing against him. He reached out groggily and sat up with a start. Lying next to him was a totally naked Laura.

"What are you doing here?" he said, immediately recognizing how stupid it sounded.

"I came here to play chess," she said sarcastically. "What do you think I'm doing here?"

"What about your parents and Glenn?"

"They don't want to play chess. Besides, their bedrooms are way on the other side of the house."

She reached over and stroked his back. He turned

toward her and they repeated the kiss they had exchanged the last time only deeper and longer.

"Here, put this on," she said handing him something he didn't recognize.

"What is it?"

"It's protection."

"Protection against what?"

"Boy, you are dumb. Just put it on. Where do you think babies come from? Do you think the stork brought you? I didn't come here to give a lecture on sexual practices to the young and foolish."

He struggled with the "protection" inexpertly until she interrupted.

"Here let me do it." Her efforts proved successful but those same efforts almost ended the moment before it began. Afterwards they lay there, uncharacteristically without conversation. They repeated the event with a fresh item of "protection" and then fell asleep. They awoke just as the sun had started to come up and Laura quickly returned to her own room. Before leaving, she told him to be sure to flush the two items of "protection" down the toilet and, somewhat matter of factly, said she would see him at breakfast. He lay there for several minutes after she had left. It embarrassed him that he had been so awkward, but felt it had been the greatest experience of his life.

On the drive back to Jackson, Glenn said it seemed as though Peter and Laura were getting along famously. Peter smiled weakly. Glenn didn't know the half of it.

CHRISTINE

PETER ALSO VISITED the Browards often. Aware of Joshua Broward's concerns, Peter always planned to arrive after dark. It was winter and very cold. It was not unusual, therefore, for him to walk to the Browards wearing a coat, cap, gloves and a scarf obscuring the bottom part of his face. Indeed, were his forehead covered in blood, he would have looked like he did when he had arrived at Froman Hospital and had been initially mistaken for being Negro.

While he very much liked Joshua and his wife, the real reason for his visits was Christine. He had grown very fond of her. She was not like Laura other than they were both beautiful. While he knew that Christine liked him, she was not a flirt. He was embarrassed about continually having dinner at the Browards. They were by no means poverty stricken, but they were also not wealthy. He had taken to picking up things at the grocery store each time he came. It was not much, as a rule; a cake or some ice cream for dessert or sometimes a container of rice pudding.

Sometimes he would walk with Christine to a little park several blocks away. There was a patch of grass, mostly brown with bare spots, a baseball cage with gaping holes in the netting and a few rusty swings. There were lights shining down on the swings and the baseball cage and there were a couple of benches. It was a far cry from the park facilities near Mrs. Grant's house, but the children who played there during the day enjoyed themselves. After dark there were only a few older children there and none when the weather was cold. Peter and Christine would sit on one of the benches and talk. The benches were not well lighted, and it would be impossible for a person casually walking by to identify the boy with the cap pulled down as either Negro or white.

The conversations that Christine and Peter had were, in some ways, similar to the conversations Laura and Peter would have, and in some ways different. They did talk about what they wanted to do with their lives, but not about owning big houses and fancy cars or what countries they wanted to visit. Doing those things was realistic for Laura; they would only be a pipe dream for Christine. They talked about the seeming insuperable difficulties a boy and girl of different color would have in dating each other, not only in the Deep South, but anywhere. There was a sadness about the conversations Peter had with Christine that was not present in conversations with Laura. But there was also a depth of feeling with Christine, an intangible sensation that was not present with Laura. One night, as they returned to Christine's house, he leaned over to kiss her on the check and she turned and offered her mouth. The kiss was sweet, not sensual, and he felt a tear on her cheek.

That night, as he walked back to Mrs. Grant's, he was lost in thought and didn't notice three young white boys walking toward him. His scarf had become unraveled and his face was clearly visible in the street lights.

"Hey, where'd you just come from?" yelled one of boys.

Peter just kept on walking.

"Hey, I'm talking to you. Are you deaf or something? What were you doing down there in Niggertown?"

The three boys came closer to him and Peter could sense that their attitude was menacing.

"I got lost. I'm new to this town. I'm staying over on North State Street. I must have gone down the wrong street.

Their attitude softened when they heard his accent. "I guess you must be new. You must be. You talk so funny. You don't ever want to go down there again. You could get hurt. You were lucky this time," they said as they walked away. Peter was shaking. He had come very close to a beating, but, even worse, he had been careless and could have hazarded the Browards.

What a mess, he thought. He liked Laura. He liked being with her. She was fun and she had introduced him into wonderful girl-boy things that he had never experienced. She was white. Her parents liked him and they were wealthy. But his feelings for Christine were different.

They were deeper and more complicated. She was Negro and her parents were not wealthy. The difference in family wealth was of no consequence, but the difference in color seemed overwhelming and impossible to overcome.

THE READING AND WRITING LESSONS

"Boss Man, can I talk to you for a minute?"

Peter cringed. It wasn't that he didn't want to talk to Eddie. He hated being called "Boss Man." It was worse than being called "limey," which was the name some of the white Mitchell employees delighted in calling him. It was noon and, although he had been going to Mrs. Potts's boarding house for lunch more frequently, on this day he had brought a sandwich and an apple that Mrs. Grant had put together for him.

"Sure, Eddie, what is it?"

"I got this here letter and I'd be obliged if you'd read it for me."

"Did you forget your glasses?"

The moment Peter said it he wished he hadn't. Eddie looked down at his feet, reached in his pocket and pulled out an envelope. "I cain't read or write. Never learned. Never went to no school."

Peter took the envelope, opened it and read the contents. "Eddie, this is from a lawyer. Seems your Aunt

Flora has died in South Carolina and in her will she left you $200."

"I never knew her. My mamma said her name a time or two. Wow, $200. I never seen that much money in my whole life. Is it in that envelope?"

"No. You have to fill out this form that came with the letter. It's easy. All you have to do is give the lawyer your full name, home address, telephone number, date of birth, sign and date and send it back to him. Then he'll send you the $200. If you give me the information he wants, I'll write it in and then you can sign it."

"I ain't got no telephone and I cain't even sign my name."

"Well that's a bit different. I can fill in the rest of the form, but I don't think I can sign your name for you. I'll ask Mr. Luther Adams what you should do. He's a lawyer and he'll probably know."

Later Adams told Peter to send Eddie to his office with everything filled in except the signature. He would witness Eddie putting an X on the signature line. He would then attach his own signed affidavit attesting to the fact that the X was Eddie's. There would be no charge. A couple of days later Peter called his team together. "Look, I don't want to embarrass any of you and none of you have to answer if you don't want to, but I'd like a show of hands from those who can't read or write."

The only hands that weren't raised were those of Dave and a couple of others. Peter was shocked. He couldn't imagine how any adult could get by without being able to read or write, but obviously these men could and did. *I suppose if you haven't known anything different, you don't realize what else is out there,* Peter thought. *Maybe it's like me in the war, with bombings, people dying, lack of food, buildings destroyed. It becomes a way of life and that's all there is. I couldn't do anything about the bombings, the food, the deaths, but maybe I can do something about this.*

"I'll teach you how to read and write, if you want me to and if you'll let me. How many would like me to do that?"

Only one man opted out. "I'm too old and set in my ways. You cain't teach an old dog like me no new tricks. I'm fifty-two and I've made it this far with no readin' and writin' and I guess I'll make it the rest of the way the same."

And so it came about that two or three times a week, during the lunch hour, a group of illiterate men, almost all of whom were old enough to be Peter's father, would gather around the eighteen-year-old boy, who himself had left school at fifteen, and learned to read and write. He bought them all writing pads and pencils and he scrounged up a badly scarred and long unused blackboard from the back of the warehouse. He talked to them, wrote on the board with chalk and gave them assignments to do at home.

It wasn't long before the white supervisors told Foster about the lessons. Foster called Peter to his office where a number of supervisors gathered. "Mason, what the hell do you think you're doing teaching them boys to read and write? This ain't no goddam schoolhouse. They're here to work, not to learn their goddam ABCs."

One of the supervisors started to say something, but Foster interrupted. "Shut your face Bates. When I want to hear from you, I'll let you know." By now Foster was out of breath and his face was bright red. "I told the fellows to lay off you when you ate lunch with the Nigras, but no more lessons, you hear me?"

"But it's not during working hours and—" Peter got no further.

"What I just told you is the way it's gonna be. And that's the end of that. You got it?"

But it wasn't the end. Mr. Mitchell, the president of the company, heard about the lessons and called Foster into his office.

"I hear that English boy, what's his name—Martin, no Mason, has been teaching the Negro workers to read and write. I like it. Let him continue to do it so long as it doesn't interfere with work. Apart from anything else, it'll help them put the goods in the right places. I think this English kid has promise. I want to encourage him."

As Foster started to leave Mitchell's office, he was called back. "I want you to make sure that none of your supervisors give the kid a hard time or hassle the Negroes about their lessons. It's your responsibility. Don't screw it up."

The lessons continued. The number of students increased. Negro employees on other teams, mostly those loading the trucks and some of the drivers, joined the class. Supervisors would periodically come out to watch the curious spectacle of this slight built teenager with the odd accent surrounded by a bunch of Negroes learning their ABCs.

The pupils faithfully came back with each of their assignments completed. They couldn't wait to show Peter what they had accomplished. Their enthusiasm bubbled over and was contagious. Peter looked forward with great anticipation to the next class. He went to the library and read books on elementary education. He carefully went over their homework and corrected their childish writings. Some of their letters were written backwards and initially the spelling of even the simplest words was wrong. But as weeks went by, the improvement was remarkable.

"You can't teach them to read and write," one of the supervisors said contemptuously. "It's like trying to teach a chimpanzee to sing opera."

"Bring me a chimpanzee and I'll not only teach him to sing opera, I'll have him write one," retorted Peter.

"Don't get smart with me you limey jerk or maybe I'll teach YOU a lesson and it won't be about reading," the supervisor snarled.

THE BROKEN FOOT

"ARE YOU GOING downtown this morning?" Peter had knocked on Glenn's door to see if he wanted to walk together to their jobs. Glenn opened the door and pointed downward. He had a cast on his right foot.

"How did you do that?" Peter asked.

"Playing basketball last night. Somebody tripped me. It was an accident, I think. I fell awkwardly and I felt something crack. They had to take me to Jackson General. I'm going to have to wear this damn thing for months. Sylvia is going to give me a ride. I can't drive with this thing on my foot. I'm sure she'd give you a ride too," Glenn responded. Sylvia was one of the women who lived during the week at Mrs. Grant's.

"I'm sorry. If there is anything I can do, just ask," said Peter.

"I may ask you to drive me out to the farm this weekend, if you'd like to and if you think you're ready to drive on the highway," Glenn said, knowing that Peter had only recently learned to drive and had little experience.

"Sure, I'll be glad to."

"I won't be able to drive for ages, so if you want to use my car any time, you can. Just don't run into anyone."

"Thanks, I might just take you up on that." And he did borrow the car with the intention of taking Christine for a ride. Her parents had the usual concerns that parents have when their daughter is dating a boy, particularly one who has had little driving experience. They had the added concern that their daughter was dating a white boy in a community that did more than just frown upon such relationships.

"I can't let you take Christine for a ride. I just can't allow it," said Joshua.

"It's okay, really. Glenn loaned me the car and I know how to drive. Look, I have a license." Peter pulled it out of his pocket.

"It's not that. Where would you go? It's one thing to go to the park a few blocks from the house. It's something else to ride around town. You get seen with a Negro girl, there's no telling what will happen. And you can't just drive off in the woods or some such place and park. She's only seventeen. I can't allow it."

Peter knew he was right and had to accept it. He was distraught that he and Christine had to be together only in her house or in the shadows of the park. He desperately wanted to be seen with her like other boys and girls. He had watched young couples together in restaurants, arm-in-arm on busy streets and at outdoor concerts. He had seen them in broad daylight sitting on park benches hugging and kissing while people walked by and mothers pushed babies in strollers. Nobody seemed shocked or concerned in any way. Of course the boys and girls were all white. When he was alone at night, he fantasized about being in a place with Christine where they could walk arm-in-arm and hug in public without any passersby being shocked or thinking anything bad about it.

Once in a while, the Browards would go to the movies, leaving Peter and Christine alone in their house. They did engage in some heavy necking (he had learned that was the term for it) but he went no further. It wasn't because he didn't want to. He adored her and merely touching her face or her hair raised overwhelming emotions in him that he hadn't ever experienced even with Laura. He was ecstatic about the sexual activity that he had with Laura, but for some reason he would not attempt to do the same with Christine. His feelings for Christine were sexual, but they were much more than that.

He did drive Glenn in his car to the farm and he managed to do so without hitting anything, although Glenn was forced to shout "watch out!" and "slow down!" a few times. The Landers had a party on a Saturday evening for some of their friends in the area. The friends were a "Who's Who" of the Jackson elite: doctors, lawyers, judges, businessmen, ranch owners, politicians and their wives. The two main topics of conversation were Peter, and Glenn's foot. The attendees were fascinated by Peter's accent. He, again, had to pretend to listen attentively to claims of English ancestry, some farfetched, some not.

Guests also oohed and aahed about the injury Glenn had suffered—how did it happen, did it hurt much and how long did he have to wear the cast? Peter could have made a lot of money were he to receive a dollar for every "y'all" and "howdy" delivered that evening. At the end of the evening they had a cast-signing session. They got a marking pen and most of the guests signed their names or a two or three word message on Glenn's cast. Glenn got Peter to write "Limey" in the one remaining space close to where his toes protruded from the end.

Peter's sexual encounters with Laura had become more inventive and daring by reason of place, position and frequency. Both his and her bedrooms were used, but they also moved outside to such areas as the stables, the wheat field and even one of the benches overlooking the lake. Based on her skill at these matters, it was quite clear that Peter was not her first or second and probably not even her third or fourth. They were sure that their trysts had not yet been discovered although a sly smile or two from some of the field workers suggested otherwise. That weekend, Glenn had wanted to leave for Jackson Sunday night, but he opted to wait until Monday morning. He preferred to chance Peter's inexpert driving in daylight rather than in the dark. They drove in silence for some time until Peter suddenly blurted out, "How do you know whether you're in love?"

The question, coming straight out of the blue, took Glenn by surprise and he could only say "What?"

"I think I'm in love, but I don't know for sure and I don't know how you tell."

"I don't know how to answer that. I've never really thought about it. I don't know of any particular items that you can check off and if they come out one way you're in love and if they don't you're not. If you want to know if you have a cold, you can check off items — I'm sneezing, I'm coughing and I have a bit of a fever so I probably have a cold. You can't do that with love."

"That's not much help."

"I'm sorry. I'm an accountant, not a love expert. Do you feel tingly when you see her? Does your heart rate speed up? Do you think about her all the time you're away from her? That's the best I can do."

"Based on that, I'm in love. I want to marry her."

"I hope you are not talking about my sister," said Glenn, to Peter's surprise.

"Why do you say that?"

"Because I like you and I don't want you to get hurt. My sister's a terrible flirt. You're by no means the first boy she's slept with and you certainly won't be the last. When you're in Jackson, she's with some of the local boys. She changes boyfriends as frequently as most people take showers. My parents are perhaps the only people in the neighborhood who don't know that she's sleeping around and I'm not sure they don't at least suspect it."

Peter was surprised that Glenn knew of his sister's sexual escapades, even though he and Laura had not gone to great extremes to hide what they were doing. "I really like your sister. She is terrific. I'm very fond of her, but it's not her."

"I didn't know you were seeing any other girl. What's her name?"

"Christine. Christine Broward"

Glenn smiled "Nice name. Where did you meet her?"

"In Jackson. She's the granddaughter of a chap I met traveling from New York."

"Where does she live in Jackson?"

"On Randolph Road."

Glenn looked sharply at Peter and the smile left his face. "You've got that wrong. She doesn't live there. You've got the wrong street name. Randolph Road is in Niggertown."

Peter suddenly realized that, thoughtlessly, he had been about to confide something to Glenn which would be abhorrent to him.

"No not Randolph Road, it's a similar name."

"Do you mean Rangell Avenue?"

"No that's not it, but close." Peter concluded it would perhaps arouse suspicion if he jumped at the first suggestion.

"How about Randal Way?"

"That's it, Randal Way, that's where she lives."

"That's a nice area. What does she do?"

"She's still in school. I don't know which one."

"I hate to say it, but she's probably a better choice for you than my sister. One day Laura will settle down and stop playing the field, at least I hope so. She's a great kid, but not someone to fall in love with, at least not until she gets a few years on her and a lot more maturity."

That was the end of that conversation. They drove the rest of the way talking of various other things. Glenn did not seem to have been suspicious about the inadvertent mention of Randolph Road, at least Peter hoped not.

That night, in bed, Peter felt ashamed that he had lied to Glenn. While Glenn was a Southerner and had said things that demonstrated some prejudice, it also seemed to Peter that Glenn was not a hard-line bigot. Sure, he had called the maid at Mrs. Grant's a Nigra, but that word was used by many people including some of the Negro employees at work. He had said "Niggertown," but that area of town was widely referred to by that name as a means of identifying the location. Peter also remembered that Glenn had gently reproved Alice Renfrew for her racial comments about Dr. James and the people at Froman. Glenn was his friend and perhaps he should have leveled with him about Christine. He might have been able to offer some helpful advice. Peter decided to think about it for a while.

THE MARRIAGE PROPOSAL

THEY DID WHAT they had done a number of times before. They had dinner with Christine's parents. They ate the rice pudding that Peter had brought for dessert. They walked to the little park down the street. They sat on the same bench they always sat on. They talked. They hugged and they kissed. But this time it was different.

He had rehearsed what he was going to say to Christine for days. He thought about it when he was walking to and from work and sometimes while he was at work. He even became so distracted that Dave had to remind him that he hadn't checked off a couple of loads being wheeled off a freight car. He fell asleep and woke up thinking about her and even rehearsed in front of the mirror in the bathroom when he was sure that Glenn was away. He had considered saying that he thought of her all the time, that he couldn't live without her and that they could overcome any problems. Everything he thought of sounded mushy and reminded him of some of the movies his mother took him to when he was small.

After they had talked for several minutes, Peter suddenly blurted out, "I love you and I want to marry you." Immediately, he could have kicked himself. It came out too suddenly, too loudly and too awkwardly. Christine looked startled and didn't say anything for what seemed like an hour, but was less than a minute. "I knew you were going to say that sooner or later and I've been dreading it."

Now it was his turn to look startled. "Why would you dread me saying I love you and I want to marry you?"

"I love you too, Peter, but it won't work. Not now, not in a thousand years; well maybe in a thousand years. But not now, not in 1951, not in the Deep South and not in Mississippi. To begin with, we're too young. That will change, but you're white and I'm Negro and that won't change."

"We don't have to stay in Mississippi. We can go anywhere—New York, California, even England. You'd love England. It wouldn't be easy even in those places. People might stare. Maybe some people wouldn't rent us an apartment. But other Negroes and Whites have married each other and they're happy. Things will change. We won't be happy if we're not together, so we have no choice."

"Let's give it time. I'll be going to college in Alabama in September," she said trying, unsuccessfully, to fight off tears. "After the first year, or maybe the second, we can see if we still feel the same and, if so, maybe figure out something—I don't know what. Maybe going to England will be the answer, but we have to wait, whatever we do. You can see that, can't you?"

He couldn't, but he said he could. They held each other tightly and the tears, which Christine had held back, flowed.

A few trickled down his face. *Why did I meet her here in Mississippi, why not in London or New York? Why can't she be white or me Negro?* he thought. *It will work out; it has to.*

THE KLAN

THE FOLLOWING Wednesday, Peter and his team had worked very late. Three new freight cars were due in the next day and two cars still on the tracks had to be unloaded before morning to make room. By the time they were finished, it was dark. Dave offered to give Peter a ride home. But first he had to drive ten miles in the opposite direction to pick up his daughter, who was visiting a friend. Peter figured that by the time Dave drove him home, picked up his daughter and then went back the other way to his home, it would be very late. He knew that Dave had to get up early and take his children to two different schools before he came to work, so Peter declined his offer of a ride and started to walk home.

The first mile of his walk took him past commercial and industrial businesses. The workers at those places had long since departed. There were no houses or shops in that area and very few street lights. The road was very dark and very quiet. An occasional car passed in either direction. He had walked about a half mile when he heard a car approaching from behind him and stop. Peter thought nothing about that until he was suddenly grabbed from behind. Someone pulled his arms behind his back and tied his wrists together. Someone else blindfolded him. He was bundled into what he guessed was the back of a car. He was jammed in between two people as the engine started and the car moved forward.

"What are you doing?" he cried out. "Where are you taking me?"

A gruff voice said two words: "Shut up."

Peter estimated that the ride took the better part of an hour and those two words were all that was said by his captors. Peter had no clue which way they were heading. He was not sufficiently familiar with Jackson and the surrounding countryside to have any idea. Even someone intimately familiar with the local geography almost certainly would not have been able to figure it out since the car made a lot of turns, once seemingly going back the way it had just come. Perhaps the driver was going in a number of different directions to confuse him. They needn't have bothered; Peter wouldn't have been able to figure it out even if they had taken a direct route.

Finally the car slowed down, drove over some very rough, bumpy terrain and then stopped. The door opened and he was roughly yanked out of the car. Someone untied the blindfold and the twine binding his hands. As scared as he was before, he was now terrified. He was standing on the edge of a very large field and about 100 yards away was a huge burning cross. It must have been ten feet tall. Around the cross stood twenty or thirty men, he guessed they were men, wearing white sheets and hoods that completely obscured them. Behind them were a number of cars parked in a sort of arc with their headlights illuminating the scene. There were four men in the car in which he had been transported. He saw that all of them wore the same white sheets and hoods. The only parts visible were their eyes and, sometimes as they walked, portions of their shoes.

He was half dragged, half pushed toward the circle of men. As they approached the circle, one of them walked toward him. That man had some kind of emblem on his sheet, on the left side of his chest. None of the others he had seen had such an emblem.

"Peter Mason, you are here to be punished for your serious and ongoing crimes against the white race," the man said in a somber monotone.

Peter started to protest. "You are to say nothing unless I ask you a question," the man interrupted.

"We forgave you going to the nigger hospital. We accept that you were unconscious and could not have known you were being taken there. We even forgave the nigger doctor who kept you overnight since, with his inadequate abilities, he thought you might die if you were moved. We didn't forgive, but we overlooked, you going to a nigger theater. You're English and you might not have known the significance of what you were doing. But we do not forgive, and we are going to punish you and the Browards for, you seeing that nigger bitch. We are going to be lenient this time, but we are going to show you what will happen to you if you do anything like this again. Take your shirt off."

Peter fumbled with the buttons, but his trembling fingers wouldn't allow him to undo them. The speaker ordered the man next to him to take off Peter's shirt, which he did. They propped him against a nearby tree, his face pressed against the trunk, placed his arms around it and tied his wrists. Someone picked up a whip and struck him repeatedly. Soon he lost track of the number of lashes. The pain was the most intense he had ever felt and he passed out. When he awoke, he was lying face down and was soaking wet. At first he thought it was blood, but then he realized that someone had thrown water on him presumably to bring him to.

"Help him up," the man with the emblem said. Two of the sheeted and hooded figures pulled him to his feet. "Now I want you to watch what is going to happen next and always remember that the same thing will happen to you if you see that nigger bitch again. We are going to hang Joshua Broward."

For the first time Peter saw a man not wearing a sheet or a hood. He was a good ways off and Peter could not see his face clearly. But he could see that he was a Negro. He was standing next to a tree with a rope hanging from a branch with a noose on the end. Two men were holding the Negro who appeared to have his hands tied behind his back.

"No, please, please, you can't do that. It wasn't his

fault. It was all my fault. They told me not to come visit, but I barged in. He said he'd call the police if I tried to see her again. The girl didn't want me around. She told me that. I forced myself on her. Oh God, please don't hurt him. I promise I'll never see her again. Not ever." Peter's voice trembled. He could barely get the words out. His knees started to buckle. He thought he was going to pass out again, this time from the combination of the pain, the terror and the impending lynching.

"It doesn't matter whose fault it is. This is not just to punish him, but to serve as a warning to others."

With that, the leader gave a signal and the two men who had been holding the Negro lifted him, whimpering and crying, onto the stool. One held him while the other put the noose around his neck. The man with the emblem gave another silent signal. One of the men pushed the Negro off the stool and the other kicked the stool away. The Negro's body jerked. It swung back and forth and then was still. The only sounds heard at that moment were the rustling of leaves in nearby magnolia trees and Peter's muted sobs.

"Take him over there and let him look," said the man with the emblem, breaking the brief silence.

Two men half pushed and half carried Peter. His legs had practically stopped working. As he stood in front of the hanging body, the man who had pushed the Negro off the stool reached up and turned the body so that Peter could see the dead man's face. Peter bent his head to avoid looking.

"Look at him," ordered one of the men. While the events of the night would never fade from Peter's memory and while there would not be a day in his life that he would not think about them, two other unbelievable things occurred at that moment. He recognized two people present at that cross-burning and murder. Somehow the Klan had made an unbelievable mistake. The dead man was not Joshua Broward. He was Jerome Washington. Peter was in too much pain and too horrified to appreciate the grotesque irony. The dead man hanging from the tree was the same man who was saved from execution by Peter's testimony. He had now been killed as a direct result of Peter's conduct in dating a Negro girl.

Peter's recognition of the second man was, if anything, more horrifying. The feet of the man who pushed Washington off the stool were uncovered as he stretched up to turn the body. As Peter looked down to avert his eyes from the awful sight, he saw on the right foot, below the sheet, a cast and on it was written the word "Limey."

THE QUANDARY

IN A TOTALLY unexpected act of seeming compassion, one of the Klansmen treated the bleeding wounds on Peter's back with a damp cloth and then applied some kind of balm or ointment. Finally he wrapped his torso in what seemed to be a bandage. Throughout his medical ministrations, the Klansman uttered not a word. This surprising show of humanity was dwarfed by the unspeakable terror that Peter had experienced and the brutal, cold-blooded murder he had witnessed.

Four hooded men placed him back in the car. For the first time, he noticed that the license plate was covered by a piece of cloth. They again blindfolded him, but they didn't tie his hands. As the car made its way out of the field and onto the road, the bumping caused him to wince in pain and cry out. The return journey was conducted without a word, not even a "shut up." They helped Peter out of the car at Mrs. Grant's and he watched as they drove away, still with the license plate covered. Slowly and painfully he made his way to the private entrance to his room. It was a few minutes after midnight. He had no thought of getting any sleep or even getting into bed. He had some potentially life-altering decisions to make that could affect not only him but also a number of other people: Glenn Landers, his parents and sister Laura; and Joshua Broward and his wife and children, particularly Christine.

He could forget everything; go on as though nothing had happened. His back would heal by itself. He was young and strong and didn't need medical attention. He could continue with his job at the Mitchell Company; continue with his friendship with Glenn and continue to spend weekends at the Landers. He could cut off his relationship with the Browards and particularly with Christine and conduct himself like a proper Southern white boy.

He quickly determined that was not an option. It might be that no one would ever find Jerome Washington's body, or if they did, they might not be able to identify it. That way the Klan would always think they had killed Joshua Broward and would have no need to look for him. But that was a very unlikely scenario. Even if the Klan believed they had killed Broward, they might find out later, perhaps by accident, that Broward was still alive. Unless Broward spent the rest of his life closeted in his house and never came out, he would be seen around town and word would probably get back to the Klan. If the body was discovered and if the Klan learned they had killed the wrong man, they still might not go after Broward. They had taught the lesson they wanted to teach and maybe they would leave Broward alone. That was a slightly more realistic scenario, but was he willing to leave the Browards unwarned, out there exposed without calling in the police? The answer came easily. It was "no" and he would have to come up with a different plan.

He could go to the police, show them his back, say he was kidnapped and beaten by hooded men who also hung a Negro, get them to warn and protect the Browards, and not implicate Glenn. He might continue his friendly relations with Glenn and his family and continue to spend weekends at their estate. It was tempting, but too distasteful.

He would tell the police that he could identify one of the hooded men and that it was Glenn Landers. Should he tell Glenn, in advance of telling the police, what he was going to do? Should he tell the police it was Jerome Washington and not Joshua Broward who was killed? He would tell Glenn in advance, but should he tell the police about the mistake made by the Klan in the killing? Of course, there was no guarantee that the police would do anything about it, even if they were convinced that Peter was telling the truth. Maybe, rather than going to the police, he would tell Assistant District Attorney Broderick. Possibly he would be more likely to take some action. It was starting to get light and his back was still hurting, but now so was his head.

THE CONFRONTATION

THERE WAS A RAP on the bathroom door. It had to be Glenn and it was a moment Peter had been dreading since he had decided to identify Glenn as one of the murderers. Another rap and Peter still did not answer. Glenn opened the door and looked in.

"Do you want to drive me to my—" Glenn stopped mid-sentence and stared at the bed which had not been slept in and at a pale and shaken Peter Mason. "What's the matter? What's happened?" Glenn's concern was so clearly etched on his face that, for a moment, Peter doubted what he had seen the previous night. But that quickly passed as he looked at Glenn's cast.

Peter related the whole story of his night with the Klan; how he had been seized by four men in white sheets and hoods while walking home; how he was blindfolded with his hands tied behind his back; how he was told he was being punished for seeing a Negro girl; how he was beaten and how he watched while a Negro man was hanged. The two critical omissions were his identification of the hanged man and of the Klansman with the cast on his foot. He held both back for different reasons; the first to protect Joshua Broward and the second to watch Glenn's reactions. *He would make a great actor*, Peter thought.

Glenn's repeated expressions of shock and surprise seemed completely genuine even though Peter knew they could not be. "Let me see your back. Take off your shirt." Glenn unwrapped the rather crude bandaging that one of the hooded men had done. "They gave you a pretty good thrashing, but it will heal. I'll run down to the drug store and get some ointment and bandages and I'll fix you up as good as new."

"No. I think I'll go to the hospital or a doctor. It could get infected or something."

"I don't think there's any need for that. It's not all that bad."

"Well maybe you're right, but one place I am going is to the police."

Glenn's expression changed very slightly. "I wouldn't recommend that. It could be very dangerous for you. The Klan, as you've already found out, is capable of anything including murder. If you do nothing, don't seek medical help, don't go to the police, stop seeing that little Negro girl and just fit in, you won't have any more trouble. But if you stir this thing up, and particularly if you continue to see that girl, the Klan may not be satisfied with just giving you another beating."

"I can't do that. Apart from anything else, a man's

been murdered. I can't just forget about that even if I could forget about what they did to me."

Glenn became more insistent, bordering on becoming frantic. "Peter, the man is dead. Nothing you do or say can change that. Remember this is the Deep South. This is what happens down here, fortunately not often, but it happens and nothing you can do or say can change that either. You've got a good life here, a nice job, friends and my sister likes you. Let it go. Take my advice."

Peter paused, took a deep breath, then stood and stared directly at Glenn.

"I saw you," he said.

Glenn didn't say a word for several seconds, frowned and leaned against the bathroom door.

"You saw me what?"

"I saw you help kill that man. I saw you push him off the stool while another man kicked the stool away."

Glenn's face turned red and he seemed to be having some trouble breathing. "You're insane. They must have beaten you on your head as well as your back. I wasn't there. I'm not a Klansman. The only thing I know about it is what you just told me."

"I saw you."

"You said all the Klansman had sheets covering them completely with hoods on their heads. How could you identify anyone?"

Peter looked down at Glenn's feet and pointed to the cast. "I saw that."

Glenn suddenly sat down on the bed. He said nothing

for a long time. "You're mistaken. The terror, the beating and seeing that man hanged has addled your brain. I wasn't there."

"You were and I'm going to have to tell the police."

"They won't believe you. Nobody will. Who the hell are you? Some foreigner who comes into our country and tries to tell us what to do. Some little nobody who goes to nigger theaters and dates nigger girls. My father is one of the richest and most influential men in the county. If you're lucky they'll run you out of here. More likely, you'll end up like that miserable nigger piece of shit."

Peter said nothing.

Sensing that his harsh approach wasn't working, Glenn's tone again softened. "My parents like you. They could do lots of things for you. They could get you a much better job, even make you a rich man. You could marry my sister and become part of one of the wealthiest families in the state. You want to throw all that away? For what? For nothing."

"You helped kill a man."

"It's well known that when the Klan sets out to kill a man, nothing and nobody can stop them. There can be no doubt that they were going to kill him anyway. There was no way I, assuming I was there, or anyone else could stop that. Assume I was involved but that I stopped them killing you. Assume that they wanted to and had already decided to. Assume that I talked them out of it and that it wasn't easy. If all that happened, then I saved your life and now you want to pay me back by trying to ruin my life. You try that and it will be you that's ruined, not me. When it's your word against mine, who do you think they'll believe?"

Glenn walked up and down across the small room and then said in an even softer, almost pleading tone, "Peter just think about it for a few days. There's no need to rush into anything. Remember this: nothing that happens, if you tell the authorities, will change a thing that has already happened. The Negro will still be dead and you will still have had the crap beaten out of you. Nobody will benefit and only you will be hurt. Just hold off and think for a while. Surely you owe me that much." Without waiting for a reply, Glenn smiled at Peter and left the room.

THE DISTRICT ATTORNEY – AGAIN

PETER SAT in his room for a long time after Glenn had left. Before he talked to Glenn that morning, he had made up his mind what he should do: turn Glenn in to the police; warn the Browards of the danger they could be in; and get law enforcement to protect the Browards. Now he was no longer so sure. Some of the things Glenn had said he already knew; some he didn't. He had been prepared to risk continued danger from the Klan, and loss of his friendship with Glenn and the great things that could come to him from his relationship with the Landers and, of course with Laura. He had been prepared for other possible consequences, such as losing his job, being ostracized, having to leave Jackson before he had enough money to go anywhere else, much less back to England. What he hadn't considered was the possibility that Glenn's actions may have saved his life.

There was no way to verify that Glenn had interceded on his behalf and had persuaded the Klan not to kill him, but it was not illogical to believe that he had. But how had the Klan found out about Peter dating Christine? He hadn't exactly told Glenn, but he had initially blurted out that she lived on Randolph Road before Glenn told him that couldn't be right because Randolph was in "Niggertown." Peter had then corrected himself, but somewhat awkwardly so that he was not at all sure that Glenn bought the change. Perhaps Glenn could have found out that there was a Christine Broward who lived on Randolph. It wouldn't have been hard, once he suspected that the girl Peter had mentioned did live there.

The only person he had ever told about her was Glenn. It seemed unlikely that anybody else except the Browards knew, but it was possible. It was hard enough to accept that Glenn was a Klansman. It was even harder to accept that Glenn was the source of the Klan's awareness of the relationship between Peter and Christine, but it seemed most likely.

He remembered his mother's advice not to make a decision until he had weighed all the pro and con factors against each other. Her advice was to line up all the "pro" factors on one side and all the "con" factors on the other and see which side predominates. But she said that you couldn't simply add up the factors to decide which side had the most. Some were entitled to more weight than others. He mentally lined up the pros and the cons and he decided, on balance, to tell, not the police, but Hinds County Assistant District Attorney Roy Broderick. The deciding factors were first that the Browards needed ongoing protection from the Klan and there was no way that could be achieved without assistance from law enforcement. It might not even be achievable then, but without it, the Browards would be defenseless. Second, Glenn Landers had played a lead role in the murder of Jerome Washington and clearly knew in advance that the murder of a Negro was to take place. He could have and should have informed law enforcement immediately.

It was close to noon when Peter got to the office of the district attorney. He walked around the block several times thinking over exactly what he would say, before he walked in.

"Well if it isn't young Mr. Mason," said Roy Broderick with a broad smile, as his secretary ushered Peter into his office. "Have you been up to more detective work seeking to undermine the strengths of another of my cases?"

Peter also smiled, but a little more weakly, and sat down where Broderick had indicated. For a minute Peter said nothing until Broderick asked "What's it all about Peter? I don't mean to rush you, but I told my wife I'd take her to lunch and she's waiting downstairs."

Peter quickly related the whole story starting with his friendship with Glenn Landers, his relationship with Christine Broward, his abduction by the Klan and ending with his conversation that morning with Glenn Landers.

"Let me get a look at your back, Peter." The smile had long since left Broderick's face. Peter took off his shirt. Broderick had seen many serious injuries, but nonetheless, upon seeing the lash marks on Peter's back, he drew a deep breath. He then called his secretary and told her to go tell his wife that something had come up and he couldn't go to lunch with her. "Do you mind if I get a picture of this?" Without waiting for an answer, Broderick called to his secretary to tell Len to come in with his camera.

After the picture-taking, Broderick tried, through Peter, to determine the site of the Klan beating and murder. Peter was not of any help, but Broderick explained that there were a number of remote areas which were known by law enforcement to be favorite meeting and cross-burning sites of the Klan. Wherever it was, Washington's body was almost certainly still hanging from the tree. It was customary for the Klan to leave such evidence as both an advertisement of the Klan's power and as a warning. Broderick detailed two investigators to explore those sites to see if they could find Washington's body.

Broderick then called in a stenographer to take down Peter's statement. "You know the drill, Peter. I'm going to ask you a lot of very detailed questions, not only about the events of the night, but also about your relationship with the girl and your relationship with Landers. You give me full and complete answers. Betty will take it all down, type it, then you'll review it, correct any mistakes and sign. Then I will have a nice long chat with Mr. Landers." The question and answer session lasted over an hour.

Broderick got up from his chair and stared out of the window before turning and saying, "Peter, this isn't going to be easy for you. The Landers family is very prominent and old man Landers carries a lot of weight in this county.

They're rich. They're powerful and, though they're not universally loved, they're respected, if not feared. The fact that you were seeing a Negro girl will not play well and the fact that Glenn Landers befriended you when you knew nobody, got you two separate jobs and took you to the family estate on weekends, is all going to make you look like an ungrateful jerk. You're a smart kid and I feel that you must have thought through all of this before you came to me. If it makes you feel any better, I think you did the right thing, although I'm not sure I would have had the guts."

While Peter was grateful for Broderick's words of support, they didn't make him feel any better about what was sure to come.

Peter begged Broderick to ensure the Browards' safety by all possible means. "If I hadn't called on the Browards and particularly on Christine, none of this would have happened. It's all my fault. Please help them. Please, don't let anything happen to them. I'll do anything you say but help them, please."

"We'll do what we can, but there's no assurance we can prevent further violence. We'll post an officer round the clock for a while, but we can't do that forever. You can help," said Broderick.

"I'll do anything you say, anything," said Peter

"Then break it off with Christine; never see her again."

"But I love her."

Broderick threw his arms in the air in exasperation. "If you love her, you'll stay the hell away from her. Goddam it Peter, if you keep it up she could get hurt, maybe killed and it will be your damn fault."

"I want to talk to my sister. After our mother died, she always knew what to do; always had good ideas. I need to talk this over with her."

"Sure, give her a call and tell me what she says."

"She doesn't have a phone, nor do I. I'll have to call her at work. Can I call from here early tomorrow? There's a six-hour time difference."

"I guess the coffers of Hinds County can stretch to a transatlantic call. Arguably it relates a little to the Landers matter. Be here at 7:30 tomorrow morning and you can make the call."

THE SISTER'S ADVICE

PETER ARRIVED on the stroke of 7:30. Broderick offered to sit in on the call if Peter wanted him to, but Peter declined, explaining that his sister would be more candid if only he was on the line.

"Beth, you're wanted on the phone. It's your brother calling from America."

Beth was more than a little surprised and she knew immediately that there had to be something seriously wrong. Peter never called her at work, even when he lived in London. He knew that her boss didn't like the employees getting personal calls. At first Peter had considered omitting any reference to the hanging or the beating and merely saying that he was warned by Klansmen that he would be punished if he continued to see the Negro girl. He decided against that approach. Beth's advice would only be meaningful if she had all the facts, particularly the hanging and beating.

Peter laid out the whole story starting with meeting Solomon Broward and ending with the Klan dropping him at the boarding house. He skipped nothing. Although Beth was a worrier, characteristically she spent little time in expressing horror or decrying that such could happen in a supposedly civilized society. She was always pragmatic and she knew that she had to think through the situation with Peter and try to come up with some logical solution. Peter assured her that he and Christine were truly in love and it was not just an infatuation that would fade. Beth noted the obvious; that the possible consequences of continuing the relationship were dire and perhaps even fatal and that the easiest and safest course for both of them and for Christine's family was to break it off fully and finally and to let it be known that such had happened.

It was precisely the same advice given to him by Broderick, absent Broderick's swear words. Peter told her that he just couldn't do that.

"I know how you feel about the girl, but you must realize that you are being very selfish. If it was only your life at stake, that would be one thing, but you may be putting a whole family at serious risk. However, if you are not going to break it off, you should at least stay away from each other for a good long time. If you feel the same about each other then, you'll need to get together somewhere else other than the southern states of America. Even that might not be safe and, if you marry, there's going to be unimaginable difficulties no matter where you live. I've read a lot about the South and I see no way that you could both live there as a mixed race, married couple. I have the feeling that you already knew all this without me telling you."

Although her advice was painful to Peter, he knew he had to do what he could to protect the Browards. He thanked Beth, told her he loved her very much, assured her that his back was much improved, and said how glad he was that she had a roommate. Peter then went into Broderick's office and told him of Beth's advice.

"Smart girl, but I wish she hadn't suggested continuing the relationship even with those conditions. It's still damn dangerous. But if you won't walk away from Christine, we can do something. The DA's office has contacts with snitches, informers and the like, and we can probably get the word out that the romance is over, information that the Klan will pick up. Whether they believe it is another question. Perhaps, if the opportunity presents itself, you can tell that to Landers, but be careful. He's nobody's fool and it is clear he was onto you about the Randolph slip."

BETH'S ROOMMATE

"MORE TEA?"

"Yes, please."

Beth and her new roommate Janet were sitting at the kitchen table in Beth's tiny flat. A good-sized man could almost touch all four walls when standing in the middle of the kitchen and stretching his arms.

"How's Peter doing in America?" asked Janet.

Beth related the phone call she had with Peter and the terrible trouble he was in because of his relationship with Christine. "Maybe I should go to America and help him. What do you think?" she asked.

"Not a good idea. He's old enough to take care of himself, and besides, it'll be too expensive for you and you might lose your job if you're gone too long. You've already told him what he should do. Either he does it or he doesn't. Either way, if you go over there, all you'll be doing is telling him the same thing again."

Beth thought for a moment. "Maybe I wasn't forceful enough. Maybe I should've pushed him harder to give up this girl no matter how deeply he feels about her. He'll ruin his life and hers."

"Well Beth, I hate to say this, but it's his own fault. He should've stuck to his own kind. He shouldn't run around with one of them."

Beth bristled. *Why is it,* she thought, *that people always preface things they are dying to say with 'I hate to say this?'*

Janet went on, "They say that Negroes can't be trusted; they lie and steal. I'm not saying that I necessarily agree with that, but they do say it. With all the white girls around and Peter being a good-looking chap, why would he do such a stupid thing?"

Beth was stunned. She had known Janet for a long time and had never heard her say anything so cruel, bigoted and ignorant before. "Who are the 'they' who told you this bloody rubbish about Negroes?"

"Well, it's a known fact, and I cannot believe that you would like to have this girl as a sister-in-law. I know if it was me and my brother married one of them, I'd have nothing more to do with him—ever," retorted Janet. "Anyway, I have to go. I'm meeting Joe. We're going to the pictures."

Beth sat for a while, finished her tea, and concluded that sharing the flat with Janet might not be lasting much longer.

It had been a tough trip getting home from work that day. The tube from Regent Street to Bethnal Green Station was packed and neither one of them got a seat. The bus from the station to their street was also packed with no available seats. They were both tired. Maybe what she said was because of fatigue. Of course, the fact that she was tired does not excuse what she said. It may have even made what she said more likely to reflect what she truly believes. Whatever the reason, maybe she should give Janet a little more time. The problem with Peter, however, was not as easily resolved and a little more time was not likely to help.

THE LULL

TWO THINGS happened that surprised Peter. The first surprise was that nothing happened. It had been over a week and he had not heard from Broderick. He had not been contacted by any reporters and there was nothing in the papers. He had not seen Glenn, although he had heard him in the bathroom, so he figured that there had been no arrest. The second surprise came as he and his team were unloading a freight car of canned goods. Ben Driscoll, one of the supervisors responsible for the loading of grocery products onto trucks for delivery to a variety of retailers, came to the platform and told him he was wanted in Mr. Mitchell's office.

Mr. Mitchell was the grandson of the founder of the Mitchell Company and had been its president for twenty years. He was born and raised in Mississippi and had lived there all of his life except for his college years. He had an undergraduate degree in economics from Georgetown University in Washington, DC and a master's degree in International Trade from

Harvard. Peter had never seen him, much less spoken to him.

This is it, thought Peter. *They've now heard about the whole thing and they're going to fire me.* He was only surprised that it had taken so long. He waited in Mr. Mitchell's outer office for about five minutes before the secretary told him he could go in. Mr. Mitchell's office was very different from all the other parts of the company that Peter had seen. It was large. The walls were paneled with dark wood and there were built-in bookshelves along two of the walls. The desk was old and ornate, holding more books and a glass decanter of dark liquid alongside several expensive-looking glasses. Mr. Mitchell was a man in his late fifties or perhaps early sixties. He was thin, elegantly dressed in a dark-blue suit, white shirt, and what looked like a university tie. He wore gold-rimmed glasses and sported a thin, well-groomed mustache. He was on the phone and he motioned Peter to sit down.

Peter looked idly at the bookcases. Mr. Mitchell obviously had eclectic tastes. There were books on American history; books of a trade and business nature; a large matched set of the works of William Shakespeare and several volumes of Charles Dickens and the Bronte sisters. His review of the literary tastes of Mr. Mitchell was interrupted as Mr. Mitchell hung up the phone.

"Hello Mason, how are you?" Mr. Mitchell said. Apparently not expecting or wanting an answer to his inquiry, he went on. "I've been hearing a lot about you lately. I was very sorry to hear of your run-in with the

Klan. I understand they beat you up pretty good. Looks like you're recovering. If you need a reference to a good doctor, let me know. I'll put you in touch with my guy. Fortunately, we have not heard of much Klan activity in these parts for some time."

Mitchell got up, walked around his desk and sat down in the chair next to Peter. He cleared his throat and said, "I got a call from my old friend Warren Landers and he was telling me all about your trouble with the Klan. He says you may have got his son in a bit of trouble." He picked up a yellow folder and opened it.

Here it comes, thought Peter, *the next words out of his mouth are going to be a gracious or not so gracious dismissal.*

"Well, I'm sorry about the mess that Glenn may have got himself into. I've known the boy since he was a baby and he's always been a decent kid."

At first Peter thought that Mitchell was making involvement in a murder sound like a high school prank, but then Mitchell went on to say, "It all looks very serious, but we'll leave it up to the courts to determine what happened. In this folder is a report from your supervisor, Mr. Foster. He says your performance on the platform has been first-rate. The efficiency in the unloading of the freight cars has improved dramatically since you took over out there, and the men on your team seem to react very well to you. When men react well to their bosses, we always see improvement in service. I called you up here to congratulate you and to tell you to keep up the good work and, most importantly, to tell you that, as of the first of next month, your wages will be increased from $32 a week to $40 a week. We're expecting big things from you, Peter."

They both stood up. Peter stammered out a surprised thank you and floated on air back to the platform.

Three days later, Mrs. Grant left him a telephone message from Mr. Broderick asking him to stop by the office at his first opportunity. When he did, Broderick told him that they had located the scene of his beating and found the body of a Negro hanging from a tree, later identified as Jerome Washington. Finally, he assured Peter that police presence in the area where the Browards lived had been stepped up. He said nothing about what, if anything, was being done regarding Glenn Landers.

THE VISIT OF THE LANDERS FAMILY

IT WAS THE following Saturday and Peter was lying on his bed reading the newspaper and trying to think of what he should do for the rest of the day. There was a small back-page article about a Negro named Jerome Washington having been found hanged. There was no mention of Peter or the beating he got. There wasn't even any mention of the Klan involvement or of the alleged presence of Glenn Landers. The front page had stories about the opening of a new restaurant and the wedding of a local socialite among other "important" items. The murder of a Negro apparently didn't warrant much notice.

He answered a knock on the door and Mrs. Grant told him that Mr. and Mrs. Landers and their daughter were in the sitting room and wanted to talk to him. This was not a conversation he had anticipated and not one he looked forward to. Momentarily he thought to ask Mrs. Grant to tell the Landerses he was out. Even if she said she would do that, he knew she wouldn't. This was just too juicy and she was looking forward to eavesdropping, or, as she would say, "innocently overhearing" as she was just passing by. Peter walked slowly toward the sitting room and walked in. Mr. Landers got up and shook hands with Peter.

"Hello, Peter, how are you? I hear you got badly beaten. I'm so very sorry. What a dreadful thing to have happened. I hope your injuries are getting better," said Mr. Landers with what appeared to be sincere concern.

"Thanks for asking sir. Yes it's getting much better."

"Well, that's wonderful. I wanted to talk to you about what you have told the authorities about thinking that Glenn had some involvement in what happened. I can't imagine the horror of that night and how terrified you must have been. I know I would have been scared out of my wits. We all know when anyone is in a situation like that, it would be the easiest thing in the world to think that something was happening or that someone was there or doing things when, in fact, no such thing was occurring. Nobody could blame you for a mistaken identification. I probably would have fainted clean away." Landers said all of this with an understanding smile and a little laugh at the remark about his fainting.

He's good, thought Peter. *He's making excuses for my being the one who made the mistake and he's actually forgiving me for it.*

Without waiting for any response to his opening salvo, Landers continued, "We like you, Peter. Don't you agree dear?" He said to his wife.

"Oh, yes, we do. You are such a nice boy, with such

good manners. I'm sure it's your English upbringing. We love it when you come to our house, don't we, Laura, dear?"

Laura just nodded, but decidedly without conviction.

"I was talking to George Mitchell, you know he's a very good friend of mine, and he tells me you're doing fine over there. I know Glenn got you that job and the one at the hotel earlier. He's been a good friend to you. I'm sure you agree. But it's quite possible that we could do more for you. Maybe get you in a position that one day you could be a rich man. Maybe fairly soon. I know it sounds immodest, but I think you know I am one of the leading citizens around here and have a lot of powerful connections."

Peter made no response. Landers shifted around in his chair as though he was sitting on something sticking him in his butt. He was used to telling people what to do and having them do so immediately and without questioning. He was not used to begging people to do things, much less trying to bribe them, and that was what he was doing and doing it awkwardly and uncomfortably.

"Let's say hypothetically, just for the sake of argument, that Glenn was present at the Klan meeting. It didn't happen, but let's just say so for the moment, and that he stopped the Klan from killing you. You would have to be eternally grateful for that, wouldn't you?" Without waiting for an answer he went on. "Again, still hypothetically, let's say that the Klan was intent on killing a particular Negro and couldn't be talked out of it and Glenn happened to be there, that wouldn't be his fault would it? They were going to kill him anyway, right?" Landers looked almost pleadingly at Peter.

"Could I ask you a hypothetical?" said Peter.

"Of course Peter," said Landers, still smiling.

"First of all you have gotta tell me what 'hypothetical' means. I never heard of that before you said it. It sounds like a hypothetical is a bunch of made up stuff that you don't know really happened that you tell someone and then ask a question based on that made up stuff."

Landers smiled even more broadly. "Well I might not have phrased it quite like that, but basically that's it."

"Well here's my hypothetical: Suppose you and a bunch of your friends were sitting around and you were all very angry with Mr. Mitchell about something—anything. I mean really angry. Your friends decided they were going to take Mr. Mitchell out to a lonely field, tie a rope around a branch of a tree, put Mr. Mitchell up on a stool and put a noose around his neck. Let's assume you are sure that they can't be talked out of it. Finally, let's assume that instead of immediately getting a hold of the police and telling them about this planned murder, you decide to join the murderers and even get into it by pushing poor old Mitchell off of the stool. Do you think that you would not be to blame since your friends were going to do it anyway? This is, of course, hypothetical."

The smile left Mr. Landers's face. "You're worse than a fool, Mason. You're the one who is going to be hurt by all this. You have no idea who you are messing with. You're trying to take down a fine boy with a great future; a boy who, if he was there, and I'm not saying he was, saved your life and befriended you and for what? Because some worthless no-count nigger got what he deserved."

"I'm sorry you feel that way, Mr. Landers. Mr. Washington didn't do anything to be hanged for, but it will be up to others, not you or me, to say what is or what isn't right. All I did was tell what I saw. I told the truth and, since it was Glenn I saw, I didn't want to say anything, but I believe I didn't have any choice."

Without another word, the Landerses got up and left, almost knocking over Mrs. Grant, who had her ear pressed against the sitting room door. As they left, Laura dropped one of her gloves. Peter picked it up and handed it to her. She snatched it away and walked out the front door. She had not said a word from the time Peter arrived in the sitting room until the time she left.

Mr. Landers had virtually promised that he would make Peter a rich man if only he would tell the authorities that he was wrong about having involved Glenn in the slaying of Jerome Washington. Now he wasn't going to be a rich man, at least not with Mr. Landers's help. Visions of a big house, an expensive car, a plush office and a huge bank account flashed through his mind and were instantly wiped out. Oddly, he was more confident that he had made the right decision after his conversation with Mr. Landers than he had been before.

THE AMNESTY OFFER

HE THOUGHT of Christine constantly, and the pain of not seeing her seemed almost as severe as the pain in his back. He had written a short letter telling her that the DA, through contacts, was letting it be known that the two of them had broken up. He told her that, while untrue, it was hoped that the Klan would hear of the planted story, believe it, and leave the Browards and him alone. He told her that he loved her and that he could not break off their relationship, but they had to be very cautious.

Except for the small buried article about the death of Jerome Washington, there was complete silence about the hanging and beating. Peter began to fantasize that the whole thing was a bad dream. The pain in his back was a frequent reminder. He went to work, but didn't concentrate as much as he should. He ate, but not nearly as much as he should and he slept, but not as much as he should. He heard Glenn Landers in the bathroom, but never spoke to him. Life went on as though nothing had happened; then the first major story broke. Soon the newspapers were full of it. LAW ENFORCEMENT INVESTIGATES BELIEVED KLAN MURDER

There was still nothing about the more or less contemporaneous beating of Peter Mason. The day the first newspaper story appeared, he got a message when he arrived home from work,. that Mr. Broderick would like to see him. He would be in his office until eight. When Peter got to the office of the district attorney at 7:30, it seemed as though nobody had gone home. Secretaries were typing away; deputy district attorneys were on the phones and investigators were thumbing through files or dictating reports into little machines. Broderick was in his office, feet on the desk and smoking a particularly foul-smelling cigar.

"Peter, you earlier told us that you couldn't identify any of the other Klansmen; that the one you did identify you did solely from the writing on his cast; that he was tall; and that you didn't see any license plates on any of the cars. Since then, have you thought of anything else?"

Peter had to admit that he could not think of anything else.

Broderick then said, "Two things you might like to know. They'll be in the paper tomorrow anyway. First we believe we know how it is that Jerome Washington was hung by the Klan. They made a mistake. They must have thought Washington was Joshua Broward. How did they make that mistake? Other than that they were both Negro, they didn't look alike. Broward was taller and lighter skinned than Washington. They lived quite a distance from each other and they had never met. At first we were mystified; then we found a bracelet in Washington's pocket. It had an inscription on the inside, 'From JB to HB with love.' We determined that 'JB' is Joshua Broward and 'HB' is his wife, Harriet. How did Washington end up with Harriet Broward's bracelet?"

Broderick leaned forward and looked intently at Peter. "Well the night Washington was hanged, Mr. and Mrs. Broward had gone to the movies with their children. When they came home, they discovered that their house had been broken into and the only things they could find missing were the bracelet and a relatively small amount of money that was on a nightstand next to their bed. So what probably happened is that the Klan arrived at the Broward house, saw Washington coming out and made the incorrect, but understandable, assumption that he was Broward. Undoubtedly Washington protested that he wasn't Broward and that he was a thief robbing the Browards, but he had no identification and they obviously didn't believe him. Washington may have been the unluckiest man who ever lived and Broward the luckiest."

"That's amazing, but it makes sense to me," said Peter. "I'm so glad for Mr. Broward, but poor old Washington. It's the second time he was in the wrong place at the wrong time. What's the other thing?"

"We offered Glenn Landers amnesty if he would give us the names of all the Klansmen at the hanging and would agree to testify against them. He turned us down. He said that he wasn't a Klansman; that he wasn't there that night and that he had nothing to do with your beating or Washington's hanging."

"That's really bad news. That leaves the Browards at risk. Isn't there some way he can be talked into naming those people? If they were caught and imprisoned for life, the Browards would be safe. If the Browards were to be harmed, that would be because Glenn wouldn't give you the names. Doesn't he realize that I positively identified him from the cast on his right foot—the cast that I signed? He could get the death penalty, couldn't he?"

"Maybe yes, maybe no. An all-white jury will listen to that one piece of identification and they may believe it and they may not. This is the son of a very prominent citizen of this state, widely known, a great philanthropist. His son is an up-and-coming college graduate who has many friends and a very bright future. The victim was a ne'er-do-well Negro thief. You're a nice kid, but the jury will know you are a foreigner and you talk funny, at least from their standpoint. They may think that Landers was very good to you and you paid him back by ratting on him. Not my view, but it could be the jury's. If Landers goes to trial for murder, he could very well be acquitted. If he turns state's evidence and identifies and testifies against the Klan, they will exercise their own form of justice and Glenn Landers will not be acquitted by that 'court.'"

"Well I was a victim, too. Doesn't that count? Even if Glenn was good to me and even if I talk funny, I got beaten and I've the scars to show."

"Yes, we're counting on that. You're a fine upstanding

white boy whose beating, despite your dating a Negro girl, may offset the fact that none of the jurors will have any sympathy for Washington. You're our star victim. You're also our star witness."

THE FUNERAL SERVICE

DAVE HAD TOLD him that there was to be a funeral service for Jerome Washington the next day at the Abyssinian Baptist Church. He had read about it in the Negro newspaper. Peter told Dave that he thought he would go.

"Boss, you got a death wish or something? White folks don't go to Negro funerals, 'cept maybe for maids or field hands who been working for 'em for years."

"I figure I ought to show a little respect."

"You don't owe them people nothing. This ain't England. It ain't even New York. You're in a very different place. You gotta go along with the way things are done here. You can't just be going to Negro movies and such like. You're young, but you gotta learn quick-like. You gotta listen to me. You ain't learned no lesson yet."

Peter realized that Dave's advice came from years of experience and was wise. He decided to go anyway. Whether it was born of a youthful refusal to conform, curiosity or something else, it was certainly imprudent and just downright foolish.

When he arrived at the church he noted that there were three white police officers standing outside and a police car parked at the corner.

"Where are you going, son?" asked one of the officers.

"I'm going to pay my respects," Peter replied.

"Wait a minute. You're that Mason kid who testified for Washington at the murder trial. Well, I guess in the long run you didn't do him much good, did you?"

"I suppose not. May I go in now?"

"Go ahead, if you think you must. You'll stand out like a sore thumb in there, but it's your funeral," said the officer, laughing at his own macabre attempt at humor.

The officer was right, though. Peter did stick out. His was the only white face in a very large congregation of Negro mourners. The church was crowded. Everyone sat on wooden, backless benches. There were no stained-glass windows, just dog-eared books of psalms, a podium next to a plain wooden cross and a small organ. He found a seat in the last row and tried to be inconspicuous, but the heads of most of the congregation turned toward him as though he were an alien presence in their midst. The service had already started when he arrived and it continued for about another half hour. There was a lot of singing and wailing. The reverend was very animated and emotional and interspersed his sermon with much raising of arms and entreaties to God.

Peter was not a regular churchgoer and he had never seen a service quite like this one. When it was over, he tried to sneak away, but he ran into Luther Adams, the lawyer who had defended Washington at his murder trial. Adams was with Jerome Washington's mother and he stopped Peter to introduce him to her.

"Mrs. Washington, this young man was mainly responsible for your son being acquitted of the murder charge."

She looked at Peter angrily and spat at him. "You mean he's the one responsible for my Jerome being dead, don't you?"

Adams grabbed her arm and said, "What on earth do you mean? He saved your son and didn't have anything to do with Jerome's murder."

"Yes he did," screamed Mrs. Washington, raising her voice so that the police down the street started to come toward her. Adams waved them back. "It's okay officers, no problems here," called out Adams and the officers backed away.

"If he hadn't been going with that nigger girl, this wouldn't have happened. The Klan wouldn't have come after her father and thought my Jerome was him. It's that white boy's fault. He got no business sniffin' around that girl."

Peter was shocked, but he was also angry and he struggled to control himself. He had expected that, despite her grief, she would have recognized that he was the one who had stood up for her son and that she would be heartbroken, but grateful to him. He was also shocked to hear a Negro person use the term "nigger."

"Mrs. Washington, I'm sorry about your son, I really am. I wish it hadn't happened, but it wasn't my fault. I go where I please and see whom I please. Your son wouldn't have been mistaken for Mr. Broward if he hadn't broken into the Broward house to steal their things."

She said something else that Peter did not hear or understand, then she stomped away. "Peter, I am so sorry," said Adams. "She had absolutely no right to say those things to you. She's just distraught and I am sure when she calms down, she'll be sorry. She's under a terrific strain right now and she is just reacting by lashing out at people. She had a few nasty things to say to me this morning, also."

As Peter walked away, the same police officer called after him, "I'll bet you're glad you came, huh?"

Clearly, he wasn't.

THE RE-CREATION — REHEARSAL

BRODERICK HAD ARRANGED for a re-creation at the scene of the hanging. It was late afternoon when Peter, Broderick, two investigators from the DA's office and Police Sergeant Timothy McIntire arrived at the field. It was quiet with nobody seemingly within miles. Peter had not seen the field in the daylight. It was quite beautiful. There were magnolia trees on the perimeter and hundreds of pink and white wildflowers. A gentle breeze rustled through the leaves and the late afternoon sun was low on the horizon and golden. It was inconceivable that acts of unspeakable horror had taken place in this tranquil, pastoral place.

Broderick broke the silence. "Peter," he shouted. "I want you to point out the tree where you were whipped and then point out the tree where Washington was hung."

Peter just stood there staring and not moving.

Broderick spoke more sharply, "Peter we don't have all day. It's going to be dark soon and I want this set up accurately, now."

Peter still didn't move.

Broderick walked over to Peter and saw that tears had run down his face. He spoke more softly, "You okay, kid?"

Peter came out of his trance and said, "I'm fine. Let's get on with it." He walked over and identified the two trees.

Peter had told Broderick that, although he was not absolutely sure, his recollection was that there were eight cars, not including the one that brought him; that they were approximately three yards apart from each other, in an arc shape with their headlights on, pointed toward the tree from which Jerome Washington was hung. Peter had described the approximate height of the burning cross and the width of the crosspiece.

Broderick's investigator had looked in the paper issued the date of the hanging to determine the phase of the moon and learned that it was almost full. On the night of the re-creation, the moon was slightly less full. Leaving nothing to chance, Broderick got a local orthopedic surgeon, who was a friend of his, to put a cast similar to Glenn Landers's on the foot of Police Sergeant Timothy McIntire, a man about the same size and weight as Glenn, with the promise that the doctor would remove it the following morning. McIntire, being a good sport and entering into both the importance and the humor of the situation, asked in mock seriousness whether he would be entitled to disability benefits.

Broderick also had McIntire fitted with a sheet that would ride up when he stretched upwards in the same way as the sheet had done when Landers reached up to turn Washington's face in Peter's direction. Finally, Broderick had Peter write "Limey" on McIntire's cast with the same type and color of marking pen and at the same location and at the same size as he had done with Glenn's cast. At each stage of the preparation, Broderick confirmed with Peter the accuracy of what they were setting up.

Before it got dark, Peter positioned the cars, the cross, the stool on which Washington stood, and the place where Glenn and he stood at the moment Glenn reached up and turned the body. After dark, Broderick had officers turn on the car lights and set fire to the cross. He asked one officer to stand on the stool and had McIntire reach upward. Broderick stood next to Peter, looked down and announced that, while it was not like reading the newspaper in your living room, Peter's writing on the cast was visible enough.

Before leaving, Broderick carried out one more experiment. He had the cars move in eight yards. Everything else remained the same. Peter's writing on the cast became even easier to read.

"I know the cars were not that close," Peter protested.

Broderick looked over at him and said, "I want to tell you a joke. A man claimed he had been hurt in an automobile accident and that as a result he could only lift his right arm to a position level with his shoulder. He was testifying in court and the defendant's lawyer asked him to show the jury how high he could lift his right arm. He lifted it to the shoulder. Counsel then said for him to show the jury how high he could lift it before the accident and, without thinking, the man lifted it straight up in the air. End of case."

"Funny story, but what does it have to do with moving the cars to a position they weren't in?" asked a confused Peter.

"When we put on this demonstration during your testimony, everybody will be out here—the judge, the jury, the lawyers, the court reporter, the court attaches, you and the defendant. I will put the cars where they are now and you where you are now and, most importantly, McIntire where Landers was, and I'll ask the court if he will have the jury step forward and look at the same cast on McIntire's foot. Maybe, just maybe, Landers will blurt out, without thinking, that the cars are too close. It's a long-shot and Landers may be too quick to fall for it, or Sinclair, Glenn's lawyer and nobody's fool, may object and stop Landers from saying anything. It's worth a shot since the only people who know whether the cars are too close are the people who were here when Washington was killed."

Peter smiled. He was beginning to realize that trials were far more complicated than just questions and answers.

"Do you think Glenn will fall for this trick?"

Broderick bristled. "It's not a trick. It's a legitimate attempt to ferret out the truth. I don't know whether he will fall for it. He's a smart fellow, but a lot of smart fellows have been tripped up by similar types of ploys."

THE BROWARDS MOVE

Mrs. Grant was waiting for him when he got home the following day. "A Negro girl dropped this envelope off for you. It's probably from Mr. Broderick about the case."

"Thanks," Peter said as he started to go to his room.

"Aren't you going to open it?" asked Mrs. Grant, whose curiosity about the contents of the envelope had caused her to come close to steaming it open before Peter got there.

"I will in a minute."

He opened it as soon as he had closed his door. The letter was from Christine. It was short and shocking.

"Dear Peter, my uncle got daddy a job in Detroit. He has to start as soon as possible and we are all leaving first thing tomorrow morning. I know this is best for all of us. We'll be safer in Detroit and you'll be safer for the same reason. I'll always love you and this is not the end. We'll be staying for a while with my uncle until we find a place. I'll send you the address. We'll keep in touch with each other and if, in a year or two, we still feel the same, and I know we will, we'll solve this somehow. With all my love, Christine."

He sat for a long time, in a daze. Although the news devastated him, in a curious way there was some feeling of relief. They *would* be safer in Detroit, and, although they would be many miles apart for a long time, he wouldn't let go of his feelings for Christine. He was determined that they would be together again. But he had to see her once more before she left. He felt there would be no danger to them. They had police protection, and the family would be out of harm's way early the next morning.

"Where are you going?" A voice from the shadows shattered the quiet stillness as a uniformed police officer stepped out of the darkness into the roadway and blocked Peter's path. Peter had thought he could call on the Browards without being seen. He had taken every conceivable precaution; taking a devious route, setting out late at night on a workday and covering most of his face with a scarf. He was wrong.

"I'm going to see Mr. Broward."

"MISTER Broward, is it," the officer said sarcastically. "And what business do you have with MISTER Broward?"

"He's a friend of mine." Peter was surprised by the confrontational tone in his own voice.

The officer shone his flashlight in Peter's face. "You're that English kid, Mason, aren't you? You gotta have a death wish or somethin', coming here. What the hell is with you? Haven't you learned your lesson yet? The Klan doesn't believe in the nine-lives theory. They gave you your only chance. The next time you come back from a Klan meeting, they'll have to put you in a wooden box. Go home, kid, and play with your toys."

This was now the second time that Peter's conduct had been referred to as a "death wish." He didn't have a death wish; far from it. He had fought hard, but was unable to resist his longing to see Christine. His intense love for her had overcome the irrationality and selfishness of his actions. He had to see her. "I'm going to see Mr. Broward." Peter stepped around the officer and walked the remaining thirty or forty yards to the Broward home.

Joshua, Harriet and Christine all came to the door.

After Joshua stepped outside and looked up and down the street, he motioned Peter inside. "You shouldn't be here, Peter. We were all lucky last time. We won't be so lucky if there's a next time," Joshua said, with a worried expression on his face.

"That's about what the officer just said, only not quite as nicely. I had to come to see you and tell you about Christine and me."

"We know about you and Christine and you know that it's impossible. Those things just don't happen here."

"Mississippi isn't the only place in the world. Aren't there other places we can go—New York, California, England? I love Christine and I hope . . . I think she loves me. Isn't that the only thing that matters?" Peter almost pleaded, his voice breaking, while he repeatedly twisted his hands in anguish.

"That's not the only thing that matters," Joshua

Broward said, with a sharpness in his voice that Peter had not heard before. "Life matters. Being able to come and go and to live your life without worrying that some racists will kill you matters, and for goodness sake, sit down before you fall over."

The long walk, standing for a long period and the misery he was suffering had aggravated the pain in his back and had made him slightly light-headed and unsteady on his feet. He sat down gingerly, making sure he didn't rub his back against the chair.

"Oh, your poor back," said Harriet. "Take your shirt off; let me see it. I've some very good salve. It'll ease the pain and make it heal quicker."

He protested that it was much better and didn't need any treatment, but she insisted. The salve did, in fact, soothe the area.

"I know Christine told you that we're leaving early tomorrow, probably before sunup. The police protection we have won't last long and I'm not sure they are all that enthusiastic about guarding us anyway," said Joshua. "Christine isn't going to college in Alabama. There's a small interracial college close to my brother's house. She's going there."

Christine looked over at Peter. "We're still very young. You stay here, or go back to England. We'll write to each other and, in a year or two, if we still feel the same way, well then, we can decide what to do," she said.

"Wherever the two of you were to go—Detroit, London, New York or even Africa, you would have trouble, not as much as you would have here, but lots of trouble, nonetheless," Joshua said, his tone softening. He wrote something down. "This is my brother's address in Detroit. You kids stay in touch if you want to. Both of you think long and hard about what you would be getting into, and we'll see what happens with the passage of time."

"All right, we'll do it your way, but I know I'll feel the same way in a year or two," Peter said, barely controlling his emotions.

Peter and Christine embraced. She was in tears and he was close. He embraced both Joshua and Harriet, and then he left. As he walked back toward Mrs. Grant's, the officer called out jeeringly, "Finished your business with MISTER Broward, have you?"

Peter said nothing, but he hoped it wasn't finished.

THE TRIAL OF GLENN LANDERS
— DAY ONE

THERE WERE some astonishing coincidences between
the trial of The State of Mississippi vs. Jerome Washington
and The State of Mississippi vs. Glenn Landers. In the first
case, the defendant was Jerome Washington. In the second
case, the victim was Jerome Washington. In both cases
the star witness was Peter Mason, first for the defense and
now for the prosecution. Both cases were tried in the same
courtroom, before the same judge and prosecuted by the
same assistant district attorney. The dramatic difference
came in the makeup of the defense team. Washington had
been defended solely by Luther Adams, who had no other
lawyers on his side, no assistants, no investigators and no
secretaries. He actually was compelled to type his own
court documents, outlines and subpoenas.

Glenn Landers was defended by an army of lawyers
led by Byron T. Sinclair. Sinclair was generally touted as the
top criminal defense lawyer in Mississippi and one of the
most prestigious in the entire United States. He had tried

a large number of capital cases, not only in Mississippi, but throughout the South. He bragged, justifiably, that he had never lost a client to the executioner. Although he dressed in hand-tailored suits and silk ties with a solid gold chain across his prodigious midsection, he portrayed himself as just a good ole country boy. His speech was peppered with "y'awls" and "how yews." Sinclair's clients invariably came away well satisfied with his services, but considerably lighter in the pocketbook.

At counsel table, he always had two junior lawyers and an investigator. In his office, he had several other lawyers and investigators, all of whom were scurrying around peering in law books, writing motions, seeking out witnesses and performing a myriad of other tasks related to the defense of Glenn Landers.

"Well, I see we have Mr. Mason back with us again. We're going to have to get you an office here if this keeps up. Maybe you should go to law school. You could take after your namesake, Perry Mason." Judge Carson had taken the bench and laughed at his own joke. The lawyers, assistants and court attaches all dutifully joined in. "Call the panel," Carson instructed the bailiff.

Sixty men and women trooped into the court and took seats in the audience section. The men and women were fairly equally divided, but all were white. The day was spent in the selection process and was not concluded by the evening adjournment. Broderick had asked Peter to be present so that he could be introduced to the prospective jurors in case any of them knew him.

None did. Glenn Landers sat at counsel table next to Mr. Sinclair. On one occasion, he made eye contact with Peter and smiled. Apparently Sinclair had told him that it would be beneficial if he showed warmth to his accuser.

Peter could not fathom why that would be helpful to Landers. He would ask Broderick. Glenn's parents and Laura sat in the front row of the audience, directly behind Glenn. They made no eye contact with Peter and showed him no warmth. Presumably warmth from the parents was not part of Sinclair's strategy.

THE TRIAL OF GLENN LANDERS — THE OPENING STATEMENTS — PREPARATION

Although jury selection had not been completed on day one of the trial, it was anticipated it would be completed reasonably early on day two and then opening statements by both sides would be made. It was late at night and Sinclair was still working on his preparation. He had a yellow pad in front of him on his antique oak desk. It had pages and pages of scribbled notes. The floor around him was littered with crumpled paper with angrily disposed of ideas. While he would be surrounded by junior lawyers, secretaries and investigators during much of the trial, he wanted no one around during his nighttime preparations for the following day. He leaned back in his chair, sighed and looked around.

The room was large with the floor covered in a thick dark-red carpet, his favorite color. The cabinets, containing casebooks, awards and victory mementoes, were of darkly stained walnut. The artwork on the paneled walls was original and expensive. There was a crystal chandelier hanging over his desk, which his wife had bought at an exclusive antique store in Paris. On his desk there was an eighteenth-century glass decanter containing single malt scotch surrounded by matching glasses. There was even an upright piano in the corner which he played to relieve the tensions of trial.

When asked by one of his subordinates how many trials he would have to handle before the heart-pounding nervousness stopped happening, he replied, "If you're doing your job to the very best of your ability and laying everything on the line for your client, you'll never be rid of that heart-pounding nervousness. I know because I've tried lots and lots of cases and I'm still not rid of it."

Sinclair subscribed to the view held by the vast majority of prominent trial lawyers that opening statements were the most important element in determining the outcome of a case, and the lawyer who delivered the most persuasive opening was very likely to win. He had agonized over how to deal with Mason's identification of Landers through the cast on his foot. It was extremely damaging and there was no even remotely satisfactory answer. He had finally settled on what he concluded was the best way to proceed. It was far from perfect, but it was the best he could come up with.

He had considered getting Landers's doctor to change the cast so that the jury wouldn't see the word "Limey." He soon discarded that idea. It would have been too easy for Broderick to line up a large number of witnesses who had seen the cast; people at the party where Peter wrote

"Limey," fellow workers; people living at Mrs. Grant's and many others. Sinclair had spoken to a close friend who was an orthopedic surgeon, who told him that there was no medical reason to change the cast and if a doctor did change it he would not be able to justify it. The jury would almost certainly conclude that the change of the cast was prompted by litigation strategy and not by medical prudence.

Perhaps as daunting, was how to handle Mason's dating the Negro girl. At first blush, this was a huge plus for Landers in front of a white southern jury. To say that an all-white southern jury would not look favorably at such a relationship would be a gross understatement. At second blush, the positive effect was not quite as clear. Landers had told Sinclair about the conversation in which Mason said he thought he was in love. Landers said that the street where Mason told him the girl lived was in a white area. On being pushed, Landers admitted to Sinclair that Mason had originally said she lived in an area which Landers knew was exclusively Negro. Sinclair assumed that Mason would testify that he had maintained absolute secrecy as to his relationship with, and visits to, the girl and that he had only told Landers, even though he had tried to correct his initial statement of where the girl lived. The jury might very well infer that Landers was not fooled by Mason's change in location of the girl's house; that Landers had then done some investigation of his own and had turned over the resulting information to the Klan.

How else could the Klan have got it? If the jury drew

those conclusions, the hill Sinclair had to climb as a result of the cast would be virtually insurmountable. It would then depend entirely on how much damage he could do to Mason's entirely plausible story. For all of those reasons, he couldn't give the jury all the information he now had about the girl in the opening. He would play it by ear and base how he would deal with the issue in his opening and thereafter, on how detailed the prosecution dealt with it in *its* opening, which preceded that of the defense.

In his office in the county building, Broderick was also engaged in preparing his opening. He was also writing on a yellow pad and there were crumpled pieces of paper on the floor containing discarded ideas. That's where the similarities ended. Broderick's office was probably no more than twenty-five percent the size of Sinclair's. The bookcases were of unfinished wood; the kind that could be purchased in most low-cost, discount stores. There was no carpet, no chandelier, no oak desk and no decanter of fine whiskey. The salary of an assistant district attorney did not run to expensive office décor.

Had he been privy to Sinclair's thought processes, he would have agreed to two things: Opening statements were almost always the most important event in a trial and frequently outcome-determinative. Like Sinclair, Broderick was also troubled by the Peter-Christine romance. It was a double-edged sword. However, that double-edged sword had different edges for the prosecution than it did for the defense. Sinclair wanted to use it to poison the jury's mind against Peter, the prosecutor's key witness, but was concerned about it aiding the prosecutor in establishing the Landers-Klan connection. Broderick wanted to use it to establish that connection, but was concerned about the adverse effect on the jury of the Peter-Christine connection.

It would be an important issue for both sides. The Klan, murderous though they were, would not have "punished" this white boy without knowing about the Negro-white romance. Broderick would have to take the chance that the jury, though probably appalled by the romance, would nonetheless conclude that Landers was the source of the Klan's information. He would bite the bullet and explore the issue fully in his opening.

It was after midnight when both men left their offices, neither one fully satisfied with the decisions they had made, but recognizing that, in trial work, as in life in general, compromises had to be made.

THE TRIAL OF GLENN LANDERS
— DAY TWO

Peter was fascinated by Mr. Sinclair. He was like a great actor, never at a loss for words, with an uncanny ability to communicate with each juror in simple, engaging language. *What a talent*! thought Peter. *I could listen to him for hours even if he was just reading the dictionary.*

The prospective jury panel was comprised of a bus driver, a tenant farmer, several housewives, a waitress, an automobile mechanic and others of similar financial status. The clothes Sinclair was wearing probably cost almost as much as any of the jurors earned in a year. Sinclair owned a yacht that he kept moored in Biloxi on the gulf coast. It slept eight and had a permanent crew of three. In addition to his palatial estate on the outskirts of Jackson, he had a beach house on the gulf coast adjoining the marina that housed his boat, a penthouse in New York City, and he vacationed in various expensive resorts around the world. Nonetheless, he seemed to be able to convince the jurors that he was one of them. He regaled them with hayseed anecdotes and talked to each one individually, as if that person was his closest friend.

Broderick's questioning of the jury was effective, if less flamboyant and clearly less entertaining than Sinclair's. As skilled as he was, Broderick was not able to convince the jury he was one of them, even though his net worth was a small fraction of Sinclair's.

Finally the voir dire examination was over and twelve jurors were selected: three women and nine men with three male alternates. Peter had taken some French lessons in school and knew that "voir" meant to see and that "dire" meant to speak. Broderick explained that those definitions were exactly what jury selection was all about. The lawyers made decisions on who to keep and who to let go based on what they saw and what they heard. It was, as Broderick said, an unscientific procedure at best.

Peter sensed that Sinclair had "won" the jury selection, not because of anything he could put his finger on, but because of the rapport that Sinclair had established with so many of the jurors. Then came opening statements. Predictably, Broderick's was well thought out and organized. It laid out what the prosecutor expected to prove and through whom. A lot of Broderick's presentation had to do with Peter and what had happened to him from the time he was kidnapped by the Klan to the time the Klan dropped him off at the boarding house. He discussed the cast, and how Landers came to be wearing one; the circumstances of Peter signing the cast with the word "Limey," and Peter's seeing the cast at the hanging and beating. An audible gasp was heard from the jury as Broderick discussed how it came about that Peter had seen the cast at the hanging and the circumstances of his savage beating.

As he had decided, Broderick laid out how the jury could infer from the evidence that it was Landers who had told the Klan of the romance; that Peter had initially told Landers that his girlfriend lived in an area that Landers knew was in the Negro part of town; and that there was no other source from which the Klan could have learned that. Sinclair scribbled an addition to his opening statement outline, now feeling that Broderick's extensive recitation of the car discussion required an equally extensive response.

The jury listened attentively to Broderick and, while there were some frowns and negative body language when Broderick talked of Peter and Christine, the prosecution's opening seemed to be received favorably. Peter noted that Broderick had been far more emotional, outgoing and demonstrative in the Jerome Washington case. Here, apparently for strategic reasons, he had toned down his approach, and Peter guessed that the changed circumstances and the different cast of characters prompted the different approach.

Sinclair was far more animated, but less so than Peter expected. He had changed to a grey silk suit with a red vest, light-blue shirt and a red tie. He still had the gold chain across his middle and had added a red handkerchief to the ensemble. He laid out two options of what might have motivated Peter to claim that he had seen Glenn participate in the murder of Washington. First, he was just plain mistaken. After all, the boy was terrified. He was staring his own death in the face. He was trembling. The light was very bad, he was forced to look at a man hanging from a tree and he just plain didn't see what he thought he saw.

The second option was more ominous, so Sinclair intentionally made it vague and less definitive than the fear/bad light/mistake option. Perhaps Peter was being vindictive. The Landerses had been extremely kind to him. Glenn had befriended him, found him not one but two jobs, and took him home for weekends. The older Landers had welcomed him to their house, fed and entertained him and Laura had shown him around, taught him to ride and had generally been a friend. And how had he repaid their generosity? He had been sexually aggressive with Laura, who had been forced to resist him.

On hearing this, Peter gasped, remembering how it all started with him finding her naked body next to him when he awoke. He tried to whisper to Broderick that it was a lie, but Broderick just told him to calm down. Sinclair stopped just short of saying that Peter had raped her before changing the subject. Sinclair told the jury that money was found to have disappeared from the Landers home after Peter had visited and the servants had all been employed at the house for many years and had never stolen anything. When asked about it, Peter became angry and defensive. Peter could now see that the Landerses were prepared to say anything, true or false, and even to perjure themselves in an effort to save Glenn, and he was to be the target of their lies.

Attacking Peter was a calculated risk. If the jury liked Peter and did not believe the attacking evidence, this tactic could backfire badly. The fear/bad light/mistake avenue was safer, but Sinclair was clearly prepared to use either. Sinclair addressed the Klan's source of knowledge about Peter and Christine, but somewhat more briefly than had Broderick. He said that Landers had no idea that the girl was Negro; that Mason had told him where she lived and it was in a white area; that Landers was not a Klansman and, even if he was, he would never have told them that the girl was Negro, even if he knew that, which he didn't. The jury seemed to receive Sinclair's opening somewhat more warmly than that of Broderick. If there was an opening statement "winner" it was probably Sinclair, but it was close.

As it turned out, Peter was not the sole witness for the prosecution. The law enforcement officers who had found the hanging body of Jerome Washington testified to that discovery and to cutting him down, and removing the body to the county morgue. They also testified to a thorough search of the field where the body was discovered. They found a stool, presumably the one on which Washington was forced to stand. They also found tire tracks and some rope in addition to that which was attached to Washington. They assumed it was what was used to tie Peter to the tree. Finally, they interviewed neighbors within a one-mile radius of the field. Predictably, nobody had seen or heard anything.

An autopsy had been performed on the body of Jerome Washington. Conscious of the tongue-lashing Judge Carson had given him in the Washington case, Dr. Silvers had performed a complete autopsy this time. Ironically, and unlike in the Washington case, a complete autopsy on the hanged man was not necessary. The coroner testified that the cause of death was asphyxiation secondary to being strangled by hanging. There were also indications that, before he was killed, Washington had been severely beaten around the face.

The dead man's nails were examined to see if there was any material resulting from him clawing at or scratching someone. The results were negative. Finally, evidence was introduced that Washington had been identified through fingerprints. Given Washington's long criminal history, his fingerprints could be compared with what the county had on file. Peter would also have been able to identify him, but Sinclair did not find it necessary to cross-examine any of the witnesses that day.

As he walked out of the courtroom at the end of the day, Sinclair looked at Peter and said with an unpleasant smile, "You had better get a good night's sleep."

"I always do," Peter managed to retort, but that night he didn't.

LIFE OUT OF COURT

Mr. Foster had told Peter that he should come to work when he could, but that it was understood that he might have to spend a lot of time in court or with Mr. Broderick. Mr. Mitchell had made a point of telling Peter that his job was safe, despite his repeated absences because of the trial.

His picture had been in the paper and people would stare at him as he passed them on the street. Several whispered to their companions and pointed. He didn't go out much at night. He was fearful and found himself frequently looking over his shoulder. A car honking or stopping behind him was startling and his heart would pound. Nights were a problem for reasons other than Peter's fear of being outdoors. He had trouble sleeping. Sometimes it seemed that he had only slept for two or three hours the whole night. Even sleep was no release. He had repeated nightmares—all of them including visions of hooded men and the dead body of Jerome Washington. Twice he woke up screaming and sweating profusely after dreaming that a giant-sized Glenn Landers, covered in blood, towered over him while laughing uproariously.

At work, Peter's team were even more solicitous to him than they had been, frequently asking if they could do anything for him or run any errands. Dave, who had occasionally driven him home from work, insisted on taking him home every night. He had offered also to pick him up in the mornings, but Peter declined. Mr. Mitchell, through Mr. Foster, had instructed both white and Negro employees not to discuss the case with Peter. The employees obeyed those instructions, although there was a palpable coolness in the reactions of some of the white employees to Peter.

Peter knew Glenn was still living at Mrs. Grant's, since he still regularly heard the key being turned in the bathroom door and the water running. He dreaded running into Glenn, and he timed his comings and goings in an effort to avoid any meeting. He wasn't always successful. On one occasion they almost collided going out the front door. Glenn said, "Hi Peter," and continued to walk. Peter gave a weak smile and a nod.

Mrs. Grant was more persistent. She came to Peter's room and asked a lot of questions about the case, including some that were very intrusive, such as what Mr. Broderick thinks the verdict will be and if Peter really did molest the Landers girl. Peter repeatedly told her that he was not permitted to discuss the case. That didn't stop her.

He had recently been having dinner at Marty's, a small café in easy walking distance of Mrs. Grant's. The food was plain, but quite tasty and, most importantly, cheap. Most of the tables were for four or six persons. A few were for two people. He would try to get the two-seat table in the corner where he would read a newspaper and hope nobody recognized him. Unfortunately, the proprietor liked to tell incoming patrons of the presence of what he claimed was a celebrity. They would then stare, but none of them spoke to him. The attention made Peter uncomfortable and he started avoiding Marty's and picking up a sandwich at the bus station to eat in his room.

His spirits were raised by a letter he got from Chuck Bradley and one from Mrs. Hamilton. He had exchanged letters with Chuck a number of times. He had only written to the Hamiltons once, primarily to, again, thank them for their kindness and to give them a brief summary of where he had been since he last saw them. Mrs. Hamilton's letter was short but sweet. She reminded Peter to be sure and call when and if he was next in New York. Chuck's letter was longer. He described his job in his father's construction company. He had gotten a promotion, but he was still at a relatively low level. He closed by telling Peter to let him know if he needed anything.

THE TRIAL OF GLENN LANDERS
— DAY THREE

PETER GOT to the courthouse early. He had arranged to meet Broderick in an attorney conference room on the third floor an hour before the trial commenced. Broderick had brought containers of coffee and some doughnuts for the two of them. They went back over what Broderick was going to ask and Peter went through what his answers would be. Broderick predicted what Sinclair's cross-examination would cover and Peter went through what his answers would be to those questions. Nothing they discussed was new. They had been over all of this several times before. Peter was nervous, but felt he would still be able to give straightforward answers.

"Take your time up there, Peter. Listen carefully to the questions and wait for the questioner to finish before you start to answer. Just answer the question. Don't ramble. A witness who rambles is like the fellow who thought he knew how to spell Mississippi but didn't know when to stop. When Sinclair is cross-examining, don't look at me.

If you do, the jury will think I'm tipping you off as to how to answer. Sinclair will try to anger you. It's a ploy. Don't fall for it. Crossing swords with him won't help. You can't win that fight and the jury will not like you for it. I'm going to start out by asking some questions about you—where you come from, how you ended up in the United States, where you were during the war and a little something about your family. Do you have any questions?"

"Yes. Why ask me a lot of questions about where I come from and where I was in the war? What's that got to do with whether Glenn was involved in a murder?"

"It has absolutely nothing to do with whether Glenn was involved in a murder. It has everything to do with getting the jury to know you. Juries frequently decide cases on things that have absolutely nothing to do with the case. Do they like you? Do they think you are cocky or respectful, combative or co-operative? Often the jury's perception of the messenger is more important than the message itself."

The fact that the scheduled start of the trial day was delayed by twenty minutes only increased Peter's nervousness. The judge had several lawyers in his chambers on another matter. When he finally emerged, he apologized to the jury for the delay and told Broderick to call his next witness.

Broderick conducted the direct examination exactly as he said he would. He started with a rather extensive review of Peter's life in England; his schooling, his years in London during the Nazi blitz, the loss of his mother at a young age and his brief employment as an errand boy. He pointed out that Peter still had a piece of shrapnel just below his left knee and even had Peter pull up his trouser leg and show the jurors the faded red mark. As instructed by Broderick, Peter would, from time to time, look at the jury and make eye contact while delivering his answers. He thought that he detected indications of sympathy from them as he told of the bombings and their impact, particularly on his mother. Sinclair objected once that the whole area of questioning was totally irrelevant, but the court allowed it. His objection was not made with any great attempt at persuasiveness, perhaps because he intended to pursue a similar line of questioning with his client.

Broderick next took Peter through his journey to and in the United States. He had Peter describe his two jobs in Jackson. The background examination had taken a little over an hour, and during that time, nothing was mentioned that related in any way to the reason everyone was present in the courtroom: whether or not Glenn Landers was guilty of the murder of Jerome Washington and the aggravated assault on Peter Mason. But the jury had clearly warmed to Peter. They sympathized with his wartime experiences. They were amused by some of his escapades, particularly the account of his difficulty in getting the elevator to stop in the right places. They seemed captivated by his accent. In short, Broderick's plan had worked so far. The jury liked Peter.

Having apparently succeeded in the initial part of his

plan, Broderick then took Peter through his association with Glenn Landers and the circumstances leading up to his signing the plaster cast on Landers's foot. Broderick secured the permission of the court to show the jury the place on the cast where Peter had signed. The jury filed out of the box and one by one looked at the cast on Landers's foot. Landers had risen from has chair and remained standing while the jury examination was taking place. Several of the jurors, who had brought their notebooks with them, made notes. Two or three took a long time to complete their examination. One pointed at the cast and whispered something to his neighbor who nodded. Landers tried to make points by smiling at each juror as he or she looked at the cast. The effort was essentially wasted as the jurors seemed too busy looking at the cast and writing in their notebooks to pay much attention to the expression on Landers's face.

Broderick then went on to question Peter about the night of the hanging. His examination was methodical. He started with the reason why Peter was walking home from work so late that night, continued to his being grabbed from behind and taken to the field where the Klan members were gathered, through the beating, the hanging and, most carefully and meticulously, how it came about that he was in a position to see, and did see, the cast with his writing on it.

Peter testified that the dead man was Jerome Washington and he explained how he was able to make the identification. While the jury had smiled a lot and had seemed quite relaxed during the preliminary part of Peter's testimony, during this part of the examination they became serious, almost tense, seemingly riveted on what Peter was saying.

Broderick knew that how the Klan had discovered the Peter-Christine relationship was a necessary step in developing the case against Landers, but he also knew that the sensitive nature of that inquiry could come back to bite him. He had earlier considered not pursuing the subject until Landers testified in the defense case, but there was no assurance that he would testify and he couldn't be made to do so.

He proceeded gingerly, phrasing his questions carefully. He asked how Peter came to meet the Browards, and that he "saw" Christine as opposed to "dated" her. He attempted, as much as possible, to phrase his questions to minimize the extent of their involvement and to make it appear that the relationship was casual and not serious. However, that effort was probably unavailing. There was no way to avoid the jury finding out that Peter had said he loved Christine. It was part of the conversation Peter had with Landers on which was based the contention that it was Landers who told the Klan about the Peter-Christine relationship. Broderick had bitten the bullet earlier when, in his opening statement, he had laid out the 'how do you know if you're in love' conversation, and the circumstances leading up to it. He had to, and did, go through the whole episode in meticulous detail.

At that point Judge Carson said to the jury, "We

are going to have an unusual day tomorrow. We won't reconvene until 5pm. Then you are going on a field trip."

The jurors looked at each other and there was a buzz of interest and excitement.

Judge Carson continued, "We are all going out to the area where Jerome Washington was found hung and we are going to see a reconstruction of what Mr. Mason says happened that night and what he claims to have seen. You are all now excused but be back promptly at 5:00 p.m. tomorrow and dress warmly. It can get cold and we might be out there for some time."

DAY FOUR — THE RE-CREATION

A COUNTY BUS customarily employed for transporting prisoners was used to take the jurors, the judge, the lawyers, the court attaches, Peter and Glenn Landers to the field where the hanging had taken place. No spectators were allowed. Glenn's father asked for permission to attend, but was turned down. There were eight cars on the field, positioned where Peter indicated they should be. The cross had been erected where Peter remembered it was located. It was covered with rags and impregnated with kerosene. A stool had been placed under the tree where Washington had been found hung and above it a straw-filled dummy hung from a noose. Police Sergeant McIntire had the same cast on his right foot that he had worn during the rehearsal, despite Broderick's promise that he could take it off immediately after the rehearsal. He was also wearing a sheet which just barely covered his feet.

Chairs had been set up for all the participants and the jurors sat in what passed for a jury box. Judge Carson announced that this was a regular session of the court, even though it was taking place in an open field, and that everybody was to conduct themselves as though they were in court. Peter was feeling relaxed and confident. Broderick previously told him that the direct examination he had conducted had gone even better than had been hoped. However, Broderick had warned him that the cross-examination would not be nearly as comfortable.

"All right Mr. Broderick, you may proceed, and remember, Mr. Mason, you are still under oath," directed the judge.

"Mr. Mason, is the cross where it was on the night you were beaten and Jerome Washington was hung?"

"Yes sir, it is," responded Peter. Broderick signaled and the cross was ignited. "Is the rope with the noose, the dummy and the stool where you saw those objects on that same night?"

"Yes, except that it was Jerome Washington and not a dummy hanging there."

Broderick had Peter show the jury where he got out of the car that had brought him to the field; where the apparent Klan leader confronted him; the tree that he was tied to and whipped and how he was pushed and pulled to the spot where the hanging took place.

"Now, please stand where you were when Mr. Washington was pushed off the stool and somebody kicked the stool away."

Peter complied. While these proceedings had taken place it had become very dark. Broderick walked out toward the cars, stopped and yelled to the drivers to turn their headlights on and to move their vehicles forward in an arc starting where he was standing. The point Broderick had indicated was eight yards closer to the noose than Peter had noted on the night of the hanging.

"Now I'm going to ask Sergeant McIntire to go to the stool and—" Broderick got no further.

Glenn Landers leaped to his feet. "That's not—" he started to yell, but Sinclair, almost simultaneously jumped to his feet and stopped Landers from saying any more by hissing something inaudible at him and pulling him back on to his seat.

"I think that, before he was interrupted, Mr. Landers was about to tell us that I had moved the cars further forward than they had been on the night of the hanging," Broderick stated, while staring directly at Landers.

Sinclair exploded. "He was saying no such thing. This is outrageous. This piece of attempted trickery and the DA's comments are totally inappropriate and unethical. It's clear, inexcusable misconduct—the worst I've ever seen."

"The comments of Mr. Broderick are stricken and the jury is admonished to disregard them. Mr. Broderick, watch yourself. I won't warn you again," Judge Carson said severely.

"My apologies, Your Honor. Mr. Mason, have I placed the cars closer to the hanging tree than they were on that night?"

"Yes, you have," answered Peter.

"Please walk out there and instruct the drivers where they should place their cars."

Peter did so and returned to the witness chair. The "how far could you lift your arm before the accident" ruse had not worked completely, but it was far from a failure. Broderick was hopeful that it had placed a seed in the minds of the jurors. Sinclair was fearful that it had, and that there was still use to be made of Landers's brief outburst.

"Now, what happened with respect to Mr. Washington after you arrived here on that night?"

"He was put on the stool. The man with the cast pushed him off the stool and another man kicked the stool away."

"At that point did you see a cast on the leg of the man who pushed Mr. Washington off the stool?"

"No, not then."

"All right, what happened next?"

"I was told to go over to get a better look at the dead man. Those weren't the exact words. I was then pushed and dragged to the tree."

"Go and stand where you were after they dragged and pushed you over to the tree." Peter complied.

"Then what happened?"

"One of the men, I don't know which one, told me to look up at the dead man's face and remember it. The body had turned and was facing away from me. The man who had pushed Mr. Washington off the stool reached up and turned the body so I could see the face. I didn't want to see it so I looked down and, as I did, the sheet on the man who was reaching rode up a bit, and I could plainly see the cast on his right foot."

"Did you see anything on the cast?"

"I saw where I had written the word 'Limey' on the cast."

"Why 'Limey'?"

"It's a slang name used for Englishmen. Years ago, English sailors ate limes to ward off some disease, I forget which, when they were on long voyages. We were at a party at the Landerses' home and Glenn asked me to write that word on the cast rather than my name."

"Is the sheet covering Sergeant McIntire precisely as long and precisely covering the same parts of his body as the sheet covering the man with the cast on the night of the hanging?"

"Yes."

"Look at the cast on Sergeant McIntire's foot. Did I get you to write your name on it with the same type of marking pen, using the same color, in the same location and at the same size as the name you wrote on Glenn Landers's cast?"

"Yes."

"Your Honor, I would ask permission for each juror to stand in the spot where Mr. Mason is now standing and look at Sergeant McIntire's right foot as the sergeant reaches up and turns the dummy."

"Proceed."

"As each juror comes up, I will ask the sergeant to reach up and turn the dummy, and Mr. Mason, if the sergeant doesn't move exactly the way the man with the cast moved on the day of the hanging, you tell us, all right?"

"Yes sir."

Each of the jurors separately came up and looked closely at the cast. Several made notes.

When the last one had finished looking and had returned to his or her chair, Broderick said, "May the record reflect that the writing on the cast put there by Mr. Mason is clearly visible as a result of the car headlights and the burning cross."

Sinclair jumped up, "Is Mr. Broderick now testifying? Whether the writing is or is not visible is a question for the jury to determine, not the DA."

"Agreed," said the Judge. "Mr. Broderick's last comment is stricken. Any more questions, Mr. Broderick?"

"Just one, Your Honor. Mr. Mason, on the night of the hanging and your beating, did you have any difficulty, any difficulty whatsoever, in reading the word 'limey' on the cast?"

"None at all."

"Then I have no further questions of this witness, Your Honor."

"Do you wish to cross examine the witness?" asked Judge Carson.

"Indeed I do, Your Honor." Sinclair took a while to get up. He then stood and looked at Peter for some time and finally said, "I would like to just ask a few questions now and save the major part of my examination for tomorrow. It's cold as a witch's ... well it's cold, and the jury has already sat outside too long to watch this dog and pony show." With that, Sinclair started his questioning.

"Mr. Mason, were you scared on that night?"

"Very much."

"You were more than scared weren't you? You were petrified, panic stricken. Right?

"You could say that."

"Never mind what I could say. Do you say that?"

"Yes."

"You had seen the Negro man hung and you thought you were next, that you were about to be killed. Correct?"

"Yes."

"With the court's permission, I'll continue my examination tomorrow."

As they walked back to the bus, Sinclair pulled Broderick aside. "Cute trick. Too bad it didn't work."

"That's disappointing to hear, especially since I thought it did," Broderick retorted.

THE CROSS-EXAMINATION ORDEAL

IT WAS EARLY the following morning. Peter and Broderick were again meeting in the attorney conference room on the third floor of the courthouse. Broderick seemed more solemn and intense than Peter had seen him before.

"Remember this: Sinclair will do his level best to rattle and anger you and his best is as good as it gets. If he can get you to be combative and lose your temper, we will have lost most of what we achieved in the last couple of days. I know I've told you this several times before and you're probably sick of hearing it, but it's important and it bears repeating. I'm sure the jury likes you. A jury liking a key witness is frequently more than half the battle. Stay calm. You can be firm in your answers, but be polite and don't rise to the bait."

The courtroom was crowded and all eyes were on Peter as he walked to the witness stand. They swiveled around so that they would not lose sight of him even for a second. Judge Carson reminded Peter that he was still under oath and motioned to Sinclair to continue his cross-examination.

Sinclair wasted no time. "Mr. Mason, some time ago you were knocked down by a car, correct?"

"Yes."

"When you woke up you were in Froman, a hospital that ordinarily treats only Negro patients, correct?"

"That's right."

"You stayed overnight and when you were discharged, you were told that you should get ongoing treatment for your head wound at an institution that treats white patients. Is that correct?"

"Yes."

"You knew that a Negro doctor treating a white patient might not be looked upon very favorably in Mississippi, right?"

"Nobody said that, but that was what I thought."

"You then went to Jackson General and your wound was looked at and re-bandaged, right?"

"Yes."

"And when the doctor at Jackson General asked you where you had been previously treated for that head wound, you said by a doctor in Washington, DC Is that correct?"

Broderick jumped to his feet. "I haven't said anything so far, Your Honor, not wanting to interrupt my esteemed colleague, but none of this has anything to do with this case."

Judge Carson glared at Broderick. "I assume that

somewhere in that little speech is a hidden objection. Am I right?'

"Yes Your Honor, objection–irrelevant."

"Overruled."

"Let me repeat the question," said Sinclair, pleased at the opportunity to repeat and hammer home his point. "When the doctor at Jackson General asked you where you had been previously treated for the head wound, you said by a doctor in Washington, DC Correct?"

"Yes."

"That was a lie, wasn't it?"

Peter wanted to explain why he said what he had said, but he remembered the warning Broderick had given him. He figuratively bit his tongue and simply answered, "Yes."

"You lied because you wanted to protect the Negro doctor from criticism, or worse, if it became known that he had treated a white patient, right?"

"Yes."

Sinclair then interrogated Peter about the speeding car that killed Mr. Fleming and Peter's testimony that ultimately exonerated Jerome Washington from having allegedly struck and killed Fleming.

Broderick knew that any further objections to this line of questioning would not be granted and might irritate the jury, so he didn't make any.

"Again, you wanted to help one of your Negro friends in the earlier situation to avoid criticism or worse, and in the later situation to avoid a murder conviction, right?"

"No, that is not right. I wasn't trying to help or

hurt him. I testified, under oath, to what I saw and Mr. Washington was not a friend of mine. I have never even spoken to him."

Ignoring Peter's denial, Sinclair pressed on. "Having helped your friend the Negro doctor to avoid criticism and your friend the Negro criminal to avoid execution, you then decided to punish some white person for the death of your friend, Washington, right?"

Despite his earlier decision not to object to the line of questioning, Broderick felt he had to protest. "Objection. Mr. Sinclair is deliberately distorting Mr. Mason's answer."

"I think that objection is well taken. Mr. Sinclair, rephrase the question."

"I'll move on, Your Honor. I think the jury understands what Mr. Mason is up to."

Broderick again objected, this time to the uncalled-for comment and the judge gently remonstrated with Sinclair. Undeterred, he continued, "Having established that you will lie when it suits your convenience, whether or not it is for friends, we cannot even be sure that you were out there on the night of the hanging, can we? We only have the word of a confessed liar, don't we?"

The tactics and the evidence that Sinclair was using in an attempt to demonstrate that Peter was a liar, were, ironically, the exact same tactics and evidence that Broderick had used for the very same purpose in the Jerome Washington cases. The odd similarities between the two cases were ongoing.

Peter was seething, but he forced himself to keep

calm, remembering the importance of not losing his temper. He did sense, from his eye contact with the jury, that their warm feelings for him were starting to evaporate. However, at the risk of violating one of Mr. Broderick's prime instructions, he could not avoid one retort, "Mr. Sinclair, do you think I put those lash marks on my back myself?"

Then Sinclair made an unimaginable mistake, one that even the rawest rookie would not have made; one he would come to regret and one that a lawyer of his skill and reputation should never have made. It had been very unwise for him to have challenged that Peter was present at the hanging, but already having seriously erred, he went on to make it infinitely worse. The only evidence of the whipping introduced so far had been a black and white photograph taken in Broderick's office. Although it was taken shortly after the beating, it did not really convey the magnitude of the injury. The contrast was not sharp and the angry red welts did not show well. Furthermore, it only showed a back between the shoulders and waist so that whose back it was could not be identified. Perhaps believing that the wound had completely healed by now Sinclair said, "We saw the picture but there isn't even any guarantee that it is a picture of your back."

Before Broderick had submitted the photograph in evidence, he had looked at Peter's back and had seen that the wounds, while healing, were still very apparent. He had considered having Peter show his bare back to the jury, but had decided against it. While he was anxious to have the jury convict Landers of aggravated assault on Peter, he was almost desperate to have the jury convict Landers of murder. The conviction of a Klansman for murder would be a major setback for the Klan. A conviction for assault would have less impact. Further, emphasis on the whipping would have prompted Sinclair to belabor the point that Peter did not claim that Landers used the whip on him. A white boy being whipped might be a dreadful thing to a white jury, but the hanging of a Negro, particularly one with a long criminal record might be … well it was a close question, but Broderick decided, at that time, that focusing on Peter's wounds might unnecessarily distract the jury from the key issue of the identification of the cast and the hanging. He had made a note to perhaps have Peter show his back to the jury during closing argument and, optimally, during the prosecution's rebuttal, which would be too late for Sinclair to respond. It was chancy. Judge Carson might not allow it in closing.

Sinclair's mistake had changed everything. Now the viewing of the terrible injury to Peter's back would be used to dramatically refute the totally unsupportable and weakly asserted contention that Peter wasn't even present at the beating and hanging. The making of that specious contention would substantially lessen any impact on the jury of the conceded fact that it wasn't Landers who beat Peter.

Now Broderick leaped to his feet. "Your Honor, given these last few questions, I ask the court's permission for

Mr. Mason to remove his shirt and show his back to the jury."

"I protest, Your Honor," said Sinclair, visibly agitated by his apparent mistake. He knew that Broderick would not have made the request if the wounds had healed. "This is my cross-examination and counsel should not be permitted to interrupt it."

"No, I think you have raised an issue that would be appropriate for clarification at this time," said Judge Carson.

Peter got down off the witness stand, removed his jacket and tried to remove his shirt. Given the length of time he had been seated and the tension he had been under, he had perspired and his shirt had stuck to his back. He gingerly and painfully pulled the material away from his skin and turned to show the jury. There was an audible gasp. Two of the female jurors started to tear up. One of the men blew his nose loudly. An elderly juror sitting at the far end of the box asked if he could get a closer look, which the court allowed. The lashes, while no longer oozing blood, were still bright red and angry-looking. There were ugly scabs that had formed and the lash marks stretched from a couple of inches below the neck almost to the waist.

Viewing Peter's back was infinitely more graphic than looking at the small black and white photograph. Broderick recognized that the reasoning he had used in deciding not to show the jury Peter's back during direct examination was an error in judgment. Now Sinclair's mistakes had turned Broderick's error into a stroke of genius.

The jurors' view of Peter's back occurred during Sinclair's cross-examination, thereby magnifying its effect on the jury and eroding the impact of Sinclair's entire cross-examination. In his long career as a deputy district attorney, Broderick had seen many gruesome sights; a small child deliberately starved to death by her parents, a man shot through the eye, people burned beyond recognition in an arson fire. He was not immune to horror, but he was hardened to it—not so the jury.

"All right, Mr. Mason, you can put your clothes back on. It is just about noon. We'll take our lunch break now. Be back at 1:30 and remember, don't discuss the case among yourselves or with anyone else."

The timing of the break could not have been better for the prosecution. It would be an hour-and-a-half before Sinclair could ask any questions to try to rehabilitate his position; an hour-and-a-half during which the morning's significant events would become solidified in the jurors' thinking. As they walked out, several of the jurors looked at Peter. The warmth seemed to have returned.

THE CROSS-EXAMINATION — CONCLUSION

THE REMAINDER of Sinclair's cross-examination of Peter consumed most of the rest of the afternoon. Sinclair had regained his composure. There were no fireworks; no unexpected developments and, for the first time, the jurors' interest seem to flag—that is until near the end of his cross-examination when Sinclair, uncharacteristically, made another serious error.

Nothing that Sinclair established in the afternoon was really in dispute; it could even have been the subject of a stipulation. Peter did not see the man with the cast take part in dragging Peter to a tree, tying his arms around it or flogging him. Peter could not identify any of the other robed and hooded men. He couldn't even say that all of them were men. The only ones there who were not robed and hooded were the unfortunate Jerome Washington and Peter. He saw no faces, other than Washington's, no clothes, hair or identifying marks. He couldn't recall how many people were present, how heavy any of them were or how tall. He did recall that the man with the cast was approximately the same height as Glenn Landers. He recalled that there were eight cars in the arc shining their lights on the hanging tree and the surrounding area. He could not identify the make, model, color or year of any of them and did not see any license plates. The only additional information he knew about the car he had ridden in was that it had four doors and was dark in color.

"Is there anything else at all that you can remember about the car that brought you to that field that might help identify it?"

Peter shifted awkwardly in his seat before responding. "It's possible that you would find the remains of a wet spot in the middle of the backseat."

The courtroom exploded in laughter. Even Judge Carson allowed himself a smile, partially hidden behind his hand. He recovered quickly and gaveled for silence. A red-faced Sinclair then asked Peter, the only other person in the courtroom who was not smiling, "Why do you think that's funny?"

"There was nothing that night that was the slightest bit funny. Peeing in my pants is something I haven't done since I was two years old. What happened that night was so horrible that—"

Sinclair interrupted, "There's no question pending, Your Honor; the witness is just volunteering."

"No, he's not. You asked him 'why' and he is entitled to tell you and the jury everything that is reasonably responsive to that question. You may finish your answer, Mr. Mason," Judge Carson told Peter.

In his anger at the laughter, Sinclair had made a rookie mistake. He had used the dreaded "why" word, something that is never done on cross-examination of a hostile witness since it allows that witness to say almost anything he wants to. As a skilled cross-examiner, Sinclair knew that it was imperative to carefully restrict an adverse witness by the use of leading questions. Such careful cross-examination in fact reverses the roles and the questioner is, in reality, testifying. Statements of supposed fact are made in the leading questions and the witness' role is limited to affirming or denying the stated facts in one word, "yes" or "no."

"As I was saying, that night was so horrible I'm sure there'll never be a day in the rest of my life that I won't think of it. I was whipped so hard that I passed out and I'm sure I'll be scarred for the rest of my life. I saw a man hanged by a bunch of cowards who wouldn't show their faces; a man who had done nothing to deserve being killed; a man whose cries for mercy are carved into my brain. I haven't slept more than an hour or two each night since this happened and I have had nightmares every night and all made worse because I saw a man, who I thought was a friend of mine, doing the killing. No, Mr. Sinclair, I see nothing the slightest bit funny in what happened that night."

The courtroom became very quiet. Two of the women who had teared up earlier dabbed at their eyes again, and the rest of the jurors looked somber.

Sinclair attempted to recover by starting a different line of questioning. He asked Peter about any conversations he had with any of the Klansmen or any conversations he overheard. He recalled the only two words spoken by his abductors on the ride to the site of the hanging: "shut up." He recalled that the apparent leader of the Klansmen told him that he was being punished because he was seeing a Negro girl. He remembered something about his having to look at the dead man and let it be a lesson to him, although he didn't remember the exact words. He remembered that nothing at all was said on the ride back to Mrs. Grant's house. He recalled nothing unusual about the speech patterns of the few words that were said, no lisps, no strange accents, nothing at all memorable.

Sinclair concluded his cross-examination by exploring his personal relationship with Glenn Landers, Landers's family, and the Browards, particularly Christine Broward. He again went over how Glenn Landers had befriended him; had helped him get two jobs and had taken him on several weekend visits to his family home where his family had welcomed him. He finished by having Peter testify how he had visited with the Browards and how he had come to know them as a result of meeting Joshua Broward's father on the bus from New York. Peter admitted that he had been seeing Christine Broward and had kissed her, but denied having sexual relations with her. Broderick objected several times to all of the questioning about Peter's relations with the defendant, the defendant's family, the Browards and Christine Broward, but the court allowed it.

The jury did not seem to register any particular interest in this testimony; even their reaction to Peter's seeing and kissing a Negro girl was mild. Sinclair had intended this conclusion to his cross-examination to be a dynamite finish that would destroy Peter's credibility. Surprisingly, the expressions of the jury; their body language and the absence of note-taking seemed to indicate that it did not have the desired effect. Sinclair was obviously surprised and disappointed.

Broderick was also surprised, but pleased. He attributed this to several facts. The jury obviously liked Peter; they sympathized with him because of the severe beating he had suffered and he was English, new to the country and still not altogether familiar with the customs of the region. Of course, Peter's dramatic and extended answer to Sinclair's "why" question was also a significant factor.

There were a few eyebrows raised when Broderick told the court that he had no re-direct examination. He explained to Peter later that a statement that there was to be no re-direct examination frequently signaled to the jury that counsel did not believe his witness had been at all harmed and that the cross-examiner had "not laid a hand on him."

Broderick then announced that the state rested. It was only a little after three, but Judge Carson stated that the trial would be in recess until Monday and that the defense would then put on its case.

Broderick told Peter that he had done a superb job and that he should take a well-deserved rest over the weekend. He also told him that it was not necessary to come back to court unless and until he was told to, but he could if he wanted to. Peter said he had been granted some advanced vacation time by his boss and, if Broderick didn't mind, he would attend the rest of the trial. Mr. Mitchell had been extraordinarily supportive of Peter. He liked this young, somewhat brash English kid. He admired his courage in coming to a foreign country by himself and with little money. It didn't hurt Mitchell's assessment that Peter was a good employee and had achieved significant increases in productivity from his team.

Peter asked Broderick when he thought Glenn Landers would testify because he particularly wanted to hear that. Broderick explained that it was not certain that Landers would testify and that, under the Fifth Amendment to the United States Constitution, a criminal defendant could not be compelled to testify and frequently did not. However, given Peter's un-contradicted testimony about the man with the cast on his right foot, Broderick speculated that Sinclair would feel he had to have Landers testify.

Peter was more relaxed that evening than he had been for some time. His testimony had been a great success for the prosecution. The pressure was off him, at least for a while, and, most importantly, Christine and her family had left Jackson and were out of harm's way. Nonetheless, that night he had the worst nightmare he had suffered.

Christine was tied to a tree. Klansmen had ripped her dress off and were beating her as blood flowed from her back. Peter woke up screaming in a cold sweat. Although it was only three o'clock, Peter got no more sleep that night.

DETROIT — ONE

JOSHUA BROWARD had driven straight through, stopping only for gas and to pick up food at the convenience stores in the stations. He couldn't wait to get out of Jackson and get settled in Detroit. Several times Harriet had offered to spell him at the wheel, but he refused.

Henry and Rosie Broward lived on a street that was much like the street Joshua and Harriet's house was on in Jackson. The neighborhood was all Negro and the houses were small and very close to each other. Henry's house had three bedrooms, one bathroom, a kitchen and a very tiny living room. Henry and Rosie had three children, twin eight-year-old girls, Gretchen and Tania, and a ten-year-old boy, Lester. Even before the arrival of Joshua and his family the house was crowded. With the addition of Joshua, Harriet, Phillip and Christine, "crowded" was a definite understatement. Henry and Rosie occupied what they euphemistically referred to as the master bedroom. It was just large enough for a queen-sized bed, an armoire and a chest of drawers. Joshua and Harriet slept in the second bedroom which was only slightly smaller than the "master." The third bedroom was the converted one-car garage. Christine and the twins had that room, which could only accommodate one bed. Fortunately, all three of them were slim, because the bed would have been too small for two full-sized adults or three large girls. Christine's brother Phillip and cousin Lester slept on a convertible sofa in the living room.

Three days after their arrival in Detroit, Henry called a family meeting in the kitchen. Phillip and his cousins were sent out to play.

"I want to give you a few pointers. Things is a bit different here, but not so much. You don't have to ride in the back of the bus, but if you can, it's best to sit with your own kind. You can shop in most white stores. Some don't allow it and Rosie can pretty much tell you where you can and where you can't. Some restaurants will let you eat there, but many won't let you in at all or will make up something about being full when they ain't. They don't mind taking your money in the shops, but they don't much like eating with you."

"What about schools, Henry?" asked Harriet. "I know Christine is going to that college she is already enrolled in. She knows which bus to take, but what about Phillip?"

"He'll go to the same school as my kids. It's not far. They can walk there.

Harriet you should go with Phillip the first day to get him enrolled. All the kids are Negro. All the elementary and high schools are separate. Not where you're going,

Christine, and that raises something else. You're going to be in school and in classes with white kids. I know you bin had by some white boy in Jackson and 'cause of that you're all here. I'm telling you—stay away from them white boys. If they know you bin had by some whitey, they be after you."

"What are you talking about Uncle Henry? I don't know exactly what you mean by being 'had' but I've got a pretty good idea. I've not been 'had' by any boy, white, brown, black or any other color and I'm not going to be 'had' by anyone except by my husband and then only after I'm married."

Joshua and Harriet were stunned. Christine was not exactly a meek child, but they had never heard her talk back to one of her elders, even if that person was saying things that were not right.

"Easy Christine, Uncle Henry's just trying to help."

"I'm grateful he's put us up here. I know it crowds us all together, but I don't like being told that I've done things that I haven't."

THE TRIAL OF GLENN LANDERS — THE DEFENSE CASE

PETER WALKED into the attorney conference room. Broderick was in there alone reading some penciled notes.

"I'm not disturbing you, am I?"

"No, come on in. I'm just going over my notes for the tenth time. Hey, you look like you haven't slept in a week. I told you to get some rest and not worry about the case."

"I wasn't worried about the case, at least not directly. I wanted to ask you a question. The other days when he was in the audience, Mr. Landers wore a suit and tie. I just saw him walking up the steps to the courthouse and he's wearing what looks like some old farm clothes. What do you make of that?"

"You're a smart boy, Peter. You'd make a mighty fine lawyer. Maybe one day you will. Mr. Landers is going to testify today. Probably Sinclair told him to dress down, try to make the jurors think he's a good old boy and one of them. Of course, he's worth a thousand times more than the lot of them put together, lives in an estate that's worth half of Jackson and on any other occasion, he wouldn't give any of them the time of day."

"You didn't tell me how to dress."

"Didn't have to. Didn't think you even had a $20 suit, much less a $300 one. No offense. You looked natural in work clothes. Old man Landers doesn't."

Peter thought. *I do have a $300 suit. Of course it was made for a 300-pound man, not a 135 pound boy.*

Before the jury returned to the courtroom, Sinclair made an impassioned argument for dismissal of the charges, claiming that the prosecution had failed to make out a case against his client. Broderick argued, less passionately, but more effectively, that the state had established the presence of the man in the right foot cast; that the cast had been signed by Peter Mason and that Mason had established, beyond any reasonable doubt, that the man wearing that cast was Glenn Landers. Finally, Broderick argued that Glenn Landers was the Klansman most responsible for the murder of Jerome Washington since it had been established beyond any reasonable doubt that Landers was the individual who pushed Washington off the stool, thereby killing him. Judge Carson, without a moment's hesitation, denied Sinclair's motion.

As anticipated, Glenn Landers's father was the first witness for the defense. Under Sinclair's questioning, he testified to having befriended Mason; that he had him as a guest in his house over the course of several weekends and that Mason had paid him back by stealing money from him and molesting his daughter. He also testified that, at Glenn's urging he had used his influence to get Mason a job, first at the Robert E. Lee Hotel and later at the Mitchell Company. He had called in owed favors from the president of the hotel and from his old friend, George Mitchell, president of the Mitchell Company. He detailed what a fine upstanding boy his son had always been; that he didn't have a racist bone in his body; that he had been valedictorian of his high school senior class; an honors student in college and he was a promising accountant with a major Jackson firm. At the conclusion it would appear that Glenn Landers, rather than being a murderer, was long overdue for a top humanitarian award.

When Sinclair announced that he had no more questions, Landers made a move as though he was getting down from the witness stand. Broderick immediately reacted. "Not just yet, Mr. Landers, if you please, sir. The law does provide me the right to ask questions also. Please resume your seat. Do you remember paying a visit to Mr. Mason at Mrs. Grant's boarding house within the last month?"

"No, I don't remember any such visit."

"You were present with your wife and your daughter Laura."

"No, I still don't remember any such visit."

"Do you remember that Mrs. Grant answered the door and ushered the three of you into the sitting room?"

Landers looked uncomfortable, but still shook his head no.

"Mr. Landers, I have Mrs. Grant under subpoena.

I can have her here in an hour. I understand she has a keen memory of those who come to visit her tenants, particularly those in the last month and particularly those as well-known as you are. I ask you again; in the last month, did you, along with your wife and daughter, visit Peter Mason?"

Sinclair resisted the urge to let fly with a curse word. He had gone over that meeting with Landers several times in great detail and he had been satisfied that Landers could handle cross-examination on that meeting without much difficulty. It was planned that Landers would say how he had seen great potential in Peter; that long before any of the Klan accusations surfaced, he had contemplated discussing with Peter how he could help him achieve that potential; and that the only reason for the meeting was to explain to Peter that nothing about the Klan accusations altered Landers's views as to Peter's potential and the ongoing fact that he wanted to help Peter. Sinclair believed that such an approach, which seemed marginally plausible and even, arguably, had the smallest scintilla of truth, could possibly diffuse any jury thoughts of bribery. Now Landers had forgotten everything they had discussed and had not only mishandled the cross-examination on the meeting but had denied it had ever happened.

Landers attempted to recover. "I do remember the meeting. My apologies, I had a busy day that day and for a moment that meeting skipped my memory. I don't remember thinking it was of much importance." His lame explanation was a long way short of being enough or even remotely persuasive.

Being the experienced, skilled and successful trial lawyer that he was, Sinclair was able, with enormous effort, to convey an outward calm and relaxed manner, but inwardly he was seething. He knew that his witness was coming apart despite all of his preparation sessions. Men of importance, used to being in command and used to giving, rather than obeying, instructions were frequently the worst and least manageable witnesses. Landers was certainly proving that age-old adage.

"Before the meeting with Mr. Mason at Mrs. Grant's, you had heard that Mr. Mason was claiming that it was your son who was involved in the killing of Jerome Washington, is that correct?"

"Yes, I had heard that."

"And it was your intention in going to that meeting to try to talk Mr. Mason out of that contention, right?"

"No. I just went to find out what the facts were."

"I'm sure you know that Mrs. Grant has a reputation for being, shall we say, curious about things. I have a belief that she heard what went on in that meeting. Do I need to call her to give us a, perhaps, more objective account of that conversation?"

A few suppressed giggles were heard from the jury box. Judge Carson had a hard time resisting the temptation to join in. Even Broderick stifled a smile since he had no idea whether Mrs. Grant had heard one word of the conversation.

"Well, I did try to reason with him."

"So when you told him that you could get him an even better job than the one he had at the Mitchell Company and that you could make him a rich man, you certainly weren't trying to bribe him, or were you?"

"Of course I wasn't trying to bribe him." Landers bristled at the question and his face flushed with color.

"You thought then that Peter Mason was a fine fellow, fully deserving of your trust and confidence and fully deserving of your getting him a great job and making him a rich man, having absolutely nothing to do with his future testimony in this case. Is that what you are telling this jury?"

"Well, yes," said Landers, with some hesitation.

"You told the jury during your direct examination that you had the belief that Mr. Mason had stolen money from you and had molested your daughter."

"Yes."

"You formulated that belief, assuming that you did, before your conversation with Mr. Mason at Mrs. Grant's house, right?"

"I don't really remember, but maybe I did."

"Isn't it absolutely clear, Mr. Landers, that you would not have made the generous offers to Peter Mason of a great new job and future prosperity if you thought, for even one second, that there was the slightest chance that he had stolen money from you or that he had molested your daughter?"

"Well, a boy can mend his ways, can't he?" Landers said belligerently, but also lamely.

"Come on Mr. Landers. Be serious! You would never, never offer those things you offered Peter, to a thief and a molester of your daughter, now would you?"

"Probably not."

"Don't you mean 'definitely not?'"

"Yes, definitely not."

"Now you can leave."

Sinclair had no redirect. Unlike Broderick's decision not to redirect Peter, since Peter had not been damaged on cross, Sinclair's decision was based on his belief that he could only make a very bad situation even worse by his further questioning of Landers.

Given Mr. Landers's barely hidden attempt to bribe him, it didn't surprise Peter that he would lie about the conversation at Mrs. Grant's. What did surprise him was how clumsily Landers had gone about it.

THE TRIAL OF GLENN LANDERS
— THE DEFENSE CASE — PART TWO

"Walter, how long are you going to let this nonsense go on?" Broderick asked. The lawyers were in chambers with Judge Carson at the request of Broderick.

"What are you talking about, Roy?"

"All we're hearing from the defense is a lot of baloney about young Mason having supposedly stolen money from the Landers and having supposedly roughed up the daughter. It's a smoke screen. Even if any of that were true, which it isn't, it would still be totally irrelevant. What does it have to do with whether Glenn Landers is a Klansman, or whether he was present on the night of the hanging and whether he participated in what went on that night? You should have sustained my objections to all of this nonsense at the outset. If Byron can offer proof that some other six-foot male broke his right foot, had a cast on it that Mason signed and was the person who pushed Washington off the stool, let's have it. Otherwise, make him rest."

"He's got a point, Byron," said Carson. "I'll let you try your own case. I know you're one of the best, as is Roy, but I must say I didn't see that anything Mr. Landers had to say was of much help to you. If you want to pursue these peripheral issues, I won't stop you. Let's get the jury."

Laura Landers made a most attractive picture on the stand. She was demurely dressed in a light-pink dress that was buttoned to the neck. She gave her testimony in a quiet, yet somewhat nervous manner, and she paused frequently to take sips of water. She displayed none of the aggressive, flirtatious speech patterns or mannerisms that Peter had seen. She testified that she had first met Peter at her father's estate and that he had aggressively pursued her almost immediately. She said that she constantly tried to dissuade him, but that seemed to make him even more aggressive. When he would find her alone, he would make suggestive remarks, touch her inappropriately and, on one occasion, tried to pull down her shorts. He repeatedly tried to kiss her and she had to fight him off. On another occasion, he came up behind her, reached around and grabbed her breast, pressing so hard that it hurt. By the time Sinclair had finished his examination, Laura had successfully painted a picture of a boorish, crude sexual predator who had stopped just short of attempted rape.

Broderick's first question on cross-examination was, "Miss Landers you do realize that you are testifying in this courtroom under oath, do you not?"

Sinclair objected on the grounds that Broderick

was trying to intimidate her, but Carson overruled the objection.

"Yes," she answered.

"The penalties for perjury in this state are very severe. Did you know that?"

"Yes."

"I don't mean to embarrass you, but given your answers to Mr. Sinclair's questions, I must get into certain delicate areas. Before meeting Mr. Mason you had sexual relations with a number of boys. Is that right?"

She blushed deeply and in a very low voice that was almost inaudible, she said, "Yes."

The judge told her in a kindly tone that she would have to keep her voice up.

"Did you ever get into bed with Mr. Mason, while he was asleep and while you were naked and without being invited to do so by Mr. Mason?"

She hesitated, then shook her head no.

"Are you saying 'no' that didn't happen?"

"It didn't happen."

"Do you deny having voluntary sexual relations with Mr. Mason?"

"Yes, I deny it."

"You never told your parents or Glenn that Mr. Mason had been molesting you, did you?"

"No, I was too embarrassed."

"You never told anyone that Mr. Mason had molested you, right?

"No I never did."

"You were here when your father claimed that Mr. Mason had molested you. Correct?"

"Yes"

"That must have come as a big shock to you since you never told him that, and if it had happened you would be the only one who could have told him, right?"

"I don't know. I suppose so."

"On the number of occasions that Mr. Mason spent weekends at your parents' estate you were alone with him a lot, going for walks, fishing, and riding horses. Is that right?"

"Yes."

"And all those walks, rides etc. were at your invitation, right?"

"Sometimes."

That ended Broderick's cross.

Sinclair asked one question on re-direct.

"Has anything Mr. Broderick asked you changed in any way your testimony that Mr. Mason repeatedly and uninvitingly touched you inappropriately and molested you?"

Broderick interrupted, "Surely that is for the jury to determine."

The judge said, "I'll allow it."

"No, none of his browbeating has changed my testimony."

Peter was not surprised, much less shocked, by Laura's testimony since it was inconceivable that Laura would deny being molested by Peter after her father had testified that she was. Of course, if Laura was too embarrassed to tell her parents or Glenn that she had been molested, how could Mr. Landers know that she had been, as he had testified?

What Peter had not seen was the barely perceptible frown that appeared on Sinclair's face when Laura denied telling her father that Peter had molested her. Earlier she had told Sinclair that she had told her father. The testimony of both Laura and her father demonstrated that consistency is much more difficult when the truth is not being told.

THE TESTIMONY OF GLENN LANDERS

GLENN LANDERS'S father had told Sinclair that he could wheel up as many alibi witnesses as were necessary, and they would say whatever Sinclair believed would be most helpful in securing an acquittal. At Landers's request, they would testify that Glenn had been with one or more of them miles away from the scene of the lynching and at the critical times. They would place that meeting at a location that would preclude any contrary evidence from potential eyewitnesses.

Sinclair had cut quite a few corners during his distinguished career, but he drew a very sharp line at putting on false witnesses who were prepared to perjure themselves. The testimony of Mr. Landers about the meeting at Mrs. Grant's would have been very close to Sinclair's self-imposed line and probably, at least marginally, over it. Sinclair seriously doubted the truthfulness of Landers's claims that young Mason had stolen money from the Landerses or had molested Laura. However, those things could have happened and Sinclair could not be criticized for putting on that evidence. The "alibi evidence" was something entirely different. It was way, way over the line, and was completely out of the question. However, Landers continued to insist that Sinclair do what Landers wanted, urging that his son's life was at stake. He even offered to double Sinclair's fee, which was already enormous, if he would go along.

"Byron, my son's life is at stake. I'll do anything to get him off. You have to do whatever it takes, and I do mean, whatever it takes," pleaded Landers.

"I'll do things for clients that can take me right up to the line and, once in a while, a little bit across the line, but what I won't do for any client, your son or anyone else, is I won't do time in jail and I won't jeopardize my license to practice. Knowingly presenting false, perjured evidence is a felony resulting in years in jail. No way will I get involved in that. You can go get another lawyer if you want. You won't hurt my feelings. Maybe, just maybe, there's some marginal lawyer out there barely scraping a living who would be desperate enough to do what you want, but not me."

"I'll triple your fee. If that's not good enough, name your own number."

"You can give me every nickel you have and everything else you own down to the clothes you're wearing and I won't do it."

Reluctantly, Landers agreed to continue with Sinclair, but with no alibi witnesses. Glenn Landers took the stand dressed in a blue blazer with his school's emblem on the pocket, a white shirt, a striped tie, light-grey pants and one white buck shoe on the unbroken foot. He looked like a fresh-faced university graduate student, which is exactly what Sinclair had planned. Although the senior Landers had testified to Glenn's achievements in high school, college and in the work place, Sinclair went methodically over the same background, only in greater detail. He covered the fact that Glenn had spent a summer as an unpaid volunteer with the county probation department, working with delinquent teenagers. He explored Glenn's relationship with Peter Mason; how he had befriended the young foreigner; obtained jobs for him and had him spend weekends at the family estate. He had Glenn explain how he had broken his foot; how that prevented him from driving and how he had loaned his car to Peter, who had only recently learned to drive.

Sinclair then moved into the central issues. Glenn denied ever having been a Klansman or ever having gone to a Klan meeting. On the night in question, a fellow worker had given him a ride home. Since he couldn't drive, he stayed home all evening reading and went to bed early. On being asked how Mason could have seen a Klansman wearing a cast on his foot with the word "limey" on it, Glenn said he had to be mistaken; that the understandable terror must have badly affected him and caused him to imagine things.

As Broderick got up to start his cross-examination, several jurors moved forward on their chairs in anticipation of what they thought was very likely to be a high point of the trial. They would not be disappointed.

"Mr. Landers, you, of course, recall the other day when we were all out in that field re-creating the night Jerome Washington was hanged and Peter Mason was beaten?"

"Yes, I remember that."

"Do you also remember I asked that the cars be moved forward to re-create where they had been on the night of the hanging?"

"Yes."

"When the cars had moved forward, do you remember that you jumped to your feet and said, 'That's not—' and then Mr. Sinclair silenced you and pulled you back in your seat?"

"I don't remember those exact words."

Juror number seven, a florid-faced, heavyset man wearing a red and white work shirt and farm overalls suddenly spoke up. "Those *are* the two words. I wrote them down in my notes."

There was a buzz around the courtroom. Judge Carson said, "I would ask the jurors not to say anything while the proceedings are going on in court. If you have a question or comment, please write it down and give it to the bailiff." Broderick looked quickly at his notes taken during the voir dire examination. He saw that juror number seven was Billy Joe Anderson who farmed a few acres in a rural area north of Jackson. He had a ninth-grade education, did not seem too bright during juror examination, and seemed to react very positively to questions asked of him by Sinclair. He had not been one of Broderick's favorites. In fact, Broderick had come within a whisker of exercising a peremptory challenge on him. He couldn't remember specifically why he hadn't done so, but he was now pleased with his decision.

Broderick smiled at the juror and went on. "Weren't you about to say that I had placed the cars too close to where Mr. Washington was hung?"

"No, I wasn't going to say that. How would I know where the cars were on that night? I wasn't there."

"Because you *were* there the night Mr. Washington was hung, and you knew that I had placed the cars too close, and you were afraid that the wrong placement of the cars would put too much light on the cast and make it easier to read. Isn't that so?"

"No, it isn't so. I've told you. I was not there."

"Mr. Landers, this case has been going on for some time now, and you've been here every day. That was the only time you said something in open court other than when you were on the stand testifying. Is that right?"

"I don't know, maybe."

"What was so important about my positioning of the cars that made you jump up and start to say something?"

"I don't know."

"What was it you were about to say before Mr. Sinclair stopped you?"

"I don't remember. It couldn't have been anything important or I'd remember. It didn't have anything to do with where the cars were. I wasn't there. How many times do I have to say that?"

"You were there."

"No I wasn't."

"All right Mr. Broderick, we've heard enough about that. You've made your point. Move on to something else," said the judge.

Both Broderick and Peter noticed with some measure of satisfaction that most of the jurors were writing furiously in their notebooks.

"Do you remember a car ride from your family's estate with Mr. Mason when he asked you how a person could tell whether he was in love?"

"Yes."

"Did you give him an explanation of what you thought about that subject?"

"Well I did my best because I'm not sure how you make that determination."

"Did he, during that ride, tell you that he thought he was in love with a girl named Christine Broward who lived on Randolph Street?"

"Yes he did, but he corrected himself when I told him Randolph Street was in the Negro part of town. He then told me the name of another street that I've forgotten, but it was in a white part of town."

"Interesting that you remember the name of Randolph Street in the Negro area, but not the name of the other street in the white area. That's because you wanted to remember Randolph Street because you intended to tell your Klan buddies that Mr. Mason was in love with a Negro girl, isn't that right?"

"No it isn't right."

"What did you say to him about his changing the name of the street where the girl lived?"

"I didn't say anything that I can recall. I didn't find it unusual that he would fall in love and, with his correction of the address, I knew it had to be a white girl. He hasn't lived in Jackson for very long and I didn't find it the least bit strange that he, a newcomer, would confuse the names of streets."

"Did you tell Mr. Mason that it was dangerous for him to date a Negro woman?"

"Why would I? I thought he was dating a white girl."

"After he told you that he was dating a girl named Christine Broward on Randolph Street, you checked and found out that there was a Negro family named Broward, with a daughter named Christine living on Randolph Street, didn't you?"

"Why would I do that?"

"Because you're a Klansman. After you discovered Christine Broward was a Negro, you informed the Klan that Peter Mason was dating a Negro girl, didn't you?"

"Objection, Your Honor. The witness said he didn't find out that the girl is a Negro and counsel is asking a question assuming he did find out. It assumes facts not in evidence."

Judge Carson recognized that the objection was probably sound but, like the jurors and everyone else in the courtroom, he was caught up in the intriguing story and wanted to hear more. He overruled the objection.

"Of course not. I don't know any Klan members and even if I did, I wouldn't tell them."

"Did you tell anybody at all that Peter Mason was dating a Negro girl?"

"No, I didn't know the girl he was dating was a Negro."

"Mr. Mason told you the name of the Negro girl he was seeing, didn't he?"

"He told me the name of the girl, but he didn't tell me she was a Negro."

"Did you tell Peter that Randolph Street was in 'Niggertown?'"

"No I wouldn't use the word 'nigger.'"

"Of course not," said Broderick sarcastically.

Broderick finished his cross-examination by confirming that there was no one who could corroborate his story of spending the whole evening and night of the killing in his room. Sinclair determined that Landers had handled himself as well as could be expected, given his outburst at the re-creation, his conversation about Mason being in love with a girl, initially said to live in a Negro area, and his inability to provide a corroborating witness. He decided that he would ask no further questions. The examination of Glenn Landers had consumed the entire day and adjournment was taken with Sinclair announcing he had one more witness.

THE SHRINK

DR. HANS GRUENER was a psychiatrist practicing in New Orleans. He had been born in Switzerland and had received his medical degree in that country. Later he moved to the United States, interned and did a four-year residency in psychiatry at the Wilson Hospital in Boston. He had written books and treatises on the short-term effects of severe mental trauma and had lectured at medical conventions on the subject. He was a neatly dressed little man with a greying goatee beard, perhaps in his late fifties or early sixties. He wore a polka dot bow tie and thick, gold rimmed glasses. He looked exactly like a character that Hollywood would cast in the role of a psychiatrist, even down to the slight German accent.

After describing his long list of impressive credentials, Dr. Gruener testified that his study revealed that persons experiencing episodes of terror and, particularly, legitimate fear of imminent death, frequently recall specific details of that experience inaccurately.

"It's not that they are deliberately lying. They may

well be convinced that they saw something that, in fact, was not there. It might, indeed, be rooted in their memory and they remember it as clearly as they remember what they had for breakfast an hour ago. But what they are certain they saw during moments of terror may very well not have been present."

Sinclair laid out for Dr. Gruener the facts of the friendship between Glenn Landers and Peter Mason, the signing of the cast on Landers's foot, the abduction of Mason by the Klan, the whipping, the hanging and Mason's admission that he was terrified and in fear of his life.

"Doctor, based on those facts do you have an opinion that Peter Mason's experience was of the type which, within the realm of medical probability, could lead to an honestly held, but mistaken, recollection of having seen something which, in fact, was not present?"

"It is precisely the type of situation that would, in many cases, lead to mistaken recollections. It's almost a textbook example. And if I might add something, I see that Mr. Mason is very young and young people without much life experience are more subject to this sort of incorrect recollection."

"Doctor, one last question: In your opinion is Mr. Mason's recollection of the cast and the writing a predictable, albeit honest, mistake?"

"Yes, again it is classic and I am quite sure that young Mr. Mason is certain that is what he saw, and he might be right I am not discounting that he might, indeed, have seen it. We are not dealing with absolute scientifically provable certainties. However, my opinion is that there is at least a probability and maybe a high probability that he didn't see it."

"Thank you Doctor. Your witness"

Broderick jumped right in. "What are you getting paid for testifying here today, Doctor?"

"My fee for today is $2,000."

There was some rolling of eyes and exchanges of glances from a number of the jurors. It would have taken each employed member of the jury in the neighborhood of six months to earn what this witness would earn in a few hours.

"In your practice, what do you charge your patients?"

"It works out roughly to $10 an hour."

"Doctor, I figure that you are going to complete your testimony here in less than two hours and for those two hours you will be receiving one hundred times as much as you would receive for treating a patient. Am I correct?

"Yes, but—"

"Never mind the 'but,'" Broderick interrupted. "And if you hadn't agreed to testify the way the defense wanted you to testify, you would have got nothing, right?"

"This is my honest opinion."

"Well, we will let the jury decide that. Would you agree, Doctor, that battle-hardened veterans in wartime, returning from reconnaissance missions, would be expected to report their sightings accurately during debriefing, despite the fact they had been under constant threat of imminent death and were very scared?"

"Yes, but your question presupposes that the soldiers had previously experienced highly dangerous situations and it would be expected that, although they were scared, they would not have the same episodes of mistaken recollection."

"So repeated exposures to potentially imminent death would immunize a person from making the kind of mistaken observations that you have described?"

"Not totally immunized, but greatly lessened."

"Doctor, were you aware the Peter Mason spent the entire war in London and experienced lengthy periods of bombing, and that he, himself, was wounded and had friends and neighbors who were killed and that he became used to the bombings, the terror and the deaths?"

"No, I didn't know that."

"Mr. Sinclair conveniently omitted to tell you that and therefore you didn't take that into account in coming to your opinion, did you?"

"No I didn't, but it wouldn't have changed my opinion."

"Why doesn't that surprise me?" said Broderick sarcastically. "Mr. Mason accurately described his abduction, the place where he was taken, the approximate number of Klansmen present, the number of cars, the position of the burning cross and the identity of the hanged man. Are you saying that the terror and fear of imminent death that Mr. Mason experienced did not affect the accuracy of all of those many details but only affected the one detail about the cast?"

"It is not infrequent that the terrified individual will only get one or two facts wrong."

"And, conveniently, you decided that he probably got the key fact wrong in this case; the fact that conclusively identifies as a murderer, the man who's paying you lots of money. Under your analysis, why did he accurately identify the murdered man as Jerome Washington? Why didn't he mistakenly believe it was Winston Churchill or Adolf Hitler he saw hanging there?"

The courtroom erupted in laughter. Judge Carson gaveled for silence and Sinclair objected to the question.

"I withdraw the question and I have nothing further."

On redirect, Sinclair got the doctor to say that Peter was not a combat veteran going through similar life-threatening events on a daily basis and what he experienced at the hands of the Klan was not remotely similar to what he had experienced in the war. He also testified that the observation of the cast was a unique shock because, unlike the other accurate observations, what he thought he saw on the foot of one of the Klansmen pointed to a friend and that created an entirely different sensation and distorted recollection. It was, he said, like a nightmare which is, of course, not real but causes one to wake up trembling and sure it was true. With this phenomenon, the belief that the nightmare is true does not fade.

Sinclair was satisfied that his redirect of Doctor Gruener, while not eliminating the impact of Broderick's very effective cross-examination, had at least minimized it. He was right, but only to a point.

Broderick had a couple of additional questions on re-cross-examination. "Doctor, you draw a distinction between Mr. Mason's experiences during the war and veteran soldiers' experiences in combat. Is that right?"

"Yes."

"The reason you draw that distinction is that Mr. Mason's war experiences were nothing like the experience he suffered the night of the Klan beating and murder. Is that also right?"

"Yes, his war experiences were not remotely similar."

"Assume for the sake of argument that Mr. Mason was a combat veteran of twenty-seven years of age rather than an eighteen-year-old veteran of the London Blitz, and that he had been subject to fear of imminent death on the frontline, would you still be of the view that he imagined seeing the cast with the word 'Limey' on it?"

"I would still believe that there was a strong possibility that he didn't see what he thought he saw because combat and the Klan hanging are so different and because of the friendship angle."

"I'm going to assume that there is no hypothetical situation that I could come up with that you wouldn't try to weasel out of, so I won't waste the court's and the jury's time with further questions along that line."

Sinclair started to explode, but Judge Carson beat him to it and told Broderick that he was way out of line.

Broderick apologized. "Do you believe that combat troops, even those who had been on the frontline for months, if not years, ever encountered a bunch of hooded and robed men, with a burning cross, hanging a man and beating a boy?"

"I don't know."

"You don't know?" Broderick asked sarcastically. "Do you entertain the possibility that the German high command had engaged the Ku Klux Klan to capture and hang Negro soldiers while wearing hoods and robes?"

The question was intentionally pointless, but it had the desired effect of causing the jurors to smile and snicker at Broderick's trivializing the doctor's opinion. Rather than saying that the question was senseless, which might have blunted, to some extent, the impact of the question, he merely denied any such knowledge. Neither counsel having any further questions of the doctor, he was excused.

THE FINAL WITNESS

Sɪɴᴄʟᴀɪʀ ᴀɴɴᴏᴜɴᴄᴇᴅ that the defense rested.

"Mr. Broderick, does the prosecution have any rebuttal witnesses?" asked the court.

"Just one, Your Honor; Mr. Mason."

Broderick had told Peter the issues he wanted to address. Peter was most hesitant to testify about Laura's contentions that he had molested her. He was embarrassed to reveal in open court that, before his initial sexual encounter with Laura, he was a virgin. Broderick reassured him. First, he said the prosecution could not leave her claim of molestation unchallenged. Second, he reminded Peter that many southerners were deeply religious and would feel that a boy of eighteen who was still a virgin was acting in a morally proper way. Broderick also wanted to re-review that conversation in the car when Peter told Landers about being in love.

Reluctantly, Peter was forced to tell the jury of his virginity and how he had lost it one night when he awoke to find a naked Laura Landers rubbing up against him in his bed. Broderick was right. The jury seemed sympathetic to his previous virginity, with the women jurors nodding seemingly with approval. He detailed Laura's sexual aggressiveness and how the two of them had intercourse in various places at her father's estate, sometimes in the open. On cross-examination he would concede, to snickers from the jury and the audience, that he had not exactly fought her off.

He next testified that he had not stolen any money from the Landerses and the first he knew of any such contention was when Mr. Landers so testified. Significantly, Mr. Landers had not raised that accusation until Peter let it be known at that meeting that he was not wavering on his contention that he saw Glenn Landers at the hanging. Also significantly, Sinclair did not see fit to cross-examine on this point.

Finally, Broderick got to the issue of who, other than Glenn Landers, could possibly have known of Peter seeing Christine Broward. "On the ride from Mr. Landers's estate did you tell Glenn Landers the name of the girl you thought you were in love with?"

Sinclair objected. "Your Honor, we've been over all this. Counsel is just plowing the same ground again."

"Overruled. You may answer."

"Yes. I told him it was Christine Broward."

"Are you sure of that?"

"Absolutely sure. I even remember Glenn saying it was a very nice name."

"At first did you tell Landers that Christine lived on Randolph Street?"

"Yes."

"What, if anything, did Landers say?"

"He said I must be mistaken because Randolph Street is in Niggertown."

"Are you sure he used the word 'nigger' and not 'Negro'?"

"I'm sure."

"What did you say then?"

"I told him I must have got the street name wrong."

"Did he tell you the names of several streets that sounded like Randolph?"

"Yes."

"Did you pick one?"

"I did."

"Why?"

"Because he's a damned liar," yelled Landers from his seat at defense counsel's table.

Broderick wheeled around, pointed at Landers and said in a loud voice, "You do like to blurt out things don't you? Maybe now you'd like to come up here and tell us what you were going to say about where the cars were improperly positioned when we were out at the Klan scene."

The judge was feverishly pounding his gavel. "Mr. Landers don't you interrupt again or you'll find yourself spending the night in jail. As for you Mr. Broderick, you know better. One more comment like that and you can spend the night in the next cell."

Broderick apologized, but he had seized the opportunity that Landers had given him and he had embellished in the jury's minds the incident at the re-creation. "Peter, why didn't you tell Mr. Landers the truth, that you were seeing a Negro girl?"

"I thought of doing that, but I decided not to."

"Why?"

"I felt that Glenn had some racial prejudices. He had used the term 'Niggertown.' He had called the maid at Mrs. Grant's a 'Nigra' and said nasty things about her and a bunch of other things. I just thought he would not like my seeing a Negro girl, although I never thought, until the night I saw him kill Washington, that he was a Klansman or would tell the Klan about me and Christine. I just never imagined that."

Peter had tried to persuade Broderick not to disclose Christine Broward's name to the jury. Broderick told him that the Klan obviously already knew about the Broward family and knew it was the Broward daughter, Christine, that Peter was dating. The Klan leader had used the name "Broward" in castigating Peter. The Klan mistakenly believed they were hanging Joshua Broward. Broderick told Peter that Glenn's knowledge of the name was important to complete the picture and would not reveal any information that was not already known.

"Did you make any efforts to hide the fact that you were seeing this Negro girl, and if so, how?"

"I would only go to her house at night and I am sure

no one saw me arriving or leaving the Broward house. The only close call was one night as I was coming out of the Negro area, I was stopped by some white boys who asked me what I was doing in the Negro area. I told them I had taken a wrong turn. I was well away from the Broward house when they saw me."

"Did you ever go with Christine to any public place, a restaurant or a movie for example, or walk down a street where anyone could see the two of you?"

"The only place we ever went away from the Broward house was the little park at the end of her street. We sat in a dark corner and nobody saw us there."

"Did you ever tell anyone, other than Mr. Landers, that you were seeing a Negro girl? Anyone at all?"

"No."

"So the only way the Klan could have known of your seeing Christine Broward is if Glenn Landers told them. Is that right?"

"Objection. Calls for speculation, without foundation and he's leading the witness."

"Sustained."

"No further questions."

Sinclair then went after Peter. "You can't swear to this jury that nobody other than the Browards saw you with Christine, can you?"

"No, but—" Peter began. Sinclair interrupted, "I didn't ask for an explanation. You can't swear that Christine didn't brag to her friends that she was dating whitey, can you?"

"She wouldn't do that."

"You can't swear to this jury that Mr. or Mrs. Broward didn't tell anybody, can you?"

"No, but I'm sure they didn't."

"In this town, a white boy dating a Negro girl doesn't go unnoticed for long. Did you know that?"

"Objection. Lacks foundation."

"Sustained."

"You told Glenn Landers that Christine Broward lived on Randolph Street and when he said you must be mistaken, you lied to him and said she lived on Randal Way in a white neighborhood, correct?"

"Yes."

"You did it to protect the Negro family, correct?"

"Yes."

"And when the white boys saw you coming out of a Negro area, you told them you were new to the area and you had gotten lost, correct? And that was a lie too?"

"Yes."

"I won't go back over the lies you told about having been treated in Washington, DC instead of at Froman here in Jackson. We've already covered that and I'm sure the jury remembers all of that. You do quite a bit of lying whenever it suits your purpose, don't you?"

"No."

"This jury will have a hard time telling when you're telling the truth and when you're lying, won't they?"

"No they won't. I'm not lying about the murder and the beating."

"We only have your word for that—the word of a proven liar. That's all, Your Honor."

Momentarily, Broderick considered asking Peter further questions to emphasize that the lies were intended to protect innocent people, Dr. James and the Browards. However he quickly decided against it because emphasizing the reasons for the lies would re-emphasize that they were lies.

That ended the presentation of evidence and the court ordered the jury to return the following morning, at which time counsel would present their final arguments, the court would instruct the jury in the applicable law, and then the case and the fate of Glenn Landers would be placed in the hands of the jury.

That night, as was true on the eve of opening statements and before each subsequent day of trial, the two lead lawyers spent solitary hours preparing for the next day. Similar to all previous nights, they each left their offices very late and each left the floor covered with discarded and crumpled ideas.

THE CASE GOES TO THE JURY

THERE HAD BEEN reporters from local newspapers present during the entire trial. Their stories appeared daily. Mrs. Grant had taken to leaving copies of the papers under Peter's door. She later explained that she had never previously known anyone who got their names and pictures on the front page. The question of the guilt or innocence of Glenn Landers, while covered extensively, seemed of secondary interest to the reporters. Headlines read, "White Boy's Secret Romance" and "The Hidden Love Story." One story was simply headed, "Forbidden Fruit." Reporters were continually waiting for Peter outside Mrs. Grant's and the courthouse. They asked him the same questions repeatedly: how did he feel, did he still love the Negro, were they going to get married, on and on. Peter smiled, and said nothing. The photographers took enough pictures of him coming and going to fill several albums. They were constantly sticking their cameras in Peter's face, momentarily blinding him with the flashes.

On the day closing arguments, instructions and

submission of the case to the jury were scheduled to occur, representatives of national wire services and a reporter from an English newspaper were present. The English reporter wanted to interview Peter, but Broderick told him that such an interview would have to wait until the verdict was rendered.

The closing arguments were surprisingly brief. Broderick explained to Peter that toward the end of a fairly long trial, the attention span of the jury characteristically gets shorter and shorter. Even with a high-profile case like this one and even with top-notch lawyers, the interest of the jurors falters. They are ready to go home or back to work and they become restless and irritable. Long drawn-out arguments become tiresome and counterproductive.

Because of the crush of people in the courtroom, Peter found himself sitting next to Laura Landers, a position that both of them found uncomfortable. The spectator benches were hard. After some time, Peter moved in such a way as to inadvertently come in contact with Laura's thigh. She made a loud commotion and insisted that the man sitting on the other side of her change places. If her conduct was intended to attract the attention of the jury and to make them think Peter had deliberately touched her, it failed. The arguments were well along and none of the jurors saw what she had done.

The arguments were predictable. Although relatively brief, they covered everything in short order. Both counsel had prepared several charts itemizing the issues that they found significant and showing how the evidence supported their side of the case. During the arguments, both counsel made liberal use of the Court's instructions to the jury as to the applicable law. Sinclair pushed hard on the requirement that guilt be found beyond a reasonable doubt and urged that various items of evidence, in his view, either demonstrated categorically that Landers was in no way involved in the hanging and beating, or at least established reasonable doubt. Broderick argued that the evidence established without any doubt that Landers *was* involved and alternatively, if there was any doubt, it had to be reasonable and not irrational.

Since the prosecutor had the burden, Broderick got the first and last arguments. Broderick made much of the cast and the word "Limey" written on it. He appealed to different senses. He wrote on the board, and he dramatically went down on his knees and pointed to the word "Limey" on Landers's cast, which was sticking out from under counsel's table. He also confronted the white boy-Negro girl issue directly.

He told the jury, "Some of you may not like that. I understand. Quite honestly I don't much like that myself, but it's their choice; their business. Peter is English. Some of you have ancestors that came over from England. He's new to this country and to Mississippi and is just learning how things are done here. No matter what, you don't kill a Negro because his daughter had a friendship with a white man, even if it was the right Negro. The law doesn't allow it. God doesn't allow it and you can't allow it. You can't beat a young white boy within an inch of his life because of his friendship with a Negro girl. The law doesn't allow it. God doesn't allow it and you can't allow it. The judge is going to read you the law after Mr. Sinclair and I are finished. Listen closely. Listen real closely, because you'll hear that Judge Carson here doesn't allow it either."

Sinclair's emphasis was that Glenn Landers was a great young man who had done great things in the community, had befriended this young foreigner, did not have a racist bone in his body and was totally incapable of the crimes of which he stood accused. He missed no opportunity to remind the jury that no contention was made that Landers had beaten Mason and to remind the jury that, while Landers had nothing to do with the killing, Washington was a no-good criminal. He spent little time on the molesting and stealing contentions, obviously recognizing their weakness and the seeming lack of jury interest in them.

Judge Carson then read a long litany of legal instructions. He had been on the bench for many years and had read these same, or similar, instructions numerous times. He read them fast and in a monotone, such that Peter wondered how a juror with no legal training could follow them at all. The jury was then asked to retire to consider their verdict and told that their first order of business when they got into the jury room was to select a foreman and then they could go home for the night. When they briefly returned to the courtroom before leaving for home, juror number seven, Billy Joe Anderson, told the judge, in answer to his question, that he had been selected foreman. Several days earlier Broderick would have been distressed by that news. Now he was delighted. He mused to himself that on such thin threads do likes and dislikes appear and disappear in trial and on such thin threads are cases decided.

The judge told Sinclair and Broderick that they could return to their offices and his clerk would call them if the jury had questions and when the jury had a verdict. He said they would have fifteen minutes from the time they got the call to be in the courtroom. Broderick told Peter he was free to do whatever he wanted. He could wait in the courtroom, in the DA's office or wherever he liked. Broderick would send somebody to get him if he left word where he would be. Broderick told him this was now the time that most trial lawyers hate—the wait for the verdict.

THE BOARDING HOUSE LUNCH

IT WAS NO LONGER required that Peter be present for any developments emanating from the jury, including, but not limited to, the verdict. Peter was going to return to work but Broderick, aware of his keen interest, told the warehouse manager to send Peter back to the court when he received a call indicating Peter's presence was requested. At the warehouse, the Negro team that worked for him unloading the boxcars was obviously pleased to see him, but all stayed away from discussing the trial with him. Peter was glad to get back to work. Even though there was the tension of the awaited verdict, which pressed on him, being able to occupy himself with matters unrelated to the trial was a relief.

There was no eating establishment, restaurant or boarding house in close proximity to the warehouse that catered to Negroes. The Negro employees brought their own lunches and gathered to eat, talk and laugh on the platform. The white warehouse employees most often ate at Mrs. Potts's boarding house which was only 150 yards from the warehouse. There were many strange and, to Peter, unusual aspects of life in the American South. One of them was the food. At Mrs. Potts's establishment, the workers sat around a very large, round communal table and plates of different kinds of food were passed from person to person. The plates contained such items as hog jowls, collard greens and sweet potatoes, all of which, until recently, were completely foreign to Peter. While he had become somewhat inured to the different tastes, he would have much preferred a plate of bangers and mash.

The day after the jury retired was the first time Peter had been back to Mrs. Potts's place since the trial began. As was customary, a group of the white warehouse employees walked together to the boarding house. On the way the employees didn't mention the trial although they didn't seem as pleased to see Peter as had been the case with his team. Peter was uneasy and tried to break the ice somewhat by making a few innocuous remarks about how it looked like rain and how hungry he was. One fellow said he thought it wouldn't rain until the evening, another said that Mrs. Potts had baked strawberry pies for dessert and that was his favorite. They took their seats around the table as two of Mrs. Potts's assistants starting bringing huge plates of steaming food to the hungry men. Suddenly, Mrs. Potts, with dyed red hair pulled back in a bun and wearing a green apron, came storming into the room.

"You get outta here!" she screamed, pointing at Peter. "I ain't gonna have no nigger lover in my place. Nobody dating some nigger bitch is gonna eat here. Go on, git!"

The room had been filled with a cacophony of several different conversations interspersed with gusts of laughter. All of a sudden everything went quiet. Peter pushed his chair back, got up without a word and started to leave. Randy Crenshaw, one of the supervisors on the loading dock, grabbed his arm.

"C'mon Mother Potts," he said in a conciliatory tone. "Peter didn't know no better. He's just a young boy and he's new to this country. I bet if you and me were to go to his country, we wouldn't know about a lot of their ways either. Let him stay."

"No. I want him outta here and I don't want him ever to come back," she retorted.

"Well, I'm out of here too," said Crenshaw. "He's our workmate and if he can't eat here, neither can I." Crenshaw pushed back his chair and got up. "What about the rest of you Mitchell Company guys? We can always go down to Wanstead's, it's right down the street and they got good food."

"It's all right, Randy," said Peter. "I'll leave. You don't have to."

"It's not all right," replied Crenshaw. "You coming or not?" he said to the others.

The other five warehouse employees started to get to their feet, somewhat reluctantly. Mrs. Potts mentally calculated the ongoing loss of revenue from the Mitchell Company employees abandoning her establishment. That seriously adverse financial impact seemed to result in a sudden liberalizing of her thinking.

"All right," she said grudgingly. "If you and the others want someone like him eating with you, he can stay." And she stalked out.

On the way back to the warehouse, Crenshaw pulled Peter aside. "Don't think for one moment we took your side because we like what you done. We don't. But you're young and new and, for good or bad, you are one of us. But if you do what you done with that girl again and the Klan string you up, ain't none of us gonna shed any tears for you. None of us will go to any funeral services for you like you done for that no good nigger."

THE JURORS' QUESTION

THE JURY had been out for four days and nothing had been heard from them. During deliberations, the courtroom staff heard no sound coming from the jury room; no raised voices, no clamor of any kind. When they came out for lunch or to go home at night, lawyers for both sides were present, trying to discern any sign of anything: a smile, a nod, averting of eyes, indications of anger, anything … but nothing at all was discernible. Peter went to work and went home. His days there were uneventful. Lunch at Mrs. Potts's resumed with their noisy conversations, laughter and Mrs. Potts scurrying around chatting with the men while pointedly ignoring Peter.

Peter's nights remained much the same. He still picked up his dinner and ate it in his room. He still did not sleep well and still had nightmares. He thought a lot about the startling similarities between his shipboard friend Chuck Bradley and Glenn Landers. They were both college graduates and approximately the same age. They were both tall and lean and they had both befriended him and offered advice. There were also startling dissimilarities. Chuck was a Yankee, and, while racism was prevalent in the North, it was of a lesser degree. Chuck was not encumbered by the pressures and prejudices of the Southerner, Glenn. It was inconceivable that Chuck would have denounced him for loving a Negro, but then again Chuck was not living in that world.

Peter thought a lot about the night he had disclosed to Glenn his love for Christine Broward. He had intended to tell Glenn that Christine was a Negro. He had got as far as revealing her name and the street she lived on. He knew Glenn harbored prejudices against Negroes and he knew Glenn would not approve of the relationship. However, he had been certain that Glenn, his good friend, would not disclose his confidence and he just felt the need to tell someone. It was only when Glenn said "Niggertown" that Peter changed his mind and tried to back away from revealing Christine's color. It wasn't that Glenn's remark surprised him. It didn't. It was the timing and the way it was said. It was clear that the backing away did not work and that Glenn was not fooled.

On the fifth day of jury deliberations, the warehouse foreman came out on the platform at a little after 2 o'clock. "Peter, they want you down at the courthouse, pronto. You'd better hurry. I'm two supervisors short today and I can't spare anyone to come out here." Then, "Dave," he yelled to the man on Peter's team who had taught him to drive. "You know how to read and write, don't you?"

"Yes sir, boss," responded Dave.

"Take Mr. Mason's clipboard and continue checking in boxes off that freight car and get it right, do you hear?"

"Yes sir, boss."

Foster told Peter to get back in a hurry and re-check what had been taken off in his absence.

The courtroom was surprisingly crowded when Peter got there. Word had gotten around that the jury had a question and, after four days of silence, that was big news. They'd had a lot of time to review the evidence and a question at this point was certain to be significant. Judge Carson took the bench. He held a piece of paper in his hand. "This is the jury question, gentlemen 'We would like to have read back the testimony of Peter Mason, starting with the time he was taken by the KKK until they dropped him off at his house. Signed: Billy Joe Anderson, Foreman.'"

Sinclair jumped up. "That includes both direct and cross-exam, right Judge?" he asked anxiously.

"To the extent that it relates to the events and the time period that the jury has asked about, the answer is yes," said Carson.

"And also Mr. Mason's testimony on rebuttal, Judge?"

"I don't recall that Mr. Mason's testimony on the rebuttal part covered anything that would relate to the jury's question, but we'll have the reporter go through the entire testimony of Mr. Mason and pinpoint everything that arguably could be pertinent to the question. Please do that, Elsie."

"It will take me a couple of hours, Judge," said the reporter.

"Shouldn't they also have Glenn Landers's testimony denying that he was at the Klan meeting?" asked Sinclair. "It's only fair to have both versions of that night."

"They haven't asked for any of Landers's testimony. I'm only going to give them what they asked for. When they ask for further testimony to be read, if ever, we'll decide what to do then," replied Carson. He added, "We'll have the jury come back tomorrow at nine to hear the reading. I'll let them go home now."

Peter didn't come back the next morning for the reading. Broderick explained that it would simply be a reading of what had been testified to. Nobody could ask the jury anything and the jury would not be permitted to speak, except to confirm that what had been read was what they wanted.

The lawyers watched the jury very carefully as the testimony was read to see if they could determine what they were thinking from their facial expressions at various times, their body language, any nods, smiles or knowing looks. They also watched to see if any jurors wrote anything in their notebooks. If either of the lawyers had detected anything by the time the reading was over, they didn't tell each other. When the reading was finished, the foreman confirmed that what had been read was what they wanted and they again retired.

The wait went on.

THE FIRST BOMBSHELL

FOUR MORE DAYS passed. What had been a completely quiet jury room changed. The courtroom staff could hear raised voices. While they could not hear what was said, they could hear angry exchanges. When they came out for lunch or to go home, many of the jurors look flustered and some exchanged glares with one another.

Meanwhile, Peter's days at the warehouse continued without incident. He still lunched at Mrs. Potts's and she even asked him once, perhaps in a moment of forgetfulness, if he wanted more lemonade.

He wrote a number of letters to Christine, never mentioning the trial, and he got a number of sweet and loving letters in return. He read them over and over again and saved every one of them. He mentally revisited the times he had spent with Christine. While Peter found her to be self-confident and unafraid to express her thoughts—even quite forcefully at times—there was also a gentleness and vulnerability that made him want to protect her. He remembered how she smiled a lot and laughed, but there was also a sadness in her face. One part of her most recent letter tore at his heart and made him want to jump on a train or bus to Detroit.

"This is a great big town. There are so many people. The school I go to has a thousand students. I have gotten to know some of them and they seem very nice. I belong to some clubs on campus and, along with my class work, I'm very busy. I'm even on the softball team. But I'm so lonely. I never knew a person could be lonely with all these people around. There are a lot of bad things in Jackson, but it was my home since I was born and I miss my friends. But mostly I miss you. I thought that would fade over time, but it's gotten worse. A parting of one or two years didn't seem too terribly long when we talked about it, but now it seems like ages. Keep writing, and often."

Occasionally Peter would hear Glenn go into their mutual bathroom, but he didn't see or speak to him. Mr. Broderick had told him that it was most unusual for a person charged with first-degree murder to be free on bond particularly when there was an additional charge of aggravated assault on a second victim, but the judge had required that a very substantial amount of money be posted and had announced that he did not believe Glenn was a flight risk.

On the ninth day of deliberation, Mr. Foster again came out to the platform and again told Peter that he was wanted in court. This time Bert, the supervisor of one of the loading docks, filled in for him. Peter was almost as nervous as when he was testifying. He was so wrapped up in thinking of things that might be about to happen that he was oblivious to his surroundings and walked three blocks past the courthouse until he realized where he was.

The courtroom was crowded and, inadvertently, Peter made eye contact with Glenn. Neither one said anything, although Glenn smiled in a way that more closely looked like a sneer. Mr. and Mrs. Landers and Laura were also present. They sat on the far side of the courtroom from Peter and made no effort to look at him. Peter figured that they all anticipated that the jury had a verdict, but in fact they didn't. What they had was another question.

Judge Carson took the bench and said, "Well gentlemen, this is one for the books. This is the question: 'May we find the defendant guilty as to one of the victims, but not the other?'" There was an uproar in the court. Despite their many years of experience and the numerous cases that they had tried, both lawyers appeared stunned. Glenn Landers turned pale and the two Landers women grabbed each other and sobbed.

"What does this mean, Judge?" blurted out Sinclair.

"For which of the two alleged crimes have they found guilt?" asked Broderick.

"Gentlemen, I know nothing more than you do. All I know is what is contained in the sixteen words of the question and it would not be proper to ask them for what, if any, finding they have made at this preliminary point. Despite appearances, they may not have found guilt as to either victim and may just be thrashing around."

Judge Carson sent the jury home early and told

them that he would have an answer to their question in the morning. The jury had four verdicts to consider. Was Landers guilty of the murder of Jerome Washington? Was Landers guilty of conspiracy to murder Jerome Washington? Was Landers guilty of the aggravated assault of Peter Mason? Was Landers guilty of conspiracy to commit aggravated assault on Peter Mason? It seemed inconceivable, and probably legally impossible, for Landers to have been present at the Klan meeting and therefore a party to what happened and be guilty as to one victim and not the other. Neither the judge nor either of the two experienced counsel had anticipated this complication. For obvious reasons, neither had made any attempt to separate out the two victims and argue that the jury could find guilt with respect to one victim but not the other. Broderick had presented a case that Landers was guilty of everything charged and Sinclair had presented a case that he was not guilty of anything.

The judge and the two lawyers met in chambers for hours, trying to resolve the unexpected dilemma. In the end the court either took the coward's way out or acted prudently, depending on one's point of view, and elected to tell the jury that they should continue to deliberate until they could finally decide all four counts.

Neither counsel was happy with the decision, which might, in fact, have demonstrated that it was the correct decision.

As they walked out of the courtroom, Peter asked Broderick what it all meant. "You could lose a lot of money betting on where a jury is headed," Broderick said. "As a guess, and it's only a guess, they might be thinking about convicting Landers for the beating and acquitting him for the murder."

"But how can that be? He wasn't the one who beat me, but he was the one who killed Washington."

"Logically and legally, if he's guilty of one he's guilty of both. It may be difficult for this jury to send a white person, who has been portrayed as a fine young man, to be executed for the murder of a no-'count Negro. It may be more palatable to send that fine young white man to jail for a few years for the beating of a fine young white boy. That's the best I can do. If you want logic and certainty, go be a mathematician, not a trial lawyer."

THE JURY RETURNS

MORE DAYS WENT BY, and on the twelfth day of deliberations, Mr. Foster again told Peter he was to report to the courtroom. Judge Carson looked more somber than usual.

"Gentlemen, I have another note from the foreman. It reads, 'We have not been able to come to a unanimous verdict on any of the charges, despite our best efforts.' I am going to call in the jury and find out whether further deliberations could help to break the deadlock."

The jury filed in, looking angry, tired and frustrated.

"Is there any possibility that, with more time, this jury could come to unanimous verdicts on any of the counts? We're in no particular hurry. You can have all the time y'all want. If the case has to be tried to a different jury, they're likely to have as many disagreements as all of you."

Billy Joe Anderson stood up. He looked very tired and disturbed. "Not a chance, Your Honor. We have gone over and over everything many times and we ain't never going to be able to agree on nothing. We tried. It's hopeless. Believe me it is. It ain't for want of trying sir. We tried and tried."

"Does anyone disagree with what the foreman said? Do any of you think a decision could be reached if you had some more time?" The judge asked. There were a few negative shakes of the head and no other response.

"Under the circumstances, I have no alternative but to declare a mistrial, which I now do. Counsel, we will have a hearing next Thursday at which time I will set a date for the retrial in the Matter of The State of Mississippi vs. Glenn Landers."

There was an audible sigh of relief from the Landers family, a smile on the lips of Byron Sinclair and a puzzled and grim look on the face of Roy Broderick.

"It will perhaps be instructive to the court and counsel, Mr. Foreman, if you tell us what the last vote was on each count," said Judge Carson.

The foreman looked at his notes. "We were 10-2 for conviction on both the aggravated assault and the conspiracy to commit aggravated assault on Peter Mason. We were 6-6 on both the first degree murder and conspiracy to commit first degree murder of Jerome Washington."

There were whispered conversations all over the courtroom. Judge Carson rapped his gavel for silence and then told the jury, "You are discharged with the thanks of the court for having performed your civic duty. I know that serving on a jury, particularly as lengthy as this matter was, is an imposition. Our thanks might have been somewhat more effusive if you had actually decided the case, but these things happen. You may talk to counsel if you wish, but you don't have to."

All of the jurors were not only willing to talk to counsel, they were obviously anxious to do so. They gathered around Broderick and Sinclair while Peter, Glenn, the Landers family and the press stood around the outside of the circle of jurors, straining to hear. A number of jurors expressed admiration for the performance of both lawyers; two even asked for their business cards. Several jurors were more talkative than the others. They said that they were very persuaded by the testimony of Peter Mason. They were convinced that he was telling the truth about what he saw at the Klan meeting. They paid no attention to the testimony of the psychiatrist, who most of them thought was talking nonsense. Broderick asked the logical question. "If you all believed Mr. Mason and thought the psychiatrist was not believable, why didn't you convict?"

All the jurors would say was that ten of them were prepared to convict, but they couldn't convince the other two. It was also enlightening to learn that the earlier question about whether they could convict on some counts, but not others, did not signal that they were prepared to convict Landers on anything. They never were. They never got closer than 10-2 on the counts involving Mason or 6-6 on the counts involving Washington.

While they hemmed and hawed about their reaction to Glenn Landers, all they would really say was that he seemed to be a nice boy from a fine family, but they had grave doubts as to whether he was telling the truth. As the jurors started to drift away, there was one last obvious question. How in the world could they be 10-2 to convict as to the attack on Peter, but only 6-6 as to the murder of Washington? At least ten of them believed Peter and he had testified that Landers had hung Washington and hadn't touched Peter. They mumbled a bit and whispered to each other, but gave no explanation for the seemingly glaring inconsistency. But as Broderick had previously told Peter, the explanation was obvious.

Broderick and Peter sat in the attorneys' conference room for some time. "They may well have persuaded the two holdouts to vote with the majority if the only crime charged was the assault on you, but there was Washington's murder to consider. Those two probably couldn't divorce the two crimes from each other, and they also probably were angry at your association with Christine Broward. Four of the ten who voted guilty on the assault, voted the other way on Washington. Why? Clearly on racist grounds. A white man being found guilty of beating a white boy is one thing. A white man being found guilty of murdering a Negro, particularly with the criminal record of Washington, is a whole different thing," Broderick said.

"This now makes less sense to me than when you were guessing what the jury was doing," said a puzzled Peter.

"Don't try to make a sense of it. I told you before that juries frequently make decisions on things that have absolutely nothing to do with the case. This is a prime example. I am sure that's true not only here in Mississippi, but throughout the courts of this country and probably in your country too, although maybe not often on racial grounds. But don't believe for one moment that there haven't been cases decided in other parts of this country on racial grounds. I'm quite sure there have. Don't worry, we'll get 'em next time."

As he walked out of the court, Peter was having difficulty coming to grips with what had just happened. He sat on the bench in the hall outside the room for quite some time. Several reporters came up to him, including the fellow from the English paper. They all wanted to know his reaction to the mistrial, whether he thought it was fair and what he thought would happen on the re-trial. Peter found the questions to be idiotic. They could figure out what he thought of the verdict and whether or not he believed it was fair, without asking, and how in the world would he know how the re-trial would come out. He said he was surprised at the mistrial and let it go.

The entire Landers family came out of the courtroom together and none of them looked at Peter. *At least they didn't gloat*, thought Peter.

Sinclair was the last to leave. He walked past Peter without a word, went about ten yards, turned around and came back. He put his hand on Peter's shoulder and said, "Peter, you're a nice kid. I like you. Want my advice?" Without waiting for a response, he continued. "Go back to England or at least get out of the South. This place isn't for you, boy. You'll never get used to the way people live here if you stayed here for a hundred years. I've watched you. I've listened to you. You've foolishly put yourself in harm's way a number of times. I don't think you've finished doing that. You don't belong here. That's not necessarily all bad."

"Are you telling me this because you want to get rid of me so I won't be around to testify against your client in the re-trial? You can forget that. I'm staying," Peter said angrily.

"You've got me wrong. I'm talking about what I think you should do *after* the re-trial, not before. Anyway, do whatever you want. It's no business of mine."

Peter had, in fact, been thinking of possibly going back to England. He had almost enough money, but he hadn't yet made up his mind. The pivotal issue was Christine. If it were possible, he loved her more deeply now than he had before she left. He desperately wanted to marry her and he would do nothing to hurt her. What would she think if he went home? Would she think he didn't really love her? Did it matter to her if they were separated by several thousand miles rather than several hundred? When the time came, he would stay or go depending solely on her reaction.

Peter sat on the bench long after everyone had gone, until a Negro carrying a bucket and mop came up to him. "Sir, they're closing up the courthouse. Don't you think you should leave? I gotta mop this floor and it'll get mighty slippery."

Peter smiled and left.

THE SECOND BOMBSHELL

Sɪɴᴄʟᴀɪʀ ʜᴀᴅ ᴍᴇᴛ with Broderick in an effort to get the district attorney to drop the prosecution against Landers and not re-try him.

"Roy, you could try this case a dozen times and you'd never get a conviction. You did a great job and the jury liked that kid, Mason. Hell, I like him. I made a mistake putting that goddam Swiss shrink on. I should have known better. He was a joke. I won't make that mistake again. Good God, I made more mistakes in this case than I've made in all the others I've tried. I won't make them again. I let that kid ramble on about his nightmares and all that shit. Next time we won't hear that or about him pissing in his pants. I screwed up about the marks on his back. I won't do that again and those marks will be pretty well healed by the next go round. All you can do is put on the same case you just did. What do you say, Roy? Will you drop it?"

"Not a chance."

"Dammit Roy, you've lived down here for your whole

life, but you're thinking like a Yankee. This is Mississippi, the Deep South. This is not Chicago. You will never get all twelve white Mississippi jurors to convict a white man of killing a Negro, particularly where the white man is the son of one of the most prominent citizens of this state, and the Negro is a no-good, long-time criminal piece of shit. I don't think you'd even be able to make it stick in Chicago or New York or anywhere else. "

"We'll get a conviction on all counts next time. Dammit, we got six votes on the murder and ten votes on the assault this time. We'll do better next time."

"You'll have nothing new. You'll just present the same case you presented last time. It didn't work then and it won't work next time. But if you want to waste your time and the county's money, be my guest."

The following Thursday, the matter came before Judge Carson for the scheduling of the re-trial. Sinclair tried again, this time asking the judge to dismiss the matter. Sinclair was no more successful with Judge Carson than he had been with Roy Broderick. The re-trial was set for a month later. Broderick told Peter he would get back to him in a couple of weeks so they could go over his prior testimony and prepare for the re-trial.

Peter got back into the routine of work. He had become quite friendly with Nick Sylvester, who worked in the dispatcher's office at the warehouse. Nick was in his mid-twenties, married, with a three-year-old daughter. Peter had been a guest for dinner at the Sylvester's house on two occasions. While Nick was a born and bred

Mississippian, Betty Sylvester was raised in Portland, Oregon. She had moved to Jackson with her parents when she was a teenager. Her father had taken a job in Jackson as an executive with the telephone company. While Betty had been in the South for some years, much longer than Peter, she still had some difficulty adjusting to Southern customs. She and Peter had long conversations about the differences both had experienced, although Betty conceded that Peter's adjustment had to be far more difficult than hers.

While Peter had not forgotten about the pending re-trial, it was far enough off that it had stopped being foremost on his mind; that is until Mr. Foster again came out to the platform two weeks before the re-trial and told him he was to be at the court the following day at 9:45 and was to meet Mr. Broderick in the third floor attorneys' conference room.

When Peter arrived the next morning, Mr. Broderick was not alone. The other man was introduced by Broderick as Alan Rasmussen. Mr. Rasmussen was a very distinguished, slim, silver-haired man, dressed immaculately in a grey striped suit, light-blue shirt and a red and blue tie. On being introduced to Peter, he stretched out his arm to shake hands and revealed an expensive gold wristwatch and gold cuff links. Broderick's clothes were never elegant, but on this day he looked more disheveled than usual. Although Broderick was quite a bit overweight, he looked drawn, haggard and miserable.

Rasmussen did the talking. "The district attorney

has agreed with the defendant, subject to approval of the court, to accept a plea to simple assault by Landers on you and to dismiss the other counts."

"I don't understand. Isn't the trial going ahead? Isn't Glenn going to be retried for the murder of Jerome Washington?"

"Not if the court approves. Again, subject to the court's approval we, I mean the district attorney, has agreed to a sentence of one year in the county jail to be suspended and one year's probation."

Peter paused and shook his head. "He's not going to jail, not even for an hour?"

"No he's not," said Rasmussen very matter-of-factly, without the slightest show of regret. "I'll see you in the courtroom, Roy," and he walked out without looking at Peter or saying good bye.

After he was gone, Broderick looked down at the floor for quite a while and finally said, "This was not my idea. I argued with him, the district attorney and others, and told them we could win it next time, but they were adamant."

"But why? Glenn killed poor old Washington. Never mind about me. I'm almost better and I'm fine. Washington stole a dead man's wallet, had it for a few minutes and got a year's probation. Glenn kills Washington and gets the same one-year probation. Who is Mr. Rasmussen and why is he so important?"

"It's not just Rasmussen. He's what's called a 'civic leader,' a wealthy local businessman who carries a lot of weight, but his views are shared by a lot of other 'civic leaders.' This case has had its critics. You and I have talked about this several times. I'll say it again, many people don't like prosecuting the son of a powerful man for the killing of a Negro petty criminal, particularly where the only witness that connects the defendant is a foreigner who was befriended by the defendant, who never saw anyone's face and has been dating a Negro girl. It's politics, pure and simple. This case is not looked on favorably by most of the influential people, not only in Jackson, but in other parts of the state. As far as Landers getting the same sentence as Washington got and for vastly different crimes, you must remember that Landers was never actually convicted of anything and Washington was. I'm sorry, Peter, but life is not always fair, as I know you've already found out."

"Why only one year, and that suspended? I thought you told me the penalty was five years for my beating."

"He was charged with aggravated assault. You were tied to a tree and whipped unmercifully and that was obviously planned in advance. He is being permitted to plead to simple assault. That's like a guy getting drunk in a bar, having an argument and punching someone in the face, breaking the other guy's nose. Spur of the moment stuff. Maximum one year for that."

"Then he is being convicted for something he didn't do and acquitted for something he did do. It would be like a man robbed another man and was allowed to plead guilty to speeding. What sense does any of this make?"

"It's called plea bargaining and it allows a court to get

rid of a questionable case and free up the judge's calendar. Sometimes it makes sense. In this case, in my view, it doesn't. This case was not questionable."

The courtroom again was swarming with the media. They had been alerted by Sinclair to a potentially dramatic development in the case. The Landers family members were all present. Judge Carson had been fully briefed on the proposed resolution.

"I am a bit surprised by the resolution that's been suggested," he said. "Absent the agreement of the district attorney, Mr. Rasmussen's support and the support of quite a number of other prominent citizens for this decision, I might have had some serious doubts about approving it. However, both sides are represented by extraordinarily talented and experienced counsel and Glenn Landers has no prior record and has displayed through the years a deep social consciousness. I therefore approve the plea bargain and resolution. Mr. Glenn Landers, please stand."

The court went through the procedures and ended up sentencing Landers to one year, suspended, with one year of probation. Judge Carson further stated that, at the end of the year of probation, and if Glenn Landers complied with the terms of probation, his conviction would be expunged and would have no further force or effect.

Peter was seething. *No prior record!* he thought. *How many murders is he allowed before he is officially a naughty boy? Deep social consciousness, my eye! Putting on a sheet and hood and hanging a man—where is the deep social consciousness? How could Judge Carson say all that and still keep a straight face?*

The Landers family were hugging each other, laughing and clapping Glenn on the back. Peter had to get out fast. It wouldn't have been very seemly for him to throw up all over Judge Carson's courtroom floor.

DETROIT — TWO

CHRISTINE had no illusions that a move to the North would bring an end to racial prejudice against her family, or that Detroit would turn out to be the "Promised Land." Outwardly, Detroit was very different than Jackson. It was much bigger, much noisier, much more crowded and much colder. When it came to segregation, there were differences and there were some similarities, as Uncle Henry had explained. There were no "Colored" or "Whites Only" signs on restrooms, restaurants or movie houses. There were no signs anywhere that Christine had seen that forbad entry or use of facilities to people of color, although quite a number of businesses enforced exclusion of Negroes. In truth, however, there were perhaps more similarities than differences; more subtle than in the Deep South, but there just the same.

Public elementary, junior high and high schools were segregated, as were most of the local colleges. A Negro lawyer friend of Christine's uncle told her that much segregation was what he called "de facto," meaning that it was not required by law, but it was observed, nonetheless. He told her that a United States Supreme Court decision had held that the races could be legally separated in schools provided that the facilities and level of education in both the white and Negro schools was comparable. It was known as the "Separate but Equal" doctrine, although any fair-minded person who had visited Negro and white schools would agree that they were separate, but in no way were they equal. There was a possible silver lining on the offing. The Negro lawyer told her that there was a case wending its way through the lower courts and that if it reached the Supreme Court, things might change.

Christine's first direct and personal confrontation with Northern prejudice occurred quite by accident and was surprisingly gentle. A couple of years earlier on her sixteenth birthday, her father had bought her a fountain pen. It was her prized possession. She was out of ink and she went for a walk to find a stationery store. She found one several blocks from her uncle's house. She went inside and started to look for the blue-black ink she preferred. The store seemed deserted and she walked up and down the aisles looking at various items and trying to find where the ink supply was kept.

A middle-aged, grey-haired sales lady came up to her, smiled, and said very softly. "I'm sorry dear, but this store doesn't serve coloreds." The sales lady then spoke even more softly and looked over her shoulder furtively as though she didn't want to be heard. "There are a number of white-owned stationery stores that *will* serve you, but I would recommend a Negro-owned store named Graham & Brent. When you go out of this store turn right, go three blocks and turn right again, you will find it in the middle of the block. I wouldn't be surprised if their prices were a bit lower than ours."

Later, Christine's aunt told her that a gracious rejection was unusual and most clerks in white-owned businesses that didn't serve Negroes would have been much less polite.

Christine's uncle, aunt and three children lived in a large area just east of the Detroit River that was exclusively Negro. The residential properties in the white areas contained racial deed restrictions prohibiting sale, rental or any occupation by Negroes, Asians and a variety of other "undesirables." However, dogs, cats, goats and pigs were welcome. In 1948, the United States Supreme Court had invalidated such restrictions. In the early fifties, that case was essentially ignored. A white realtor who showed a property in a white area to a Negro would probably be very soon looking for employment in a different line of work. That probability never became a reality because no realtor was foolish enough to test it. There was, of course, no restriction, legal or otherwise, against a white person acquiring a home in a Negro area. But since that never happened, it too was purely academic.

Christine's college was private and purportedly inter-racial, and, to some extent, it was. Negroes and whites went to the same classes, had the same professors, ate in the same food hall and attended the same sports events in the college's small stadium. Before the war, the college had excluded Negro students. During the war, and in the years following, student enrollment had dropped precipitously. Despite substantially dropping tuition fees the free fall continued. The board had very reluctantly opted to open the enrollment to Negro students in order to keep the school afloat. There was nothing about a striving for equality or the protection of human rights that motivated the change. It was all about money and it was not very successful at that. There were not that many Negro families that could afford even the reduced tuition fees, but a number of them mortgaged their houses or took out loans at inflated interest rates in order to provide a college education for their children. Solomon Broward had saved a tidy sum over the years and had insisted on paying his granddaughter Christine's tuition.

Other than permitting the admission of Negro students, the board did nothing to create a climate of true integration. Professors who employed seating charts uniformly separated the races. In classes without seating charts, white and Negro students separated themselves without being ordered to do so. Between classes, in the quad, the dining hall, and on weekends at college football and baseball games, it was tacitly accepted that whites would congregate in one area and Negroes in another. It was not formally required by the school board. This was just the way it was and the authorities did nothing to change it.

On her way to school one morning, Christine was

carrying all her books for the day's classes. Ordinarily she would have put the books for later classes in her locker, but she was late and she decided to head straight for class with all of her books. In her hurry, she tripped and fell. The books scattered all over. A white student that she recognized from class helped her up.

"You okay?"

"Yes, I'm fine."

"Here I'll get your books." He started to gather them up.

"There's really no need. Thank you."

"No problem. You're in Psych 101same as me. I'll carry them."

"Please don't."

He ignored her protest. "What's your name?"

"Christine Broward"

"Mine's Jake Curtis. You like football? I'm on the team, halfback. We're playing Rossmore Saturday. Why don't you come?"

When they got to class, instead of going to sit in what was the white area, Curtis put Christine's books on her desk and sat down next to her. There was an audible gasp throughout the room and the Negro and white students stared at what they had never seen before. Professor Switzer did a double-take when he saw Christine and Jake. He said nothing and launched into his lecture. As they walked out of class, Curtis said to Christine, "I'll see you at the game. Don't forget."

Christine just smiled. She was immediately

surrounded by a group of Negro girls from the class. "What the hell do you think you're doing, girl? You making up to that white boy is gonna get you in a whole mess of trouble," said one of them as the others nodded.

"Nobody gonna sit still for what you just done—not nobody," said another.

"I wasn't making up to him, whatever that means. I fell and dropped my books and he helped me. That's all. I've got a boyfriend back in Mississippi and I'm gonna marry him. I'm not interested in any other boy whether he's white, black, green or purple."

"Well that's more like it," said the first girl. "You stick with that guy from Mississippi and don't hang around with whitey if you know what's good for you."

"I told you once I'm not interested in him and I'm not going to hang around with him so what's all the commotion about?" Of course she didn't tell the girls that the boy back in Mississippi that she planned to marry was white.

As it turned out, the "commotion" would not be limited to the Psych 101 class.

THE FAMILY BLOW UP

CHRISTINE'S BROTHER and her three cousins had been sent out to play. Uncle Henry strode back and forth in the family kitchen, periodically thrusting his finger angrily at Christine. The episode with the white student hadn't remained a secret very long. Nothing remained a secret very long in this compressed overcrowded neighborhood.

"You almost got your whole family killed by messing with that white boy in Jackson and now you come here and put us all in danger by doing the same damn crazy things all over again. Don't you never learn nothing girl? Can't nobody ever get through to you. Now you've come to Detroit and you're gonna get all of us killed here. You gotta—"

"Now hold on, Henry," interrupted Joshua.

"No you hold on. You hold on. I ain't nearly finished," yelled Henry. "You all come to my house to escape what she done. Remember, I specifically told her to stay away from them white boys and the first thing she does here is do all over again what she done down in Jackson. She goes into a whites-only store as bold as brass and then she goes after some white boy just exactly like she done in Jackson. Can't she get it through her head that a lot of things here are much the same as Jackson? There are things you can do and lots more you can't."

Christine was a quiet-spoken young lady and very slow to anger, but now she was past angry—she was enraged. "Now just minute, Uncle," she shouted, stunning herself with her own vehemence.

"I ain't finished yet, young lady."

"Oh yes you are, and you're going to pipe down, stop marching up and down, and listen to me, you hear, and you're going to listen good. I didn't trip over and drop my books on purpose. I didn't want that boy to pick them up. I tried to stop him. He insisted on carrying my books to class. I tried to stop him doing that, also. I didn't want him to sit down next to me in class, but he just did. I didn't try to talk to him, he started talking to me. How is this any of my fault and what is it you think I could've done or should've done? Just tell me, if you can. Just don't you bellow at me and don't you wag your finger in my face."

Uncle Henry was stunned into silence. The bellowing, blustering, pacing and finger-pointing were over. Uncle Henry retained his composure, harrumphed a couple of times and left the room followed by Aunt Rosie. Joshua and Harriet looked at their daughter with wide eyes. This was now the second time Christine had refused to be intimidated by Henry and they were worried about the consequences of the interchange they had just witnessed. They were, however, secretly proud of how she had stood up to the unjustified and factually absurd attack on her.

Harriet put her hand lovingly on Christine's shoulder.

"Don't worry child. You did nothing wrong. Your uncle, he gets mad from time to time for no good reason. He don't really mean nothin'. It's just him." Joshua said, "It's going to be all right. I think I found us a nice little house to rent not too far from here. It was kind of your uncle and aunt to let us stay here, but we'll all be better off if we are in our own place."

Christine's unexpected combativeness melted away and the tears came. Both Joshua and Harriet hugged and consoled her and the tears stopped. That they were going to move was really good news. Uncle Henry was more than a little hard to take. Christine was very grateful to him and to Aunt Rosie for letting them stay at their house, but her relationship with her uncle was not good and the crowded conditions didn't help. The two men and the five young people all left for work and school at about the same time every weekday morning. The line for the bathroom and the crush in the tiny kitchen for a quick breakfast made for a mad scramble and some short tempers.

It had been an eventful couple of days and Christine was grateful for the quiet after everyone had gone to bed. She sat in the kitchen and wrote a long letter to Peter. She told him of her classes, her winning hit in the softball game against Rossmore and the plans to move into their own rented house. What she didn't tell him was her mistake in going into the white stationery store or about the incident with the white male student and the unpleasant aftermath.

THE PARTY

ALTHOUGH THE COURT session was over very quickly, and Peter had not stuck around either to watch the celebration or to talk further with Mr. Broderick, he did not go back to work for the rest of that day. He called Mr. Foster from a public phone booth and told him that he wasn't feeling well. While he didn't have any diagnosable illness, he definitely didn't feel well. He walked around for hours, not remembering where he had been, and not having any clear idea where he was going. He sat for a while in a local park watching small children play with their toy boats in the pond.

Later, he walked by the county building which housed the district attorney's offices. He wanted to go in. Still there were a lot of things he didn't understand and he dearly wanted to explore those things with Broderick. He decided that Broderick had his own disappointment to deal with and he didn't want to bother him at this moment. It was starting to get dark and he thought he should stop someplace and get some food, but the thought of eating was not attractive and he decided to go home.

As he approached Mrs. Grant's house, he heard a lot of activity; people laughing, loud noise and car doors slamming. There were lots of cars, in the driveway and up and down the street. The front door was open, which was unusual. He decided that, instead of weaving in and out of the cars in the driveway and going into his room from the garden, he would go through the front door, and he was curious as to the source and reason for all the noise. Mrs. Grant's house was always very quiet and, if there was ever any protracted noise, she would put a stop to it in short order. Perhaps she was not home and when the cat's away, etc.

Once inside the front door, Peter could tell that the noise was coming from the sitting room. He looked in and saw that the room was crowded with mostly young men and women and a few older people. To his complete surprise, one of the older people was Mrs. Grant herself, sitting in an armchair drinking from a bottle of beer. The rest of the people were also drinking and the way some of them staggered around or talked in a slurred manner, Peter was sure that they hadn't just started.

Peter slowed down, but didn't intend to stop when one of the young men he didn't recognize reached out and grabbed him by the arm. "Come on in," he shouted. "Have a drink. We're celebrating."

Looking around, Peter did not immediately see anyone he knew, other than Mrs. Grant. The room was so crowded that most of the people could not be seen from the doorway.

"What are you celebrating?"

"Dontcha know? Where've you been? On another planet? We're celebrating Glenn beating the rap and sticking it in the ear of that miserable little English rat."

Peter pulled his arm out of the grip of the drunk and, as he did, Glenn Landers emerged from the crowd. "Don't say that, Kyle," shouted Landers. "This is my English friend. We all know he was wrong, but he thought he was doing the right thing and you can't ever blame a person for doing what he thinks is the right thing."

For the second time in just a few hours, Peter felt like throwing up.

"Yes but—" Kyle started to protest.

"Lay off him," interrupted Landers. "All of you just lay off him. He's my friend, and he always will be, and you must be prepared to forgive a friend for an honest mistake. Peter, come on in and drink with us to show there's no hard feelings. You know your fellow tenants, who are all here, and you certainly know Mrs. Grant, who is also here and has given us dispensation for the night to kick up our heels."

"No thank you," Peter responded and he walked away quickly, went into his room and closed the door. Immediately there was a knock. Without waiting for an invitation, Landers walked in.

"I want to tell you something, but before I start, I want you to remember, this conversation never happened. If I ever hear that you have told anybody about it—well I'll leave what can happen to your imagination. I saved your life. They wanted to string you up beside that no good piece of garbage. I had to call in a lot of chips to get you off the hook."

Peter bared his back. "You call that getting me off the hook?"

"Look kid, it could have been a whole lot worse if it wasn't for me."

"I heard all this from your father and you, only both of you were talking 'hypothetically' then, and now you're not. When did all this 'getting me off the hook' conversation take place?"

"Three days before it all happened."

"You could've stopped what happened to me and what happened to Jerome very easily."

"No way. Not a chance. No amount of talk or calling in chits would've prevented the hanging or the beating. I pleaded for you. I very nearly went down on my knees. Other than me, they started out being of one mind. They were going to hang you. I've never known them to change their minds. This was the first time."

"You're a hypocrite. You claim that you saved my life, but you wouldn't have had to if you hadn't told the Klan that I was in love with a Negro girl. Jerome Washington would be alive today if you hadn't given Christine Broward's name to the Klan. Even after you had done all that, you could still have stopped my beating and Jerome's hanging by going to the police before it happened. Do you want to know why you didn't stop it? Because you wanted it to happen. You enjoyed it. You loved it. You wanted to be a part of it."

"That's not—" Landers started to protest.

"Don't bother to deny it. You're a smooth talker but you couldn't convince me in a thousand years. Don't think for a moment that you convinced those jurors who voted for you that you were innocent. You know as I well as I do that those votes had nothing to do with guilt or innocence. It wouldn't surprise me it if those six people would have voted to acquit you even if they had actually seen you kill Washington. You were there. You killed a man and you admitted it in open court. Everyone knows that."

"What in blue blazes are you talking about? I didn't admit anything, in open court or anywhere else, except maybe just now in this room and nobody better ever find out about that."

"You admitted to simple assault on me. It wasn't even a rap on the knuckles but it demonstrated that you were there and were part of what happened. The only time and place that could have happened was at that Klan hanging. I was never beaten anywhere else, ever. They can call it a plea bargain or whatever they want. The court can erase the conviction if you're a good boy for a year, but they can't erase it in my mind or yours or anybody else's who heard anything about the trial. But don't worry, you have an advantage that a lot of murderers don't have and I'm not talking about your money, or your father's position or your ability to hire the best lawyers available. "

Landers anger turned to puzzlement. "What are you talking about?"

"I'm not a psychiatrist like that Swiss bloke you

bought and paid for, but I think many murderers later are sorry for what they did and it eats them up, not because they are going to be executed or spend the rest of their lives in prison, but because they have a conscience. You won't ever be sorry for what you did because you don't have a conscience. You'll go on with your life of luxury, marry a beautiful woman and have lots of kids. You'll live in a fine home with many servants. Once in a while, but not often, you'll think of Jerome Washington and me and the murder you got away with. You'll have everything but the one thing that counts. Because you have no conscience, you have no honor and a man with no honor is an empty worthless shell. Now go back to your friends, because you don't have one in here, and celebrate your 'victory.'"

The two of them stood there looking at each other. Glenn, the articulate, the well-educated, the well-liked honor student, the man of wealth, never at a loss for words, had nothing more to say. Peter, the younger man, the not so well-educated, the not so articulate and the not so wealthy, betrayed by a man he had greatly admired, a man he considered a good friend and benefactor, also had nothing more to say. The only sounds came from the sitting room where the noisy celebration continued and would not end until the early hours of the morning.

Glenn started to offer his hand to Peter, thought better of it, turned and left.

THE TEAM

L IFE WENT ON pretty quietly for Peter. He had looked into the possibility of going to the local community college at night. While his financial situation had improved—he had received another relatively small raise—he had concern about the expense. He filled out forms for admission the next semester, but decided to wait before submitting them. He continued his frequent correspondence with Christine. The tone of their letters clearly indicated that their feelings for each other had not changed. Indeed, they appeared to have strengthened. Her letters arrived at Mrs. Grant's without a return address, although the postmark showed that they came from Detroit. Mrs. Grant wondered who Peter knew in Detroit and, while she was again tempted to steam open the one of the envelopes, she resisted the urge, albeit with some difficulty. She could not bring herself to ask him right out since that would confirm what everyone knew anyway, that she was an inveterate nosy parker.

One day Dave came to Peter on the platform. It was an unusually slow day and there was only one car to unload.

"Boss man, me and the men would like to tell you something, if you've got the time."

"That's fine, Dave, but only if you all stop calling me 'Boss man.' All of you except Jimmy are old enough to be my father. I'm barely old enough to get a driver's license and not old enough to vote. My name's Peter, not Boss man, not Mr. Mason, just Peter. OK?"

"OK, Mr. Peter," Dave responded.

Peter groaned in frustration, but was finding out that age-old customs and hierarchical attitudes were hard to break.

The men gathered in a circle around Peter. "We just wanted you to know that it took a lot of guts to do what you done in trying to get justice, not only for you, but for Jerome," said Dave. "Some of us might have a question about your dating a Negro girl. Some of us don't like that, but I think that's your business. My only worry about that is that you got yourself in a packet of trouble already and we don't think it's a very good idea for you to do that no more. But, we all think you're a hero for saying them words about what happened like you did."

Peter decided he would not tell the men that, despite everything, he had every intention of marrying Christine.

"I'm no hero. I only told what happened and, as it turned out, it didn't help. I was scared to death. Heroes aren't supposed to be scared to death."

Julian, one of the oldest and quietest members of the team, spoke up. "I think in some ways it was a victory. I know that none of them hooded men is ever going to get punished for what they done to you and Jerome and even Mr. Landers got nothing but a light tap on the knuckles, but it was a victory of sorts anyhow."

"How could that be?" said Jimmy, the youngest of the group and the most outspoken. He was going to a Negro college in Jackson at night and was a little less subservient than the others. "They're all walking around free as the breeze and you say it was a victory? Don't be a fool, old man. You don't know what you're gabbing about."

Julian smiled at Jimmy and went on, "Jerome Washington was a Negro and not one of the best men in the Negro part of this town. He got let off by a white jury when they tried him because they said he done killed that white man. But more important was the trial of that Klansman for killing Jerome. Glenn Landers is a white man and the son of one of the most powerful men in this state. He had the best lawyer money could buy. That man could charm a bear into doing a jitterbug. For all that, six white folks voted that that rich white boy done murdered some no count, thieving Negro. Tell me when that has ever happened before anywhere in the South, let alone here in Jackson. Tell me that ain't progress," said Julian. "Things is changing. Not all at once and not quickly, but they is changing. You're gonna see more people like Mr. Peter and fewer like Mr. Landers as the years go by."

Mr. Foster, the warehouse manager came by at that point and saw Peter surrounded by his team. "Don't you boys have any work to do? Lunch break is over. Let's finish unloading that car."

Peter was overwhelmed by the affection shown him by the team. It brought him out of the despair he had felt when Glenn Landers walked free. Julian, a Negro, whose grandfather had been a slave, and who had virtually no education, had shown a positive side to the decision in the case; a side Peter hadn't thought of, and that even Broderick couldn't verbalize as eloquently as Julian had done in ungrammatical Negro patois.

Peter blew his nose hard and wiped a tear off his check. "Thank you all for what has just been said. You can't imagine how good it makes me feel. We'd better get back to work."

THE END OF A FRIENDSHIP

IT WAS A BEAUTIFUL warm Saturday morning and Peter decided to take a walk to see the Sylvesters. He had borrowed a book from Nick about the American Civil War. The subject fascinated Peter. In school, Peter had learned about the Civil War, but it was about the War of the Roses and not the American conflict. He was puzzled by the antipathy of the present day Southerners to the "Yankees." The War Between the States had ended almost a hundred years ago but there was still apparently a residual bitterness. There was no such bitterness in England concerning the War of the Roses, but that conflict had ended centuries earlier. Peter was also intrigued by England's support of the American South during the Civil War, until he came to realize it had been based on economics—the need for cotton for the English textile mills—rather than slavery or other issues dividing the states. The support of England during those times had still not been forgotten by grateful Southerners and what warmth and forgiveness was shown Peter for his transgressions was a perhaps, to some extent, a reward for his national origin.

While the Sylvesters had no rich relatives or a sprawling palatial estate similar to the Landers, they were more than adequate replacements as close, warm friends to Peter. They had long talks, went for hikes in the country and Nick was teaching Peter how to play tennis in one of the public parks. Peter had even baby sat for young Andrea, although taking care of a three year old girl was not something he knew much about. On this morning, as he approached the Sylvester house, book in hand, he saw Betty puttering about in their small front garden. He called out what he thought was a cheery greeting, only to see her look up and abruptly turn and almost run into the house.

Maybe she didn't recognize me. I was still quite a long way away, he thought. He knocked on the door and, after what seemed an inordinately long time, Nick opened it but stood blocking the doorway. "Hello Nick, it was such a nice day I thought I'd stroll over and return your book, maybe see if you wanted to go for a walk or something. Great book. I really enjoyed it. I knew so little about your Civil War."

"Sorry, Peter, I have things to do today." Nick paused and looked down at the ground as though he wanted to say something, but didn't know how. Finally, he said haltingly, "I don't think we can be seeing you, at least for the time being. Something has come up."

Peter was stunned. He couldn't think of anything

he had done to offend Nick or Betty, but maybe he had. "Tell me what it is. It's obviously something very serious on your mind and I think you had better tell me about it."

Nick walked out to the porch, looked at the ground, kicked a few pebbles and cleared his throat, "This is not going to be easy and I don't know quite how to say this. I don't want to hurt your feelings."

"What is it?"

"A couple of tough-looking guys came up to Betty when she was in the park with Andrea. They told her that the two of us shouldn't be friendly with you. That you are a dirty nigger lover as is anyone who hangs around with you. They said that Andrea was a beautiful child and that they hoped that she would grow up to be a fine lady. It wasn't exactly what they said. It was more how they said it. Betty told me that the way they said it sounded menacing and she got a chill when they looked at Andrea. Look, Peter, if it was just me I'd tell them to go to hell, but I've got Betty and Andrea to think of. You understand, don't you?"

At first Peter was at a loss for words. He knew from bitter experience that the Klan was perfectly capable of carrying out their threats, however thinly veiled. He couldn't let that happen. "Of course, I understand, Nick. It's okay. Tell Betty not to be upset about me. If I was in your shoes I'd probably do the same thing. Give Andrea a kiss for me."

With that, Peter turned and walked away. He had smiled and shaken Nick's hand, but the rejection hurt like the devil. Nonetheless, he didn't blame Nick. As he told

Nick, if the positions were reversed, he almost certainly would have done the same thing. Still somebody had to stand up and say this is not right and be a leader that people would listen to and follow, but he wouldn't be there to see it and join in. For some weeks he had been thinking, off and on, about when and if he should go back to England. Recently the focus had become more on the "when" than the "if." On that beautiful warm Saturday morning the conversation with Nick Sylvester had finally eliminated the "if" and all that remained was the "when."

What about Christine? It was bad enough being in Jackson and her in Detroit. He didn't know how far that was. All he knew was that it was an awful lot closer than London. He had reassured himself from time to time that he could always take a train to Detroit. It wouldn't cost much, although it would break their agreement to stay apart for a considerable period of time. It would be much more difficult to go to Detroit from London, if not impossible. He barely had enough money saved to get to England.

CHRISTINE'S DECISION

Mrs. Grant was in the hall when he got to the boarding house. "I've got a letter for you. It's another one of those from Detroit. You get a lot from up there don't you? Who is it you know in Detroit?"

"It's an old friend of mine from school. He came over to America with his parents some years back. His dad works at something in the car business."

"He sure does write a lot of letters. Must like you very much."

When he got back to his room, he read Christine's letter six times. She wrote, "My dearest Peter, I love you as much and more than ever. Us being apart is hard, but it will only make us closer. I think of you all the time. Things are going well here. Daddy likes his job. He makes a lot more money here than he did in Jackson and the work is interesting. However, things are a little more expensive. School is okay. College is a lot tougher than high school, but I like the challenge. This is going to be short because I'm writing this before breakfast and I've got to be in class in a half hour. I love you. Keep writing. The time will pass and we'll be together forever. All my love, Christine. PS, Although I've gotten to know a whole lot more people and have a bunch of new friends it's still awful lonely without you."

While Peter's response was full of expressions of love, it also laid out the possibility of his returning to England, and that he always believed that their lives together would be better in England. He assured Christine that he would stay in America if she would be upset with his leaving and he further assured her that the added distance of their separation wouldn't cause that separation to be any longer than what they had agreed upon. Finally he told her that he would live anywhere she wanted the two of them to go.

The wait for her reply was painful to Peter. He was fearful that she would misinterpret his reasons for leaving America and that, despite his protestations to the contrary, she would believe that his feelings toward her were cooling.

Her reply elated him. She fully understood why he would return to England. When the time came, she would live with him anywhere in the world that he wanted.

It was time to book his return trip.

GOING HOME

There was quite a stir when his decision to return to England surfaced. At work, his team learned it directly from Peter even before he told Mr. Foster. They were devastated. They had never worked for anyone like Peter before and they didn't think they ever would again. He had treated them as equals, something that no white man had ever done. No white man had ever insisted that he be called by his first name (although they still had not been able to bring themselves to refer to him as "Peter" and compromised with "Mr. Peter") and no white man had ever consulted them as to how to do his job as Peter had done.

Mr. Foster was far less distressed by Peter's decision, although he would just as soon Peter stay. For whatever reason, Peter's tour on the platform had resulted in improved performance. Foster could not fathom the reason for such improvement and had made no effort to divine the causes. He was just satisfied that it had occurred and that the success also benefited him. Peter's white co-workers had gotten used to what they considered to be Peter's eccentricities. While they were far from enthusiastic about the stories of his associations with Negroes and particularly a certain Negro girl, they tolerated it, although that tolerance did not rise to the level of acceptance. They had assumed that he was no longer seeing the girl and tolerance would have been short-lived if they had been made aware that he was planning to marry her.

Peter had suggested to Foster that he quit in thirty days, but said he would leave earlier if Foster preferred, or leave later if Foster had not filled the vacancy. Foster said thirty days would be fine. The thirty days passed quickly and his last day on the job arrived. It turned out to be a grand and memorable day but one that was bittersweet.

To Peter's surprise, the white co-workers who ate at Mrs. Potts's boarding house, hosted a lunch in his honor. Several of them made short speeches saying how pleased they were to have met him and how sorry they were to see him go. They gave him a card signed by all of them. Mrs. Potts had even made a cake for dessert, which she had topped with icing that spelled "Good Bye & Good Luck." Just so he knew that she was not forgiving him, however, she made a point of saying that Mr. Mitchell had commissioned the cake and was paying for it. When he got back to the platform he had a message that Mr. Mitchell wanted to see him.

The first time he had been to Mr. Mitchell's office he had been in fear that he was about to be fired. This time was different. He liked Mr. Mitchell and had been treated very well by him. He was particularly sad to be saying good-bye to him.

"Peter, I'm truly sorry to see you go. You've done an excellent job here and I want you to know that you can come back to work here whenever you want to, but that was not the only reason I wanted to see you. Of course, I want to wish you well but I also want you to know that I think you've handled the difficulties you encountered admirably. I know your encounter with the Klan was horrendous and you will bear the scars on your back forever, but hopefully there will be no scars in your memory. It's difficult living in the South for people who were not born to it. I was, but I spent some time in the North and a lot of things that go on down here I don't think I will ever get used to. You should know, however, that like places all over the world, not everyone in the south thinks alike on everything or holds the same views about race relations. I know it must have been infinitely more difficult for you. I want to wish you the very best of luck. Stay in touch and I hope one day you'll come back."

They shook hands and Peter went back to the platform for the last time.

As the work day ended, the team gathered around him. Dave was their spokesman. "Peter," he said and everybody laughed and smiled. "Not Boss man, not Mr. Mason, not even Mr. Peter, but just Peter. We wanted you to know that we think you are the best thing that has ever happened to the Mitchell Company and we're going to miss you. We want you to have this card that everybody signed. Jimmy here did the art work."

Jimmy handed the card to Peter. It had a picture of the platform and the team at work. In a prominent place, it showed Peter holding a clipboard. Underneath it said, "To Peter, a truly great man. We will never forget you. Please don't ever forget us."

Peter didn't know whether he trusted himself to say anything without crying, but he managed to thank them for everything. He told them that when he got home he would have their card framed and hung in a prominent place in his house. He assured them that he couldn't forget them even if he tried. Finally, he gave each of them a key ring with a metal disc containing the word "London" and a small replica of the Union Jack. He'd had his sister send them to him. They weren't much—the type of trinkets that tourists bought at airports and railway stations in England— but they were from the heart.

Later that day, he stopped by the DA's office to say good bye to Roy Broderick. Broderick again urged Peter to consider a career in law. He said that Peter obviously had an affinity for the law and would make a fine barrister or solicitor in his own country.

Peter thought long and hard about going to see Dr. James, but decided against it. He owed the doctor a lot and dearly wanted to thank him again, but he had already caused the doctor enough trouble and he didn't want to compound it by being seen going to Froman Hospital. He would write to him.

His last tasks were to finish packing, thank Mrs. Grant for letting him stay at her house, and get ready to leave. Although he heard Glenn Landers come and go at the house, he never saw or spoke to him again.

THE RETURN TO LONDON

Shortly before Peter left for England, his sister wrote him that her friend Janet continued to share the flat and the rent. Beth had forgiven, but not forgotten, Janet's racist comments. Nothing more had ever been said about it. When Janet found out that Peter was returning, she immediately offered to move out, but Peter would have none of it.

When he arrived in England he rented a cheap room in a poor area of Stepney and immediately looked for a job. The market was still tight, but he was lucky in answering an advertisement placed by a firm of solicitors looking for a clerk and was immediately hired. There were three partners of the firm comprising three generations of Simpsons; Walter, the grandfather, Colin, the son and Leonard, the grandson. Peter's duties were similar to what they had been at the real estate firm, getting coffee and tea, running errands and delivering documents—in this case taking documents to be filed in court and served on other lawyers.

The staff referred to the three lawyers as "Mr. Walter," "Mr. Colin" and "young Mr. Leonard." The three lawyers took an immediate liking to Peter. They were fascinated by his stories of his life in America and, in particular, the two cases in which he had been the star witness. After he had worked at Simpsons for several months, Mr. Walter offered Peter the chance to study to, perhaps, eventually become a lawyer.

"It will be long and hard," Mr. Walter warned. "You'll have to perform your regular duties and then study at night, on your lunch hour and weekends. I won't hold it against you if you don't want to, but I see something in you, Peter, that tells me you could make it."

Peter eagerly accepted. It was long and hard, but all the Simpsons helped, especially Mr. Walter. The old gentleman spent hours going over legal principles, assigning reading materials and answering questions. He was a wonderful mentor. Although well into his seventies, he was still tall, straight and energetic. He was a talented lawyer and very well thought of in the legal community. Despite the adversarial nature of his chosen profession in which he was superbly effective, he was always gentle, kindly and soft-spoken. Mr.Walter explained to Peter that, unlike the United States, England had two categories of lawyers – barristers and solicitors. He told Peter that barristers appeared in all the courts in the kingdom and solicitors could appear in most but not all the courts, and that solicitors also performed legal services in a variety of other areas that barristers did not

The schooling was tough. Peter barely had enough energy to eat his dinner before falling into bed exhausted each night. The Simpsons were very generous in raising Peter's salary and giving him bonuses. That generosity allowed Peter to rent a one-bedroom flat and, for the first time in his life, to get a telephone. He found out that he could call Christine in Detroit, station to station after midnight on Sundays at a low rate, and he called every single Sunday. They would limit their calls to ten minutes, but in that time they would tell each other over and over how much love they felt and how much they missed each other. Peter would tell her of his work and studies. Christine would tell him of her schoolwork, her family and how she was doing on the softball team. Peter would sit by the phone as the time for the call approached in eager anticipation. It was the most important time of his entire week.

One Tuesday morning, Peter got to the office late. Mr. Colin had asked him to stop on his way in to pick up some legal supplies from a shop in Holborn. When he arrived, Greta the receptionist told him that Mr. Walter wanted to see him the moment he arrived. He knocked on Mr. Walter's door and went in. Mr. Walter was sitting behind his desk reading a legal document.

"Peter, did you see that young man sitting in the waiting room?"

"I did, sir."

"I'm giving him your job."

Peter was shocked. For a moment he didn't know

what to say, then, in a shaky voice, he said, "Did I do something wrong? I'm sorry . . ."

"You have nothing to be sorry for," Mr. Walter replied, smiling. "You did nothing wrong. Quite the contrary. We all think the world of you. You're as fine a young man as I have ever known, and with all my years, I've seen a lot of fine young men. We're relieving you of all your duties other than those preparing you to becoming a lawyer. In addition to your studies, you'll be attending court sessions with us and going to client and witness meetings. You will be doing legal research on our cases and writing drafts of briefs. How does all that strike you?"

Peter was overwhelmed. His legs felt weak and he could only stammer out his thanks. As he turned to leave, Mr. Walter said, "By the way, there'll be an extra five pounds each week in your pay envelope."

In the weeks and months to come, Peter had many opportunities to visit the courts. If time permitted, he would sit in one or another and listen to the proceedings. Often he would accompany one of the Simpsons to a court appearance. Frequently they would be arguing motions or presenting briefs that he had drafted. He would take notes and discuss the outcome of the hearings with one or more of his bosses. On one occasion, the judge complimented Mr. Walter on the excellence of his brief—one that Peter had written. Mr. Walter thanked the bewigged and robed elderly jurist and told him that his young colleague beside him was the one who should be receiving the plaudits since he was responsible for the brief's preparation. The judge looked at Peter and said, "Well done, young man. Seems to me that the Simpsons have secured the services of a future legal star."

It was a memorable moment for Peter; one of many to come.

TWO YEARS LATER

IT HAD COME full circle. Peter was once again standing on a pier in Southampton, but a number of things had changed. He was wearing a suit that was not made for a man three times his size, nor was it tailored on Savile Row. It was purchased off the rack at Marks & Spencer's at a much lower price. He now had a car he'd bought used. It had a lot of miles on it, but it ran well. He still rode the bus to work because of the price of petrol, but for this occasion he had filled it up and driven it the hundred miles from London. Unlike the last time he had been on this pier, he was not embarking on an ocean voyage.

He frequently recalled what he had been told by Solomon Broward on the bus trip from New York that there would be experiences that were pleasant and some that weren't. There were lessons he had learned that had proved to be valuable in his achieving a degree of maturity. He thought back to the pleasant experiences often: the trip to America and sharing a cabin with Chuck Bradley; going to the theater and having dinner with the

Hamiltons; playing ball on the Mall in Washington with the boys from Minnesota; Dr. James; Roy Broderick; Mr. Mitchell; Solomon Broward and the Broward family, Dave and the platform team; the baseball game; the memories flooded back.

The unpleasant experiences could not be suppressed, some as minor as the nasty immigration agent or the Broadway scam artist, but some as major as his encounter with the Klan. Some were mixed; the initial pleasantness of his friendship with Glenn Landers and the Landers family that turned as bad as anything could turn; his friendship with the Sylvesters before they were frightened away by the Klan. He would lie on his couch looking at the framed card that Jimmy had drawn and all the team had signed. It was his most valuable possession, even more than his car or the set of law books that had been given to him last Christmas by Mr. Walter and occupied the bookcase in his office at Simpsons.

Solomon Broward was right, there were pleasant experiences and there were unpleasant ones too, but they all taught important lessons. What Solomon Broward could not have foreseen on that bus ride was what would be Peter's most pleasant experience of all. As he looked up, she was coming down the gangplank. He ran to her. They hugged and kissed and cried. They stepped back and looked at each other. Then they hugged and kissed and cried some more.

Three days later in a small church near Peter's flat in front of Solomon, Joshua, Harriet and Phillip Broward,

Peter's sister Beth, other relatives, his childhood friends, the staff of Simpsons and the Messrs. Walter, Colin and Leonard, Peter Mason was married to Christine Broward. Did they live happily ever after? Not completely. Few do. Life, after all, is not a fairy story, although Peter had married his princess. There were stares, a number of unpleasant remarks, and two or three apartment owners who would not rent to them. Despite all this were they happy together, at least most of the time? Yes—they could not have ever been happy any other way.

AUTHOR'S NOTE

Somerset Maugham, the great and prolific British author, once said that everything he wrote was based to some extent on his own life experiences. He noted that, not infrequently, he found the line between what was fact and what was fiction to be blurred. Although modesty has not been one of my vices, I would never have the audacity to compare myself to Mr. Maugham. Nonetheless I have found that in the book just completed I have leaned quite heavily on my own personal experiences and very occasionally the line did blur.

I did come to America shortly before my eighteenth birthday; I did meet "Chuck" and shared a cabin with him. Unfortunately, he didn't give me any money and I could have used it. I was wearing a suit given to me by my 300-pound uncle although I was only 135 pounds at the time. I did end up running the elevator at the Robert E. Lee Hotel in Jackson and was just as inept in that job as Peter. I did supervise a team of black workers at the Mitchell Company (not its real name) when I was eighteen years of age and all but one of them were all old enough to be my father. Neither the hotel or the grocery company are still in existence, at least in the form I knew them.

"Dave" did teach me to drive. I did share a bathroom in a boarding house but the fellow with whom I shared the bathroom did not become a close friend and was not a Klansman. I never met his parents or had sex with his sister, assuming he had one. I did encounter the depths of unopposed segregation and I did ignore its written and unwritten rules from time to time, more out of youthful foolishness than bravery.

I was never hit by a car or treated in any hospital. I did not see a car accident which led to a murder prosecution. I was not abducted by the Klan nor did I witness a hanging. I did not marry a girl I met when I was in Mississippi. (Years later, I married a girl I met in California.) Many of the other events and people are fictional. Segregation was absolute in the Deep South at the time but not any longer. I have been back to the Deep South numerous times in recent years and things, happily, are now very different and have been for a long time.

One of the fundamental differences between Peter and me is that I never went back to England, except for visits. Since I was in the United States on a permanent visa and was eligible for the draft, I was drafted into the U.S. Army toward the end of the Korean War. I was told that, since I was not an American citizen, I need not serve in the American army, but if I elected not to serve I would have to go back to England, where I would have been drafted into the British Army. I stayed because, like Peter, I loved it in the U.S. Service in the United States Army made me eligible for accelerated U.S. citizenship and the GI Bill, that permitted me to go to University (UCLA undergraduate and Law School) and I have practiced law in Los Angeles for fifty years.

While "Peter" and I had much in common and shared many of the same experiences, there was much we didn't have in common. I must admit that while I was as foolish as Peter, he was braver than me. He has scars on his back to prove it, and I don't. Would I have been willing to subject myself to extraordinary danger, to beatings and even possible death, had I fallen in love with a black girl in those days? I'd like to think that I would have, but I don't know, and I never will.

ACKNOWLEDGMENTS

To my wonderful family, my wife Margie, my daughters Jill and Katie, my sons-in-law, Mark and Aleksander (Sasho) and my grand-children, Amelia, Chet and Paula-Marie. Their kindness and love overwhelm me.

To my editor, Ellen Willard, whose attention to detail and thoughtful, intelligent suggestions for corrections and changes were truly extraordinary. Among the many lessons I learned from her was when to use 'which' and when to use 'that,' a puzzle which has confounded me as well as many others for ages. She caught errors in the manuscript that (or should it be which!) had escaped me despite my having read it numerous times.

To the remarkable Jose Ramirez and his company, Pedernales Publishing. I am awed by the depth of his knowledge and expertise. He was constantly and promptly on top of the complicated procedures for getting a book published and ready for sale. Nothing was too much trouble for him and his advice was always spot on. He was most kind, thoughtful and patient in answering my many questions, some of which were not exactly of the most intelligent variety.

To Sarah Robarts and her associates for their services in promoting this book, I am grateful to their creative planning in an area, one of many, with which I have little familiarity. It doesn't hurt that Sarah is a fellow Brit!

To Virginia Lawrence who has provided excellent counseling and services in the confusing (to me) world of technology. Since my most detailed knowledge and use of technology involved using a new type of pencil sharpener, her expertise in the baffling worlds of social media, web sites and the like were and are invaluable.

To my dear friend David, 'The Wall' Waller who I prevailed on to read an early version of my manuscript, my thanks. His enthusiasm and encouragement were very important to me. Among other things, he caught the fact that I had given the same character two different names in two widely separated portions of the book!